I plunged on, than go along wit it. I was committe...

Silence hung palpably in the room. Outside, the rain beat against the windows like distant applause. The resonant murmur of retreating thunder caused the prisms in the chandelier to tinkle playfully.

Grant shifted and stood up, stretching lazily like a great panther climbing down off his rock to prepare for the evening hunt. I watched him, knowing with resentful embarrassment that I had placed myself unconditionally in his hands.

Before he could open his mouth to speak, however, I rushed on. "This marriage, of course, will be no more than a piece of paper and will not take place at all if it isn't understood by everyone that it will be on my terms."

"Well," he said finally. "I guess we should all be grateful to Suzanna, eh?" His eyes sparkled with something akin to malice, and I turned my look on the others.

Grant came to stand next to me and placed a strong arm around my shoulders, giving me a squeeze that hurt. He was still smiling. "So, you've come down off your regal throne, my girl, and deigned to bestow your gracious gifts upon mere mortals such as ourselves?"

"Grant, don't!" I muttered, shaking off his arm and retreating to a chair into which I sank gratefully.

"What's the matter? Can't put up with a hug from your fiancé?" He snorted and bent to retrieve his glass, downing the last of his whisky in one gulp. "Well, my dear adoptive relatives, has it ever occurred to any of you that I have an equal say in this decision which Suzanna has so magnanimously taken upon herself?"

I looked up at him in surprise.

"Yes, that's right," he said, seeing me blush. "You've been so keen to bemoan your own hideous fate that you forgot it takes two people to tango."

Shadows in the Mist

by
Maureen M. McMahon

Avid Press, LLC   Brighton Michigan USA

Published by
Avid Press, LLC
5470 Red Fox Drive
Brighton MI 48114-9079 USA
http://www.avidpress.com

Shadows in the Mist
ISBN 1-929613-36-9

© 2000 by Maureen M. McMahon

Cover illustration ©2000 by Diane Augustine-Grau

To Peter, my love, for all his unwavering support.

PROLOGUE

Between the idea
And the reality
Between the motion
And the act
Falls the shadow.

Thomas Stearns Eliot
The Hollow Men

Looking back, I realize that the first time the apparition appeared to me was the night of my father's death. At the time, I thought it was my imagination or some strange hallucination, but now I know otherwise.

I'd rented the cabin as a retreat. The seclusion was meant to force me into completing a second novel that I'd been commissioned to write. Instead, it had simply served to accentuate the prickling sense of disquiet that had been afflicting me for months. Since my arrival I'd done a lot of pacing, a lot of smoking and a lot of thinking, but my laptop still lay untouched in its leather case.

It happened on the second night. The cabin, hidden deep in Michigan's Manistee Forest, was rustic to a fault: there was no phone, the electricity worked when it felt like it, and the water had a tendency to change color daily. I remember there was a chill in the air that night. A mist had worked its way down through the trees and settled in opaque gauze close to the ground. I'd lit a fire in the ample fireplace and it crackled warmly, but still I shivered.

I was drawn to the window. Had I heard something? Was it the wind creaking in the boughs? Or the snap of a twig? I turned out the lamp so that I could see more clearly into the darkness beyond. The firelight danced, making shadows flick across the walls and ceiling. I cupped my hands and peered out through the glass.

The mist slithered between the tightly packed pines and cloaked the thick underbrush. Fingers of it stretched up trunks and crept across the meager plot in front of the cabin. The pine boughs hung heavy and still; there wasn't a breath of wind to stir them. The night blackness was dense and impermeable, the tangled forest canopy allowing not a trace of moon- or starlight. The fireglow from my window cut a shimmering rectangle across the needle-strewn yard, and lit the encroaching mist into ghoulish patterns.

My eyes found him immediately, dark against the swirling fog, but somewhat indistinct amid the shadows of night and forest. It was the figure of a man, faceless, featureless. He didn't move, but I felt his intensity. It reached out to me and beckoned me, pleaded with me—beseeched me with silent urgency. Surprisingly, I wasn't afraid. Something in me responded. I wanted to go to him, to comfort him, but my body was frozen and my limbs had become numb. So instead, I opened my mind to him and somehow, in the deepest recesses of my consciousness, I felt him touch me. The touch chilled me, turned my insides to pulp and left me reeling and dizzy. And if I were to translate that touch, it would spell two words; two words screamed like a banshee wind in a hurricane of agony and desperation. The words: "Help me!"

ONE

I shall not see the shadows,
I shall not feel the rain;
I shall not hear the nightingale
Sing on, as if in pain:
And dreaming through the twilight
That doth not rise nor set,
Haply I may remember,
And haply may forget

    Text by Christina Rosetti
    Set by John Ireland
    When I Am Dead, My Dearest

I hit the stop button and pulled the tape out of the machine abruptly. David automatically handed me the plastic case.

"Are you all right?" he asked.

"Sure," I lied, fumbling with the cover, unreasonably irritated by his penchant for such ancient and sentimental recordings. "Are we nearly there?" It was a stupid question. I knew the roads as well as he did.

He took no notice. "Nearly there," he said.

Good old reliable David, always calm, always predictable. I was glad he was the one to tell me; he had a way that always soothed me. Unfortunately, on this occasion, there wasn't much he could do to lighten the blow.

"Your father has had a terrible accident, Suzanna," he'd said. "I'm afraid he's…dead."

His voice had been emotionless. The words had slipped easily from his lips, like acid over steel. My first impulse was to laugh. The thought of Leopold Dirkston being mortal like the rest of us was preposterous. Yet I knew that David rarely joked, and would certainly not do so about something as macabre as my father's death. Disbelief was quickly replaced by horror.

"How?" I asked. We were sitting in the cabin. He'd appeared on my doorstep unexpectedly and I knew before he'd even opened his mouth that something was amiss.

"I'm afraid it was just one of those horrible things, darling. I found him in the swimming pool. He must have fallen and hit his head and…"

I tried futilely to visualize this fantastic concept.

"You found him?"

"Yes. Colin and I stopped by to go over some business and, well, he was just floating there, in the pool. Naturally, we pulled him out and started CPR right away. For a while we even thought…" he shrugged helplessly. "Dad came over right away and rode with him in the ambulance, but I'm afraid he died on the way."

I didn't hear the rest. An anthill of thoughts burst open and I felt my head reel with the effort to focus.

"I'm truly sorry, Suzanna."

He reached over and his long fingers engulfed mine with a warm, dry strength that I found strangely unbearable. My eyes lifted to his face and I saw that, for the first time in my life, David couldn't comfort me. This thought sent a bolt of panic through me, and I snatched my hand away and fled to the bathroom to be sick.

That had been only a few hours ago. I'd had no choice but to pack my few things and head for home. Now it was just after one a.m., and the towering steel gates of Beacon, Leo's estate, had just come into view. I wasn't eager to be back. I'd grown to resent Beacon nearly as much as I resented its creator. At times I wondered if it was, in fact, some sort of extraneous limb of my father's. Fortunately, there were parts of it that weren't entirely permeated with his dynamic personality. There was High Dune, my bedroom, the lighthouse—these places were mine and mine alone. Just knowing they were there waiting made my homecoming more palatable.

David pressed a button on the intercom affixed to the gatepost. "It's me, John," he said.

I could see the security guard peer out the window of the small gatehouse and, recognizing David's car, he waved acknowledgment. Seconds later, the gates slid smoothly open, allowing us to pass.

I hadn't met John. I did know that we permanently employed two guards at Beacon, one to screen visitors at the front gate and one to patrol the grounds. Grant Fenton looked after that side of things. I rarely saw them, but I always knew the guards were there, making it impossible to feel completely private.

"You said he asked for me?" I said dully. I was still searching for answers.

David glanced at me. "Yes. He seemed to come to briefly, just before the ambulance arrived. He said your name; that was all."

"But why? Why would he?" I felt sick again.

His hands tightened on the steering wheel. "Dad says he's sure it was an accident, Suzanna. Leo had had a few drinks, stumbled on something by the pool, fell and hit his head on the concrete edge."

I frowned. Leo didn't have accidents. He'd built an empire with his ability to use good judgment and sound logic. He'd risen from the slums of Chicago to a position as owner and president of one of the largest shipping firms on the Great Lakes. No, I couldn't believe that he had simply made a fatal "mistake." But if not an accident, then what? Once again I shivered, afraid to follow the path my instincts chose. Instead, I took a different approach.

"Had he had a lot to drink?"

David shrugged. "I don't really know. Dad seemed to think so. You know how it once was…after your mother died? We think that if he'd been sober, he might not have stumbled."

I hesitated. "Had he…had he been drinking often? I mean, since I left?"

He didn't answer immediately and I noticed a muscle tighten in his jaw. Finally, he looked at me.

"Suzanna, don't do this to yourself. It wasn't your fault. It was an accident, that's all; a tragic accident. Blaming yourself will do no one any good."

"You haven't answered my question," I insisted stubbornly.

He let out his breath in exasperation. "Okay, okay…yes, I suppose you could say he was drinking than usual! But it wasn't as much or as often as before."

My palms began to perspire and I gripped the door handle, remembering the last time I'd seen my father.

"A writer? You want to be a writer?"

He'd sat behind his heavy mahogany desk and stared at me as if I'd just announced I wanted to have my leg amputated for cosmetic purposes. The huge wall of glass behind him looked out over the bay and South Chicago's Calumet district. With the sun framing him, he looked like Thor, ready to hurl his golden hammer and smite the traitor before him.

I didn't flinch, forcing myself to be calm. After all, I had expected this, hadn't I? His hair was thick and clung together in gray bouffant perfection, dramatically streaked with black. With wry amusement, I noticed he'd let his sideburns grow and was now sporting a moustache. Despite all his old-world ideals, he still wanted to keep up with the younger set.

"Yes, Dad." My voice was steady and I lifted my chin, a gesture intrinsically his. "I've had my novel accepted by Charlotte Press in New York. It's to be released in a few months."

I was excited, but I tried not to sound like a schoolgirl on her first date. This contract was the realization of my greatest dream. I was being accepted as a writer on my own merits, without benefit of any influence from my father or his powerful name. With this goal achieved, I was now ready to take on the world.

"They told me they might be interested in second novel," I added, as if it would make any difference.

"Charlotte Press." He said the name as if it were melting ice cream. "What the hell do they publish? Comic books?"

I felt my resolve begin to crumple.

"They publish…" It was too late. I knew what he would say, and finished the sentence in barely a whisper, "…romances." I chewed my lower lip. His bushy eyebrows flew up and suddenly he was roaring with laughter.

Molten rage welled up inside me and I turned on my heel to go.

"Wait, Suzie!" He struggled to regain his composure. He blew his nose and wiped his eyes, chuckling occasionally. "Romances!" he repeated to himself.

I stood woodenly. I certainly wouldn't give him the satisfaction of responding to his outburst.

"Well," he finally said, "this is a surprise! And has dear David helped you research this romance of yours?" His sarcasm wasn't lost. It was a savagely vulgar thing to say, and I knew he was baiting me for a fight. Instead, I chose to ignore the implication, telling myself that he must truly feel threatened to resort to such cruel tactics.

"I wish you'd try to understand." I said, my voice much calmer than I felt. "If you love me like you keep telling me you do…" I stopped. Now, I was sinking to his level. It hardly mattered. His voice cut in like a thunderclap.

"Don't you give me that, young lady! Everything I've ever done was for you—and your mother, God rest her!" A fleeting shadow passed over his face and as quickly as his anger had erupted, it abated. He leaned back in his chair, drained and looking suddenly old. He gazed at me, puzzled.

"Why won't you come to me?" he asked quietly. "Hell, I'd buy the damn publishing company for you if that's what you want! Why do you have to grovel?"

I sighed. It was no use. How could I ever make him see that I had my own ambitions; that I needed to earn my own applause? He was so very brilliant in his own world of import, export and finance, and yet so very naive when it came to human nature.

As I looked into his confused eyes, I felt like weeping. "I'm sorry, Daddy." It was all I could manage, and the helplessness of that utterance merely widened the vast chasm gaping between us. I could suddenly see with pinpoint clarity that we would always be strangers.

That had been almost six months ago. Since then I'd been back to Beacon only once, and had stayed for less than three hours. Leo was away—a meeting in Amsterdam or something, I couldn't remember—but I'd only returned to collect some of my things, and made certain I wouldn't have to face him again. Tears trickled down my cheeks now, as I realized we'd never again have the opportunity to patch up our differences.

David guided the car down the long gravel approach. The house towered before us, a huge crouching lioness, impervious to wind or weather. Gardens curled around a sleeping fountain. The flagpole stood stark against the night sky, its empty rope clanking rhythmically in the steady breeze that blew in off Lake Michigan. The only signs of life were the lights pouring from the downstairs windows, and the floods that illuminated the circular approach and portions of the carport and garage.

David pulled his aging Mercedes around in front of the steps and I glanced at him, wondering what he was thinking. His face was shadowed and expressionless. I sighed inwardly. It was this very inscrutability that had attracted me to him in the first place. David had always been a paradox; a tower of unreadable complexity; a challenge to my insatiable curiosity. However, after a nine-year relationship fraught with continuous power struggles and unresolved conflicts, I had somehow lost any desire to understand him. I knew now that we weren't meant for each other. As much as I admired him and wished I could be like him, marriage to him would have been a big mistake, and I knew I had been wise to break off the engagement. Still, whenever I looked at him, I felt that dull ache of loss and I wished again that there was some way that we could make it work.

Feeling my eyes on him, he turned and half smiled. "Here we are. I'll let you off and see to your things. Colin and Alicia are inside with Grant. They wanted to wait up for you."

He held open the door, and I sighed and stepped out. My eyes found his and for once, our thoughts found common ground. He took me into his arms and held me close. I squeezed my eyes shut to keep the tears back, and wished desperately that I could stay there forever, safe from the confrontations waiting inside.

His lips brushed my hair briefly, then he put me from him resolutely. "It'll be all right," he said. "You'll see."

I nodded acquiescence and took a deep breath to bolster my wavering courage.

The great sweeping veranda of Beacon spread out before me, skirted on all sides by gleaming white steps. I mounted them slowly, acutely aware of the stone lions crouched beneath all ten of the slim white pillars, their malevolent eyes watching me. I shivered. The ponderous, solid oak door was adorned with another lion's head, this one gripping a huge iron knocker in its mouth. I didn't look at it, but fumbled in my purse for my keys.

Suddenly, without warning, the door swung open and light streamed out, blinding me.

"Suzanna, dear! I thought I heard David's car. It does make such a racket. It's just as well we don't have close neighbors, they'd certainly complain, don't you think? Oh, my, you must be simply devastated! All this is just too shocking!"

"Alicia," I managed to slip in as she drew a breath, "how are you?"

I endured her embrace that was accompanied by the inevitable clink and chink of a dozen bangles and the smell of heavy musk that I guessed she bathed in daily. Stepping past her into the foyer, I scanned the familiar surroundings, ignoring her continuing prattle.

The entrance hall was impressive, to say the least. The floor was a mirror of onyx black tiles marbled with gold. The ceiling was vaulted and decorated to excess with coffers of plaster cherubs and nymphs, all delicately gilded and framed with twining grapevines or roses. A wide staircase, carpeted in immaculate, impractical white, swept up to the second floor gallery. Near me, against the wall, a rare Grecian urn was displayed on a marble pedestal. The roses in it were wilting, and a few petals lay scattered on the floor. If Leo were here, those roses would never have been allowed to reach such a state. It was tangible proof that things weren't as they should be.

Sliding double doors opened off either side of the hall, to the left onto the living room, to the right onto what we grandly referred to as the ballroom.

"You must come into the library," Alicia was saying. "Grant and Colin are waiting. No one wants to go into the den. It's too close to where it happened. The police were here for hours!"

"The police?"

"Why, yes! Of course, they said it was all routine; but still, it was simply ghastly, all those strangers crawling around…and the questions! Why, it makes me dizzy. You must need a drink, love, to calm your nerves."

I accompanied her down the short spacious passage, marveling anew at the vast differences between Alicia and Colin. Her propensity for the dramatic was evident under any circumstances. Even her appearance screamed of Hollywood glitz. She was tall and overly thin with golden-bronze hair that frizzed riotously to her shoulders. Her eyes were almond-shaped and made very green with tinted contact lenses. The lashes, which most certainly weren't her own, fanned out from lids defined in shades of aqua and mauve. Her nose was small and straight over a kitten mouth, her lips carefully outlined and coated with a rich tangerine gloss. Her hands were dainty, with fingers made much longer by perfectly manicured nails painted to match her lipstick. A collection of gold and diamond rings winked and gleamed as she gestured erratically.

My half-brother, Colin, had met Alicia on one of his jaunts to California in the days when he was trying to be a jet setter. She was a would-be actress, doing bit roles in soap operas and TV commercials to pay the rent. I couldn't guess what kind of spell she cast over Colin, but after sharing her apartment for only a few months, they drove to Los Vegas and were hastily married. Whether by choice or at Colin's insistence, Alicia gave up her acting career almost immediately and before the year was out, she was comfortably installed at Beacon. That same year, Colin and David hatched out a plan to open a chartered fishing business and, thrilled that Colin was finally making an effort to curb his irresponsible ways, Leo happily loaned them the capital to get the enterprise off the ground.

I don't know exactly when Alicia started to drink, but the alcohol was beginning to leave its marks on her fine features. The makeup she used no longer hid the smudges beneath her eyes or the tiny lines at the corners of her mouth. She seemed to be growing thinner by the day so that her clothes, despite being the height of fashion, hung limply.

Colin and David were doing reasonably well with their business, from what I could tell. They had acquired two new cabin cruisers, and had opened a sideline canoe rental for the Pere Marquette River. It meant nothing to Alicia, however. She still lived for the day when she could return to the stage.

Alicia's unpredictable moods and incessant chatter were tolerated by everyone more out of pity than any magnanimous feeling of goodwill. It was common knowledge that Colin was obsessively jealous and viewed her career as a threat. If she blamed him, however, she never said so. Instead, she invented her own little world to live in and ignored the hopelessness of her existence. I could almost empathize with her, for I knew what it was like to live under the smothering influence of a domineering man.

"Everyone is positively strung out, Suzanna." she was saying. "Poor Colin is still suffering from the shock. It was Colin and David who found him, you know. He was just floating there in the pool. They thought he was dead already, but…" She glanced sideways at me, expectantly. I didn't respond, but pushed open the mahogany doors and stepped into the library.

Colin stood gazing at the bookshelves, his hands thrust into his pockets, absently jangling coins and keys. His shirt was wrinkled at the back and his curly brown hair was matted on one side.

He was every inch his mother's son. Only his short husky build belied his paternity. His nose was thick, and slightly crooked from a break that happened during his school days. His complexion was uncharacteristically pale, accentuating the shadow of stubble on his chin. Though his eyes were wide-set and colored an indistinct hazel-brown, the thick fringe of lashes softened them and made them, in my opinion, his most endearing feature.

Across the room was Grant Fenton, my father's right-hand man. He leaned against the bar, one foot propped on the chrome rail that ringed its base. He wasn't a tall man but was well proportioned, with a broad chest and tapered waist. He was dressed in faded denims and a burgundy shirt and, like Colin, hadn't shaved. His dark brown hair was sun-streaked with auburn and stood on end, as though he'd been running his hands through it. His eyes, in contrast to his weathered complexion, were a startling marine blue and, despite the lines of fatigue creasing his face, they always lit with amusement when he looked at me. It was a habit that I resented deeply.

Now his gaze unnerved me and I felt an uncontrollable blush creep up my neck to my cheeks. It would be just like him to make some sarcastic remark. Instead, he merely sloshed a healthy portion of brandy into a snifter and extended it in my direction. "Here, Suzie, you look as though you could use this."

I crossed the room and accepted the drink with a polite murmur.

"We would have rung you," Colin said, perching on the arm of a chair, "but I understand that your little hideaway didn't provide the modern convenience of a telephone. And your cell-phone wasn't working." His voice was petulant.

"I'd switched it off," I replied as calmly as I could. "I wanted it that way."

I knew that Colin was baiting me. I felt defensive, but refused to be drawn into a quarrel at a time like this. It seemed as though everyone was silently accusing me—as though my absence had somehow caused Leo's accident. I gulped a bit of the brandy and grimaced as it burned its way down my throat.

"He was such a wonderful man," Alicia piped up. Reclining cat-like on the settee, she downed the remainder of her martini and waved the empty glass at Colin. "Darling, do be a love and fetch me another. I'm simply a nervous wreck."

Colin rose to accommodate her, more out of habit, I guessed, than a sense of duty.

"I still don't understand how this could have happened," I said quietly.

"Why, my dear! Surely, David told you?" Alicia warmed to the subject. "It was all a horrible accident. You know how your father loved to swim in the evenings? Well, he must have tripped on something and hit his head on the side of the pool…"

"Oh, shut up, Alicia!" Colin barked. "Dad was drunk, we all know that. He was also fully clothed, so I doubt that he'd intended to take a 'dip'." He handed his wife the martini and sat down beside her, roughly shoving her sprawled legs aside. She shrugged, unperturbed.

Grant was silent, intent on swizzling his brandy, but I sensed an undercurrent. What were they all hiding? I looked from one face to the next, but they avoided my eyes. I opened my mouth to demand an explanation, but was put off by David, who appeared in the doorway.

"I've taken your bags to your room, Suzanna," he said, oblivious to the tension, "and I'll have someone bring your car back tomorrow."

For once, I was grateful for his faultless practicality and appreciated the arm he dropped around my waist, leaning into it for support.

There was no room for conversation after that. David quietly relived the episode for everyone's benefit. Leo's drinking wasn't mentioned again, and eventually an uncomfortable silence fell. There was nothing more to be said. The light discourse that usually linked our separate lives no longer seemed appropriate, and no one was willing to touch on the personal emotions that pulsed like electricity just beneath the surface. Even Alicia was, for once, without words. It was Grant who broke the spell.

"I think we could all use some sleep," he said, placing his empty glass wearily on the bar.

The others were quick to murmur assent, welcoming an excuse to escape.

"Come on, Alicia," Colin said, pulling her to her feet,

"let's pour you into bed."

David gave me a squeeze. "I'd better be going, too. Dad will need me. I'll come by to see you after you get some rest. Will you be all right?"

"I think so," I said and raised my cheek automatically for his kiss. He left on the heels of Colin and Alicia and I turned to follow, looking forward to some privacy, but Grant stopped me.

"We need to talk, Suzie."

I stiffened. This would probably be another one of Grant's big-brotherly lectures. I waited. He was silent for so long, I began to get impatient. He was standing at the window, his back to me. Beyond him, the sky was becoming a little less black as the moon slumped low over Lake Michigan. I went to stand next to him, drawn by the beauty of the star-studded sky, and the moonlight rippling on the sliver of water just evident beyond the rear gardens. In a few more hours, the sun would appear to paint the horizon pink and lavender and tinge the rolling swells with gold. Leo had rarely missed a sunrise. He'd said that each one was a work of art and not to be wasted. It suddenly occurred to me that he would never see another, and a choking sob caught in my throat.

Grant glanced down at me and his eyes softened. "For what it's worth, Suzie, I'm sorry."

If he hadn't said that, I would probably have been able to ward off the tears, but his sympathy amplified my own self-pity and, before I knew it, I was sobbing shamelessly, my face buried in his shirt-front.

How long I cried, I don't know. I cried until there were no tears left, too bereft to appreciate the irony of finding comfort in Grant's arms. I'd never thought him capable of tenderness. He seemed too unbending, too ruthless—a carryover, I suspected, from his childhood amid the dock-side slums of Chicago.

Grant's father had disappeared when he was a baby, leaving him and his mother to fend for themselves. By the age of six, he'd learned a lot about surviving on the streets. Stealing came naturally and was his only means of putting food on the table.

It was probably his greatest luck that he happened to choose Leopold Dirkston as a target one day. Leo caught the skinny lad's wrist as he attempted to make off with his wallet, and dragged him kicking and screaming across the wharf to his warehouse where he paddled him soundly. Afterward, he gave Grant fifty dollars to buy himself some decent food and sent him on his way.

After that, Grant became Leo's shadow. When Leo appeared on the docks to oversee the loading or unloading of cargo, Grant trailed a few paces behind, watching and silently digesting everything that went on. Surprisingly, Leo enjoyed the boy's curiosity. It must have reminded him of his own checkered youth. Eventually, he put Grant to work unpacking crates and sent money secretly to Grant's mother, stipulating that some of it be used for the boy's education.

When Grant's mother died six years later, Leo brought him to live with us at Beacon. I remember him then as a scruffy urchin who had no manners and carried a huge chip on his shoulder. As time went by, though, and he threw himself into his schooling, some of the rough edges disappeared and he grew into a formidable asset to the firm. Now, years later, having risen to the position of Senior Corporate Attorney for Dirkston Enterprises, he still found time to visit the docks once or twice a month, to work alongside the crews and keep abreast of the climate within the unions and among the laborers. This periodic link to his roots was essential to him and seemed to revitalize him, like a grounded sailor needing the smell of salt air and the feel of a rolling deck.

Colin tolerated Grant, but there was no love lost between them. In one sense, he was relieved that Grant had taken on the onus of succession. He'd never wanted to become involved in the business, much to Leo's chagrin, so

Grant was a welcome replacement.

But Grant wasn't an easy man to understand. I remembered one of his court battles: a small fishing combine sued Dirkston Enterprises for some real or imagined breach of navigational courtesy. Like a maggot, Grant had picked away at the meat of the testimony until everyone, including the judge, squirmed uncomfortably. The case was thrown out and the fishermen departed, red-faced. I was appalled and embarrassed. I thought him cruel and unfair. It would have cost Dirkston relatively nothing to have settled out of court, but Grant wanted to make an example of it and seemed to care less that the fishermen involved might lose their reputations as well as their livelihoods.

This was the same man who now offered me compassion and understanding where no one else had, and I began to doubt my poor opinion of him. I resolved to be more open-minded.

Once my tears were under control, he dropped his arms and handed me his handkerchief.

"Feel better?" he asked.

I nodded, mopping my eyes.

"I'm sorry," I said. "I guess it's supposed to be good therapy to cry, but I should have done it in private. Now, I've saturated your shirt." I dabbed futilely at his tear-stained pocket.

He turned away abruptly and I sensed that he was irritated.

"There is something we need to talk about," he said, "but it can wait until later. Go to bed now, and get some sleep."

I stared at his back, my hand still poised, shocked by the terse dismissal. My jaw clenched. This was the Grant I knew—cool, remote and unfeeling. I tossed the handkerchief onto a nearby chair and, without another word, stalked off before he could see the hurt in my eyes.

It was peaceful on High Dune. I'd named it when I was very young, when I'd come here with Mother—before her accident.

She would sit and write in her journal while I clambered up and down the shifting mountain, pretending to be a General in the French Foreign Legion or one of the Arabian Knights, conquering an enemy stronghold. Sometimes I would lie at the top and see how far down I could roll, careless of the warm sand sifting through my hair and clothes. They were golden days.

After her accident, I avoided the place for many years until the pain abated and I was able to put things into perspective. Now, it seemed to bring me closer to the past, as though a part of Anna still smiled from her shaded spot beneath the yellow birch, her pen poised, her eyes proud and possessive as she watched me play.

I breathed deeply of the fresh breeze whirling in off the lake. The air tingled with clarity and the waters seemed to stretch endlessly. The waves drifted onto the shore far below, leaving huge dark arcs along a hard-packed opaline beach.

I could see the house far to my left, a fat toad squatting atop a weathered bluff. It was truly an abomination of architecture, jumbled together in a chaos of arches, gables, columns and balustrades, with chimneys sprouting everywhere, capped by a glassed octagonal belvedere, its foul-weather shutters turned back.

Leo's dreams were far from modest, and Beacon was a testament to that fact. It was obvious that there had been no real aesthetic theme to the design so that, while the house was indisputably breathtaking, it was also decidedly vulgar—an aberration in an otherwise harmonious landscape. But I respected Leo for the audacity and courage it must have taken to wave the red flag of nonconformity in the face of rigid midwest conservatism. He'd worked hard to attain his position in the world, and he had every right to do as he pleased with his money and his house. But my father's tastes were very different from my own, and I couldn't help feeling he'd gone overboard when constructing a home for a family of four.

Below and to my right stood the ancient lighthouse. Perched upon a stony outcrop, its blind eye stared dully over the waves as it had for nearly a hundred years. It would have been nice to refit the lamp and bring the ponderous bulk to life, but it was much too late for that. Its bleached stone skirt was beginning to crumble, and there were fissures in one side where mortar had fallen from between the blocks. The continuous buffeting of wind and tide had eroded the rocky shelf on which it stood, making the whole structure tip very gently to one side.

"I thought I might find you up here."

David sat down gingerly, conspicuous in crisp white trousers and turquoise shirt. I'd watched him approach from the direction of the house, not really welcoming the company, but too apathetic to avoid it. There was no point in trying to evade him. He was as much a part of Dirkston as anyone, especially now that he and Colin shared the partnership.

"How did you know I'd be here?" I asked.

"We all used to call this 'Suzanna's Spot' not so long ago. I figured you'd want to come here first. I hope you don't mind me butting in?"

I sifted sand idly through my fingers. "No, I don't mind. I was just thinking about going back. It must be getting close to dinner time."

He leaned back on one elbow and squinted at the glittering lake. The sun was a huge yellow balloon invisibly tethered to the horizon. "It's beautiful, isn't it?"

I nodded, watching a white gull soar above the spume. It dipped abruptly for some real or imagined tidbit, caught the edge of the lapping waves with experienced precision, then resumed a lazy patrol.

"I suppose you'll be going away again when this is all

over," he commented.

I sighed. "No. I've decided to stay for a while. It wouldn't be fair to leave a lot of loose ends for Colin and Grant to tie up."

"It's mostly business. I'm sure they'll have things well in hand. After all, Grant is an attorney. He's used to handling these things."

I glanced at him, puzzled. He was treating my departure much too casually. I thought he'd be pleased about my decision to stay. Now, I wondered if he was the least bit affected by our breakup. Logically, I should have been relieved that he was taking it all so well, but some primitive instinct in me longed for him to collapse in desperation at my feet amid anguished pleas for reconciliation. Or, at the very least, give some indication that he wanted me near.

I turned my gaze back to the house, trying to think of words to explain my decision. Finally, I sighed. "I need to get rid of the ghosts," I said.

He regarded me levelly for a moment. "Yes. I think I understand."

I doubted it.

We fell silent and when he spoke again, the gravity was gone from his face. "Well, I can't say I'm disappointed to have you back. I have missed you."

I smiled sourly. Well, here it was—no begging, no groveling, merely a toe in the water to test the temperature. It was this very practicality, this irksome, unemotional, unbending and never spontaneous nature of his that always brought out my most obstinate and irrational qualities.

"David…"

"No." He touched my hand. "I'm not trying to change your mind about us. I love you, Suzanna, you know that; but I also think I understand what you want and, until you find your own niche in the world, I'd only be a weight around your neck. I do want you to know, though, that when the time comes, I'll be here for you. Until then, I hope we can still be friends. We've shared too much to pretend it never existed."

It was a sad attempt on his part. I knew he was only saying what he thought I wanted to hear, but I couldn't help responding to the tug of old-fashioned romance. My own novel would have used his words as a cue for a tearful reunion and a passionate 'and-everyone-lived-happily-ever-after' finale. But this wasn't a novel, and the complexities of our past problems couldn't be overlooked.

"Of course, we'll always be friends," I said brightly. "How could we not? If I refused, you'd probably put another dead fish in my bed!"

He laughed, remembering the incident, and his mood lightened.

"Come on, let's go back," he said. He stood up, brushed the sand from his trousers and offered me a hand. Together, we made our way down the steep dune to the beach.

TWO

In ancient shadows and twilights
Where childhood had strayed,
The world's great sorrows were born
And its heroes were made.
In the lost boyhood of Judas,
Christ was betrayed.

Dinner was nearly ready when we arrived, and I hurried upstairs to change. I paused briefly at the door to my father's bedroom, toying with the urge to open it and give myself over to the haunting presence within. But I quickly overcame the impulse. There were some things I just wasn't ready for.

My room hadn't changed much in the years since that lanky, brown-limbed child had lived there. The pink canopied bed remained like an old friend, quilted and draped with sweet girlish frills and lace. It was a perfect example of how totally Leo had misjudged me; such frippery was as foreign to my nature as feathers on a greyhound. But, as with everything else he'd thrust upon me, I accepted it with quiet goodwill and eventually absorbed it into that myriad of impressions that meant 'home' to me.

An enormous collection of stuffed animals and dolls

smiled expectantly from their positions about the bed and shelves. I had long since packed them away, but some-one—I suspected Martha, our housekeeper—had resur-rected them. I felt ridiculously sorry for betraying them.

At one side of the bed, double doors opened onto a bal-cony that ran the entire length of the second floor, con-necting the bedrooms from the outside but divided by intri-cate lattice partitions of wrought iron.

Against one wall was a dressing table, and my eyes fell on the small shell dangling by its chain from one corner of the mirror. It was a simple tiger shell, the kind that wash-es up on the beach frequently but rarely survives intact. David had given it to me on my thirteenth birthday. He'd polished it to a high gloss and bored a small hole in one edge so that I could wear it as a necklace.

I turned the shell over between my fingers and read the worn words inscribed inside the pink leaf: For Your Collection—David. At the time, I'd worn it covertly. My infatuation for him was a child's crush and a mortal secret. The gift had meant nothing to him, merely a token, but I had treasured it and dreamed of a David that I now real-ized was as much a fantasy as the relationship I hoped we could have. They say that love is blind, and at that tender age when adolescence begins to blossom, I was walking proof of it. The old tenderness tugged at my heartstrings as I fingered the smooth surface—tenderness mingled with that sense of sadness which inevitably occurs when dreams are doused by reality.

I put the shell into a drawer and turned to the immedi-ate distraction of dressing for dinner.

Dinner was a tense affair. Grant was preoccupied.

Alicia and Colin were at odds with each other. Even David seemed more subdued than usual. Only Giles Lancaster, David's father, appeared unaffected. Giles had been a lifelong friend of my father's. A retired medical practitioner, he and David were our nearest neighbors. Their estate, Spindrift, wasn't nearly as palatial as Beacon but possessed that quiet, homey appeal that Beacon lacked. I was particularly glad that Giles had come by that night. His uncomplicated compassion was just what I needed now.

"Have you made any plans for the future, Suzanna?" Giles asked.

"Not really," I replied. "I think I'll stay on here for a while, though—until I get my bearings."

"A wise decision, though I'm sure it won't be easy. Beacon must hold some sad memories for you."

I nodded, grateful for his frank perception.

Giles was probably somewhere in his early sixties, yet still good looking despite the obvious marks of time. His hair was pure white and his face was pleasantly lined beneath a deep tan. He kept fit by sticking to a regimen of an early morning jog, followed by (weather permitting) a swim in the lake. Giles's wife, Bethany, had died after a prolonged illness many years before. I didn't remember her, but I was told she'd meant the world to him. Our housekeeper, Martha Simms, compassionate by nature, took on the additional responsibility of Spindrift and, for her convenience as well as at the insistence of Lottie, our cook, Giles and David were regular dinner guests at Beacon.

I smiled warmly at the concern in Giles's eyes. "It's not as bad as all that," I said. "Beacon still holds a lot of good memories, too."

He nodded. "Well, if you ever feel you need to get away for a while, you're welcome to stay with us at Spindrift. It's been ages since the old place has felt a woman's touch."

Martha rattled the serving caddy noisily and glowered. He winked at me slyly and added hastily, "…besides our lovely Martha, of course."

"That's an excellent idea, Dad," David put in. "We'd love to have you, Suzanna."

I smiled across the table at him. "I'll keep it in mind. It's a very kind offer."

"Well," Alicia roused herself, "I for one just don't know why you'd want to leave." She glanced at Colin from beneath lowered lashes. "After all, this place is your home. Now, more than ever."

I looked at her, but she avoided my eyes and picked daintily at her food.

"What do you mean?" I knew she was playing games with me, but my curiosity was piqued.

Her eyes widened in mock surprise. "Why, darling, hasn't Grant told you...?"

"Alicia," Grant cut her off sharply, "I think you've said enough." He sent a dark look in my direction. "But I would like to discuss some matters with you, Suzanna. Privately."

I glanced around the table, feeling once more like an outsider.

"It seems as though we should talk," I agreed, "and the sooner, the better. After dinner?" My voice was bitter, but I didn't care. How dare they keep secrets from me?

Grant merely nodded and lapsed into brooding silence.

The rest of the meal was wrapped in tension. Colin scowled at his untouched dinner, then pushed back his chair, tossed his napkin onto his plate and strode from the room. This seemed to please Alicia and she smiled her feline smile at me, as though we had somehow contrived his hasty exit. David looked confused, and once again, it was only Giles who seemed willing to establish some semblance of rapport.

"I'll be jogging later, Suzanna. If you're not busy, perhaps you'd like to join me—just like old times?"

I grimaced. "I'm afraid I haven't kept up with it. I'm probably so out of shape, I'll collapse at a hundred yards! But, I'd love to give it a try if you promise not to laugh."

He nodded benignly, but his eyes held a message. "Maybe we could just talk, then. About seven-thirty, shall we say?"

I agreed and he made a polite exit via the kitchen for a word or two with Martha. It was obvious to us all that he held a deep admiration for her and I was certain, despite her coy protestations, she reciprocated the feeling. At least that was one area that was untouched by gloom.

Grant excused himself by bluntly stating that he'd be in Leo's study when I was ready. I resented his dictatorial manner and, though I hardly tasted the food, made a point of taking longer than necessary over my dinner.

"What's this all about, Alicia?" I asked. But even she seemed suddenly uncomfortable.

"Really, Suzanna, how could you ask me? I wouldn't dream of taking that pleasure away from Grant."

She also stood to leave, but paused and glared at me with a venom that took me by surprise. "You two really wouldn't get along, honey. He's not your type. Believe me, I know."

I stared, dumbfounded, as she sauntered away. What in heaven's name was she talking about? Grant and me? How absurd! I pushed my plate aside and hurried off in the direction of the study.

He sat behind Leo's desk, the tall back of the black leather chair turned against me as he apparently perused the gardens and the few golden chips of lake twinkling through the thinning foliage of hedgerow beyond the plate-glass windows. A thin string of smoke rose from the recesses of the chair, which explained the butt-filled ashtray on the desk.

"Come in, Suzie," he said at the sound of the door. He didn't bother to turn, and his arrogance ignited my smoldering irritation.

"Don't call me that!"

He swiveled around and his stony blue eyes met mine. "Don't call you what?"

"Suzie," I said, then faltered under his questioning gaze. "Dad called me that."

I couldn't explain to him that the nickname was something I'd discarded along with my youth. When Leo called me Suzie, it was an endearment that made me feel loved and protected, but when others used it, it seemed somehow demeaning. I didn't want anyone to find that child still alive in me. I was still too vulnerable.

"All right, Su-zann-a," he said sarcastically. Then, in a less belligerent tone, "You're really going to let this thing affect your whole life, aren't you?"

"Yes, and why not?" I fumed. "Am I supposed to ignore it? Of course, it affects my whole life. He was my father, for God's sake!" All the pent-up tensions of the past week boiled up. I couldn't have stopped them spilling over if I'd tried. "Who are you to judge me, anyway? He's dead and, whether it matters to you or not, I happen to have loved him. But what would you know about love?"

I was never one to give in easily to tears, but it seemed I had no control over them any more. I looked away quickly as my eyes misted, all the more angry for my weakness. Grant got up and went to the cupboard, and produced a bottle and two glasses. A short time later, he shoved a drink into my hand.

"Here," he said gruffly, "it seems all I do lately is give you alcohol to sooth your nerves."

I was sorely tempted to toss the drink in his face. Instead, I glared pointedly at him until he dropped his eyes and shrugged. "Okay," he said, "I'm sorry. I guess we're all a bit on edge."

Slightly mollified by my victory, I sat down in the nearest chair.

"Perhaps it's time someone told me why everyone is on edge," I said. "I thought something like this was supposed to bring a family closer together, but I get the impression that it's driven us to each other's throats. What's going on?"

He straddled the corner of the desk and turned his glass between his hands; his eyes were downcast, his face looked positively haggard.

"Drink up," he muttered, "you'll need it!"

I complied, suddenly chilled by that same sense of foreboding that had overcome me when David appeared at the cabin. I wasn't at all sure now that I wanted to hear what he had to say. I saw he was struggling for words and knew that, for someone practiced in law and used to speaking on sensitive matters, a loss of words wasn't a good sign. When he finally did speak, his voice was strained.

"I don't know how else to tell you this but straight out," he said. "Leo's will is to be read tomorrow, as I'm sure you know...."

I nodded. Of course I knew, and I knew what it would say: Colin and I would share equally in Leo's holdings, while Grant would undoubtedly receive a substantial settlement as well as a good percentage of the business itself. Everyone knew that Leo had groomed him to take over.

"I'm afraid," Grant continued, "that your father was rather upset about this new independence of yours. I'm sure that, in his own way, he thought he'd be guaranteeing your security as he thought it should be. He often changed his will. It was a quirk he had. He'd always say, 'If I should die tomorrow...', never really seeing past today, but arranging the world just as he would want it to be if he were still here."

I was getting impatient. "Please, Grant, don't pretend to explain my own father to me. If you're trying to say that he cut me out of his will...?"

I hadn't really thought of it until just that moment, but now, as I looked back at that last encounter, it seemed an obvious conclusion.

"No." He hesitated. "Not exactly. Your father left everything to three beneficiaries: you, Colin and myself."

I smiled, relieved. "Yes, I..."

"But that's not all." He moved to the windows so his back was to me once more. "There's a stipulation."

"Stipulation?" I parroted weakly.

"Yes. To make a long story short and to put it as simply as I know how, if you and I don't...marry, all liquid assets will be divided up between the stockholders, the state and a large number of charities; the rest will be put up for public auction." His voice was cold and emotionless. "We here at Beacon would be, as they say, up a creek without a paddle."

I blinked. "Excuse me, but did you say marry? Us? You and me?" I paused, then laughed. "Why, that's ridiculous! You can't be serious?"

He smiled thinly. "I wish I weren't."

Silence hung like ice as I stared aghast. In an instant, cold rage gripped me. I leapt to my feet.

"It's unthinkable! Who does he think he is? How dare he try to manipulate me like that?" I slammed the glass down on the desk top, sloshing the liquid heedlessly. My heart was pounding and I felt suddenly claustrophobic. I took a deep breath and tried to regain some composure. "I don't want the blasted inheritance! Let it go to the state; why should I care?"

He smiled sadly. "Because you aren't the only person involved," he said quietly. "Because if you throw this inheritance away, you'll be sentencing Colin and Alicia, Martha, Lottie—everyone, including David—to certain bankruptcy. You'll destroy their lives."

I glared at him, feeling more trapped than ever. I knew he was right, and hated him for it.

"Let's not forget your own precious stake in the fortune!" I spat.

He dropped his eyes and a muscle played in his jaw, but when he spoke, his voice was reasonable and detached.

"Think what you like about me, Suzanna; it really makes no difference in the long run. The facts still remain the same. A lot of lives hang in the balance, and you hold the key to it all. Don't make any decisions right now. Think it over. Perhaps you'll be able to come up with some alternative. God knows, I've tried."

I stood for some time, still dazed, then moved blindly toward the door. I needed time to think. It all seemed like madness. Surely, in this day and age, these sorts of things didn't happen? I'd contest the will! I'd claim Leo was insane! I'd… I paused, my hand on the knob as a new suspicion occurred.

"Why did you go along with this in the first place?" I asked. "You were Dad's attorney, his confidante; surely…?"

He raised his eyebrows in surprise, then laughed loudly. Still chuckling, he came around the desk and took my shoulders in his hands. I felt small and helpless in his solid grip and, looking up at him with his eyes sparking steel into mine, I was suddenly aware that he could easily squeeze the life out of me. His teeth were very white and very close, and I could almost feel the rough stubble on his chin. Abruptly, he stopped laughing and his eyes narrowed.

"Do you think," he said tightly, "that I want this any more than you? Leo Dirkston liked to use people. To him, the world was his chessboard and everyone in it his pawns. Perhaps in your case, he honored you with a slightly higher esteem, but you were a toy just like the rest of us." He stopped, and the pressure in his hands increased until I nearly cried out. Abruptly, he released me and turned his back. I inched away mechanically, rubbing a spot where a bruise was already forming.

"I had nothing to do with Leo's will," he said, once more a study of calm indifference. "He didn't want me involved in his personal affairs. It was just as much a shock to me as it was to you. He had a different law firm draw up the will and handle his domestic accounts. If you don't believe me, you can ask Colin. Or better yet, ask darling David."

He paused, then chuckled. "Speaking of David, I read in

one of those cheap society columns that you and he are no longer an item. What a pity!"

I felt my cheeks burn and, before he could say any more, I stumbled from the room.

"I see he's told you."

Giles was waiting patiently at the bottom of the steps that led to the beach. He was dressed in running shorts and a warm-up jacket, and looked as if he had already had his workout. The sun had sunk deep into the lake, so that only a sliver remained glowing like a red ruby chip over blue velvet. The air was already cooler, and I shivered.

"He's told me," I said dully.

"Let's talk."

He took my elbow and steered me down the beach. We were both silent for a long time. I knew he was waiting for me to speak.

"How is it that I'm the last to know?" I asked.

He shrugged. "I don't think anyone purposely meant to exclude you. You were away, and Colin found out from some source connected with the law firm holding Leo's will. We all thought it was pretty heartless of him to check on such a thing right after finding Leo dead but, well, you know Colin. Grant followed it up, and I'd say he wasn't too pleased with what he found. I think he wanted to make sure it was all valid before putting any additional burden on you."

I mentally added one more resentment to the list that was rapidly growing against Grant Fenton. Giles rubbed his chin reflectively.

"You know, Suzanna, your father was my very good friend. I've known him since long before you were born. I'm sure you must be feeling a great deal of anger toward him right now, but I think I can almost understand why he did what he did."

I listened halfheartedly.

"He wasn't always so ruthless. You must appreciate what it did to him to watch his whole family die of an influenza epidemic just because they couldn't afford a doctor. He was very young then, and grew up blaming himself and the society he lived in—the rich getting richer and the poor…well…."

I knew the story already. Leo had worked hard as a manual laborer on the Chicago docks for a small company owned by a Greek immigrant named Dimitri Agropolis. Using his wits and charm, he was able to manipulate his way up the ladder and eventually managed to snatch the ultimate prize, Agropolis' only daughter, Carmen. Colin was born a short nine months after their wedding; six months later, Dimitri had a stroke and died, leaving Leo the business.

There were rumors that Leo had dealings with the mob in those early years. No one knew for sure, but the company certainly prospered under his boundless ambition and soon, he had taken over three other struggling shipping firms and combined them all to create Dirkston Shipping. Later, when the company grew and sprouted subsidiaries, the conglomerate was named Dirkston Enterprises.

Carmen turned a blind eye to most of Leo's dealings purely, I suspected, out of self-preservation. She realized that her marriage was a mistake, but pride and a certain amount of greed kept her from abandoning it. Instead, she turned her frustrated affections on Colin, smothering him with attention.

Beacon was a dream long before it became a reality. Colin was two years old before the architects were hired and construction begun. The construction took almost three years.

It was assumed that Leo fell in love with my mother, Anna Kempton, Colin's governess, right under Carmen's nose. I still find it hard to believe that my father could be capable of such cruelty to his wife, but Giles assured me that Carmen was blatantly indiscreet in her own illicit affairs long before Leo strayed. The day they were to move to Beacon, there was a vicious argument. At the end of it, Carmen lay at the bottom of the stairs, her neck broken. There was speculation that Leo pushed her, but he maintained that she lost her footing and fell. A cursory investigation proved little, and the incident was officially deemed an accident. Shortly thereafter, Leo, Colin and Anna moved into Beacon where, after a barely discreet interval, Anna and Leo were quietly married. I was born a year later and immediately became Leo's pet.

"Your mother, Suzanna, was very good for Leo," Giles continued. "She was a delicate, shy little thing who depended entirely on him. Leo loved her completely. I think it was she who helped him find a heart. Before Anna, he was a very cold and ruthless person." He glanced at me, noting my frown. "No, I don't believe he killed her. If Carmen were going to push him to the point of murder, it would have happened long before then." He grimaced, then bent over to pick up a smooth, pearly stone, turning it over between his fingers. "I witnessed a few of her tantrums. She could be extremely malicious, even using Colin as leverage against him."

"What do you mean?"

Giles tossed the stone out into the rising tide. "It's not important. I just wanted you to know that your father changed after he found Anna, and he never lost that goodness. When your mother died, I thought he would go to pieces."

"I remember," I murmured.

It was a silly accident. Mother was never the superb equestrian that Leo was. They went out riding together one morning while I stayed behind under Martha's supervision. I was playing in the sand on the beach, building my own scale model of Beacon, when I looked up to see Leo carrying my mother's limp body in his arms. I remember he was crying, and knew immediately that she was dead. It was a painful memory.

I loved my mother totally, but she loved Leo so intensely that there was little room for anyone else. I missed her desperately when she was gone, but grieved for Leo even more. He began to drink and Giles, the only person he allowed near, sat with him for hours, afraid to leave him alone. It was arranged that Colin and I should attend boarding schools. What else could be done? Leo was certainly unable to take up our rearing on his own, in his state of mind.

"I think the only thing that saved your father in the end, Suzanna, was the realization that you still needed him. The fact that you were a part of Anna and a product of their love for each other became his lifeline, and gave him the will to go on."

I winced, remembering the naked hurt in Leo's eyes when I turned down his offer to help with my writing career.

"This will," Giles continued, "is a product of Leo's need to secure your future, and what he thought would ensure your happiness."

"How could he possibly believe that forcing me to marry Grant would make me happy?" I demanded. "Especially when he knew that Grant and I barely get along as it is. I wonder if he understood me at all, or if I was just another pawn in his game?" Grant's words, spoken from my lips! It grated to believe they could be true.

I didn't want to believe that Leo could be so heartless, but there was no other way to describe it. Deep down, I sensed that there was a Leo Dirkston that I'd never known. An entity quite different from the father-figure that he presented to me; someone who'd accept help from criminals or overrun small businesses with no thought for the struggling individuals he was ruining. Worst of all, someone who could callously use a woman's love as a stepping stone to power.

Giles touched my arm sympathetically. "I know it's

hard for you to understand, but just remember that Leo loved you more than anything on this earth. In his day, marriages were arranged as a matter of course, and children were content to have the decision taken out of their hands. He would never do anything to intentionally hurt you. He did what he thought best for you."

I didn't reply. Nothing anyone could say would diminish my sense of betrayal and disillusionment.

"Don't try to solve anything right now, my dear. You're tired, and I'm sure things will look clearer in the morning. Let's go back now; it's getting late."

I said goodbye to him on the beach and thanked him for trying to help. "You're right about one thing," I admitted, "I am tired."

He nodded. "Just keep in mind that Leo might have been stubborn, selfish and bullheaded, but he rarely made rash decisions. Perhaps you shouldn't be too quick to denounce this arrangement."

I gritted my teeth. Marry Grant? The idea was totally preposterous! It seemed doubly ridiculous that Giles, of all people, should encourage it. He was David's father, for heaven's sake, and only a few short weeks ago my prospective father-in-law!

To avoid further discussion, however, I said I'd consider the matter carefully. This seemed to satisfy him, and he patted my hand affectionately and jogged off down the sandy expanse toward Spindrift.

I stood briefly at the base of the steep rise of log steps that led up from the beach and breathed deeply of the crisp, early-autumn air, heavy with the tang of decomposing seaweed and fish, wet sand and spray. There was no use brooding tonight. My mind was too weary to tackle much of anything.

I turned and climbed slowly, remembering each step as if I were ten years old again. Now, however, my legs felt heavy and the energy that had once seen me fly up and down with agility had deserted me. I vowed silently to try to get back into shape.

When I reached the top of the ridge, I glanced back over my shoulder at the darkening sky. The moon was already rising, despite the slowly fading glow of sunset. It hovered like a slim ivory pendant above the lighthouse, cold and distant, yet untouchably exquisite. I sighed. How I longed to be able to stand aside and view the whole sordid situation objectively. I was too involved—too close—to see it clearly as Giles seemed able to do.

I trudged up the narrow path that wound through the rippling razor grass and tangled, low-growing shrubs at the top of the cliff. Short, delicate catkins raised their furry golden heads and danced in the breeze. The shifting sand gradually gave way to a darker, harder earth where briar bushes had taken root and intertwined to form a formidable barrier along the base of the iron fence, marking the rear boundary of Beacon's rolling grounds. Grasshoppers and crickets whirred and chirruped restlessly from their prickly hideouts, their voices rising in a unified crescendo over the clacking reeds and the mournful shriek of a gull. The wind lifted my hair and brushed my temples soothingly. I stood with my hand on the gate, loath to enter the structured world beyond. But, it was no use balking and, with grim conviction, I pushed through and strode briskly across a vast expanse of meticulously manicured lawns to the rear gardens.

As with everything at Beacon, these gardens were magnificent though strangely out of place with their distinctly European flavor. Gravel walkways edged in brick meandered aimlessly, lined on both sides by blocked and trimmed evergreen hedges that rose to almost six feet and served as a windbreak against the raw weather that swept in off the lake. At corners where the paths intersected, the hedges were clipped into spheres at the top to resemble corner-posts. Leo had imported a topiary expert from Rome to sculpt them, and I was grateful that in this one area he hadn't gone overboard. The paths themselves met occasionally in miniature roundabouts that circled flowerbeds thick with marigolds, asters, zinnias, lavender and roses. The flowers were updated seasonally so that, except during the frigid winter months, there were blooms all year. Grotesque porcelain gnomes squatted here and there below ivory birdbaths and, somewhere nearer the house, a miniature statue of Apollo posed above a small round lily pond where Leo's cat, King Kong, loved to idle away the afternoons batting at goldfish.

Leo had painstakingly imported truckloads of dark loamy earth from further inland to enrich the otherwise sandy soil, and an army of landscape artists from all over the world had been given free rein in designing it. Now the grounds were tended meticulously by Rudy Coleman, a reclusive spindle of a man who lived above the old stables.

Rudy had originally been hired as stableman when Leo purchased his first prized stallion. The stables were to the east of the main estate, on the edge of the forest, with a good acre of untended pastureland between them and the main house. After Anna's accident, Leo sold all the horses and refused to acknowledge the existence of the stables. Rudy, however, remained and became our permanent gardener and general maintenance man, showing a surprising aptitude for both.

I followed the paths, knowing well the way through the puzzle of greenery. It hadn't always been so, and I could remember wandering, teary-eyed, for what seemed hours before being rescued by Martha. Now I wandered absently, knowing the gazebo lay just ahead. It stood in the center of Leo's lavish garden, a miniature Gothic temple with a domed roof and six slim ivory pillars. I mounted the steps, sat down on one of the stone benches that joined the pillars, and pulled my knees up to my chin, allowing my thoughts to wander.

It was cool and dark. A circle of mock orange and lilac crowned the grassy knoll surrounding the building and cast clenched shadows across the cold floor. The winds were blowing strongly, still balmy and heavy with the excesses of honeyed pollen and overripe fruit, and the thick, cloying smell of full-blown roses.

I leaned my head back against the stone and gazed over the hedges toward the darkening horizon. Grant's face filled my mind and I wondered, before closing my eyes, what marriage to such a man would be like.

THREE

My care is like my shadow in the sun,
Follows me flying, flies when I pursue it,
Stands and lies by me, doth what I have done.

Elizabeth I,
On Monsieur's Departure

I can't be sure how long I slept. The moon was high in a blue-black sky and Venus shone brilliant in its usual place below. Lightning bugs flickered on and off and crickets chirped rhythmically, undisturbed by my presence. I shivered, uncurled my legs from their cramped position and swatted futilely at a mosquito as it whined near my ear. I had to go back; everyone would be wondering where I was.

It was then that I heard the voices drifting quietly on the night air. I listened with halfhearted curiosity. The murmuring came from some spot beyond the bushes and hedges, nearer the house. I could make out Alicia's unmistakable tones, but the other voice was muffled and I turned my head in that direction, my interest piqued.

"Of course it's impossible, darling," Alicia was saying in a sickeningly transparent whine. "Leo was a tyrant!

Besides, she'd never make you happy."

It was Grant's voice that answered impatiently. "That's the least of my concerns. The problem now is how to accomplish this charade without anyone getting hurt."

I caught my breath as I realized they were talking about me.

"You don't plan to go through with it, do you?" She suddenly dropped her stage drawl and seemed genuinely agitated.

"There's nothing else to do. If I explain it to her logically, I'm sure she'll understand. You should be the last one to object, considering that Colin will stand to lose the most if we don't go through with it."

"I don't care! I couldn't stand to see you with her!"

"Alicia," his voice was exasperated, "what I do with Suzanna has nothing to do with you. And whether you could 'bear' it or not is really irrelevant to me!"

"Oh, Grant!" She was pouting again. "Don't say such things. You know how I feel."

He laughed coldly. "Cut the act, Alicia. I know exactly how you feel, and I also know what you're doing. Does Colin know about your little games? Or are you playing them for someone else's benefit? One of these days you're push him too far, and then you'll be out on your ear."

She chose to ignore the warning, for when she spoke again, her voice was low and inviting. "Let's go to the gazebo, Grant, just once—for old time's sake!"

"Alicia…" he began, but she interrupted and her voice was almost a whisper. I shuddered, imagining her fingers stroking his shirtfront coaxingly.

I chose the momentary lapse in conversation to hurry from my hiding place. I didn't want to hear any more. I was sickened by the inferences of the conversation, and stunned that Grant would consider trying to talk me into going along with a farcical marriage. It seemed they were all playing games, and my father was the mastermind behind them all. I wondered if Leo had known about

Alicia's involvement with Grant. Now, I could understand why Colin was so remote. Alicia, too transparent to hide her flirtations, seemed to savor the excitement of a juicy scandal, especially when she was in the spotlight. My already shaky respect for Grant plummeted. It made me ill to think he could fall for her shallow seductions.

I hurried through the darkened paths and came out on the sweep of lawn at the other side of the garden. The grass was soft underfoot and damp from the automatic sprinklers that must have recently turned off. I didn't glance back toward the patio where I knew they were. I didn't want to know if Grant had succumbed to Alicia's pathetic pleas, and gone with her to the gazebo.

I always knew he had no scruples! I thought, but somewhere deep inside, I felt a hollow disappointment as another childish dream dissolved and bitterness hardened like a stone in my heart.

I crept in through the servants' entrance at the side of the house and climbed the narrow stairs to the second floor. A round, stained-glass window dropped moonlit colors onto the landing, but I hardly noticed, running on to open the door to the hall and eventually gaining the blessed sanctuary of my own room.

According to the clock on the bureau, it was nine-thirty. I sat wearily on the bed, refusing to give in to my curiosity and peer out the window. I would not let Beacon and its ill-played melodramas interfere with my life.

With renewed purpose, I went to the desk and pulled my laptop onto it. Ideas for my new novel were beginning to form in my head and I set to work, grateful for the distraction.

I awoke late the next morning, surprisingly refreshed. The night had been a restless one, even though I was bone-tired after I finally put aside my writing. When I opened my eyes, the sun was streaming through the windows and the smell of fresh coffee filled the room.

"I thought you might like some breakfast." Martha was busily uncovering dishes on the table near my bed.

"I haven't had breakfast in bed since the time I had the measles!" I exclaimed, propping myself up on the pillows and pushing a stray lock of hair out of my eyes. "What's the occasion?"

She smiled and lay the tray across my lap. "No occasion. It's just so nice to have you home again! We've missed you here."

I was touched and grateful for this one openly friendly face. After my mother's death, Martha had ministered to most of my needs. I couldn't imagine Beacon without her, and often wondered how she managed the extensive supervision needed here as well as the additional demands of Spindrift.

For its size, Beacon had a meager staff. There was Lottie Wilson, the archetypally ponderous cook who worked Wednesday through Sunday and, since the death of her husband a few years before, lived alone in a small cottage some five miles away. Rudy Coleman, besides his gardening and handyman duties, doubled as a chauffeur on the odd occasion that Leo had to make a public appearance on this side of the lake. Martha ran the house entirely, except for the help of one part-time maid, a position that constantly changed as the girls came and went from an agency in Ludington. At the moment, the position was vacant since Polly, an eighteen year old from Scottville, had gone away to college. The agency was having trouble locating anyone willing to move to the relative isolation of Beacon.

By providing servants' quarters in the house itself, Leo had outdone his impracticality. There were enough rooms on the third floor to house a staff of twelve but, aside from Martha, who lived alone in a small corner room, the rest were vacant. It was a real waste. Leo had expected to fill the house with lavish entertainment—grand parties and regular gala festivities like those held by the upper classes in the bigger cities of Chicago, Los Angeles or New York. It obviously hadn't occurred to him that grand parties meant little to the simple folk who lived in this neck of the woods. Of course there had been parties, but nothing so often or extravagant that it would require permanent staff.

Martha sat down companionably in a chair near my bed. "I haven't really had a chance to welcome you back, Suzanna. Things have been so hectic." She frowned and looked down at her hands, folded neatly in her lap.

She wasn't a small woman. Despite her plumpness, she exuded a solid strength, developed from years of manual labor. Her face was pleasant, falling into the gentle folds of age and lined delicately around a thin liquid mouth that was usually set in indulgent determination. Her hair was a soft crown of silver waves. Her eyes, behind thinly framed glasses, were a sparkling gray and, magnified by the lenses, attested to a beauty muted only by time.

"It's just not the same without your father," she said quietly.

I played with my scrambled eggs. "I find it all so unbelievable. Maybe you could shed some light on what happened that night?"

She looked up, surprised. "Why, surely you've been told…?"

"Yes, yes. David told me the facts, and the others, well—it still doesn't seem possible that Dad could be so careless. Did he seem upset to you? Had he been drinking a lot?"

"No." She hesitated. "I mean, not like before but, well, that night he did seem a bit tipsy. You know he always liked to have a drink after dinner. He said it relaxed him." She looked up at me thoughtfully, then added, "I don't know for sure, dear, but I think something was bothering him. He seemed so…so restless."

"The business?" I queried.

She shook her head. "No. Well, maybe. I don't know. I guess it's just a feeling I had." She plucked nervously at her apron for a moment, then stood up abruptly.

"But listen to me ramble on!" She smiled. "How we do prattle when we get older. It was an accident, that's all. Just a horrible, senseless accident. Can I get you anything else, dear?"

She didn't sound very convincing, but I knew it was pointless to pursue the issue. I'd only alienate her, and I wanted as many people on my side as I could muster.

"No, Martha, everything is lovely. Thank you again."

She smiled and left, obviously anxious to get away. Puzzled, I watched her go. Perhaps she wasn't as 'open and honest' as I'd assumed.

It was nearly eleven o'clock when I finally went downstairs and wandered into the rear parlor. This was one of my favorite rooms, and I often came here to read or write or just think. Sunlight streamed in through the sliding glass doors that accessed the stone-paved patio and pool. Plush cream rugs were scattered about a buffed hardwood floor, and a comfortable two-seater sofa and twin chairs, upholstered in a refreshing peach and cream floral, were grouped before a white marble fireplace. In the winter, heavy draperies were drawn across the doors to keep the warmth from escaping. Now, however, only the fly screens were shut and a warm breeze swirled in, carrying the scent of chlorinated water and damp earth.

I glanced at the mirror over the hearth, self-consciously fingering my dark hair. I was Leo Dirkston's daughter, there was no doubt. I had his stubborn chin and Greek coloring. My eyes, however, were my mother's, a rich brown flecked with gold. They tended to show my emotions too readily, so I learned early in life to veil them discreetly with my thick fringe of lashes. Still, I'd always secretly envied Alicia, who was as fair and glamorous as I was dark and unsophisticated. I often tried to convince myself that practicality and intelligence were traits far superior to sexiness and physical beauty, but I still coveted those pouting lips and that slinky body.

My eyes dropped from the mirror to the neat display of framed photos covering the mantle top. One in particular stood out and I picked it up. It was a shot of my mother taken shortly before her death. She looked lovely, captured candidly on the beach, her fawn-brown hair loose and drifting in delicate fingers about her face. She had turned, laughing, toward the camera and her eyes sparkled in wild abandon. I smiled back sadly. I had rarely seen her so carefree. She'd always been timid and skittish, like a doe caught in an alien environment. I guessed that the gossip surrounding Carmen's death and Leo's marriage too soon after had caused a lot of pressure, and was probably responsible for that nervous disquiet that forever surrounded her.

I set the photo back and glanced fleetingly at the others. There was myself astride Dimmy, my pony. Another of me in my graduation cap and gown, and one of the whole family posed in front of Beacon. The rest were of Colin and Grant, and one studio print of Leo that had been taken for the cover of Business Week. I turned away brusquely.

"A bit of useless nostalgia, eh?" Colin smiled wanly, coming in through the patio doors. I assessed him cynically: Frayed and patched, cut-off blue jeans, faded yellow T-shirt, bare feet—he looked every bit a beach bum, except for his pasty complexion, which was odd, considering the time and effort he'd once put in to sun-tanning.

"I thought you'd be at the Marina," I said. "What are you doing home?"

"David's minding the store," he replied absently, fingering the photo of Anna. He rubbed his thumb along the face of the glass, a frown creasing his brow. "I suppose Grant has told you the wonderful news?"

I nodded mutely. There was no point in trying to avoid

a confrontation. Colin had every right to feel slighted. Still, I wasn't entirely ready to deal with his feelings yet. I'd hardly had time to deal with my own.

"What do you plan to do?" His voice was guarded.

Once I might have felt sorry for him, even tried to offer sympathy, but over the years he'd made it quite clear that he didn't want my concern or any other emotional bond between us. I suppose that to him I was devil's advocate—Leo's favorite—that alone was enough to create a rift. The ten-year difference in our ages served to broaden it.

"I don't intend to marry Grant, if that's what you mean." I chose to be as blunt as he, hoping he would drop the subject and leave me alone. Instead, he gazed at me with eyes full of sadness and resignation. He sat down slowly and ran his fingers through his curly hair. My defensiveness ebbed and I sat down nearby, assessing him less harshly.

"Do you think I'm wrong?" I asked.

He sighed and shrugged. "No. I suppose if I were in your shoes, I'd be insulted. But, I had hoped…" He smiled sheepishly. "I have my own neck to look out for, you know."

I cocked a brow. "I hate to be trite, Colin, but money isn't everything. Surely, the marina is doing well enough?"

A shadow passed over his face and I frowned. This wasn't like Colin. I had expected sarcasm, accusations, demands. I could cope with those, but this quiet defeatism was so out of character that I was bewildered. Dare I hope that the rebellious Colin of old had mellowed? Had he lost some of that dark broodiness?

"You know I'd like to save this place," I said, "but, well, maybe it's time we all quit living in Dad's shadow and made lives for ourselves."

"I think the problem goes a little beyond that." He picked up a small figurine from the table and turned it around in his hands nervously. "I know you've never thought much of me. I guess I deserve it. I've never gone out of my way to treat you fairly." I opened my mouth to speak, but he waved his hand impatiently. "I never meant to take things out on you. There were times, though I never told you, when I wished we could have been closer—like brothers and sisters are supposed to be—but my damn pride always got in the way and, after a while, it was just too late."

He leaned toward me, his eyes very serious, and I realized with distaste that he was pleading with me, something I would never have thought possible. It left a sick feeling in my gut.

"I'm sorry, Suzanna. I guess it's sort of hypocritical of me to say all this now, but—well, I really mean it, and no matter what happens, I want you to know that I've never meant to hurt you."

I knew why he was saying all these things, and my mind worked furiously. What sort of desperate situation would make him grovel so? At the same time, I was surprised how little empathy I felt. I nodded my head inanely, unable to think of what to say. I felt as if I'd been dumped on stage before a packed house and had suddenly forgotten my lines.

He didn't seem to notice my discomfiture but continued on hurriedly, as if too long a pause would cut off the words forever. "You of all people know Leo and I were never close," he snorted at the understatement, "but I won't say that he didn't try. In the beginning, I think he tried too hard. I guess I just couldn't forgive him for what he did to Mother. Eventually, he gave up, which was a relief to us both.

"I've never been good with money. He was always there to bail me out. It was sort of a truce we had—I could do what I wanted, as long as I kept the name clean and stayed out of his hair." He hesitated, and I noticed that his hands were trembling.

"I always wanted the best for Ali. In the beginning, I would have done anything—and I can tell you, she likes spending money! There were new cars, acting agents and coaches, wardrobes for every occasion and parties..." He set the glass ballerina down and began to pace. "I moved here to try to stop all that. You're right about having to make our own lives. It took me a while to realize it, but that's what I wanted to do when I came back here. Leo bought the marina and set us up. I really wanted to make it work, but…" His voice trailed off and I suddenly felt my palms begin to perspire.

"What are you saying, Colin?" I asked hoarsely.

"I'm saying," he said, almost angrily, "that I'm broke and in debt up to my ears." He turned on me fiercely. "I'm saying that if you don't marry Grant, I'm washed up! Finished! Kaput! Me, Alicia, David, the marina! I don't own a cent of it!"

I stared at him in alarm. "But surely…?"

He leaned over my chair so that his face was inches from mine, and I shrank back at the desperation in his eyes. "I need time, Suzanna. Leo pulled out too soon! I could have done it—still can—but I need more time!"

I didn't speak. He finally seemed to recover himself, fell back onto the sofa and covered his face with his hands. My mouth was dry. Guilt flooded me and I tried to block it out—tried to find some escape from the knowledge that this man's life was in my hands. At the same time, I was furious that he had put me into such a tenuous position by shoving the responsibility for his poor judgments squarely onto my shoulders. It was his own fault! Why should I feel responsible? I looked at him sitting there in abject despair and something melted inside. Perhaps I still had some compassion left.

Eventually, he dropped his hands and looked up, drained. "Sorry," he muttered. "I just wanted you to know."

He stood up and straightened his shoulders. "I won't beg you, Suzanna. I've made my own bed, and I won't blame you if you tell me to lie in it. But the will does state that the marriage need only last one year. No one's life need really be changed." He studied me, trying to read my stricken face, then shrugged. "I just wanted you to know."

I watched silently as he left the room, more confused than ever. I hated him for telling me those things, and hated myself for wanting to reach out and help him. I knew it had taken a lot for him to break down and confide, and I also knew that, seeing his predicament, I'd never be able to refuse Leo's will without accepting the blame for the consequences. But perhaps that was all part of Colin's plan? Could he have staged the whole episode? I wouldn't put emotional blackmail past him.

I went out onto the patio, squinting against the bright sunlight glinting off the pool and the distant lake. I could barely make out a small fishing vessel bobbing on the horizon. Leo had taught me the rudiments of game fishing years ago from the deck of his yacht. The thought of casting out pretty baubles to snag a living creature seemed barbarous at the time. I used to wonder how it must feel to be caught and dragged, in a frenzy of panic, into a foreign atmosphere, measured, gawked at, ripped and torn and, eventually, tossed back while strange creatures laughed unconcernedly. I preferred sailing.

With that thought, I went back into the house and up the stairs to my room. I changed into my swimsuit, pulled on a matching light blue cover-up and slipped on a pair of deck shoes.

The boathouse and dock nestled comfortably in a small cove to the east of the main beach. It served as protection for Beacon's smaller recreational watercraft. The yacht was berthed in Chicago, and was used primarily for entertaining clients. There was also a company seaplane, which was on call continuously in case Leo was suddenly needed at the main office in Chicago.

I grabbed a set of keys off the hook in the kitchen and headed for the beach. The sun was warm, and I removed my wrap as I descended the steps to the beach. Already, the sand burned my feet, and I was grateful for the cooler touch of the pier.

I unlocked the door to the boathouse and pushed it

open, allowing my eyes to adjust to the darkness within. There were four boats here: a sleek black speedboat with red flames painted down its sides, a twenty-two foot yacht with real teak-wood trimmings, a twin-hulled, fully equipped fishing boat, and a small, two-man catamaran. This last I approached with a half smile. It probably hadn't been used since I'd left Beacon, but its bright fiberglass hull still gleamed, even in the relative gloom.

I stepped onto the center platform, unsnapped the canvas covering the boom and sail, and used the paddle to maneuver it out into the sunlight. I tied it loosely to a pylon while I checked that all the rigging and safety gear were intact. Two gulls screeched overhead, and I saw them reflected in the crystalline waves.

Within minutes, I was ready. I paddled a short way out before raising the bright multicolored sail. The gusty breeze caught it immediately and I was off, skimming across the sparkling waves.

The day was perfect. There were only three small marshmallow clouds adorning the sky below a plump golden sun, whose pulsing heat shimmered in the air and beckoned moisture up from the earth. The water was sapphire blue, and I let one hand trail in the frothy wake. Despite the warmth of the days, the chill of late August nights had settled like a reptile into the vast freshwater depths, stirred oh so gently with each tide.

I leaned back, holding the rope tightly so that the sail bloomed and the boat skipped smoothly over the soft swells. The opposite pontoon lifted slightly out of the water. Today, the lake was tame, but before a storm it could rise up like a primeval beast, ripping viciously at its long-suffering borders. In the winter, it was even more predatory, writhing with cold-blooded purpose around the rocks and dunes with frigid, sinewy intent, waiting patiently for prey. Now it was puckish, playful—as though full bellied and content, in need of diversion. I knew the lake too well to fear it, but I had also learned to respect it.

I could translate the first signs of foul weather.

I shaded my eyes and scanned the shoreline. Beacon was entrancing from this angle. Sandy cliffs rose like sandbox sculptures, interwoven with green fingers of forest and grassy knolls. Atop the tall rise stood the house, its windows watching the horizon with vacuous patience, almost as though it was were waiting—waiting for Leo to return. The glass winked silver while the garden hedgerow underlined the looming white walls.

I loosed the rope slightly and let the sail flap, drifting gently. I never failed to be amazed at the magnificence of this view. Often, larger yachts and schooners strayed from the crowded shores further south to sidle by for a glimpse of the house or to train their zoom lenses on it, hoping for some exclusive photos of Leopold Dirkston's private life. It suddenly occurred to me that, if I let the estate go, those same greedy sensationalists could snap it up and turn it into anything they desired: a tourist trap, a public landmark, a museum. I frowned, trying to imagine the unmarred beach strewn with gaudy umbrellas and sun-worshippers with their coolers of beer and blaring radios. I shuddered, and was swept by a sudden possessiveness.

I pulled the rope tighter still. The swells were getting larger and the skiff fairly skimmed the surface. I leaned far out over the side for ballast. The wind whipped my hair and cleared my head. I was suddenly aware that I had made my decision, and the realization flooded me with relief, as though all my concerns had been blown away with the breeze.

For what it was worth, I loved Beacon more than I despised it. I knew that, despite my reservations, the place was my home and to let it go would be like abandoning an ailing pet. This reasoning allowed me to shoulder the burden my father had placed on me without submitting to him. The game wasn't over. He had merely placed me in a temporary stalemate. After the year was out, we'd see who would make the final move!

FOUR

For we are strangers before thee, and sojourners,
as were all our fathers:
our days on the earth are as shadow,
and there is none abiding.

   King James Bible, 1 Chronicles 29:14-15

The funeral was a monstrous affair. Leo had request-
ed that his body be cremated and his ashes buried at
Beacon. The estate held my mother's remains as well, and
for that reason alone, I could never allow it to be put up for
sale. The more I thought of the will, the more I accepted
it, telling myself time and again that one year wasn't long
and, in Colin's words: "No one's life need really change."
He was right, and I was prepared to go along with the condition, but only on my own terms. At least Leo couldn't
force me to like it.

   There was a memorial service that the whole family
attended, along with hordes of well-wishers, acquaintanc-
es and gossipmongers who had heard of Leopold Dirkston
and wanted to see who remained to inherit the fortune.
There were also reporters from dozens of newspapers, as
well as television camera crews and journalists. These

people weren't allowed inside the church, but crowded about the steps and entrances like maggots.

For appearance's sake, Grant enlisted the services of two limousines to transport the Dirkston clan. At the church itself, police and security guards held back the crush of onlookers and media until we were all safely inside and seated in black-draped pews at the very front.

Alicia was primed for an Academy Award performance. She leaned delicately on Colin's arm, pressing a lace-edged handkerchief to her nose with a black-gloved hand and sniffing pathetically. She was dressed in black chiffon that flowed like mist about her fragile frame. Her head was hidden by a wide-brimmed black hat with a snood in the back (that completely covered her golden hair) and a demiveil in the front. She wore extremely high heels and seamed black stockings that displayed her slender legs to perfection.

David accompanied me at my request. I felt I needed his stolid support to get me through this ordeal. I wore a black tailored jacket and skirt devoid of frills and decorations, with a modest velvet pillbox hat. I despised hats but, not wishing to create discord, bowed to Martha's and Alicia's advice.

Grant followed us into the church. He seemed out of place and uncomfortable. It was an environment I knew he abhorred. As I was wont to do often these days, I appraised him critically. But I had to admit he was actually quite handsome in his dark suit with his hair neatly combed and his face newly shaved.

The ceremony took the better part of two hours. The minister was Greek Orthodox, though it hardly made any difference. Leo had disdained organized religion since early childhood, almost as if it posed some sort of threat to his ambitions for worldly success. If he had thought to do so, he would most certainly have disallowed any sort of service. Luckily for the rest of us, he hadn't. Despite a mysterious sense of apathy, the memorial lent a greater reality to his demise, and for that, I was thankful.

At the front of the church, surrounded by wreaths and bouquets, stood a small, onyx-black urn that held Leo's ashes. The smell of burning incense mingled with the thick, sweet perfume of hundreds of flowers was stifling. I tried to take slow, deliberate breaths, barely aware of the droning voice of the minister, concentrating instead on the steady grip of David's hand and my own disassociated thoughts.

The church was full to overflowing, lending further discomfort, and I wasn't the only one relieved when the eulogy was completed. Grant left silently before anyone else to waylay reporters and give them some incomprehensible jargon to take back with them. This allowed the rest of us time to reach the sanctuary of the cars and move off for the private ceremony to be conducted over the burial of the urn within Beacon's grounds.

I was dry-eyed and because of it, I suspected that the crowd condemned me as heartless and unfeeling. In truth, my emotions were blank. The little black urn meant no more to me than the impersonal words that had been spoken by the pompous, balding priest. I knew that it would take some time to put my father to rest in my own heart. I still felt his presence throughout the estate, as if I might come around a corner and find him striding toward me, grinning, or dictating to some junior executive scurrying to keep up, his clear, deep voice echoing resonantly. Perhaps if I had been able to see Leo in death, I might have accepted it, but it wasn't to be. There had been a brief lying-in, but the body was draped—also at Leo's request—so that it was no more familiar or recognizable than the impersonal black urn.

King Kong was waiting in the entrance hall when everyone straggled back from the burial. He was a typical feline, in that he came and went as he saw fit and displayed little loyalty to anyone. After Leo's death, he had disappeared. This wasn't surprising, since he often embarked on personal business that sometimes kept him away for days. He always returned, however, not much the worse for wear, and adamantly refused to give any hint as to where he'd been or what he'd been up to. Such was the case now. He sat perusing us with aloof dignity, his thick satiny fur blending with the black marble floor, his eyes slitted into yellow-gold chips and his huge, fluffy tail curled around him with just the tip twitching with some inner annoyance.

Alicia drew in her breath when she saw him and clutched Grant's sleeve. "Lord, I'd forgotten about the cat!"

I looked at her curiously, then back at the huge Persian.

"Poor old Kong." David smiled sympathetically, squatted and stretched out a hand.

Kong regarded him lazily for a moment, then stood, stretched, blinked twice and turned his back. He stalked regally down the hall and disappeared in the direction of the kitchen without a backward glance. David smiled ruefully and stood up.

"Don't bother with him," Colin snorted. "Leo's the only one he paid any attention to. Cats are too stupid to appreciate anything."

"I wonder if he knows," Alicia mused ominously.

Grant looked at her and his eyes glittered. "Oh, he knows all right. He's probably the only one who does know exactly what happened that night by the pool."

The words echoed hollowly through the large room, and I shivered. "I'm going up to change," I announced. "There'll be more reporters on their way, not to mention friends and associates. I think Grant had better brief us all on what he's told them already, so we can get our stories straight."

Grant nodded agreement, obviously impressed by my seemingly cool logic. We all agreed to meet in twenty minutes and I escaped just in time, shutting my door solidly and giving in to an unreasonable fear that pulsed through me like lava.

A strange sensation had come over me. I noticed it the minute we stepped into the entrance hall, and it remained even after Kong had disappeared. To describe it exactly was impossible, but it was a feeling akin to being watched from the shadows by covert eyes.

I moved to the closet and pushed the hangers this way and that, aware that my hands trembled. Abandoning that, I fumbled in my drawer for a cigarette, lit it and inhaled deeply, trying to calm myself. I tried to pinpoint a logical reason for my disquiet, and finally settled on the lame excuse that the memorial service and funeral had shaken me up more than I realized. Having accepted this, I crushed out the half-smoked cigarette disgustedly. Up to now, I'd done pretty well at giving up!

Turning once more to the closet, I chose soft tan slacks, a cream crêpe blouse with full-length draping sleeves, and comfortably low brown shoes. For ornament, I clasped a thin gold chain with a floating heart about my neck.

I brushed my hair and studied my pale face, not impressed by the dark smudges beneath my eyes and the anxious tightness about my mouth. Yes, certainly I was in a worse state than I realized and, despite my self-assurances, it took all my courage to descend the stairs some minutes later. I let my eyes scour every inch of the foyer, but the feeling was gone. I breathed easier and, somewhat satisfied that it might only have been my vivid imagination, hurried off to join the others.

The official reading of the will took place the next day and, despite the fact that everyone already knew its contents, reactions were high. Grant paced like a caged lion, Colin sat, splay-legged, cracking his knuckles nervously, while Alicia fidgeted with her bangles. David wasn't present. I decided it was time I quit leaning on him and faced the music alone. I listened impassively, keeping my face blank, all too aware of the furtive looks that were cast in my direction by all eyes.

The officiating attorney was Henry Legget of Garth, Garth and Legget. He wore cut-down bifocals and eyed Grant and me over the tops of them.

"There will be a ten-day period from this date in which to file for contest of this document but, should the will be accepted, stipulations must be complied with before the end of the month. Is this understood?"

I nodded woodenly and Grant shot him a look that made the little man cough nervously.

"Well, then," he said, tidying his papers and placing them in his briefcase, "are there any questions? No? Fine." He snapped the case shut. "I'll show myself out."

No one spoke for some moments. I think we were all too dazed. Finally, Alicia proclaimed that she needed a drink and scurried off to the library. Colin and Grant eyed me speculatively, probably hopeful that I'd announce some decision. Instead, I excused myself and, after grabbing a copy of the will from the desk, escaped before anyone could question me.

David was waiting for my call. He said he'd be happy to see me, but that he'd be working at the marina all day. In the end, we agreed to have lunch together. It was already after ten, but there would be enough time to stop off at the law offices in Manistee before meeting him. I didn't intend to leave any stone unturned.

There was a definite chill in the air when I left the house. I was grateful for the warmth of my white cardigan. I realized with a twinge that it would be winter in less than two months, which meant long periods of time cooped up indoors. I hoped that, if indeed this marriage to Grant was inevitable, he'd at least have the courtesy to move into the Dirkston penthouse in Chicago. Such an arrangement would certainly be more practical. Not only would he be closer to the company offices at this inevitably busy time, but it would also help to ease the embarrassment of our situation.

My little red Mazda zipped down the drive, and I paused only briefly before turning north on the main road. I felt relieved to be away from the tense atmosphere at Beacon. It would be so nice to just keep on driving and never look back. I thought of Kong and the easy assurance with which he rejected everyone. I wished I had the confidence and audacity to do the same.

The drive to Manistee took only fifteen minutes. It was a relatively small town, about the same size as Ludington, with its own small commercial port, but fewer curiosity shops for tourists and more supermarkets and chain stores for locals. Quaint, attractive restaurants dotted the harbor-side and main streets, while a number of old centennial homes had been refurbished as bed-and-breakfasts, displaying a unique blend of austere Puritan lines set off by frivolous rococo ornamentation.

Despite its prime location, Manistee didn't seem to rely on sun-worshippers and sports enthusiasts as did many of the other coastal towns. It thrived on its commercial enterprises and kept to itself as much as possible. I'd decided to take Leo's will to a law firm there, where I'd be less likely to run into anyone directly associated with Beacon. I certainly wasn't going to trust Grant's word that it was useless to contest it. For all I knew, Grant had arranged this whole ridiculous affair just to get his hands on Leo's money and the corporate assets. It was quite clear to me that he would stand to gain the most from this marriage, acquiring the power to influence the running of Dirkston Enterprises, as well as virtual control of Leo's private fortunes. I wouldn't be at all surprised to find he was the one who suggested the idea to Leo in the first place.

It didn't take long to present my questions to the attorney. If he was surprised at the demands set down in the will, he didn't show it. In the end, he merely agreed to study the document at length and phone me as soon as possible. I thanked him, feeling no more comforted than when I'd arrived, and returned to my car to begin the return journey.

The sun broke through a scattering of gauzy cirrus clouds and dropped warmth across the tree-lined bitumen. I guided the car absentmindedly, enjoying the quiet isolation. I passed Beacon's shadowed drive and continued on toward Ludington.

It was minutes later that I saw him. I don't know where he came from, but there in the middle of the road was a man. He didn't move, merely stood as though waiting for the car to reach him. His face was indistinguishable, his clothing dappled by the rapidly moving clouds overhead. He seemed to shimmer like a mirage and I blinked, half expecting him to disappear. His appearance was so sudden that I gasped and slammed my foot on the brake. The tires squealed plaintively and the automobile veered to the right and onto the shoulder of the road. My heart was pounding furiously, and I threw open the door to confront the man; but when I looked, he was gone.

I stood by the side of the car and scanned the shrubs and forest on either side. Shadows danced through the woodland recesses and a brisk wind whipped my hair. There was no sign of anyone. Climbing back into the car, I locked the doors and sat for some moments, waiting for my hands to steady. The road stretched ahead, a gray ribbon that cut the forest in half. I began to wonder if I had seen anything after all, or had merely conjured the image in my mind. I couldn't have described the figure that had loomed so suddenly. I couldn't even be sure now if it had been a man or a woman. Perhaps a deer? It was highly unlikely. Deer were often seen along this stretch of highway, but very rarely at midday.

I started the car and, with one last furtive glance about, continued on my way. I was troubled. Something about the figure in the road had been unsettlingly familiar, like a flash of déjà vu, yet inexplicably different. I made a mental note to ask David if there were any campers in the woods near Beacon or Spindrift.

Ludington was small in comparison to the better known Michigan cities of Detroit, Lansing, Grand Rapids and Ann Arbor, yet larger than many other coastal towns such as Pentwater, Montague or Whitehall. Many of these little villages were all but deserted during the winter months, catering primarily to summer visitors who were looking for sun, sand and water. A large percentage of the population lived permanently elsewhere, maintaining holiday homes near the lake which they shut up during the winter. Ludington, a commercial port for vessels trading the Great Lakes, maintained a less transient populace. This was home to me and I felt secure in the familiarity, enjoying the continual summer stream of out-of-state license plates affixed to cars with urban faces pressed against the windows, seemingly viewing nature for the first time.

Colin and David's marina was situated just north of the main street. A tee intersection took my car along the lake road where sandy white beaches, dotted with children's swingsets, playground equipment, tall lifeguard chairs and brick barbecues, stretched indolently. About a mile later, rounding the bend that would take me out of the city, was the irregular oak sign announcing: Blue Fin Marina. Dangling beneath this sign on heavy chains, smaller signs read: Charter Fishing, Pleasure Craft and Canoe Rental, C. Dirkston/D. Lancaster. I turned the car down the short gravel drive and parked in front of a white, weather-board building labeled: Office. David appeared almost at once, smiling a greeting as he opened my door.

"I thought you'd never get here!"

I looked at my watch. "David, I'm a half-hour early!"

He chuckled. "I know, I know. It's just been so slow this morning. Only one group of canoes and a few bookings for next summer."

"It's usually quiet this time of year, isn't it?"

"I suppose." He nodded agreeably. "Where would you like to go for lunch?"

"I thought you were working all day. Who's going to mind the store?"

"Colin's on his way. He can take over for an hour or so."

Colin arrived before we had time to go inside, roaring down the drive and making twin furrows in the gravel as he skidded to a halt. I noted with a twinge of annoyance that he drove Leo's silver Maserati, which seemed somewhat presumptuous of him so soon after the funeral, but I kept quiet, not wishing to start any arguments.

"Hello, Suzanna." he said, and noting my apparent look of disapproval, added, "If I'd known you were coming here, I'd have gotten a lift with you."

"I had other errands to do."

I ignored his curious look and turned to David. "Shall we get a couple of sub sandwiches and go down to the beach?"

"Good idea. Just give me a minute with Colin and I'll be right with you."

They disappeared into the office and I leaned idly against the car, breathing deeply of the clear, crisp air sweeping in off the lake.

"Got a light, Miz Dirkston?"

The voice was so unexpected that I jumped, dropping my purse so that its contents spilled onto the ground. Mike Kensington smiled at me, his eyes slitted against the sun, a cigarette hanging from his mouth. I stooped to pick up my scattered belongings, chiding myself for being so nervous, yet irritated at him for coming up on me so suddenly.

He didn't bother to help, but waited until I stood up.

"About that light?" he persisted.

"Sorry, Mike, I'm trying to quit," I said, though I knew he had seen my lighter and cigarettes among the litter in the gravel. He shrugged and put the cigarette back in its pack, relocating it to a pocket of his blue windbreaker.

He wasn't an unattractive man. Average in height with black, rumpled hair, his gray-blue eyes were overshadowed by heavy black brows and his face, lined deeply from constant squinting, was tanned almost hickory. He sported an impressive moustache and sideburns which were peppered with gray.

"Sorry to hear about Mr. Dirkston. I was pretty shocked myself. Flew him to Chicago just a couple of days before it happened. I never would have guessed that…" He stopped at my expression. "Anyway, I'm sorry."

"Thank you," I said stiffly; then, feeling guilty for my irrational irritability, added: "It was a shock to all of us."

I expected him to go, but instead he looked at the ground and drew lines in the gravel with one toe.

"I was wondering if, well, if you know whether you'll still be needing a pilot?"

The question took me by surprise, and I realized with some degree of sympathy that he'd probably been on tenterhooks since Leo's death, not knowing if he still had a job. I smiled reassuringly.

"Mr. Fenton will be running the show—for a while at least, until the will has been probated—and he'll undoubtedly want to keep you on. After that, well, I can't say just yet, but I wouldn't worry if I were you."

He seemed relieved and smiled suddenly, breaking his angular face into an interesting pattern of creases and showing a beautiful set of teeth.

"That's good to hear, Miz Dirkston. Thanks." He touched a hand to his forehead in solute. "You have a nice day, now," he said, and sauntered off around the building toward the docks just as David reappeared.

"I hope he wasn't bothering you," he said, frowning.

"Not at all. He's just worried about his job, which is understandable."

"I already told him you'd be keeping him on the payroll, and I've put him to work around here, too. Guess he wanted to get it straight from the horse's mouth. By the way, how did it go this morning?"

I eyed him curiously. "It all went just as we expected."

He didn't seem at all concerned about the will, which surprised me. If he still felt anything for me, it certainly didn't include jealousy. Then realization dawned and I grimaced. No one had told him!

"David… " I began, but his look of quizzical innocence so disarmed me that I couldn't continue. The others had obviously tried to 'protect' David, just as they had me. What surprised me most was that even his own father hadn't had the foresight to prepare him for the shock. Like the cowards they were, they had left it up to me.

"Let's go to lunch," I said. "We've got some talking to do."

David paced up and down, his black, highly polished shoes shedding sand like an oilcloth shedding rain. He rarely indulged in cigarettes, but now he puffed angrily, blowing smoke out through his nostrils like a dragon. He had loosened his tie sometime during our conversation, and it hung at angles across the front of his white shirt. It was the first time I could remember him looking rumpled. The tail of his shirt had come loose from his finely creased gray trousers, and he'd rolled the sleeves up above his elbows. Little beads of perspiration dotted his forehead and upper lip and he wiped them absently with a handkerchief.

"I can't believe this!" he muttered. "The old coot must have been mad!"

I bristled at this unkind attack on my father, but I understood his anger. Hadn't I reacted in just the same way?

"No, David, if he were mad, we'd have grounds to dissolve the will." I was trying my hardest to remain calm.

"Oh, that's right, Suzanna, make jokes! Don't you care at all? Do you have any idea what this means?"

He stopped in front of the picnic table where I sat,

hands on hips, cigarette clamped in one corner of his mouth, his fair hair lifting in the wind. I had never seen him so angry.

"Yes, I do," I replied evenly. "And I wasn't making jokes. You seem to think that you're the only one who's been upset by this. How do you think I feel? Do you think I want to marry Grant Fenton?"

He continued to glare at me until gradually my dilemma registered and his expression softened.

"I don't know what to think," he said at last. "I just can't believe that Dad or Colin didn't tell me about all this before." He turned his head and gazed down the beach, which was dotted with the last of the truly dedicated sun worshippers.

I shrugged. "I'm sure they thought they were protecting us." This had been Giles's argument, and I hoped it would work on David.

He snorted. "From what? From the truth? What—did they think that by not telling me, it would all go away?"

I grimaced, recalling my own identical but futile tirade. "They're just cowards, I guess."

He began to pace again, stooping to pick up an occasional stone and heaving it violently at the azure waves. Finally, his rage spent, he came to sit down beside me and took a deep, steadying breath.

"What are you going to do?"

I looked away, knowing I couldn't tell him just yet and add another blow to his already battered ego.

"I've taken the will to an attorney in Manistee to see if there's anything I can do to get out of this. Until I hear from him, I don't intend to do anything."

"And what if he says there's nothing you can do?"

I frowned. "Well, I'll make a decision then."

Thankfully, he didn't pursue this line of questioning, lapsing into thoughtful silence. When he did speak again, it wasn't what I had expected.

"Has Colin spoken to you about the marina?"

"Yes."

"It sure puts me in one helluva mire! If we go along with this farce, I lose my girl. If we don't, I lose my business."

I chose not to take exception to his use of the word 'we.' This wasn't the time for petty grievances. Perhaps it would make him feel better to think he had a say in the matter.

"You know," I said hesitantly, "the will says that the marriage need only last one year. I've been thinking that, well, that's not really so long—and it would, of course, be a marriage in name only."

He didn't reply immediately, which disappointed me. Again, I'd hoped for an outraged declaration that he couldn't bear to see me wed to another man, no matter how innocent the arrangement—anything to indicate that he felt some sense of devotion to me. Instead, that calm logical side of him that I hated so much switched on and he sighed, taking my hand absently.

"I suppose if it's the only way…" he said resignedly.

"Besides," I added haughtily, "you seem to have forgotten that I broke off our engagement!"

He smiled infuriatingly. "I haven't forgotten."

His very attitude was patronizing, and I suddenly I knew that he'd never taken our breakup seriously. I was livid, jerking my hand away and bundling up the remains of our sandwiches to take to a nearby rubbish bin.

He stood up and watched me. "Have I said something?"

I squinted at him against the sun. "Not at all," I replied, through clenched teeth. Then, I added shortly, "But I really must be getting home."

Always the pacifist, he followed me silently back to his car. We didn't say much on the short drive back to the marina but, as I made to get out of the car, he caught my wrist. "You'll let me know as soon as this lawyer gets back to you?"

I searched his face, but found nothing there to ease my

irritation.

"I'll let you know," I replied briskly and, with an aplomb that even Kong would have been proud of, turned on my heel and marched to my car, driving off before my frustration got the better of me and I said things I'd regret.

On the way home, I inspected the roadside thoroughly, glancing down the many fire trails cut through the forest. There was no sign of the figure that had given me such a fright. On impulse, I swung the car into the drive leading to Spindrift. There were no iron gates barring the way here. Giles loved his privacy, but wasn't obsessed with it as Leo had been and, being simply a retired physician who had inherited a comfortable sum from his wife, didn't have to worry about being invaded by reporters or sightseers as did someone with a powerful name in high finance.

Spindrift wasn't small by any means, but hugged its dimensions compactly, surrounded closely by stands of pine, maple and oak. Its brick walls blended with the rusty autumn leaves, and the shadows dancing playfully across its face mottled it into near invisibility. A little stream gurgled past one corner and cut across the front yard to lose itself in the forest. The drive traversed this stream with an arched wooden bridge which barely let out a groan as my car rumbled across.

There was no lawn, only a modest rock garden artistically set around a stone path which led from the drive to the front door. Rambling ivy stretched parasitic tentacles across the entire south wall, surrounding the recessed front door.

I pressed the doorbell and waited, breathing in the musty aroma of decaying leaves, moss and pine. A squirrel darted down from an oak tree nearby and paused to eye me suspiciously, his tiny paws pressed to his chest, his tail flicking nervously. Eventually deciding that I was no threat, he scurried along, nose to the ground and snatched an acorn in his teeth. Just at that moment, the front door opened and the squirrel dropped his prize and darted back up the tree.

"Suzanna!" Giles smiled warmly. "What a surprise! Do come in."

He held the door open and I went past him into the cooler recesses of the house. Here the earthy autumn scents followed, tinged by a richer medley of linseed oil, leather and wood. The hall in which I stood was dark, except for the muted sunlight filtering in through narrow etched and frosted windows at either side of the door. The floor was gray slate, the walls paneled in rich cedar, and two potted palms contributed to the wooded atmosphere.

Giles appeared genuinely glad to see me.

"I had lunch with David, and just didn't feel like going home yet," I explained.

"Well, I was only cleaning up a bit," he said. "Martha will be here soon, and I do like to help as much as possible. Unfortunately, I'm hopeless when it comes to domestic chores. She'd be furious if she knew."

I laughed, knowing as well as he that his meager attempts at tidying the house would go unnoticed under Martha's critical eye.

I followed him down the long, narrow passage to a huge living room which was dazzlingly bright in comparison. A massive wall of glass rose to a cathedral ceiling, very reminiscent of a Swiss chalet except that, instead of the expected view of snow-capped mountains and grassy foothills, it framed rolling dunes, forested windbreaks and the glittering turquoise of the lake beyond.

The house was split-level. The room we now occupied jutted out from the hill supported by heavy uprights that created a cavern-like area below. This was paved with brick and screened in as a patio. From one side of the house, wooden steps followed a steep, winding descent through overhanging trees to meet up with a path to the beach. It was a far cry from Dirkston's meticulously manicured lawns and gardens, but it suited the environment and I found it charming.

I descended the two steps to the sunken sitting area, which was carpeted in soft blue and bordered by cream-colored overstuffed sofas and chairs. I accepted Giles's offer of coffee and sat down as he disappeared into the kitchenette. Bordering the sitting area were huge rectangular planters, lush with a variety of greenery that obviously delighted in the warmth and light of the room.

"How did the reading go?" he asked, placing a steaming cup before me and settling down in a nearby chair.

I shrugged. "I was hoping that it would be different from what we'd all expected, but unfortunately, Colin's sources were all too accurate."

He frowned. "And have you decided what you're going to do?"

I shook my head. I was getting weary of answering the same inquiries. Besides, I had something else on my mind.

"Giles," I began hesitantly, not quite certain how I should approach the subject. "David didn't know about the will," I said, and left the statement to pose its own question.

He set his cup down and looked appropriately sheepish. "I know. I just couldn't find a way to tell him." He looked at me and his even, white brows came together. "You told him?"

I nodded.

He sighed. "I suppose he's furious."

"He has every right to be."

His expression changed to worry and I softened. "I think he understands now, though. He'll just need time to adjust." I swirled the coffee in my cup, watching the reflections dance on the lip. "I think if we all just look at this as one short year, it will be easier to accept."

"So, you have decided."

I tilted my head. "If I have no other choice, yes."

He was too obviously relieved and I wondered why. But, of course, David's business future would probably be most important to him. Love and marriage, to an old-fashioned man like Giles, was quite definitely secondary to financial success. It was a common belief among men of his era that career, money and power were the keys to happiness, and that a wife and children were simply ornaments attesting to that success. There was no point in resenting this attitude, for it wasn't one that he had consciously adopted. Giles was set in his ways. It would take another generation to open the way for change.

"Well," I said at last, "we've still got ten days to decide. Perhaps we'll find a more recent will before then."

I'd meant the remark to sound light and jovial, but Giles choked and nearly dropped his cup.

"I was only joking!" I exclaimed, pounding him on the back until he caught his breath. He smiled apologetically through watery eyes and finally recovered himself.

"Don't surprise me like that!" he gasped, half laughing, "You don't really think…?"

"Of course not! Dad was too organized."

He nodded, satisfied, and rose to pour another cup of coffee. I watched him with a puzzled frown, wondering why I was suddenly so suspicious of everyone—even Giles, whose reaction smacked of something more than just surprise.

I didn't stay much longer at Spindrift. I could see a bank of black threatening clouds piling up in the distance, and knew there would be rain before long. He walked with me to the car, mentioning that he wouldn't be around for dinner since he had a previous engagement in town. I thanked him for his hospitality and put the key in the ignition.

Suddenly, I remembered the incident on the highway. "Do you happen to know if there are any campers in the woods between here and Dirkston?"

"No, not that I know of. Why? You haven't had any trouble?"

"No, no, nothing like that. I just thought I saw someone standing in the road." I smiled, realizing how silly that sounded. "The more I think about it, the more I think it was just my imagination."

He shook his head. "You've had a lot on your mind, Suzanna. But perhaps it was a hitchhiker. You know, there are more and more of them around these days."

"Yes. Perhaps you're right," I said. But I didn't think the person or thing I'd seen was a hitchhiker. He had stood quite immobile in the center of the road, and had disappeared too suddenly after I'd stopped.

"Do try to get plenty of rest," he said concernedly. "If you need anything to help—a mild sleeping tablet or something—please let me know."

I thanked him, bid him farewell and headed for home.

I passed Martha's little pink car, honked and waved. It must be nearly three. I wondered idly if Martha and Giles would ever tie the knot. They seemed so suited to each other, and Spindrift literally cried out for a woman's presence. But, as I turned in at Dirkston and waved to John, I scolded myself for matchmaking when my own life was turned upside down just because Leo had attempted to do the same.

A warm front blew up from the Gulf Stream while a line of cooler polar air descended from the north. The two met, mingled and fluffed up into a turmoil of confused thunderheads that became quickly saturated as they moved like giant living sponges across the huge sweep of Great Lakes. Having noted the unexpected warmth of the winds that replaced the cooler morning gusts, I'd changed into jeans, T-shirt and canvas shoes to stroll down to the little plot where Leo's ashes had been so recently buried.

It was a modest grave. A marble slab about two feet square was set flat into a fresh mound of earth. The dirt was neatly smoothed, but much too stark and raw. The other stone was identical, except that its surface was well weathered and comfortably lackluster. It blended naturally, having sunken over the years into the thickly established grass surrounding it.

I gazed pensively at both stones. Giles had overseen Anna's cremation and subsequent burial. Leo had refused to even attend the ceremony, having retreated to his study with a case of whisky to deal with his overwhelming sense of grief. Even after his recovery from that tormented period of mourning, he rarely visited the grave.

The spot was shaded by a huge, gnarled black cherry tree. A scattering of the tiny, bitter berries lay squashed into dark purple stains on the path where they'd been trodden upon by attendants at the funeral. It struck me suddenly that only a few days ago, Leo had been alive and well. His name, with the dates of his birth and death so newly etched in the stone, leaped out and seemed such an inadequate testimonial to the man he was. If only he hadn't gone out to the pool that night! If only someone had been with him!

I put a hand to my face and swept away tears. "If only I'd been there!" I hadn't meant to say it aloud, and the sound of my voice was loud in the stillness of early evening.

"Wouldn't 'ave done no good, even if you was there."

I spun around, startled. Rudy Coleman stood a little way off in the darker shadows at the forest's edge. As I turned, he moved closer, limping noticeably from some ancient injury that stiffened with each change of weather.

"God, you frightened me!" I exclaimed. "You shouldn't creep up on people that way, Rudy!" Then, realizing I'd been unnecessarily rude, I softened. "Sorry. I guess I'm pretty jumpy these days. How are you?"

He inclined his head slightly and dropped his eyes to the stones at my feet. "I reckon I'm as fit as can be expected."

We were both silent and I, too, looked down at the markers.

"Wouldn't 'ave made no difference if you'd a-been

here," he repeated. "When He says it's time t' go, well, there ain't nothin' no mortal can do 'bout it."

He took his battered brown hat from his balding head, rubbed a gnarled hand over his scalp to smooth back the few wisps of white hair that danced in the rising wind, then settled the cap more comfortably in place.

"I was gonna drop some grass seed here," he said, as if it were a normal continuation of the conversation. "Seems there's a storm comin' though, so's now I'll have t' wait 'til mornin'"

I noted the seed bag in his hand and nodded. I couldn't honestly say I'd ever understood Rudy. He was a loner, happiest when left to go about his business undisturbed, yet he was part of the very foundations of Beacon, putting every bit of his own patient endurance into the upkeep and perpetual regeneration of the estate. He rarely bothered anyone, yet seemed to be everywhere at once—clipping hedges, weeding garden beds, patching, painting, mending, hammering. It seemed an impossible amount of work for just one spindly old man.

But Rudy was by no means frail. The lean, stoop-shouldered, leathery veneer he presented belied the lithely muscled, tough individual he really was. I had no idea how old he was, but could swear his appearance hadn't changed in all the years I'd known him. I would have been disappointed if he'd appeared before me dressed in anything other than the familiar old bib overalls, heavy work boots and shapeless brown cap.

A flicker of lightning cut across the converging clouds on the horizon and not long after, a rumble of thunder rolled in. I turned my face to the sky and saw the first fingers of black edging their way over the trees. The wind carried the damp musky smell of rain.

"Guess we'll have to get in out of this," I remarked casually.

Rudy didn't shift his gaze from the stones. "Y' know, Miz Suzanna, it don't seem t' me that it was his time t' go."

I stiffened and looked at him sharply. "What do you mean?"

He shrugged. "I reckon that this might not o' been th' doin' o' the Almighty."

"I don't understand."

He looked at me, but I couldn't read his eyes in the shadows.

"I had a dream, missy," he said. "Mister Dirkston, he comes t' me and says: 'Rudy, don't let 'em get away with it!' His head's all bloody from where he fell, an' he just points to it an keeps sayin': 'Don't let 'em get away with it!'"

I shivered and he shook his head. "Can't say as I know what t' make of it, but I don't think your Daddy's restin' comf'table down here."

He turned his head toward the approaching curtain of rain, and another lightning streak threw his face into strobe-like relief. The crack of thunder that followed was much closer this time.

"Best find shelter, Miz Suzanna; looks like this one's gonna stir things up a mite."

Before I could collect my thoughts, he was gone, striding stiff-legged across the lawns in the direction of the stables. I stared after him, his words repeating themselves in my mind. For the first time, suspicion filled my mind. Rudy's instincts, less influenced by grief, had uncovered a snake-pit of doubt that up until now I'd ignored.

The wind whipped viciously, sending my hair swirling about my face. Dry leaves ripped from the tree and swooped about like disembodied wings. The branches groaned and creaked as they swayed stiffly and the first tentative drops of rain spattered across the face of Leo's stone, bringing out the color so that it shone in the lowering gloom. Another streak of lightning slit the sky directly above me—so close that I could hear it hiss as it cut the air. The clap that followed made me jump with fright and I turned to run for cover. In that brief moment as I whirled, however, my eyes raked the forest's edge and there, immobile against the blackness behind, I saw him again, shadowed and obscure. This time, I knew he was no a camper or hitchhiker. And this time, I didn't want to find out who he was. I spun and ran back toward the house as fast as I could, just as the clouds opened and spilled their contents in a blinding, soaking torrent.

FIVE

Envy and calumny and hate and pain,
And that unrest which men miscall delight,
Can touch him not and torture not again;
From the contagion of the world's slow stain
He is secure, and now can never mourn
A heart grown cold, a head grown grey in vain.

  Mary Godwin Shelley
  Adonis, stanza 40

I announced my decision that evening after dinner. There was no point keeping the family in suspense any longer. They were gathered in the living room. At first, this room had been called the front parlor, but since its introduction to all the latest recreational gadgets, it had become a favorite place to retire after dinner, to relax and enjoy a bit of frivolity. Alicia spent many hours here viewing old movies on videos, or practicing dance steps to musical soundtracks. Colin whiled away the odd moment playing computer or video games, and Grant often settled in with Giles for a game or two of chess.

It was a large, long room opening off the entrance hall and stretching across the western face of the house. It had been smartly arranged with individual groupings of furni-

ture to accommodate varying pastimes. The TV and entertainment center was in the far corner. A huge stone fireplace filled the center of the inside wall, while just inside
the entrance stood an ebony grand piano, its wrought iron
bench covered in emerald velvet to match the draperies.
When drawn, these draperies covered the entire north wall
and hide the three sets of French doors that looked out
onto the pillared front porch. At the moment, the veranda
was dark with night shadows and wet with the rain that
still pelted down relentlessly.

I released the tie that held the draperies and pulled the
drawstring to shut out the raging storm. The lights were
dimmed to lessen the glare on the television screen, and
the trio lounging indolently in front of it hardly noticed my
entrance.

Colin was sprawled on the couch with Alicia curled on
the shaggy rug at his feet, painting her toenails from a bottle placed precariously on the corner of the Victorian coffee table. Grant perched on the edge of a nearby chair, a
cigarette and a glass of iced whisky at his elbow. The television droned out a weather forecast of "continued rain
with thunderstorms clearing by morning," followed by a
series of advertisements with inane jingles that set my
teeth on edge. I took the opportunity to switch off the set
and faced the group. They stared at me with mixed surprise and irritation.

"Hey! What's the idea?" Colin griped.

Alicia opened her mouth to speak but, seeing my
expression, shut it again and put the brush back carefully
into the bottle. Grant was silent, but his eyes were slitted
and he watched me with interest.

"I've something to say," I announced, feeling suddenly
nervous and somewhat silly. They waited expectantly, and
I clasped my hands tightly behind my back to keep them
from shaking.

"I know you've all been waiting for me to decide about
this ultimatum of Dad's, and I thought it was time to put

your minds at ease. I went to Manistee today and left a copy of the will with a lawyer there to see if anything could be done to get around it." I looked at the floor, anywhere but at Grant, though I still felt his eyes burning into me. "It's not that I don't trust you, Grant; it's just that I wanted an unbiased opinion." I risked a glance in his direction and noted that he seemed quite unperturbed, concentrating on extinguishing his cigarette.

"Good for you!" Alicia piped.

I continued, more confidently. "I don't hold out much hope in that direction and, officially, I won't be deciding anything until I hear from him. But, unofficially..." I paused, realizing with rising panic that once the words were out of my mouth, I wouldn't be able to take them back.

"...unofficially," I plunged on, "I've decided that I can do nothing less than go along with the terms of the will." There, I'd said it. I was committed now. There was no turning back.

Silence hung palpably in the room. Outside, the rain beat against the windows like distant applause. The resonant murmur of retreating thunder caused the prisms in the chandelier to tinkle playfully.

Colin let out his breath slowly, whispering, "Thank God!"

"It's not God you need to thank!" Alicia spat.

Grant shifted and stood up, stretching lazily like a great panther climbing down off his rock to prepare for the evening hunt. I watched him, knowing with resentful embarrassment that I had placed myself unconditionally in his hands.

Before he could open his mouth to speak, however, I rushed on. "This marriage, of course, will be no more than a piece of paper and will not take place at all if it isn't understood by everyone that it will be on my terms."

My look challenged him to deny this, but he merely smiled and with rising indignation, I could see that he found my statement amusing.

"Well," he said finally. "I guess we should all be grateful to Suzanna, eh?" His eyes sparkled with something akin to malice, and I turned my look on the others. Colin was obviously relieved, his eyes radiating puppy-like gratitude. Alicia, on the other hand, was stricken. Her face was ashen and her mouth was clamped tightly shut. She didn't gaze at me but at Grant, and the look she sent him was one of spite.

Grant came to stand next to me and placed a strong arm around my shoulders, giving me a squeeze that hurt. He was still smiling.

"So, you've come down off your regal throne, my girl, and deigned to bestow your gracious gifts upon mere mortals such as ourselves?"

"Grant, don't!" I muttered, shaking off his arm and retreating to a chair into which I sank gratefully.

"What's the matter? Can't put up with a hug from your fiancé?" He snorted and bent to retrieve his glass, downing the last of his whisky in one gulp. "Well, my dear adoptive relatives, has it ever occurred to any of you that I have an equal say in this decision which Suzanna has so magnanimously taken upon herself?"

I looked up at him in surprise.

"Yes, that's right," he said, seeing me blush. "You've been so keen to bemoan your own hideous fate that you forgot it takes two people to tango."

Alicia's cheeks had regained some of their color, and her eyes shifted to me victoriously. Her words, however, were sympathetic. "Really, Grant, how can you be so horrid? Of course, Suzanna knows you would want to go along with this. We all know that you stand to gain the most in the long run."

"Don't pretend to know my mind, Alicia! I can think of easier ways to come up in the world."

Alicia laughed lightly. "Oh, Grant! You can be so silly!"

He shot her a venomous look and strode from the room. I watched him go regretfully. He was right. It hadn't occurred to me to speak to him first. I just assumed that he had already made his decision. I'd even mentally accused him of somehow being a party to the plan for no other reason than to humiliate me.

I excused myself and followed him. As I guessed, he was in the library hunched over the bar with a bottle in front of him and a brimming glass in his hand.

"It won't help to get drunk," I admonished.

He glared at me and defiantly swallowed the entire contents of the glass, grimacing only slightly. "Don't tell me you're going to start nagging me already!"

I couldn't help but smile at that. "I suppose I have to start somewhere." Then more seriously, "I'm sorry if I didn't speak to you first. I was wrong to assume you'd already accepted the will."

He tipped the bottle over his glass. "Want some?" I shook my head.

"I should be used to being the 'odd man out' around here," he said bitterly. "But then, no matter how we look at it, the blessed Dirkston blood will never flow through my veins!"

Briefly, like the flicker of lightning beyond the windows, I glimpsed a hurt, resentful child beneath the armored shell in which Grant cloaked himself. Hesitantly, I laid a hand on his arm. He instinctively tensed, as though my touch was somehow threatening.

"I'm sorry, Grant. I'll go along with whatever you say."

He glanced at me dubiously, as if waiting for me to add some unsavory condition. When it was evident that I would say no more, he smiled, a tired, lopsided smile, and nodded.

"Okay, it's a deal." He held out his hand. "Shall we shake on it?"

Our hands met in silent accord, lingering slightly before I pulled mine away and went to the windows to hide a confusing, illogical rush of emotions. The sky was black. Only the retreating blink of lightning outlined the roiling clouds and slanting veil of rain. I watched, fascinated, and counted the seconds until the thunder rumbled in. Already the rain seemed to be abating, pattering more sedately on the bricks outside. I could barely make out a corner of the pool. It, too, was dark, though lights from the windows glinted off its surface, displaying the radiating ripples generated by each raindrop.

Suddenly, the sky lit up again as if in a final effort to split the night. The lights in the house flickered and went out. The thunder cracked.

I froze, rooted to the spot, fingers splayed against the glass, mouth agape. I stared unblinking while the horror of what I had just seen registered. In a burst of possessed energy, I sprinted across the hall to the rear parlor, threw open the door to the patio and flung myself out into the rain. I reached the gate to the pool and fumbled numbly with the latch, then shook it in desperation. It opened and I burst through, my eyes darting wildly, searching.

I'd seen him! I was certain! Leo—floating face-down in the rippling water! Instinctively I plunged into the frigid pool, flailing madly as I searched frantically. I couldn't find him. I couldn't see for the darkness and the rain. My thrashing slowed. The weight of my clothes became unbearable, my breath came in gasps, my limbs went numb. I think I was sobbing and, eventually, in utter exhaustion, I let the waters close over my head.

There in that total silence of the water's depths, I heard it distinctly, as if he was very near. His voice called to me, pleaded with me, lured me down, until darkness and his voice were all that existed. "Help me, Suzanna! Help me!" he called. But I couldn't find him.

~ ~ ~

When I awoke, I was shivering uncontrollably and aware of three things: the rain beating down on me, the rough bricks scratching my cheek, and a great weight pinning me flat. Someone was breathing heavily, and I felt myself being squeezed relentlessly. I coughed, vomited water, and groaned. Instantly, the weight shifted and I was rolled over onto my back. I opened my eyes and Grant's face loomed in front of me. His deep blue eyes were dilated with shock and confusion, his hair was plastered to his head like a sodden mitt. Water dripped from his nose and chin in large, lazy drops.

I laughed, or at least tried to. I couldn't call the sound that issued from my mouth any more than a strangled choke, but something must have told him that this was a laugh, for he laughed, too, with undeniable relief.

"Are you all right?!" he gasped after a moment.

I nodded weakly. "What happened?"

He scooped me up in his arms and carried me toward the house. "Christ, Suzie! I don't know what came over you!"

I puzzled over this response for a moment, then let my head fall against his shoulder, feeling pleasantly lethargic and wonderfully secure.

Giles was called at once and appeared within minutes, clumsily dressed and with his medical bag in hand. Martha was also present and wrapped me snugly in a blanket, while someone else thrust a glass of bourbon into my numb fingers. The lights were back on and everyone seemed to be hovering over me at once. I still shivered, but not as violently. I was appalled that Giles had been summoned from his home so hastily to tend to me, when I knew I'd be fine in a few minutes.

"What happened here?" demanded Giles.

Colin and Alicia stared helplessly and turned to Grant, who in turn looked at me.

"I...I don't know," I stammered. My teeth were still chattering.

Giles studied me thoughtfully, noting the glass in my hands. "I think that will do you more good than anything I can prescribe."

Obediently, I put it to my lips and felt the liquor cut a

warming path to my stomach. It did make me feel better. Gradually, the shivering abated and I was able to speak coherently.

"All I know, is that I saw something floating in the pool. It looked…" I hesitated, "it looked like a body and…and I was sure it was Dad." I shook my head slowly, trying to remove the image from my mind. "I don't remember much more, just that I knew I had to get to him…to save him. I must have jumped in the pool."

Giles listened, frowning, and I saw him glance toward Grant, who nodded confirmation. Alicia blanched and covered her mouth with her hand. Martha's face was frozen. Even Colin had paled considerably.

David appeared in the doorway and, hurrying to my side, hunkered down in front of me, his face a study of worried concern. "Are you all right? What happened?"

"I'm all right," I repeated brusquely. The inanity of what I had done was beginning to dawn, and I felt ridiculous.

"I'd like to be alone with Suzanna," Giles said quietly.

They all acquiesced with sympathetic murmuring, but Grant hesitated, glancing at me inquiringly.

"Don't worry," I reassured him. "I'm all right." It pleased me that he was worried, although I didn't entirely understand why.

It didn't take me long to convince Giles that I had merely suffered some sort of nervous hallucination brought on by the pressures of the past days. He left a bottle of sleeping tablets, adamant that I use them, then ordered me to bed.

After he left, David returned, but I dismissed him impatiently, claiming that I was very tired and needed to get some rest. In actuality, I wanted to be left alone. The reality of my little drama was suddenly very vivid, and it frightened me. I could still see with total clarity the body floating in the pool, and feel the overpowering presence that beckoned to me in the silence underwater. I wondered, with a wave of panic, if I might be losing my mind, remembering the other episodes that day involving strange, fleeting figures.

Grant came in after Giles and David departed and sat down opposite me, fixing me with a penetrating stare which undoubtedly read my confusion.

"We've been wrong, Suzie," he said quietly. "We, and especially I, should have been more sensitive to your loss."

I gazed at him. The sedative which Giles had prompted me to take was beginning to take effect, and a comfortable languor was creeping over me. I assessed Grant's features hypnotically, admiring his chiseled jaw and his wide mouth with the small scar at one corner. I smiled.

"You saved my life," I said. "I guess that means I owe you one."

He cocked a brow distractedly, then smiled, too, softening his face so that it was suddenly warm and compellingly attractive.

"You do pick a helluva time for a swim!" he said, and we both burst out laughing until tears ran down my cheeks and I leaned back in my cocoon of warmth, closed my eyes and sighed, truly exhausted.

"Up to bed with you," he ordered and, despite my feeble protests, scooped me up easily and carried me upstairs.

I was asleep before we reached my room and, for once, did not dream.

I awoke early the next day still in a haze of lethargy which I refused to give in to. I was determined to pursue a new course of action, one that I'd hatched before the episode at the pool.

By seven, I was dressed and downstairs, careful not to disturb the rest of the household. The heady aroma of perking coffee beckoned me to the kitchen. I had over an hour before I needed to leave.

Lottie Wilson had obviously been busy for some time. Two apple pies cooled on a rack in front of the window, while a batch of cinnamon buns were rising in their trays, nearly ready for the oven. She opened her mouth in surprise at the sight of me and wiped her hands on her apron, her face beaded with perspiration, a smudge of flour vivid against her ebony skin. Her hair was pulled back severely and contained in a fine mesh net.

"Why, Suzanna! I didn't 'spect you to be down so soon! Shouldn't you still be in bed?" Her soft brown eyes assessed me with concern.

"I'm fine, Lottie," I grunted. It never failed to amaze me how quickly news spread through the house. I had almost hoped I'd get away without being reminded of last night's performance. "Is that coffee ready? It smells beautiful."

She smiled and her broad face melted into gentle folds. "Why, you just sit down, honey, and I'll get it for you. Seems ages since you've been in here to visit me. I was beginning to wonder if you might have forgotten old Lottie!"

She poured the dark, steaming liquid from the blue speckled pot on the stove, and set the cup before me with a jug of fresh milk and a bowl of sugar. I smiled apologetically.

"I should have come in to see you sooner, but things have been so crazy around here…" I ignored the sugar, but poured in a healthy dollop of milk and took a sip. No one could make coffee like Lottie!

She sat down across from me, her ample frame bulging over the sturdy, straight-backed chair. She studied me intently.

"How're you doing, dear?"

"To tell you the truth, I really don't know anymore. I thought I was handling things pretty well…until last night." I glanced up. "You heard?"

She nodded, dropping her eyes. We were silent for a moment.

"It seemed so real," I said finally. "I could swear I saw something in the pool. And yesterday, the man standing in the road and then, again, at the edge of the woods by the grave..."

"Wait a minute, honey. What man's this?"

"I don't know. It was all so sudden." I described the two events and Lottie listened with a frown, her huge hands laid flat on the tabletop.

After I finished, she shook her head and clucked her tongue. "You might think I'm loony, Suzanna, but it sounds to me like someone's tryin' awful hard to scare you. Otherwise...." She stopped abruptly.

"Otherwise what?"

She twisted her lips, embarrassed. "Oh, it's nothin'. There's no such thing...."

"No such thing as what?"

"Why, ghosts, dearie. Could be your daddy's tryin' to say a proper goodbye to you."

I nearly laughed out loud, but collected myself in time, taking a quick gulp of coffee to squelch the smile that threatened.

"Well," I said, "If Dad is trying to speak to me from the grave, why doesn't he just do it instead of all this non-sense?"

She stood up and moved to the oven, shoving the tray of buns inside.

"Go on, now," she grumbled. "Laugh if you like, but there's plenty of people who believe that the spirits of the restless dead come back. And it's not for us to say how they do it, neither!"

"I'm sorry, Lottie. I didn't mean to make fun. I guess I'm just not very superstitious."

She nodded. "Never you mind, honey. It's probably just what Doctor Lancaster says: nerves. You know, there's no tellin' what a passel of strung nerves can do. When my James got sick, well I nearly went 'round the bend myself—all them doctors and hospitals—and all they could say was: 'There's nothin' we can do, Miz Wilson. Jes try 'n make him comfortable.' Well, I did like they said but, in the end, it was merciful he didn't last much longer."

She rambled on and I sipped from my cup, mumbling agreement from time to time, but letting my thoughts wander down their own paths. If someone were trying to frighten me, they were certainly going to a lot of trouble. Who would want to do such a thing? And why? Could someone be that spiteful, or did they hope to gain some perverse satisfaction from making me suffer? My mind lit on Alicia as I remembered the conversation she'd had with Grant in the garden. Could jealousy of some sort be the catalyst for these horrible tricks? Could she feel so threatened by the marriage that she'd resort to revenge?

And Grant himself? Would he stand to gain by arranging these shocking episodes? Perhaps if he drove me completely mad, he could inherit the whole estate! No, it was a ridiculous thought. I'd been reading too many of those mystery thrillers!

"...my own mama claimed she saw my daddy workin' in the garden in the moonlight, and daddy had been dead close to three years."

I looked up. "What?"

Lottie threw a mound of dough onto the pastry board and sent a cloud of flour billowing up. She began to knead it expertly. "I was just sayin' that I know quite a few folks who've been visited by their dead kin. You wouldn't be the first. And what with Mr. Dirkston comin' by his end so sudden, I expect he had plenty of unfinished business he'd be wantin' to tidy up."

I grimaced and downed the last of the coffee.

"I've got to be going, Lottie," I said abruptly. "Thanks for the chat. I'll see you soon."

"But Suzanna!" she called after me. "What about a bun? They're nearly cooked!"

I was already too far away to reply and my mind was working furiously. Ghosts! What rubbish! Yet, Lottie's words had raised the hackles at the nape of my neck and sent a shiver up my spine. I zipped up my windbreaker and let myself out the front door.

"I'm sorry, Miss Dirkston, we really aren't allowed to show you our files."

The uniformed man who sat behind the desk spoke calmly, as though my request was merely one of many that passed through his office daily. He was a tall man with long, gangly arms that hung from shirtsleeves a fraction too short. His hair was blond, clipped regimentally short so that his head appeared to be too small atop his broad shoulders. His long-fingered hands were folded neatly on the desk in front of him.

"What makes you think there's something unusual about your father's death?" he asked at my look of perplexity.

"I didn't say I did."

"Well, I can see no other reason why you'd like to see the investigation file."

"Sergeant," I said, "we're speaking of my father here, not some stray cat that was run over by a car. I think I have a right to see what the police have found out about his death. Or, is there some deep secret you're keeping?"

"Of course not, Miss Dirkston! If there were anything out of the ordinary, the family would be notified."

I raised my eyebrows. "Well? What's the problem, then?"

He shifted his gaze and drummed his fingers nervously. "It's just that…well, it's against official policy. We can't just open our files to anyone who comes in. We'd have to put on a whole staff of clerks just to cater to the whims of every Tom, Dick or Harry!"

He seemed genuinely apologetic, and I relented. "All right, then perhaps you could at least tell me what the coroner's report says."

He eyed me speculatively, then with a sigh, stood up and went to the filing cabinet behind him.

"I really should tell you to go to the coroner's office for that, Miss Dirkston, but since I'm not entirely heartless…"

He laid a file in front of him and leafed through the papers, selecting one and passing it across the desk. "It's all spelled out in medical jargon, but help yourself. I have to attend to some business. I'll be back in a few moments."

He left the room, shutting the door behind him, and I studied the report. Much of it I didn't understand, but the overall profile seemed to be that "the victim died from a slow, cerebral hemorrhage resulting from a severe concussion to the side of the head."

Setting the paper aside, I reached across the desk and pulled the rest of the file in front of me. I suspected that the good sergeant had left it conveniently accessible on purpose, and I made a mental note to repay him some day.

The folder contained a number of reports that offered mostly useless facts relating to the position of the body, age, weight, height, build, hundreds of measurements and, separately, notes of interviews with various members of the family. There was nothing there to substantiate my budding suspicions. The very fact that there was no evidence to show how Leo had struck his head puzzled me. It was as if the accident had been too neatly packaged and forgotten. There was nothing to say that Leo had struck his head on the side of the pool. There had been blood found on the concrete near the edge, but that could have spilled anytime, possibly even after someone had struck him.

I shivered. Why was I questioning the evidence? Surely, the police knew more about these things than I did. But, a voice at the back of my mind argued: "They may know more about the laws, but you know more about Leo Dirkston." I could not—would not—believe that he had died simply because of a stumble and fall. The only alternative was that someone had caused the accident and that, I realized with icy clarity, was tantamount to murder.

The sound of approaching footsteps made me jump, and I hastily shoved the papers back into the file and across the desk, plastering a serene smile on my face as the police officer resumed his seat in the swivel chair opposite.

"Find anything?" His eyes glittered knowingly.

I shook my head. "Like you say, it's all very technical. I do have one question, though, that perhaps you can answer?"

"Yes?"

"How do we know that my father hit his head on the side of the pool? Isn't it possible that someone struck him, then pushed him into the water?"

His reaction to my bluntness was one of supreme tolerance. "I don't think that's plausible, Miss Dirkston. With all the advanced equipment we have these days, that avenue would have been well looked into."

"But was it?" I persisted.

He stood up impatiently. "Look here. I realize you're a novelist and that you must need to spend a great deal of time cultivating a creative imagination, but it seems to me that you're looking for trouble where there is none. Your father was an influential man. If there was any question of foul play, we'd know about it." His eyes softened. "I know this has been a trying time for you. Believe me, I've had a lot of experience with bereaved families and in most cases, refusal to accept an unexpected or violent death is quite common. There's a psychologist here in Ludington who's extremely qualified and has dealt with this sort of thing before. Perhaps...?"

"No!" I rose abruptly, clutching my purse white-knuckled. "I'm not crazy! You all seem to think...!" I didn't finish, for the look in his eyes told me that my reaction had simply reinforced his opinion. "Thank you, Sergeant," I said more calmly, and held out my hand.

He took it gently. "If there's anything I or my staff can do, Miss Dirkston, don't hesitate to call. Perhaps a holiday might be in order, eh?"

I gritted my teeth but managed a smile.

"Perhaps," I grated, then hurried out, collapsing with relief onto the seat of my car, still cursing my stupidity. Of course, no one else would be suspicious; why would they? I hardly knew myself why I was so disquieted. I felt as though some inner force was egging me on, despite the possibility of unpleasant discoveries or general disapproval. It was unlike me. I was usually a prime example of innocent gullibility. Perhaps they were right; maybe I did need some professional help. But I still believed that my father's death might not have been accidental and, despite what anyone thought, I wouldn't rest until I knew for sure what had actually happened that night.

"Suzanna! Hey!"

I was startled out of my reverie and looked up. Jenny Hampton was running toward me, her straight blonde hair flying like a curtain behind her as she waved excitedly. Delighted, I got out of the car to meet her.

"Jenny!" I cried as she flew up and threw her arms around me. We embraced warmly.

"I thought it was you, but at first I wasn't sure!" she said breathlessly. "You're hair's shorter."

"You've hardly changed at all," I rejoined. "What's it been? Almost eight years?"

She nodded, pushing her long locks away from her face.

She was quite a bit taller than I, with a sweet oval face and shining blue eyes fringed with thick dark lashes. What I remembered in her as gawky lankiness, had developed into svelte beauty. But if she were aware of her attractiveness, she didn't show it. Her face was free of makeup, and she wore simple jeans and a sweatshirt.

"What are you doing back here?" I questioned. "Last time you wrote, you were in New York!"

She shrugged. "I didn't like it. It was just too crowded. As a matter of fact, I'm kind of taking a break at the moment. I've decided to look for a teaching position in the area. Don't laugh! I know I told you that I'd probably never use my teaching certificate. Anyway, I'm staying with Mom for the time being."

Suddenly her smile faded and she placed a hand on my shoulder. "God! I heard about your dad. I'm so sorry."

I nodded. The offer of genuine sympathy caused tears to well up in my eyes. I fumbled for a tissue.

"I'm sorry," I said. "I've hardly cried at all. It all seems so…so unreal."

"I can understand," she agreed. "When my father died, I felt the same." Then, to lighten the mood: "Come on! How about getting an ice cream at Bender's—just like old times?"

I gave a sobbing laugh. "But it's only ten in the morning!"

She set her face determinedly. "Since when were you Miss Logical? I want a pistachio nut and coffee-ice. And you'll have…what was it? Oh, yes…butter-pecan and chocolate-chip-mint!"

We both giggled like schoolgirls and, linking arms, strolled the few short blocks to Bender's Ice Cream Parlor.

Once seated at an outside table with our individual indulgences, we eyed one another appreciatively. Jenny was like a breath of fresh air, and for once I felt able to talk and laugh freely. The nagging doubts of the morning vanished temporarily into oblivion. We compared notes on our lives since going our separate ways. Jenny, after graduating from the university, had followed a dream of modeling to New York where she quickly discovered that the competition was overwhelming, and her chances of rising to any degree of recognition were slim. She'd made enough money to keep a tiny apartment in the suburbs, but was able to save very little and eventually had to admit that there was no future for her there. Besides, she detested

New York, and felt alien and insecure amid all the hustle and bustle.

"If I ever had to actually drive into the city," she said, laughing, "I'd have to take along a crow-bar just to get someone to pry my fingers off the wheel! It was a nightmare!"

I nodded. "I know what you mean. I think you have to be born and bred to the city to feel comfortable there."

I told her about myself. About my decision to eke out a living on my own. About my novel and my career hopes. "Unfortunately, since this thing with Dad, everything has turned topsy-turvy. I hardly know whether I'm coming or going, let alone how I'll ever finish this new manuscript on time." I frowned, remembering how my father had disapproved of my aspirations.

She reached across the table and took my hand. "Don't worry. It does get better—it just takes time."

I smiled gratefully and squeezed her hand in return. "There's more to it, unfortunately."

She cocked a curious brow and I told her everything—about the will, about the man on the road and near the grave, and about last night's incident at the pool. "I was just at the police station trying to find out if it could be possible that Dad was…" I hesitated.

"Was?" she prompted.

"Well, that maybe his accident wasn't an accident."

"Oh, no! Do you really think it's possible?!" She shuddered violently. "But who would do such a thing? And why?" She paused, considering. "Your dad might have had a few enemies, eh? I mean, being involved in a huge corporation like Dirkston Enterprises, he was bound to have stepped on a few toes."

I nodded, relieved that at least she hadn't immediately thought I was mad. "It just doesn't sit right with me, Jenny. Call it a hunch, but I just think there's something more to this than meets the eye. And everyone at the house seems so—so—odd lately."

"I can't believe they all kept you in the dark about your father's will! I'd be so furious. What do you think you'll do now?"

I shrugged. "I don't know."

"Are you sure you're doing the right thing by going along with it?"

"I don't know that, either. I used to think it didn't matter. After all, it's only a piece of paper, and the conditions say the marriage only has to last a year, but now, with this notion that someone—maybe even Grant himself, could have contributed to Dad's death! Well, I wonder if I'm making a big mistake."

Jenny didn't speak for a moment, weighing the possibilities. "Look, for what it's worth, I'll help you out. I don't know what I can do, but you can count on me."

I smiled gratefully. "Thanks, Jen, you've already made me feel a lot better. I was beginning to think that I was losing my mind."

"No way, José!" she said lightly. "If you're crazy, then that makes two of us!"

We laughed again, comfortably pleased with each other. We reminisced for a short while longer, and parted only after making a date to go canoeing the next day.

Before heading home, I stopped into the marina to arrange to pick up the equipment for our outing. David was busy with ledgers when I arrived, but he shut the books immediately and greeted me with concern.

"I was worried about you all night," he said. "Shouldn't you spend a day or two recuperating? Dad reckons you need more rest."

"I've had plenty of rest, David. Do stop worrying! I'd like to forget last night ever happened. It was just a stupid mistake."

"One that came close to drowning you!"

I changed the subject. "How about you? Have you recovered from the shock of losing me to another man?" I tried to make my voice light and frivolous, but it sounded cold and accusing.

Fortunately, his phlegmatic poise remained unshaken. "I guess I did rant on a bit yesterday," he said. "I didn't mean to upset you. It just came as a bit of a surprise."

"I thought you were quite in control, considering," I said wryly.

"Well," he said, "I'd still like to apologise. I'll go along with whatever you decide, of course, though I wish it were me instead of Grant on the receiving end."

I cocked my head, eyeing him knowingly. "Colin's already told you, hasn't he?"

He shifted uncomfortably. "Well, yes, he mentioned that you'd made a tentative decision to go ahead with the marriage—though I'd prefer to call it a temporary partnership."

"Yes, well, there's no point in going over it, is there?" I said briskly, before that familiar irritation could take hold.

"Have you set a date?" he asked innocently.

This was the last straw. "Set a date? For God's sake, David! Doesn't it matter that I have to marry Grant Fenton? Or does this damn marina mean more to you than...than us?" My cheeks were flaming. "No! No, I haven't 'set a date!' I haven't even got used to the idea of being joined in matrimony to a man I can barely tolerate. Are you in such a big hurry to get rid of me?"

He was around the desk instantly to envelop me in his arms, but I stood rigid with frustration. I didn't stop to think that I was being unreasonable, that I myself had broken off our engagement before any of this had come about, and here I was accusing him of discarding me.

I pushed him away violently. "Leave me alone! I don't need your sympathy." I raised my chin stubbornly and took a shaky breath, feeling no pity for him despite his dejected, helpless expression. "I want a canoe for tomorrow. Jenny Hampton and I want to do the lower reach."

He hesitated, confused, then atypically chose to ignore the problem. He retrieved an appointment book from somewhere under the counter and flipped the pages, scribbling an entry.

"Okay," he said, "you're all set. I'll have Mike arrange to have the cushions and paddles at the landing with the canoe, unless you want to take them with you now."

"Mike?"

"He's helping out around here. Probably still worried about his job. Anyway, we can use him since young Jim left to go back to school last week."

"Never mind. I'll take the stuff with me now."

He nodded. "Come on, then. I'll load them in your trunk."

Minutes later, I was once more on the road. Despite my anger, I knew that David was right. I had to discuss the particulars of this 'partnership,' as he put it, with Grant. The sooner we got it over with, the sooner the year would be up and I could put the whole sordid affair behind me.

SIX

Or your shadow at evening rising to meet you;
I will show you fear in a handful of dust.

Thomas Stearns Eliot
The Waste Land
Pt. 1, The Burial Of The Dead

I stopped impulsively at a small flower stall on my way through town, choosing a large bouquet of burgundy and orange chrysanthemums combined with daisies and soft baby's breath to place on Leo's grave, and a second arrangement of delicate pink and white rosebuds to place on my mother's.

I parked the car in its usual place in front of the garage. I was in no mood to talk to anyone, so I slipped around the side and followed the path across the rear garden, flanked by its high hedgerow. It was a beautiful day. Except for the soft earth and thick, rain-soaked smell that steamed up from the ground, one wouldn't have guessed that a storm had raged nearly all night. Following the tangle of lilacs that crowded behind the swimming pool, I rounded a bend and was brought up short. Poised in the center of the gravel, Kong gazed at me with feline nonchalance. I smiled.

"Hello, Kong. Nice kitty."

For once, he responded with a low chirrup, coming to rub himself against my ankles, his purr vibrating smoothly. I bent to caress his head and ears, surprised by his sudden amenity.

"Good boy," I crooned. "What a good boy."

He didn't accept my fondling for long, but padded off to the side of the path with an inviting glance over his shoulder. I watched, bemused, as he disappeared into the dense bushes. I was about to go on when his plaintive yowl piqued my curiosity, and I got down on my hands and knees to peer into the darkness after him.

The shrubbery was heavier than I'd imagined, some three feet thick and snarled in twisting profusion right to the ground. I struggled to push aside the curling branches, cursing as my arms and face were scratched. Finally, by lying flat on my stomach, I was able to tunnel far enough in to make out the cat's yellow eyes gazing fixedly back. He, too, was crouched low against the ground, his ears laid back and his mouth opening again and again in that grating cry.

"What is it, kitty?" I wheedled, reaching out a tentative hand. He backed away, swishing his tail and yowled again. Puzzled, I noticed a long cylindrical shape lying on the ground where he had been. It glinted metallically, and I reached out and pulled it to me. Glancing about, I realized disconcertedly that Kong had disappeared, so I began my slow retreat, wriggling back out the way I'd come.

Once more on the path, I stood up, brushed at the layer of dirt and wet leaves stuck to me, then bent and retrieved the implement I'd rescued. It was a fireplace poker. I turned it over in my hands curiously. How it had come to be out here in the bushes? By the look of it, it hadn't been here long. The handle was still shiny and the other end…

I gasped and dropped it as though it were red hot. Clamping a hand over my mouth, I backed away. The essence of my nightmares stared back at me and my mind whirled in confused spirals. There was blood on the poker. I was certain that it was blood, despite the faded brown color. Clinging to the blood was gray hair—my father's hair.

How long I stood staring at the implement, I don't remember; but it was some time before I was able to calm myself enough to think rationally. I must take it to the police at once—quickly, before anyone else saw it! I picked it up gingerly and, with a shiver of revulsion, hurried back along the path toward my car, ignoring the bright bouquets that now lay discarded on the path. I had only one thought. The word I'd been avoiding flashed like neon in my mind: murder!

I was so set on my purpose that by the time I paused in my headlong flight to look up, it was too late. I stopped abruptly as I rounded the corner of the garage and there was Grant, just alighting from his car, lifting a hand in greeting.

"Suzanna. How are you? Lottie said you were up with the birds, so I assume you've recovered from last night's…?" He didn't finish the sentence; the pallor of my face and my stricken expression must have been all too apparent.

"What is it?" he asked, concerned. He approached me slowly, one hand extended, as though I were a wild animal ready to wheel and run at any moment. For in truth, I did feel trapped and drew back instinctively, my mind searching frantically for some means of logical escape. I clutched the poker behind my back, knowing I mustn't allow him to see it, all too conscious that the strong hand he held out toward me could easily have been the one that had gripped this very poker and brought it mercilessly down upon my father's head.

I spun to flee, but it was too late. With a bound, he was upon me, his hands like steel bands on my upper arms.

"What's the matter with you?" he demanded. "What have you got there?"

I was near panic now. I wrenched helplessly, even as he reached behind my back and jerked the poker from my grasp. I grabbed at it frantically, trying to keep him from inspecting it, yet fearing he already knew what I'd just discovered. His eyes narrowed as he looked at it. Was it recognition I saw flit briefly across his face? I stood before him like a despondent child, rubbing my wrist where he'd twisted it during the struggle. His face was hard as he looked at me.

"Where did you get this?"

When I didn't answer immediately, he shook me sharply. "Where did you get it?"

Just as a defenseless animal draws on its final resources and turns to face the attacker, I grew suddenly very calm and an icy numbness took control.

"Let go of me." My voice held no compromise, and probably in sheer surprise he complied, dropping my arm but not shifting, his frame blocking any hope of escape. I was trembling, but whether from fear or rage I couldn't tell.

"I found it in the bushes," I said with amazing composure. I knew there was no point in lying. If he was the one who had used the poker to kill Leo, he would obviously know of its whereabouts. And if he wasn't, well, what difference did it make?

He was inspecting it more closely now. "In the bushes?" He seemed surprised.

As his eyes lit on the hooked, charred end, I wondered if indeed there had been anything there, or if my all too vivid imagination had once again been playing tricks. His expression remained neutral and he lowered the rod to his side. I flinched inwardly, half expecting him to raise it suddenly and bring it smashing down on my skull. But he seemed to have dismissed it and my heart slowed its beat. Perhaps he hadn't noticed.

"Where were you going with this thing?"

My mind reeled. "I...I don't know," I hedged. "I guess I was just going to put it back."

"Don't lie to me, Suzie." He spoke calmly, but it was obvious that he was holding a tight rein on himself. I saw a muscle bulge in jaw and his free hand was clenched at his side.

"Where were you going? To the police?"

This is it! I thought. Now he knows I've seen the evidence, and he'll have to kill me, too.

"Yes," I retorted boldly. "I was going to the police!"

Unexpectedly, he smiled. "Good. At least you've got a bit of common sense! How long have you suspected?"

"What?" I was confused.

"Oh, come on, Suzie, don't play games! How long have you suspected that Leo was murdered?"

I hugged my arms around me and stared at him dumbfounded. "I...I guess since...I really don't know."

He nodded. "Don't move," he ordered and strode to his car, opening the rear door and depositing the poker carefully on the seat. He shut and locked the door and returned, taking me around the corner and into the shadows at the side of the garage. When we were well out of range of prying eyes, he faced me, both hands hard on my shoulders, his dark face only inches from my own.

"Now, listen to me, Suzie. It's important that you tell no one about this. Do you understand?" His voice was low and urgent. At my look of mixed fear and obstinacy, he sighed. "I know what you're thinking, but it's not true. You can trust me. I can't tell you everything, only that we've suspected foul play all along, and there's a very large investigation going on."

I still stared at him, disbelieving.

"For your own safety, Suzanna, you have to stay out of it. Do you understand?"

The intensity of his voice frightened me. If he was telling the truth, I would go along with him, and even if he wasn't, I couldn't risk angering him. If he thought that I trusted him, he might leave me alone until I could expose him. I nodded and he looked relieved.

"What about…that?" I asked, inclining my head in the direction of the car.

"I'll take care of it."

I clamped my lips together to stifle a retort.

"Don't worry, it will get to the proper authorities. We've been looking for something concrete and it looks as though you've given us just what we need." He smiled. "You've saved us a whole lot of work."

"May I ask who 'we' refers to, Grant?" He couldn't know that I had already been to see the police, and that they were not conducting any 'investigation' as he so alleged.

He looked away, across the unused paddock with its jumble of weeds and grasses only partially mown, to the stables where Rudy Coleman was undoubtedly tinkering with the tractor that had broken down before completing the job. When he turned back to me, I knew he was going to tell me a lie, but I kept my face under rigid control as perspiration soaked my armpits and palms.

"The police, of course," he said. "I'm working with the police."

The Pere Marquette River was named after Father Jacques Marquette, the French missionary and explorer who founded missions at Sault Ste. Marie and St. Ignace. The river lies like a flattened spring between Ludington and Baldwin, looping and twisting randomly to cover miles in what would have been a short distance as the crow flies. It isn't a wild river like the Pine, located a little further north, but not as placid as the Manistee, also north, making it a favorite among amateur canoeists who want an exciting but less treacherous challenge. During the summer holidays, the Pere Marquette swarmed with people. Now, with the peak season finished, there were only a few remaining tourists, so Jenny and I could enjoy our outing without the clamor of crowds.

It's an exhilarating experience to spend a day navigating the labyrinth of low hanging boughs, shallow shoals, felled logs and rocky protrusions reaching out from the steep banks. At times, it's all you can do to cling to the sides of the craft as it bumps over rushing rapids or twirls helplessly in deep, slow eddies. I was looking forward to the afternoon, if only to ease my mind of the overwhelming sense of dread that haunted me.

Thankfully, I'd not seen Grant since our meeting in the drive, which was a relief. I needed time to think, to put things in perspective. I wondered if I was jumping to conclusions too quickly. It was easy to read answers into unrelated expressions or gestures, and I couldn't afford to jeopardize my credibility any further. It was imperative that I gather evidence methodically. There was no point in running off to the police again, spouting theories of murder and bloodstained weapons. Grant would probably only deny the whole affair and, with the entire community already thinking me unstable, who would believe me? I would bide my time and watch until Grant made that inevitable mistake that would substantiate my suspicions.

But there again, the argument returned. Who was to say for certain that Grant had killed Leo? He certainly had a lot to gain—a vast inheritance of wealth as well as power. He had shown himself since childhood to be unscrupulous, and was no slouch when it came to putting on a believable charade. I half suspected that he may even have convinced Leo to rewrite his will so that he'd have free rein over the estate and business. But the only way he could do it, I thought ruefully, was by manipulating me once we were married. He obviously considered me very pliable!

Still, there was something intrinsically trusting in me which continued to jump to Grant's defense. I simply couldn't imagine that the man who had dragged me from the pool, worked frantically to revive me, and watched over me with concern could be the same man who had struck Leo brutally and left him in that same pool, dead.

Perhaps it had been a burglar? Had anyone checked to see if there was anything missing from the house? I remembered the figure standing in the road, and the other by the trees near Leo's grave. Perhaps this person had killed Leo and returned to search for the murder weapon, afraid that he might be traced by his fingerprints on the handle? I shook my head. It was no use. Anyone could have perpetrated the act. For now, I would put the puzzle aside and try to relax, for I suspected that my stamina would be sorely tested over the next few weeks.

Jenny was waiting for me at the appointed time of nine o'clock. She'd left her car at the completion point, and begged a ride back with one of the rival canoe-rental trucks which was making its early morning deliveries and pickups. These trucks held up to twenty canoes on their racks and the boats, despite their unwieldiness, were lifted and stacked expertly by finely muscled young men whose job it was to match client with canoe at the start and finish of each leg of the journey.

Having grown up in the area, we both knew many of the boys working the river and, despite the fact that Colin and David were in competition with many of them, they were all friendly enough and happy to help out where needed. For most, these were merely summer jobs, meant to supplement them until school recommenced in the autumn.

"Hi!" Jenny called cheerily. She was dressed in a flattering pink swimsuit cut high at the thighs and topped by a T-shirt which said: "New York" over a picture of the Statue of Liberty. Incongruously, her feet were encased in beat-up old tennis shoes, her toes peeping out through twin holes. Despite being obviously unfashionable, these were necessary for walking safely along the rock-strewn riverbank. On the ground beside her lay a waterproof bag containing various items of consequence: jacket, towel, sun-block, insect repellent, all the things that might be needed during the six-hour journey.

I returned her greeting and lifted the lid of the trunk to retrieve my own supplies and the necessary cushions and paddles.

"Lottie has packed us a feast, I think," I said as she helped haul out the cooler. We struggled with it down to the waiting canoe and loaded it in, securing it to the center strut with a bungie cord so the lid wouldn't come off should the canoe overturn. Next, the bags and equipment were fastened in, and Jenny climbed aboard. I pushed off, catching my breath as the icy water rushed about my ankles.

The current was swift and caught us as though we were flotsam. Having mastered the art of teamwork in earlier years, we straightened the craft expertly with myself at the stern using my paddle as a rudder to steer around small obstacles, and Jenny in front, poised to help turn the bow should any major barrier arise.

It was another beautiful day. The air was moist with the scents of moldering leaves, moss and river mud. The sun glittered down through a spackling of overhanging foliage and lay in twitching fingers across the gentle brown of the water. The breeze was deceptively warm. The rush and gurgle of the river lent a peaceful, soothing tempo to the rustle of leaves overhead, the creak and groan of swaying branches and the incessant chirp of crickets. Occasionally, a frog let out a throaty belch while sparrows and wrens chittered from thickets and a jay squawked his displeasure at our infringement on his territory. The only sound that seemed out of place was the sharp clank of wood on metal when the paddles accidentally clipped the side of the canoe, or a tree limb smacked across the bow.

There wasn't much time for idling. The river gripped and carried us rapidly, unconcerned that the fallen trees, shallow stones or sharp bends might impede our rigid nine-foot craft. We were kept constantly busy weaving in and out of the continual bombardment of obstructions and kept our conversation, of necessity, to a minimum. Before long, however, the river widened to form a deep, indolent pool and pulled over onto a sandy bank. It was ten o'clock and time for a rest and a snack.

"I can't believe you brought all this food!" Jenny exclaimed, examining the contents of the cooler. There were ham sandwiches, chocolate cupcakes, sliced avocado, a medley of salad vegetables and fruit. "Who did you tell Lottie you were going with? Bigfoot?!"

I laughed. "What did I tell you? And the worst part is that she'll be hurt if it's not all gone when we get back."

She groaned. "Well, we can always feed the fish."

We each selected a piece of fruit and a can of soda, and sat down on the warm sand to eat and gaze languidly at the constant current.

"Any new leads on your mystery?"

I didn't answer immediately. The discovery of the bloodstained poker had changed that simple mystery into something imminently more threatening. There was a real danger now, and I didn't want Jenny involved.

"Nothing really," I hedged.

She studied her feet. She'd taken off her shoes and was wiggling her toes, which were distorted by the shallow ripples lapping over them. The water was always frigid in these swift-flowing estuaries, but it felt good in contrast to the sun's intense rays.

"Have you talked to Grant yet?"

I tensed momentarily, then realized what she meant. "No." I waved a hand impatiently as she opened her mouth to protest. "I know, I know! I'll have to do it soon. It's just so…so hard."

I bit into my apple, relishing the crunch and rush of juice. Confidentially, I wondered how I could possibly go through with the marriage now, suspecting Grant as I did. Still, it made sense that I'd probably be safer married to him than not. As his wife, I could be pretty sure that he wouldn't bump me off immediately; at least, not until he had managed to manipulate the Dirkston fortune out of my hands and into his own. If I didn't marry him, there would be no reason for him to want me alive, and a very good reason to want me dead.

"Yes," I said, almost to myself. "I believe I'll have to set a date right away."

Jenny squinted at me in mild puzzlement. "What are you hatching in there? Whatever it is, I suspect it's dastardly."

"Yes." I laughed. "I suppose it is. But not any more so than Leo or Grant deserve."

"Poor Grant," she sighed. "I doubt that he'll stand much of a chance against you. Anyway, if it were me, I wouldn't worry so much about having a year of legal love with him. He's not such a bad catch, you know."

I nearly choked. "Are you serious?"

She looked at me levelly. "Well, don't you think so?"

I considered the idea. If it weren't for my rampant suspicions, I'd have to admit that Grant Fenton did have a lot going for him and, up until recently, I'd almost come to like him. I pushed the thought aside. There was no room for idle dreaming. The instance of our recent encounter had painted a darker portrait of him in my mind, and those early days seemed far removed.

As if to underline that thought, a loud crack sounded in the distance and, almost immediately, the twig of a tree above us snapped off and fell into the water at our feet. There was another crack, and a loud thud as something struck the riverbank behind us. We froze, uncertainly. Then, I saw the glint of metal between trees at the top of a rise some distance ahead, and I choked.

"My God, someone's shooting at us! Get back, Jenny!"

The next few moments were confusion. Instinctively, I leapt to my feet and clambered up the sharp bank behind me. I fell flat at the top and squirmed deep into the shadowy protection of the forest. At first, I sensed Jenny following closely but, when I took the time to look back, I was alone and an ominous silence surrounded me, broken only by my own heavy breathing and thudding heartbeat.

"Jenny!" I hissed urgently. Silence.

There was a rustling in the underbrush and I whirled, catching my arm on a sharp briar. I cried out as the thistles tore my flesh. The movement I heard was only a chipmunk foraging among the fallen leaves for food. I lay still for some time, straining my ears for any sound of my friend or the gunman. When nothing eventuated, I carefully turned myself around and crept back to the edge of the bank. I was horrified at the sight that met my eyes

Jenny lay on her back at the river's edge. One hand was flung over her head into the water. The other was out to one side, tightly clutching a small tree root, undoubtedly broken off in her haste to scale the embankment. Her eyes were shut, though her head nodded with the lapping of water around it. Long strands of her golden hair trailed out like tongues of flame into the dark pool. The sand beneath her back was slowly turning red.

Heedless of the shooter who might still be waiting on the distant hill, I half rolled, half fell down the incline in my hurry to reach her. I pressed my fingers to the side of her neck and was relieved to feel a strong pulse. She didn't stir at my touch, however, and I knew I'd have to find help quickly.

I pulled Jenny farther up onto the shore, into a slight niche formed at the base of the rise. Then, I rummaged through my own bag of belongings and pulled out a towel, which I wadded up into a compress. Lifting her prone body slightly, I was able to fix the padding tightly against the wound with one of the elastic cords used to secure the cooler. As a last measure, I covered her with what few bits of clothing and towels remained, stripping off my own light coverup to add what warmth I could.

I glanced around. The river was unusually empty, though I remembered a number of canoes lined up at the starting point. There was bound to be someone along at any moment, but I couldn't wait. I had a better chance of hailing someone from the river's edge as I made my way back on foot. There was no point in going down-river; there would be no help in that direction for at least five miles. I only hoped the gunman had taken leave and wasn't waiting to finish the job.

Taking to the woods and keeping the river in sight, I hurried as quickly as I could, running where possible, regardless of the underbrush that tore at my unprotected legs, and the small branches that whipped my face and arms.

Less than five minutes later, I heard the sound of voices and the rattle and clank of canoes. I ran faster and skidded down to the water's edge just as three crafts approached. I hailed them frantically and, seeing my obvious urgency, they paddled closer. I explained the situation as briefly as possible. There were three couples, and all of them listened with growing concern and agreed to remain with Jenny until I was able to return with help. One of the men was a radiologist who knew first-aid and would do what he could. I hurried on, my mind filled with the image of Jenny's life seeping away like the blood from her wound.

When at last I found help, it wasn't at our starting point, but rather a road that bridged the river about a mile up. It was a dirt road and, though fairly wide and well kept, it stretched empty in both directions. Temporarily indecisive, I finally struck out east toward Scottville, for I knew it was closer than Ludington to the west.

I continued running, wishing I had kept up my beach jogging with Giles. Sweat dripped from my face and neck, and the small dust clouds kicked up by my pounding feet clung to my skin until I was gray with it. The sun beat down on my bare flesh and, though the black and yellow bikini I wore was cooler than heavy clothing, it provided no protection from the burning ultraviolet rays.

Fortunately, I didn't have to go far before a small white

rickety pickup overtook me. I managed to wave it down and, within seconds, was seated alongside the elderly farmer, gasping out my story as he drove swiftly to a near-by house to call for help.

The rescue wasn't an easy one. Paramedics had to weave their ambulance down one of the fire trails cut to accommodate firefighters, should there be a need. These trails crisscrossed everywhere, and it was only with the help of the local ranger that they were able to find their way to within yards of the place where, by now, a crowd of canoeists and inner-tubists had gathered.

I refused to go ahead to the hospital as suggested, insisting that they allow me to accompany them. They conceded merely, I suspected, because I was the only one who knew the exact location and could direct them. Once we arrived, I was shunted aside as a stretcher and miscellaneous medical equipment were hastily handed down to where Jenny still lay unconscious.

I watched in shock. The man who had claimed some knowledge of first-aid came to stand near me and assured me that he had done what he could, but there was no way to know how bad the wound was. When I didn't respond, he touched my shoulder gently. "You should have someone take a look at those cuts, miss."

I looked at him vaguely. He was a middle-aged man with graying sideburns, a round nose and a slightly sagging waistline. His eyes were sympathetic, and I looked down at myself dazedly. My arms and legs were cut and bleeding, and bruises were already darkening. I put a hand to my head and felt a rising lump where I'd run into a branch, and there was a deep scrape on one cheek from where I'd fallen in my rush to Jenny's side.

I nodded at the man's suggestion, but completely forgot it as the medics brought Jenny up on the stretcher. An oxygen mask covered her mouth and nose, an intravenous drip swung from a hook above and a heavy blanket was wrapped around her under the retaining straps. She was so very pale.

"Is she…?"

"She's alive," one of the men responded in clipped haste.

They loaded her into the ambulance and, having been forbidden to ride in the rear with the attendant, I climbed into the front seat. We set off at a painfully slow pace over the rutted forest track. The revolving red light on top cast ruby shards across the sun-speckled trees. Once we reached the road, the siren was switched on and we sped urgently toward the hospital.

SEVEN

Of calling shapes, and beckoning shadows dire,
And airy tongues, that syllable men's names
On sands, and shores and desert wilderness.

    John Milton
    Comus, A Mask

I found a new spot where even David would be hard pressed to find me. I was never allowed to come here as a child without supervision, which made it all the more inviting. The lighthouse stood behind me, a protective fortress between me and the house, which squatted atop its perch, dark windows watching my every move. This spot belonged to the lighthouse. She'd stood on this rocky jetty for years, weathering storm after storm, her mortared bulk rooted inescapably. I felt a strange companionship with her, like one convict for another. We were both prisoners: the lighthouse, standing steadfast against the continual buffeting of nature's whims, and me, braced strongly in my own right against the onslaught of murder, suspicion, fear and frustration.

    Winter was approaching, I could feel it in the breeze. The sky was overcast with gray autumn clouds that blan-

ket everything in shapeless mist. Even the lake was
moody, swirling perversely as though waiting impatiently
for some cue to rise up. It, too, must have sensed the
approach of winter, nibbling skittishly at my rocky throne.

The outcropping on which I sat was formed entirely of
huge gray and black boulders, brought in over a hundred
years ago to serve as a platform for the lighthouse. The
rocks, smoothed by the constant caress of waves and tumbled together randomly, offered a labyrinth of crevices and
cracks where one slip could cause serious injury. In some
places, moss and algae grew green and blue, blending
together in a woolly blur. This softened the surfaces, but
made the footing even more perilous.

It had been three days since the shooting. Jenny still
clung stubbornly to life. The bullet had punctured a lung,
and lodged precariously close to her heart. It was a mira-
cle that the loss of blood hadn't killed her, but her youth
and strength had saved her until a transfusion could be
administered. They didn't operate until her condition had
stabilized some eight hours later, and then the surgery
itself took over six hours. The prognosis afterward was
uncertain.

I'd stayed at the hospital throughout the rest of the
day, and would have stayed longer had the situation per-
mitted. I hardly noticed the young intern who insisted on
patching my abrasions, or the nurse who, after giving up
on trying to persuade me to go home, wrapped a warm
blanket around me and placed a steaming cup of coffee in
my hands.

Jenny's mother arrived within minutes of being notified,
and I told her what I could. She was a tall, big-boned
woman with veins showing in her pale arms, and eyes that
seemed too large for her face. Her hair, which had once
been blonde like Jenny's, was dyed a darker, brownish
shade and was wound loosely on top of her head. Her
clothing was limp. She had come directly from work, a
Dirkston regional office in Ludington where she was cler-

ical supervisor. She'd aged considerably since I'd last seen her, and the stress of worry further accentuated the lines around her mouth and eyes.

Leo had tolerated my friendship with Jenny. Jenny's father had been a foreman at the docks in Ludington and, though he brought home a comfortable wage and was a kind, likeable man, Leo didn't consider the Hamptons suitably classed for me. Even as a child, however, I was strong-willed, and he finally relented and allowed our relationship limited scope. When Jenny's father died of a heart attack, the Hamptons were thrown into a financial dilemma. Leo, despite his snobbery, helped them out where he could and gave Jenny's mother a job within the firm. Meanwhile, Jenny did waitressing part-time and, with hard work and determination, managed to earn a scholarship to Michigan State University.

I was never sure exactly what Mrs. Hampton thought of me. She was always impeccably polite, but there was a hint of stiffness, perhaps resentment, that I found sadly impregnable.

After I spilled out my story to her, she lapsed into silence, seemingly intent on pacing the small waiting room or gazing blindly out the window that overlooked the main street. I wondered if she blamed me for the accident. I figured that I might have been indirectly responsible. It seemed plausible that whoever had fired those shots might have been aiming at me, and I suspected that it was the same person who had killed my father. Somehow, they knew that I'd found the murder weapon, and they were bent on revenge. However, Mrs. Hampton didn't know any of this, and her accusing attitude hurt and puzzled me.

When the police came, I still didn't voice my fears. It was Sergeant Davison, the same officer I'd spoken to at the station, and he seemed uninterested in any hypothesis I might have, continually demanding in television stereotype that I "...stick to the facts." I asked him matter-of-factly if Mr. Fenton had by any chance been to see him recently, and wasn't surprised when he shook his head no.

Mrs. Hampton listened to the police interview silently from the far side of the room. When he was finished, the officer approached her and spoke softly, so that I could barely piece together the conversation.

"…hunters out this time of year," he said. "…amateurs…accidents happen…investigation…"

I stood up, incensed. "That was no accident!" I exclaimed. The two turned to look at me in surprise. "That man was aiming at us; I saw him! He was trying to kill us!" I hardly knew what I was saying. My hands trembled, and I felt weak as I clutched the blanket around me.

Mrs. Hampton went even more pallid and placed a hand on the back of a chair for support. "What are you saying, Suzanna? Who? Who would want to kill my Jenny?"

"No!" I cried desperately. "Not Jenny! He wanted to kill me! I know it! First, he killed my father, and now he wants to kill me!" I burst into tears.

The floor nurse, who heard my raised voice, hurried in and tried to comfort me, pulling me aside and urging me to sit on the brown vinyl couch.

"Take these," she said, holding out two tablets and a paper cup with water. "You'll feel better."

Numbly, I did as I was told, my outburst leaving me totally drained. When the nurse was sure that I was calmer, she left, casting a scowl over her shoulder at the sergeant.

He turned back to Mrs. Hampton and proceeded to assure her that my allegations would be looked into, but that "Miss Dirkston is obviously suffering from shock, on top of grief over her father's recent demise, and can't be taken seriously."

I lapsed into sullen silence, realizing that nothing I could say would convince this small town police officer that there was a murderer loose in the area. Besides, I had to admit that there was a slim possibility that he was right. All I'd actually seen was the flash of the gun on the distant ridge. I didn't even know for sure if the shooter was male or female. But it seemed a bit far-fetched that an innocent hunter would fire so many misplaced shots. One, perhaps, but not three.

Sergeant Davison left shortly thereafter, with a few more reassuring words to Jenny's mother, and promises to me that he would have my claims thoroughly investigated. We both watched him go with dubious expressions, then fell once more into our own separate distractions.

David arrived some time later, his face a picture of concern. I was never so glad to see him, and ran into his arms wordlessly, sobbing silently as he led me back to the couch and sat with me. He wanted to take me home at once—in fact, he insisted. But I refused, determined to remain until we had some word on Jenny's condition.

"Everyone will be worried about you, Suzanna," he argued. "Besides, you look ghastly. You need to get some clothes and something to eat."

"I'm all right, David," I insisted. "Call the house and tell them not to worry. I have to stay."

He knew all too well that once I'd set my mind on something, it was useless to argue, so he compromised, insisting on phoning the house to arrange for the clothes and food to be sent up and, if I would be all right without him, he'd go and see what he could do to assist the police. At least, he didn't seem to think my notion of a deliberate attack was unreasonable. My claims that Leo was murdered were met with less credibility, but at least he listened, and his eyebrows lifted when I quietly told him about the poker, how Grant had wrested it from me and then claimed he would take it to the police.

David pulled me close and smoothed my hair back gently. "No wonder you've been so strung out lately," he murmured. "But you don't have to worry any longer. We'll solve this thing together." He pulled back and looked into my eyes seriously. "If what you say is true, Suzanna, I think you should consider getting out of that house and coming to stay with Dad and me for a while. I don't want you anywhere near Grant Fenton."

I nodded with relief. It was a comfort to have someone else shoulder the burden of doubt and suspicion for a while, and I wondered why I hadn't turned to David from the start.

After he left, I was content to sit quietly. I was only just beginning to feel the throb of my multiple injuries, though the pills that the nurse had given me seemed to wrap me in a cloud of peaceful apathy.

An hour later, Jenny's mother was escorted down the hall to the Intensive Care Unit while the same nurse gave me a brief summary of Jenny's condition, and told me that only the immediate family was allowed to visit. They were preparing Jenny for the operation.

"I believe someone is on their way with some clothes and food for you," she said, smiling. "Mr. Lancaster wanted me to tell you."

I nodded and thanked her. Probably Martha or Lottie would bring my things. I'd be glad to change, but doubted that I'd be able to eat a bite.

It was Grant who came. He barged into the waiting room with such ferocity that I jumped. At the sight of him, my heart began to thump erratically, fear filling my veins like hot oil.

"What's going on here, anyway?" he demanded, his voice filling the room. "I can't get a coherent explanation from anyone! Are you all right, Suzie? What's happened to Jenny?"

As if you didn't know! I thought, clutching the blanket tighter. Aloud, I said meekly: "Jenny's been shot."

He drew a quick breath and his eyes narrowed. "Shot? My God! How? By whom?"

He sat down next to me, and it was all I could do not to cower away. I told him the story again, my voice weary from the aftermath of trauma combined with the mild sedatives.

I was too tired to fight when he escorted me out of the hospital to his car. Something told me that he'd certainly not try to kill me in front of so many witnesses. To my credit, though, I did protest feebly at first, wanting to stay until after the operation, until I was certain Jenny would be all right, but Grant's air of command swept my words aside and I knew that if I didn't go with him willingly, he'd probably carry me out bodily.

The young intern who had tended my wounds met us at the reception desk with a vial of tablets similar to those the nurse had pressed upon me, and, chauvinistically directing his conversation at Grant, indicated that I should be given one as needed to calm my nerves.

Still huddled in the blanket, though dressed more appropriately in a cotton tracksuit, I eased my aching body into Grant's car, with a compulsive glance at the back seat for the poker. It wasn't there. I dismissed it for the moment and opened the glove compartment, groping inside. Grant started the engine and we left the darkness of the parking complex.

"What are you looking for?" he asked, noting my aimless shuffling amongst the maps and miscellany.

"Cigarettes," I said. "I know you keep some in here."

He smiled. "Sorry. I'm trying to quit."

I stared at him in frustration, yet when he glanced at me and our eyes met, the irony of the situation overcame us simultaneously and we began to laugh.

"I'm trying to quit, too!" I sputtered inanely.

"We sure picked a great time, eh?" he responded, still chuckling.

When we looked at each other again, it was as if a taut bow had been loosened. The release of laughter had eased the tension considerably, and suddenly, I was no longer certain that Grant was the man I should fear. I found it so hard to mistrust him when every facet of his face, every gesture, the sound of his voice, were all so familiar and had been part of my life for so many years. How could I think that he could commit murder?

"I didn't do it, you know," he said, reading my mind quite adeptly. "I can't blame you for suspecting me, but I swear on my mother's grave, I didn't do it."

I didn't reply, merely looked at him. I should ask about the poker, demand an explanation; but I knew he'd only lie to me again, and I didn't want to deal with that right now. At the same time, I knew that I wouldn't rest peacefully until a lot of questions were answered.

He pulled into the little corner store on the way out of town and disappeared inside for a short moment. When he returned, he deliberately drove off in a direction I knew wouldn't take us to Beacon. Immediately, my suspicions and fears returned.

"Where are we going?"

"Just a little detour," he said as he swung the car off the main road onto a dirt track.

We bumped along for about a mile until the track came to an end on a grassy stretch of land bordering a lovely, deserted little lake. If I had been less weary and more in command of my feelings, I would most certainly have been close to panic. As it was, I sat stiffly, clutching the door handle, ready to leap out and run should Grant make any attempt to touch me. But he turned off the engine and sat staring straight ahead, his hands still on the wheel.

"We need to talk," he said simply. When he looked at me, his eyes were grave. "There's a lot you don't know, and I think it's time you did."

He reached into his coat pocket and I drew back instinctively. He smiled ruefully. "Don't worry, it's not a gun!" He produced a packet of cigarettes and, at the sight of them, I relaxed and half smiled.

"Seems kind of silly to worry about these when you've just spent the day dodging bullets." he mumbled around one of them. He lit two, handed me one, and we puffed decadently for a moment. When he spoke again, he chose his words carefully.

"I didn't want it to come to this, Suzie. If I'd thought for one moment that you might be in danger…" He paused, frowning. "When your father was killed, I knew right away it wasn't an accident. There had been attempts before, twice that I know of."

I choked. "What? When?!"

"Once about a year ago, then again, less than four months ago. Both times, they were set up to look like accidents, but Leo and I knew better. There were letters and phone calls, threatening ones. Leo just wanted to shrug them off, but I insisted that we go to the police."

"But the police don't know anything about…"

"I know, I know. That's what they told you, and that's what they want you to believe." He twisted his mouth wryly. "You can blame Leo and me for that. He insisted that you know nothing of what had happened, and made me promise not to involve you."

"Not involve me?" I cried incredulously. "Of all the hypocritical, pataronising, contemptible…"

"Yes," he sighed. "I suppose we deserve that. Still, a promise is a promise, and I did my best to keep you out of it. Actually, the local police know very little about the investigation. They merely gather the evidence and pass it on to the FBI." He nodded at my stunned expression. "They've got an undercover team set up in the area. I'm sorry, but I'm really not allowed to tell you who they are or where they work from. Anyway, I took the fire-iron directly to them yesterday, and it's now being analyzed. We're pretty sure that you found the murder weapon."

My mind worked sluggishly to take in the enormity of these revelations. It all seemed so farfetched…and yet, all the pieces fit.

"Do you…they…have any idea who…?"

He shook his head. "I don't think so. They're very hush-hush about their investigation, but as far as I can tell, there's a bit more going on than even I know about. We just have to trust that they know what they're doing."

I laughed bitterly. "If they know what they're doing, how come Jenny is lying in the hospital with a bullet in her?" I turned my head to stare out at the lake so he wouldn't see the tears blurring my eyes.

Silently, he ground his cigarette butt out in the ashtray. When he answered, his voice was heavy. "That should never have happened," he sighed. "It seems that we're dealing with a real nut-case. It makes no sense to me that whoever killed Leo would want to kill Jenny—or you—unless…"

"Unless what?"

He frowned. "Unless they don't want the inheritance to go through."

I mulled over this theory. "Who could possibly want Leo's fortune to be auctioned off? And who could have known what was in Leo's will in the first place?"

Then, I remembered that Colin had acquired this information quite easily from some secret source. Colin? I shuddered, trying to picture my own half-brother as a murderer. It was no more farfetched than Grant. But what could Colin possibly have to gain?

"That presents another area I think we should deal with," he continued. "If it's true that someone wants to prevent Leo's estate from passing on to you, it follows that the sooner we secure the inheritance, the better. Hopefully, it will put you out of danger and in a position where we can keep a closer eye on you."

I frowned and fumbled for another cigarette. I was chain-smoking and I didn't care. He automatically produced a lighter. I rolled down the window, blew a long trail of smoke out into the gentle breeze and watched as it quickly dispersed.

It was nearly dusk. The sun was perched over the trees at the opposite end of the lake, sending a mercurial rainbow trail rippling across the water's surface. The trees were magnificently clothed in the reds, yellows and oranges of late September and were mirrored in the shallows. Fish tickled the surface as they fed off mosquitoes, water-spiders or grubs dropped from overhanging foliage. Two herons waded quietly among a stretch of lily-pads, ducking their long necks periodically to snap up passing fry. Frogs and crickets tested their voices, preparing for the evening chorus.

I'd been dreading this moment, yet knew it was inevitable. I couldn't submit quietly until I knew every avenue had been explored. "How do we know that the murderer doesn't just want me dead because he thinks I know too much?" I asked lamely. "I mean, if he knows I found the murder weapon and have spoken to the police, perhaps he—or she," I added pointedly, "just thinks I'm onto his trail."

Grant nodded. "I've thought about that, too, but it just doesn't tie in with Leo's murder. Besides, if this fellow," he glanced at me, "or woman," I smiled, satisfied, "wants you dead because of what you know, then why haven't they tried to do me in, too?"

"Why, indeed?" I said pointedly.

He groaned. "Christ, Suzanna! Don't tell me you still suspect me? Would you be happier if I went out and got myself bumped off?"

I shrugged airily. "Well, at least it would prove beyond a doubt that you're not guilty."

He snorted. "Yes, and it would leave you in a fine pickle by giving the real culprit just what he wants!"

"Or she."

He sighed.

"But that's just it, Grant. It doesn't make sense. Why don't they just do away with you? It would serve the same purpose."

"Sorry," he said, "but I'm afraid you're wrong there. If I should die, the estate drops directly into your lap."

"And if I go?"

"It goes to Colin and myself."

"Colin," I repeated. Again the web tightened. I shivered. "It couldn't be Colin!" I muttered.

Grant shrugged. "We have to start looking at every possibility. I'm sure the Feds are. I wouldn't be surprised if
you aren't right up there at the top of this list!"

"Me?" I squeaked. "But they must know I couldn't have
possibly killed my own father! Besides, I wasn't even in
the area."

"Where's your proof?"

"I've got a witness. David would verify that I was at the
cabin."

He laughed. "David, eh? Your fiancé? Come on, Suzie,
do you think he'd turn you in?"

I glared at him. "Ex-fiancé," I corrected. "Everyone
knows I broke the engagement off."

"Very convenient," he rejoined calmly.

I fumed silently. "Well, what was my motive, then, Mr.
Detective? Did I kill my father for his money because I felt
unwanted and unloved? Or perhaps I just went a little
cuckoo and felt like killing someone!" I ground my cigarette out in the ashtray.

"Don't be ridiculous. I don't think you had anything to
do with it. I'm just saying that, from a non-biased point of
view, anyone could be under suspicion."

I sat back, mildly assuaged.

"So, what you're saying, Grant, is that you think we
should get married right away."

"I think it's the safest route."

I contemplated this for a moment, then sighed. "All
right. But I want it clear from the start that in exactly one
year we have the marriage annulled."

"Of course."

"And," I added, "during that year we live our own lives.
This is only a business venture, which means our relationship stays just the way it is now."

He smiled. "What are you afraid of, Suzie? Do you think
I'd insist on conjugal rights?"

I blushed furiously. "No, I...that is...oh, I don't know

what to think! I just want to make things clear."

"You've done that," he said bitterly. "Anyway, what do you say to the day after tomorrow?"

"What?"

"Friday. We can go get it over and done with."

"But, what about blood tests? And...and the license and...?"

"That can all be taken care of," he said assuredly.

I felt my palms perspiring, and wiped them on the blanket that still hung loosely from my shoulders. There was no putting it off.

"All right," I agreed resignedly. "Friday."

He nodded. "There's no need to tell anyone. I don't particularly want a big shindig, do you?"

"Good God, no! But we'll need witnesses."

"I'll take care of that, too."

We fell silent. Then, unexpectedly, Grant reached over to touch my cheek where a strip of white gauze covered the scrape.

"How do you feel?" he asked.

I shrugged. "Numb. I feel like I'm still out there on the river, but this time with no paddle and no way to fight the current." I looked down at my hands. "It's like I don't have any control over my life anymore."

He gazed at me and his eyes were tinged with sympathy. "I think you're doing extremely well," he said. "And, by the way, I liked your first novel."

My eyes widened. "You read it?"

He nodded. "It's not the sort of thing I would have picked up at the bookstore, but I wanted to see whether you were any good. Once I got started, I couldn't put it down. I'm really impressed."

I realized that I was blushing again and put a hand to my face, ridiculously embarrassed.

"Well," I said modestly, "it's my first. I expect to get better with each one."

"Have you started another?"

"Sort of. But I'll have to put in some long hours soon, or I'll never meet the deadline."

"You'll have plenty of time now," he said. "I want you to take it easy and keep a low profile for a while; at least, until all of this is over. Perhaps even a trip abroad…"

"No!" I snapped automatically. I was wondering if he was already trying to manage my life, and I was determined to fight him if need be.

He dropped the subject, sensing my reluctance, and turned the key in the ignition. I immediately felt guilty, realizing that he was probably only being kind. I turned to him impulsively.

"Grant, I…well, David thought it best that I move out of Beacon and into Spindrift."

I left it as a statement, but I was asking his opinion. He thought for a moment; then, much to my surprise, nodded.

"If that's what you want to do," he said. "You'd probably be safer." Then, he turned to me and his eyes were a dark, turbulent blue. "Can you trust David?"

I opened my mouth to speak, but shut it, puzzled. Trust David? "Well, why couldn't I?"

He cocked a brow. "Like I said, everyone is under suspicion. He'd have a vested interest in this inheritance, too—because of the business. He is Colin's partner."

I frowned. He was right, of course. I had to start thinking more ruthlessly, and not let emotional bonds or habits color my judgment. Deep down, I was unwilling to suspect anyone close to me, but logically I knew that the chances of someone totally alien being to blame were slim. It was hard to imagine that such coldblooded methodical brutality could lie concealed beneath a familiar face.

I glanced into Grant's eyes again and saw a cloud of emotion warring within, held in check by a rigid face and an iron will. Here was a face that could hide a lot, and I felt suddenly and more desperately alone. Apprehension gripped me.

"Let's go home," I said, keeping my voice steady.

Thankfully, he put the car into gear and edged back down the bumpy track. I watched him covertly. I would marry him. If he was my enemy, the best way to fight him was with feigned innocence. If he considered me malleable, I'd pose no threat and therefore he'd have no reason to harm me. I could only hope that murder was a last resort rather than a pleasure. In the meantime, I would wait and watch and hope that the culprit would show his or her true colors soon.

So now, I sat alone on the flat rock that backed up to the lighthouse and let the rhythmic crash and suck of the waves lull my troubled mind. I closed my eyes. The steady force of the wind, with its fine mist of spray, wet my face and made my clothes limp and my hair frizzy. I felt almost ethereal, as though by sheer willpower I could detach myself from mortality and drift lightly in the up-drafts, or gambol and soar across the cream-capped waves. My muscles relaxed, and I blocked out those red webs of worry that had held me in their clutches ever since my return to Beacon. I filled my lungs again and again with clean moist air and savored the tang of sodden sand, algae and seaweed. Finally, I opened my eyes, relaxed and refreshed. For the first time in days, I felt safe. I was sure no one had seen me leave the house, and was equally certain that no one had followed.

Since my talk with Grant, I had decided against moving into Spindrift. Once the shock of that day had diminished, I felt stronger and better prepared to face the future squarely. I realized that my original motives for the move were based on fear and that, once again, I was using David as a crutch. It was unnerving to think that I might be doing this for the rest of my life. It was a habit—like smoking—and the only way to stop was to refuse to give in.

David considered my decision foolhardy and said so directly, showing more concern and emotion than I'd expected. It pleased me that, despite the battering our relationship had taken recently, he still obviously cared for me. Perhaps in the end the pressures afflicting us would bring him to realize just how important I was to him, and the fondness he felt for me would blossom into something deeper. Already he was spending more time with me, insisting that I be left alone as little as possible in case whoever shot Jenny might still be after me. It was touching to know he'd appointed himself my protector, but I quickly began to feel smothered. It had been ages since I'd been able to enjoy some solitude other than the four walls of my room at night. At least I had made some headway on my novel, managing between ten and fifteen pages each evening.

Grant had irritatingly disappeared, leaving word that he'd be staying at the Chicago penthouse for a few days to clear up some stockholder unrest. I knew that the business was suffering. The newspapers had gotten hold of Leo's eccentric bequest and were having a field day, speculating what would happen to Dirkston Enterprises. Shares were falling rapidly, and it was imperative that Grant reassure the remaining investors that there would be no major upheavals and that management was well in control. I prayed that this was true for, if the bottom fell out of the stock, we'd all face tenuous futures. Even though Leo's private wealth was massive, it was mostly tied up in investment. Divided between the three of us, the meager liquid assets probably wouldn't even cover the upkeep and maintenance of Beacon. It was all very legal. I found it tedious poring over the documents and pamphlets that Grant occasionally left lying around. It amazed me that anyone could dedicate their lives to the practice of corporate law. In my mind, it was dry, dull and decidedly boring and I quickly lost interest, relying on the troupe of attorneys and sub-attorneys on staff to keep Grant on the straight and narrow.

Despite my annoyance at Grant's precipitous departure, I was somewhat relieved, not having entirely settled his guilt or innocence in my mind, and still much too ready to place him as the hazy figure outlined on the crest of the river, rifle to his shoulder, cold determination in his ice-chip eyes. I'd managed to keep a somewhat cool ambivalence to the situation, but my imagination was constantly working, fitting that cold steel poker into the hands of everyone I knew. Undisputedly, Grant and Colin held it most convincingly and, though I forced myself to keep an open mind, I was always grateful for David's presence when face to face with either of them.

Rain was beginning to fall in misty drops, and I uncurled my cramped legs and stood up. My multitude of abrasions and bruises were still visible, but had become decidedly less dramatic and, aside from some stiffness, I hardly felt them at all. I was relieved that Jenny was on the road to recovery, and considered my own wounds a minor inconvenience. I fought daily with the irrational sense of guilt over the affair. I knew the bullet was meant for me and, if I hadn't involved Jenny, the incident would never have happened. It made me all the more determined, in a self-punishing, reckless way, to expose the perpetrator of the attack.

I picked my way over and around the slippery rocks, using a hand for leverage now and then when I had to span a large pool. The wind whistled through the empty crown of the lighthouse like a spirit keening through hollow halls. Within minutes, I was safely on the beach. I stood looking up at Beacon. Only the top floors could be seen from this angle, and they were shrouded in a swirling cloud as were the tops of the trees. Even the sandy cliffs were muted gray. The beach itself drifted away in a dreamy velvet gauze, the juncture between water and sand indistinct except for the rhythmic splash and lap of tide.

I walked slowly, undisturbed by the saturating drizzle. I relished the solitude, feeling pillowed and protected by nature. I took off my shoes and the cool lips of the tide crept up to nibble at my toes, then gently receded, coaxing me to follow to the distant deep. When I looked up, I was struck by the eeriness. The beach ahead was almost entirely swallowed up by a rolling fogbank which seemed to have taken on an odd animation. It moved against the wind in a spiraling motion that defied any laws of nature. I stopped and stared, fascinated—like a sleepwalker—happily unconcerned by the inexplicable phenomenon taking place.

The cloud thickened and its core became darker until, as if squeezed from some inner depth, a black mass manifested itself: a figure—tall, stocky, faceless and shadowed—motionless except for a crown of windblown hair. I didn't move, frozen by some intangible force emanating from the figure, as though it were trying to communicate but hadn't mastered the language. Again, I wasn't afraid, just as I wasn't afraid beneath the dark waters of the pool. I opened my mouth to speak but, as though a delicate balance were upset, the figure melted slowly into obscurity, leaving only the steamy mist which was eventually driven to ground by an increased pelting of rain.

"Suzanna!"

David hurried toward me from the direction of the cliff steps. There was nothing left of the apparition now. Even that overpowering sense of presence was gone. I felt strangely empty and unusually exhausted, as though my own energy had conjured the image, fed it, then released it. I was trembling uncontrollably by the time David reached me, still frozen to the spot, my eyes riveted on the distant rain-soaked beach.

If he found my dazed expression peculiar, he didn't say so, but threw a huge, somewhat damp towel about my shoulders, hurried me up the climb and across the gardens, chiding me all the while for standing out in the rain.

By the time we reached the back patio, the rain was pouring down with a vengeance. I had regained my senses, and shivered all the more as my mind incredulously relived the experience. I would not, could not, tell David. He simply wouldn't believe me. No one would. I suspected that the figure on the beach was the same as the others I had seen, and now I was equally certain that what I had seen wasn't made of flesh and blood.

"You're drenched!" David scolded, dabbing at my face with a corner of the towel, "And shivering! We'll have to get you into some dry clothes right away."

"I'm okay, David," I mumbled, pushing his long fingers away irritably. He looked at me with a wounded expression and I put a hand on his arm, forcing a reassuring smile. "Thanks," I said, "but I'm really all right. I'll go up and change right away."

I left him there abruptly, for I was fairly bursting with residual shock and amazement and unable to trust myself with sane conversation. He would only have to look into my eyes to see the awe and wonder of it all, and I knew I couldn't face any questions now.

~~~

Awe and wonder were quickly replaced by doubt and depression. I was going mad. It was the only explanation. First, the vision at the cabin; then, on the highway and by the grave; the strange experience at the pool; and now...now an apparition on the beach. I was most certainly losing my mind.

I stepped out of a hot bath and toweled myself off. My eyes caught my image in the bathroom mirror and I moved closer, rubbing a hole in the steam. My face looked hideous. Despite a pink tinge brought out by the warmth in the room, my complexion was unnaturally sallow. My cheekbones stood out too prominently, and my eyes were sunken and underlined by dark shadows. My lips were pale, and the lump on my forehead had spread and turned purplish-black. My hair hung, still dripping, to my shoulders, making my features appear even more drawn.

Yes, that was it. I was having a nervous breakdown. I sighed, almost wishing I could believe it. Unfortunately, the reality of my experiences was still too fresh and told me otherwise, adding a new set of fears to my already extensive collection. I had to think logically!

I opened the door from the en suite connecting my room, and hurriedly donned a warm, fleecy white bathrobe. Tying it securely, I sat down at the dressing table to work on my disheveled hair when there was a knock on the door.

"Who is it?"

"It's Alicia, Suzanna."

I grunted in annoyance, but beckoned her in. She appeared with a round tray balanced on one hand, a steaming mug tilting precariously on its surface.

"Martha was bringing this up, so I thought I'd save her the trouble. She's not as young as she used to be, you know. I wouldn't be surprised if those stairs don't give her trouble. Besides, she has enough to do."

She set the tray down beside me, then flopped on her stomach across the bed, her stilt-like legs raised and crossed at the ankles behind her, her chin propped on the backs of her be-ringed hands. She smiled benignly.

"My, you do look a mess, Suzanna!"

"Thanks," I said.

"Oh, you know what I mean. You look pooped, and who wouldn't after all you've been through?" She cocked her head to one side. "How's Jenny? Did you see her today?"

I nodded. "Yes. She's still critical, but they think she's out of danger."

"Thank God for that! I still say, you were terribly lucky to get out of it alive. You must have been petrified!"

"I didn't really have time to be."

She examined her nails critically for a moment. "When are you and Grant going to…?" She lifted one brow.

I pulled the brush relentlessly through my hair, feeling the rip of tangled strands.

"Get married? Tie the knot? Do the deed?" I snapped. "Why?"

"No reason, darling, I was just curious. No need to get

irritable."

I sighed. I knew that she'd naturally be worried about the division of Leo's wealth, and had every right to be. I must make an effort to be less touchy about the inevitable.

"I'm sorry, Alicia. I seem to have a short temper lately."

Thankfully, she didn't pursue the question, but seemed pleased to have forced my contrition. "Well, you know you're not the only one who's been under a strain lately. Just look at these hands." She held one out in front of her, and it shook exaggeratedly. "I can't stop them trembling, what with Jenny…and you falling into the pool. Why did you fall in? I never figured it out. I know you can swim better than most of us." She paused, considering; then a devious smile crept over her lips. "It was rather romantic, though, the way Grant saved you, don't you think?"

I fought to control my rising anger and turned to face her directly. "Look, Alicia, I don't know what crazy ideas you've got buzzing around in your brain, but Grant and I are merely agreeing to this arrangement to save Beacon and the people in it from ruin. Nothing more." At her look of smug disinterest, I added spitefully, "You might also remember that you're married to Colin. Perhaps if you centered more of your attentions on him and less on other members of the household, everyone would be happier!"

This broke her veneer of calm and her eyes narrowed. She uncurled herself and I could see that I'd struck a nerve. "What are you talking about?"

"I heard you fawning over Grant on the patio a couple weeks ago."

She was silent, obviously trying to remember the incident but drawing a blank. "I don't know what you heard, darling, but I hope you learned a few things from it. You could certainly use a few pointers. You think anyone's worried about you and Grant?" She snorted. "You couldn't hold his attention for two minutes! You're too interested in your precious career and your so-called 'independence' to ever be attractive to a man! Why, you couldn't even hold onto your pompous little David!"

I stood up, rigid with fury. "I think you'd better go, Alicia," I said through tight lips.

She rose, too, and faced me. She was inches taller than me, and seemed utterly composed; the only sign of tension was in the slight sheen of perspiration on her brow and upper lip.

"I'll go," she said. "But, just remember what I said. Grant doesn't want you, so for your own good, leave him alone. And if you're looking for someone to be jealous of, try his new secretary. I, personally, could care less."

With dramatic aplomb, she swept from the room, closing the door firmly behind her. I stood staring after her, still livid with rage. Up until now, Alicia had been merely an interesting but unimportant decoration at Beacon. What few conversations we indulged in had been trivial and rife with her tiresome exaggeration. This encounter surprised me as much as it angered me. When she threw aside her facade, she showed a calculating core. I had no doubt that she was involved with Grant, even if only in her own imagination, so much so that she would drop her carefully cultivated act to fight for him. I was certain that her comment about a new secretary was merely a ploy to throw me off the track.

I sat down on the bed and covered my face with my hands. My heart was pounding rapidly. Much of what Alicia had said rang painfully true. I had to admit that romantically, I was a bad risk. David had been my excuse to avoid other involvements. He was the only one I'd ever felt comfortable with—though that's not to say I was unaware of those lingering looks and tentative inquiring smiles that often came my way. I always answered them with a blank shuttered stare, or turned quickly away, squelching any chance of further flirtation. It hurt deeply to face the truth, and it made me wonder just how cruel Alicia could be.

EIGHT

Out, out, brief candle.
Life's but a walking shadow, a poor player
That struts and frets his hour upon the stage,
And then is heard no more. It is a tale
Told by an idiot, full of sound and fury,
Signifying nothing.

William Shakespeare
Macbeth, act 5, sc.5

Friday dawned bleak and cool. Despite my exhaustion, I'd slept little. David had come up to see me safely to bed and, noting my overwrought state, presented me with a soothing cup of tea and insisted that I take one of the tablets the doctor had prescribed. It did relax me, and I sank almost immediately into a black void. But some time after midnight, I awoke and thrashed restlessly until the dull light of dawn lit the windows.

Now, my head ached and I felt weak and lethargic. I lay quietly for a moment, trying not to think of the event scheduled for that day. Rain still drizzled outside, lending a dismal atmosphere.

Alicia's voice pierced my reverie. "Colin!" she shrieked. A door slammed nearby, accompanied by the muffled mur-

mur of Colin's voice. This was followed by a furious tirade
from Alicia. Firm footsteps passed down the corridor outside my room. Alicia scrabbled after him, still screeching,
but there was no response and within moments, the front
door slammed and she subsided into loud, heart-wrench-
ing sobs.

I got out of bed and, wrapping myself in my robe,
stepped out into the hall. Alicia still wailed pathetically.
She lay in a heap, clinging to one of the uprights to the
banister. Her hair was matted, and a pink satin wrapper
hung carelessly open to reveal a daring lace negligee.

"What is it, Alicia?" I asked, trying to be solicitous,
hoping to put our recent argument aside.

She looked up at me and I frowned with concern. Her
face was moist with sweat. Mascara ran down her cheeks
and grotesquely ringed her eyes. Tears stained her face a
mottled red. She looked haggard. But it wasn't her
appearance that shocked me as much as the look in her
eyes—a wide desperate look, like that of a starving animal. I knelt down to help her up, but she pushed at me
viciously.

"Get away!" she hissed. "Leave me alone!"

She stood up, swaying unsteadily, and I could see she
was shivering. Her eyes darted about desperately, then
settled on me again and, suddenly, her expression changed
to one of hope.

"Please," she said softly, "Colin and I—we've had an
argument. I need something for my nerves. You've got
pills. Could I…?"

I frowned, hesitating; then, assessing her distress, I
nodded and went to my room for the vial. I gave her two of
the sedatives and she snatched them greedily. Then, wiping a trembling hand across her brow she made an attempt
at a smile.

"Thanks. I'll be all right now," she said. She started
back toward her own room, then paused and looked at me.
"Look, I'm sorry about—about yesterday, Suzanna," she

said. "No hard feelings?"

I shrugged. "No hard feelings." I watched as she shuffled off down the hall. I'd have given anything to know what she and Colin had argued about, but knew it wasn't the time or place to ask.

Grant's return was anything but inconspicuous. He roared up the drive like a teenaged hot-rodder, gunning the engine, then coming to a screeching halt in front of the house. I watched him from the piano where I was methodically practicing a Chopin etude. He bounded up the steps, whistling gaily, threw open the front door with a bang, then slammed it with another. I half expected him to pitch a top hat onto a nearby hat stand and execute a brief tap-dance. Annoyed, I turned back to the music and pounded the keys loudly. How dare he be in such high spirits?

Hearing the piano, he strode into the room, a mischievous grin on his lips. Seeing me alone, he sat down on the bench and spoke quietly in my ear.

"Ready for our big day, darling?"

I slammed the lid down on the keys, narrowly missing his fingers.

"Get away!" I grated, shouldering him until he nearly fell onto the floor.

This display only served to further amuse him. "What's this? Last-minute jitters?" He clutched his hands over his heart. "Please, Suzanna! Tell me you haven't changed your mind!"

I stifled a smile at this totally ridiculous charade. I'd rarely seen him in such a frivolous mood, and it suited him, smoothing the harsh planes of his face and making his eyes dance. I had to admit, he could be charming when he wanted to be.

"What's gotten into you?" I asked, trying to hold my dignity. "Have you been drinking?"

He pulled a pack of cigarettes from his pocket, offered

me one and, when I shook my head, put them away again.

"No. I haven't been drinking. Aside from the fact that I'm looking forward to a very important merger today…" he winked slyly, "…I also think I've convinced our primary shareholders that Dirkston Enterprises isn't a sinking ship."

"That's wonderful," I said, only mildly relieved at the news. "I assume you had to tell them about our…this 'merger'?"

He nodded happily. "Looks like there's no way out now!"

I didn't reply. The attorney from Manistee had called this morning to tell me the will was airtight, and offering his regrets. Now that the stockholders knew, it would be in every newspaper by evening.

"Do I have any say in this affair, or are you planning to organize the whole thing?"

He spread his hands in a magnanimous gesture. "Your wish is my command. What would you like? A cathedral wedding catered to by the Vienna Boys' Choir? Or perhaps a garden nuptial with a brass band? How about a honeymoon in the south of France?"

"Don't pretend you haven't already made all the arrangements!"

"Who's pretending? I just so happen to have a friend who's a retired judge. He'd be happy to perform the ceremony any time today. I told him we wanted it kept quiet for the time being, so he agreed to do the honors at his house here in town. But, if you'd rather…?"

I cast him a withering look. "No," I replied sullenly. "We may as well get it over with as soon and as simply as possible, unless you have other appointments?"

"Nope! I'm as free as a bird today." He cocked a devilish brow. "Cheer up. It's not every day you get married! Why don't you go up and change into something more suitable for the occasion while I freshen up?"

"Black mourning clothes would be suitable!" I mumbled, but he didn't hear me as he strode off whistling the wedding march to himself.

If I had discovered it was Friday the thirteenth, I wouldn't have been surprised. It seemed an apt date for this most tragic of marriages. But it was the last Friday of the month, and held no special significance one way or the other.

Despite my insistence that the ceremony meant nothing to me, I chose one of my favorite dresses: a flowing affair of lime-green chiffon with scalloped hemline, cinched waistline and cross-draped bodice. I even went so far as to fasten on a gold bracelet and matching necklace with gold and diamond earrings that my father had given to me for my twenty-first birthday. There wasn't much I could do with my hair, except scrunch it into tousled waves and slick it back at the temples. After applying a minimum of makeup to cover my fading injuries and the dark smudges beneath my eyes, and to bring out some color in my cheeks, I was ready.

Grant didn't comment on my appearance, but his cool appraisal left little doubt that he approved. He had merely changed his shirt and tie and tried to run a brush through his thick hair, but it was determined to do as it pleased and lent him a somewhat roguish air.

We spoke little on the way to the judge's house. I sat stiffly upright while Grant concentrated on his driving, seemingly intent on getting there as quickly as possible.

The ceremony itself took less than thirty minutes. Two witnesses, neither of whom I'd met, were on hand to sign the certificate and, after the briefest of declarations, it was all over and Grant and I departed as man and wife. Strangely enough, I felt next to nothing. I gazed down at the plain gold band on my finger, thinking that it should at least feel alien. Then, I risked a look at Grant, his chiseled profile unreadable, and wondered what he was thinking.

When he stopped the car, it wasn't at Beacon, but at a popular little restaurant that looked out over the lake and specialized in clam chowder. He didn't ask for my opinion, but said simply, "I'm starving. We can get some lunch here." I didn't argue, feeling hunger gnawing at my own insides.

Once we were settled in a quiet booth with a modest view, I began to relax. It was a monumental relief to know that the dreaded moment was over and there was no point in worrying about it anymore. Still, something about this new slant to our relationship embarrassed me, and I found it suddenly difficult to meet his eyes over the menu. Eventually, he took the card from my hand.

"You've been poring over that since we arrived," he said. "You can't avoid me forever, you know."

"I'm not trying to avoid you."

He raised a skeptical brow.

"Well," I relented, "I just don't have anything to say."

He smiled. "And this is the girl who insisted that our relationship should remain the same?"

I frowned. "It is the same. How often have we ever had more than fifteen words to say to each other?"

He couldn't deny it. "It seems a shame, doesn't it? That after all those years growing up in the same house, we can't even talk to one another."

"We have our separate lives."

"So do a lot of friends, but they still communicate."

"I don't want to argue with you."

He sighed. "No. It's not the best way to start off our new arrangement. Maybe I'm hoping for too much."

It was my turn to raise my brows. "And just what are you hoping for?"

He shook his head. "I don't really know. Perhaps that we could learn to like each other a little?"

"I've never disliked you."

"Nor I you," he responded. "But I'd like us to be friends."

I hesitated. "Grant, I just don't know. There's too much going on. I don't know who to trust or who to fear. My best friend is in the hospital. My father is dead. What's left of my family seem to only care about Dad's money, and I've been seeing...well, never mind. Just don't make me choose sides right now, okay?"

He nodded resignedly. "Okay. But do try to keep an open mind."

I didn't reply, for the waitress appeared with pencil poised over her pad and I gave her my order. Grant asked for a bottle of champagne, which he said was the least we could do to celebrate our wedding day.

All in all, the afternoon progressed pleasantly enough, and I felt almost comfortable as I sipped the bubbling wine and listened to Grant expound proudly on his powers of persuasion at the stockholders' meeting. I discovered a new and fascinating side to him, enjoying his conversation and laughing at his quips. I even found myself talking candidly about my newest novel, somewhat surprised at his keen interest and encouraging comments.

By the time we were ready to leave, almost three hours had elapsed. The bright sunlight nearly blinded me as I stepped out of the darker restaurant. The clouds had broken up into floating islands, their shadows lumbering like huge dinosaurs across the dark blue of the lake. I was grateful for the light raincoat I'd brought, for despite the blaze of the sun, the wind was chilly.

We arrived back at the house, still amiably reminiscing about early days at Beacon when the front door flew open and Martha ran down the steps to meet us. She was wringing her apron, her face lined with anxiety.

"Suzanna! Grant! Thank heavens your home! It's Alicia. She's been locked in her room all day, and she doesn't answer when I knock. I'm so worried! I heard her and Colin arguing this morning, and she seemed so upset. I've got the extra key to her room, but I didn't think..."

I stiffened, remembering all too well Alicia's earlier

state. Grant started for the stairs, but I grabbed his sleeve. "Maybe I'd better go."

He frowned, then nodded and I stepped past him, key in hand, and hurried up the stairs.

Despite my loud pounding on the door, there was no sound or response, so I inserted the key and opened the door. Alicia lay sleeping on the bed. Her face, though still streaked with mascara from her earlier tears, was peaceful. She lay on one side with an arm thrown out in front of her so that her fingers hung over the side of the bed. It was below those fingers, just peeping out from under the dust ruffle, that I saw the familiar bottle and my throat constricted. I lifted her limp wrist and felt for a pulse. It was faint, but still there. I shouted urgently for Grant and Martha while fishing numbly for the prescription bottle and frantically searching for spilled pills. There were still a number of the tablets left. If this had been a suicide attempt, it had been a feeble one.

Grant bounded into the room with Martha on his heels.

"Call an ambulance!" I ordered. "She's taken some of my tranquilizers. She's unconscious."

Martha flew from the room to make the call while Grant took the bottle and inspected it.

"How did she get hold of these?"

"I gave her a couple this morning. She was so upset…she asked for them. But I left the bottle in my room."

"Good God, Suzanna! How could you do something like that?"

I stared at him dumbfounded. "What are you talking about?"

"The last thing Alicia needs are pills! You know as well as I that she has a drinking problem! Can't you read?"

He thrust the label under my nose and the words Not To Be Taken With Alcohol leapt out.

"But she wasn't drinking!"

He grunted. "I find that hard to believe! And even if she

wasn't, don't you know you're not supposed to just pass around prescription drugs to anyone? I thought you had more sense!"

I glared at him incredulously. "Are you trying to blame me for this, Grant Fenton?"

At that moment, Martha reappeared. "The ambulance is on its way. I also phoned Colin, and he'll meet them at the hospital. Is she all right?"

Temporarily sidetracked, I turned back to Alicia and felt her pulse again. It was steady.

"I think so. But I think we should try to wake her, don't you?"

No one responded, so I sat down on the edge of the bed and shook her, repeating her name over and over. Alicia groaned once, but didn't open her eyes, so I continued to shake her hard.

"Perhaps if we get her on her feet?" I looked at Grant. "Would you care to lend a hand, or should I do it by myself?"

Ignoring my acid tone, he stepped in and lifted her easily, draping her arm over his shoulders and supporting her at the waist. I put her other arm over my own shoulders and together, we dragged her back and forth across the room, her bare feet trailing uselessly. By the time the ambulance siren could be heard, she was moaning irritably and, once the paramedics were ushered into the room, she was attempting to open her eyes.

Within minutes, the attendants had her strapped onto the stretcher and hurried her to the ambulance. I looked on, my thoughts helplessly comparing this to the scene at the river's edge. I hugged my arms around me to keep from shaking. It was all becoming too much. One drama on top of another. Grant's callous accusations had touched a guilty nerve and, try as I might, I couldn't convince myself that I wasn't to blame for most of the recent mishaps.

Wordlessly, I flew down the hall to my own room and shut the door solidly, giving way to a torrent of tears.

Grant watched me go but didn't attempt to follow, striding instead to his car to set off in pursuit of the ambulance. The afternoon was shattered, and our good intentions had gone up in smoke. I knew it would take a long time before we'd ever be able to repair the damage done.

Life at Beacon changed little after my marriage to Grant No one appeared the slightest bit surprised or, in truth, much interested that the deed was done. They'd all known it was inevitable, and the incident with Alicia overshadowed any impact it might have had.

The media, on the other hand, snatched the story greedily and played it to the hilt. Headlines like: Dirkston Heiress Weds For Wealth, and Dirkston - Fenton Marry To Free Fortune appeared across national newspapers and tabloids. Scandal sheets went even further, using touched-up photos of Grant and myself, or caricatures suggesting every conceivable (and some inconceivable) slant to our relationship. Somehow, Alicia's close call had remained hushed and I thanked God, for I could well imagine what stories might have been woven around that.

I tried to ignore the publicity, but found it difficult. Where once I could move about freely, relatively anonymous, now I met reporters and cameramen everywhere, some of them shouting questions that were positively rude. The gates to Beacon were kept securely locked, but there was often a small group milling about, just waiting to catch someone coming or going. I wished fervently that I could go back to my little cabin in the woods, but I knew that that part of my life was gone and that, even if I wasn't personally controlling the machinations of Dirkston Enterprises, I played a major role in its success or failure. It was a responsibility I resented.

Grant was elated by the press coverage, gloating over the fact that Dirkston was receiving some of its best, most extensive advertising for no cost whatsoever. After an initial dive in stock values, business began to rally until it was literally booming. More and more industries threw their shipping contracts Dirkston's way, intrigued by the aura of success and wealth that the media never failed to exaggerate. Consequently, and much to my relief, Grant spent a large percentage of his time at Dirkston Towers in Chicago, working around the clock and using the penthouse to snatch what little sleep he could. If I'd thought it feasible, I'd have gone back to my cabin, but I felt obliged to take over the running of Beacon and help sort out some of the confusion there.

Lottie, when she heard of Alicia's close call, didn't come to work for a week, claiming that the house was surely jinxed. I had to coax her personally before she'd agree to return. Martha was showing the strain and tension of disorganization, and seemed to have aged overnight. I insisted that she take a couple of weeks off, which meant finding someone to fill her shoes. In the meantime, I took on most of the work myself.

Colin spent the majority of his waking hours either at the marina or at the hospital. He, too, seemed to blame me to some extent for Alicia's overdose. He spoke very little and made obvious detours to avoid me. I guessed that Alicia had done nothing to change this unfair prejudice, but I refused to let it get to me. The only person who seemed unaffected by it all was Rudy Coleman, who continued to drift about the estate tending to his regular duties methodically. I watched him with a mixture of respect and incredulity, for it seemed to me that no one should be quite so composed.

David still shadowed me but, since Colin spent long hours at the hospital with Alicia, he was obliged to put in a larger share of time tending to business. Giles took over in his place, visiting Beacon regularly on the pretext of boredom or loneliness, trying to help out where he could. Most times I was grateful for his company, though naturally I would have preferred David. Still, there was a comfortably casual air about Giles that made it easy to relax in his presence, and I needed that to sooth my raw nerves.

It was less than a week after that fateful Friday that Darla LaTrobe descended upon Beacon. I was rummaging in the attic, trying to inventory the furniture stored there, when the doorbell rang. There was no one around, so I raced down the three flights of stairs to answer it myself. When I threw open the door, I was out of breath, streaked with dust and perspiration and clad in my oldest clothes, a frayed bandanna tied over my hair. The woman poised statuesquely on the veranda regarded me with unconcealed surprise. Then she smiled remotely, adjusted her fashionable little leather shoulder bag and spoke in a husky purr.

"Good morning. I'm Darla LaTrobe. Would you be so kind as to inform Mrs. Fenton that I'm here?"

My first thought was that one of the reporters had found her way onto the grounds; then I noticed the leather suitcase at the bottom of the steps, and realized that she couldn't have gotten past the guard without a pass. I regarded her suspiciously. She was strikingly attractive in a crisp, tailored sort of way. Though not tall, her posture and high heels disguised this fact. Her hair was a dark chestnut which gleamed like satin in the sun. Cut bluntly and tapered at the sides, it neatly followed the line of a well-defined jaw. She wore a cream beret of soft angora and a two-piece suit of lightweight gray wool. In one hand, she held a briefcase with the initials "D.M.L." engraved in gold. Her large brown eyes assessed me with arrogant confidence from beneath perfectly shaped brows. I disliked her immediately.

"I'm Suzanna Dirkston," I said coolly. "You must be looking for me. I don't use my husband's name."

Her gaze never faltered and her smile merely widened a fraction. She held out a graceful hand. "Ms. Dirkston," she said readily, "I'm Mr. Fenton's secretary."

I wiped my own hand on my jeans and shook hers. So, this was the woman Alicia had referred to!

"Nice to meet you...Miss LaTrobe?"

At the questioning inflection, she nodded. "Yes, it is Miss, but please, call me Darla."

I noted disconcertedly that she could turn up the corners of her mouth quite beautifully without actually parting her lips. It gave her a decidedly feline appearance.

Determined not to let her intimidate me, I lifted my chin and smiled back. "Won't you come in? I'm sorry I'm such a mess. I was just doing a bit of inventory in the attic. If I had known you were coming..."

I left the sentence dangling with its inferred accusation. Darla lifted her chiseled brows. "Don't tell me Grant didn't tell you? But of course, he's been so busy...I'm so sorry. Should I come back later?"

"No, of course not. Perhaps you'd care for a cup of coffee while we discuss...whatever it is you've come for?"

My voice held a chilly note. It annoyed me that Darla used Grant's first name so familiarly. I wondered if it was purposely meant to convey a degree of intimacy.

"I'd love something. But would you possibly have tea? I've never acquired a taste for coffee."

"Certainly. Come with me."

Ignoring the luggage, I led the way down the passage to the rear parlor. Darla gazed about admiringly. "My! It's certainly imaginative, isn't it—the house, I mean?"

"Yes. Isn't it."

I excused myself after motioning her to a seat. Lottie was in the pantry making a list of items for her weekly trip to the supermarket.

"Lottie, could you please arrange a tray with coffee and tea and some of those little biscuits with jam?"

"Why yes, Suzanna. We got company?"

"You might say so," I grunted. "Grant's new secretary, Miss Darla LaTrobe."

She pulled a silver tray out from a corner cabinet. "I've heard of her. Seems she's not too bad to look at."

I eyed her quizzically. "Where did you hear about her?"

"I don't really remember." She glanced at me slyly. "Heard tell, though, that Mr. Grant thinks mighty highly of her."

"I'll bet he does!" I muttered. I was becoming increasingly irritable. "I'm going upstairs to change. Just bring the tray into the rear parlor when it's ready. Thanks!"

I strode out of the kitchen, pushing aside the swinging doors so that they banged against the dining room walls. Lottie was baiting me, and I had no patience for it.

"You really didn't have to change on my account," Darla said as she raised honeyed tea to her lips and sipped daintily.

"I didn't," I replied bluntly. "I was just about to change anyway when you arrived. Another biscuit?"

"No. Thank you. I have to watch my figure."

And I'm sure you're not the only one who watches it, I thought. Out loud, I said, "Now, what brings you to Beacon?"

She set the china cup back on its saucer and raised her eyes. "I really feel terribly bold, Miss, er, Miz Dirkston."

"Call me Suzanna."

"Thank you, Suzanna. Anyway, I expected that Grant would have already explained to you. I hardly know where to begin."

By now, my patience was worn very thin. "Is it some papers or documents that Grant wants? Has he sent you to fetch them?"

"No, no. I, that is, Grant has, well…Grant actually sent me here to work on a number of contracts. You see," she lifted the corners of her mouth again, "he thinks that I might accomplish more if I worked out of his lovely home—less distractions, you know. And it would also save him the trouble of having to travel back and forth so often." She laughed, a husky chuckle. "It seems that Mr. Dirkston—that is, your father—kept much of the company's paperwork here, and Grant finds it such an annoyance to flit back and forth just to find things."

I was sitting rigidly in my chair, hardly able to believe what the woman was saying. "Why doesn't Grant simply move the paperwork to the office, then?"

She turned her hands palms upward. "I can't tell you that," she replied. "I suppose he wants to leave things as they are for a while. As a matter of fact, since the stock-holders meeting and his election as company chairman…"

"What are you talking about? What election?"

Darla looked surprised. "Why, last week, the AGM," she said. "You must remember—Grant did have your proxy."

I stood up abruptly. "I signed a proxy voting affirmative to the company officers remaining as they were."

"And so they did," she said quickly. "But Mr. Dirkston held the position of chairman, and it was necessary to call an emergency election to fill the vacancy. It was mentioned in the covering letter. Your proxy authorized Grant to vote in your absence. Naturally, we all knew you would want your husband in the position."

I sat down again slowly, thinking back to the day Grant had presented a ream of papers for me to sign. It was shortly after Jenny's brush with death, and I hadn't read the documents as thoroughly as I should have. Grant had given me a condensed explanation of it all, but I hadn't paid much attention. If I had been aware that the leadership of Dirkston Enterprises was at stake, I most certainly wouldn't have allowed anyone to vote on my behalf. Grant must have known this, and used my preoccupation and worry to his own advantage. I was appalled. Already he was manipulating me, and I had fallen for it. I didn't want Darla LaTrobe to see my annoyance, however, so I forced my face into some semblance of calm.

"Yes," I lied, "I remember now. How silly of me. And you're right, who else would I have voted for, even if I had been able to attend?"

Darla took another sip of her tea and eyed me over the

rim. Quickly, I changed the subject.

"Of course, you're welcome here, Darla," I said, trying unsuccessfully to lift the corners of my own mouth. "I'm sure Grant knows exactly what he's doing!" And pigs can fly! I added to myself.

"Yes, I'm sure he does." She hesitated. "I think, Suzanna, that it's his wish to continue just as before by allowing the company to run under its own steam. He's not one to ruin a good thing, and your father had things arranged so that the position of chairman required minimal hands-on duties. He was quite wonderful at delegating authority, you know. It's only reasonable that Grant would prefer to spend more time here with you, don't you think?"

I bit back a cutting retort. I knew that the woman must be well aware of the reason for our marriage, and I sensed that a gauntlet had been thrown to the floor between us. Creditably, however, I didn't back away from the challenge but replied calmly, if a little stiffly, "Luckily, Grant and I are adult enough to accept temporary separations, but it will be nice to have him home more often. And having you here to tend to the paperwork will certainly give us more time for each other."

I watched with a sense of victory as Darla lowered her eyes, pleased that she obviously had no rebuttal. Enjoying her discomfort only briefly, I rose. "You must be anxious to freshen up. Have you brought your luggage?"

"Only one case, I'm afraid. I left it outside. The rest will be delivered tomorrow."

"Fine," I said. "Shall we fetch it, and I'll show you to the guest room?"

She nodded and we retraced our steps. I picked up the obviously expensive case and lugged it into the house and up the winding stairs.

"Don't you have servants to do that sort of thing?" she asked pointedly.

"We have servants." I replied through stiff lips, "but I wouldn't dream of bothering them with something so trivial."

I refused to let the woman goad me. I saw no reason to explain our current domestic situation. Instead, I quickened my pace and flung open the door to a guest room that was as far from my own room as possible, at the opposite end of the upstairs corridor. Grant's room was nearby which, I thought, would make it very convenient for the two of them. It could only give me reason to gloat, should they be discovered in some compromising position.

"Here you are," I said, and heaved the case onto the dark spreaded four-poster. "I hope you'll find everything you need."

It was a man's room, decorated with heavy antiques. The walls were a rich, dark walnut and the parquetry floor was softened only by a scattering of plush, Indian rugs. The windows didn't face the lake, but overlooked the garage and the paddock beyond. The draperies were of gold velvet tied back with tasseled cords. From the center of the ceiling hung an ancient five-pronged chandelier. There was a small en suite with no bath, only a shower. The room was also renowned for being the coldest one in the house in winter. I felt decidedly smug as Darla looked about. I knew I was being petty in choosing this room, but I didn't care. It was my way of telling Miz LaTrobe and Grant that I wasn't someone to be easily reckoned with.

Surprisingly, Darla appeared thrilled with the decor and assured me that she would indeed be comfortable. I apologized for not airing the room, but added that if I had known she was coming, a great many things could have been pre-arranged.

After a brief account of the household's dining schedules, I left her to her own devices and went to my own room to pound out some pages on my manuscript. It seemed the only way to get my mind off Grant's underhandedness.

Darla made herself at home immediately. Within hours,

she had met and ingratiated herself with Lottie and Rudy and, more especially, Colin, who made her acquaintance over an informal lunch in the kitchen. I came upon them laughing comfortably over ham sandwiches while Lottie smiled complacently as she stirred a large pot of soup. I was famished myself but, upon seeing the cozy scene, merely mumbled a sullen greeting, snatched slices of ham and cheese and a can of soda and retreated before anyone could comment. I did have time to notice that Darla had changed into pink slacks and a soft, designer-knit sweater. The beret was gone from her head and her slick, shining hair swung as she chatted candidly. My hasty departure bordered on rudeness, but I didn't care. I'd been unable to type a single, sensible word, so furious was I at Grant and even more ready to find fault with him. So, I changed back into my work clothes and returned to the attic. There were some pieces of furniture and bric-a-brac that I hadn't even known existed, and it was soothing to sort through them and consider whether they should be kept or disposed of.

It was some two hours later that I discovered the trunk. It was made of cedar, with a beautifully carved and inlaid lid. It seemed somehow familiar, but I couldn't quite place where or when I'd seen it. It was gray with dust and practically hidden among a pile of old straight-backed chairs and cardboard boxes filled with books. I managed, with considerable difficulty, to shift the surrounding debris so that I could drag the chest free. It was dark in this particular section of the attic, with the shuttered window nearby blocked by more stacked boxes. The afternoon sun beating down on the roof made the air almost unbearably stuffy and warm, despite a strong wind that moaned over the gables.

I removed my bandanna and wiped my face and neck, then attacked the pile in front of the window, eventually making enough room to lift the pane and throw open the shutters. The breeze was unbelievably refreshing, and I knelt there for some time while the perspiration dried on my face and my lungs took in the fresh air. Finally, I turned back to the trunk. Thankfully, it was unlocked and, except for a minor protest from long disused hinges, it opened readily.

I was slightly disappointed to find nothing of great value. It seemed to be full of clothing, and I pulled them out one at a time and held them up to the light. I knew immediately whose clothes they were and, at the same time, remembered why the box was so familiar. It had stood at the foot of my parents' bed until my mother's death and, in fact, had been one of the only pieces of furniture that my mother had brought with her to Beacon.

Most of the clothing was stained brown and would be useless. Nearer the bottom, however, lay her wedding dress and, although it was extremely wrinkled and limp, it was preserved admirably, wrapped in blue tissue paper and sealed in a cardboard box. Beneath this was a jewelry box containing an assortment of unremarkable baubles that I assumed she had purchased prior to her marriage to Leo. The expensive pieces which he had lavished on her later were locked safely in the family vault at the bank. I made a mental note to inventory those as well.

Next to the jewelry box lay a number of tattered spiral notebooks, and my heart quickened as a flash of memory took me back fifteen years to High Dune where I'd nestled drowsily next to my mother. The sun was warm on my face and I was happy, though weary from running up and down the steep hill. She'd smiled at me lovingly and chucked me under the chin with the end of her gold pen. On her lifted knees was one of these notebooks—the journals that she wrote in so diligently.

I caught my breath. I'd all but forgotten about them. Leo, in his grief, had ordered all her things removed, but somehow these had been overlooked. I pulled them out one by one and dragged a chair over near the window to read.

NINE

The other shape,
If shape it might be call'd that shape had none
Distinguishable in member, joint, or limb;
Or substance might be call'd that shadow seem'd,
For each seem'd either, - black it stood as night,
Fierce as ten furies, terrible as hell,
And shook a dreadful dart; what seem'd his head
The likeness of a kingly crown had on.
Satan was now at hand.

John Milton
Paradise Lost

The diaries began when Anna was seventeen. I was enthralled as I skimmed the pages, sharing her joys and tragedies, insecurities and frustrations. For the first time, I began to glimpse a mother I'd hardly known. Through her writing, she became more than just a pleasant maternal memory; she became a complex, interesting woman, far different from that gentle but vague entity that I'd locked in my heart. Her essence shone through with each entry, and her vivid emotions revealed a depth to her character that I'd never before suspected.

I was surprised to discover how like me she really was. Despite her somewhat stifled upbringing at the hands of strict, devout parents, she suffered many of the same frustrations and self-doubts as I. She spoke of writing—of how she longed to make it a career, but knew it wouldn't provide a suitable future for a young woman. I had to smile at this knowing that, had times been different, she probably would have made a greater success of it than I. In her era, marriage had been all-important. Propriety and respectability were the cornerstones of life. She was trained to believe that virtue and piety were a woman's greatest assets, yet deep inside, rebellion bubbled. She was often lonely, and fought daily to quell desires she had been taught were sinful.

As she grew older, the turmoil of youth mellowed. Her parents died, leaving her little in the way of financial security and, with no training in any solid profession, she turned to child-minding as a means of support. Her interview for the position of nanny to young Colin Dirkston precipitated a rash of excited entries tinged with anticipation and uncertainty. I longed to have been there for her at that time to offer her sympathy, for I understood all too well those feelings of inadequacy.

I flipped forward a few pages and my eyes lit on Colin's name.

"…Colin is a sweet young thing, though I'm afraid he's been terribly spoiled by his mother and neglected by his father. I sometimes wonder if I'll ever be able to manage him. He's so used to having his own way. It will be a challenge to win him over. He's still very young, and perhaps in time, he'll learn to trust me."

That was the end of this particular journal. I closed it gently and sat gazing absently out the dormer window. The view from this height was magnificent, encompassing a panorama of Beacon's tailored grounds, the fiery woods on either side, and the strip of white beach edging the vast expanse of rose-pink water. It was getting late. The sun was descending into its liquid lair, dressed in sleepy red and gold and trailing gauzy skirts across the sky, so that the tumble of clouds on the horizon resembled gilded dumplings. Almost directly below, the swimming pool mirrored the hues of the sky in miniature. A rising breeze rippled the surface into goose-flesh and I shivered in sympathy.

Surprisingly, organized religion hadn't stifled my imagination. Unlike Anna, I'd grown up with a less severe image of eternity and the Almighty. Despite my mother's insistence that I attend Sunday services as well as regular instruction on Christian doctrine, I took it all with a grain of salt and even actively studied other beliefs and theories on the occult and supernatural at University. It was perhaps this very open-mindedness, interwoven with the basic conviction that there is an afterlife, that allowed me the comfort of believing that my mother and father were with me—perhaps on another plane, but still able to watch over me and guide me. Sitting there in the cooling breeze with the world stretched at my feet and heaven so close, I could almost feel Anna's gentle hand on my shoulder. I closed my eyes and let my mind go blank, half-hoping that the presence which had engulfed me on those other occasions would overtake me.

A sudden gust of wind rattled the open shutters and flung itself about the attic, kicking up dust, ruffling papers, and tipping one of the haphazardly stacked journals onto the floor. I opened my eyes, disappointed and somewhat disgusted with myself. My logical side still scoffed at the incident on the beach, yet another part of me wanted to cling to it. I refused to believe I was losing my mind, though the various suggestions that I was suffering from nervous stress seemed all too probable. I didn't want to believe this, either, so instead I ignored it, shutting my mind as I shut the window and turning the slide lock at the top.

I replaced the journal from my lap and bent to retrieve the one that had fallen to the floor. I froze as my eyes scanned the words on the page that lay open.

"…sometimes I can feel him watching me, and it makes me frightened. It's as if he knows that I see through him and is waiting patiently, like a cobra ready to strike. I don't know what to do. If I tell Leo, he'll undoubtedly laugh and tell me that I'm imagining things."

At that moment, a movement near the side of the chest sent me stumbling backward in fright. I half expected to see a snake coiled maliciously there, but instead King Kong sidled up, rubbing his thick coat on the corner of the box and purring like a faulty engine. I let out my breath in relief and reached for the journal again, but footsteps suddenly sounded nearby and I peered into the lowering gloom to see David, picking his way gingerly through the mounded furniture.

He smiled amiably. "You certainly pick some damnable places to get to these days!" he said.

"And you certainly know how to scare the wits out of me!" I rejoined, though I was pleased to see him.

He reached down and picked up the fallen journal. "What's this?" he asked, thumbing through it.

I took it away from him a little too hastily. "It's nothing. Just some old college notes. I don't know why Martha saved them."

I don't know why I felt compelled to lie to him. I only knew that I wanted to keep the journals as my own secret for the time being. They were my mother's, after all, and not meant for public scrutiny.

I put the books back into the trunk and shut the lid.

"Can you believe all the junk up here?" I exclaimed. "It'll take days to go through all of it."

He nodded, his eyes sweeping the room. "I'll bet there's plenty of antiques lurking about. Probably a collector's dream, eh?"

"Well, I don't know about that. So far, I haven't really found anything I would want to 'collect.'"

"Mmm, perhaps not. But you'd be surprised at what some of these items are worth. Take this chest, for instance." He ran his fingers over the engraved lid. "This is all etched by hand. Early Dutch, I'd say. Could bring you a couple of thousand."

I looked at him with sudden respect. "Do you really think so?" Then I cocked a brow suspiciously. "Since when did you become an expert on antiques?"

He smiled wryly. "I'm no expert. But I've been to a few auctions in my day, and they sort of piqued my interest." His eyes lazily roamed over my face, and he lifted a hand to rub a dust smudge from my nose. I expected him to take me in his arms, but instead he merely gave my cheek a gentle caress, then frowned reprovingly. "Do you happen to know what time it is?"

"About dinner time?"

"About half past dinner time! Lucky for you, Darla LaTrobe has diverted everyone's attention, or Lottie would be furious. As it is, she agreed to try to keep things warm while I scoured the house for you."

I grinned mischievously. "What do you suppose would happen if we didn't go down, David? How long do you think it would take for anyone to find us?"

He smiled. "Not long, I'm afraid. Darla said that you were, uh, shall we say, in somewhat of a mess when she arrived and that you'd mentioned the attic."

I scowled. Darla! Just like her to bring up my untidy appearance!

"Come on, then," I said abruptly. "We'd better get going."

We left the attic together with Kong stalking regally ahead, tail high, ears pricked. I fully intended to return as soon as possible to retrieve the journal. That brief excerpt had left me thoroughly unsettled. It was my first indication that there had been a cloud over Beacon long before either of my parents' deaths.

As circumstances dictated, it was some time before I could

return to the journals. Shortly after sitting down to dinner, served by a glowering Lottie, a commotion in the front hall brought me curiously to my feet. I slipped quietly out of the dining room and down the passage.

"It's none of your concern!" It was Colin's voice—loud, angry. Someone—a woman—was weeping. Then, there was another voice.

"It is my concern if it's going on under my roof!"

I shrank back into the shadow of a doorway, recognizing Grant's clear, officious tone.

Colin snorted. "Your roof, is it now? I see you're not wasting any time taking over, eh?"

"Don't change the subject. I know that Alicia's been taking drugs for some time, and I want to know where she's getting them."

"Why don't you ask Suzanna? As I recall, it was her pills that put Alicia in the hospital."

At that, the sobbing rose to a crescendo. "Stop it! Stop it! I can't listen to it anymore!"

To my amazement, it was Alicia herself and, concerned at the desperation in her voice, I left the protective shadows and strode determinedly into the fray.

"What's going on here?" My eyes moved from Colin, rigidly red-faced, fists clenched at his sides, to Grant, tense, wary, mouth tight, eyes uncompromisingly riveted on Colin, and finally to Alicia, slumped in a wheelchair, her pale face blotched, a handkerchief clutched to her nose. She raised stricken eyes to mine and, as if she had uttered a verbal cry for help, I moved defensively to her side and glared furiously at the two men.

"What's come over the two of you? Can't you see what sort of state you've put her in? I assume she's just come from the hospital. Is it your intention to put her right back there?"

Grant shifted his gaze to me, briefly bewildered. Colin unclenched his fists and, as if suddenly remembering his duty, moved solicitously to his wife's side.

"I'm sorry, honey," he said quietly. "Are you all right?"

Alicia nodded, but the slump of her shoulders belied her exhaustion. I was shocked at her appearance. She seemed to have shrunken into herself, as though she'd been ill for a very long time instead of just a few days. There wasn't a trace of the glamorous actress, only a listless invalid, frightened and confused. I laid a hand on her shoulder comfortingly.

"It's good to have you home, Alicia. Are you able to walk? Perhaps you'd prefer to use the downstairs guest room until you can manage the stairs?"

She shook her head. "I want to go to my own room," she said, and turned her eyes up to Colin beseechingly. He understood and nodded.

"I'll carry her up. The doctor wants her to stay in bed for a few more days, and she'll be more comfortable in familiar surroundings."

He lifted her easily in his arms and, with a brief nod in my direction and a spiteful glance at Grant, he mounted the stairs and disappeared. I glared at Grant. He hadn't moved, watching Colin's back as he carried Alicia up the stairs, his face set tightly with irritated frustration.

"I never realized you were so callous," I said, my voice low.

He dropped his distant gaze to my face as though noticing me for the first time. I could see he was still angry.

"There's a lot you don't know about me, Suzanna. But perhaps if you'd quit interfering, we'd straighten some things out around here!"

"Oh, I see. You expect to straighten things out by browbeating Colin and compromising Alicia's health, is that it? Well, I'm sorry, but you'll not do it in my house!" His eyebrows rose in surprise and I added vehemently, "Yes, my house. And don't forget it!"

Our eyes locked in a silent battle of wills. I challenged his cold blue gaze with my own stubborn glare and finally, after a tense moment that I thought would never end, he lifted a corner of his mouth in a conciliatory smile and made a sweeping bow. "Whatever you say, Ma'am!"

I ignored his sarcasm and plunged on while my anger gave me courage. "I'd like you to explain to me why you didn't tell me about the election at the stockholders' meeting."

He shifted uncomfortably, but met my eyes unflinchingly. "I did tell you."

"You only told me there was to be a vote to retain the current officers; you didn't tell me there would be an election for a new chairperson."

He shrugged. "I assumed you'd realize that the position was vacant and would have to be filled. If you'd taken time to read…"

"You intentionally used my preoccupation with Jenny's accident to get my vote."

"Don't be ridiculous!" It was his turn to be angry. "What do you take me for, anyway? Do you think I care so much about the blasted position? Don't you think I have enough to do without taking on that responsibility as well? Or maybe you thought you could do a better job?"

"Maybe I could. At least, it would have kept you from getting your money-grubbing hands on Dad's business!"

It was anger mixed with grief that brought tears to my eyes, though above and beyond both emotions I felt an overwhelming sense of betrayal. Visions of that evening by the lake in his car and the afternoon laughing over champagne all seemed so farcical now, and it hurt. Had I begun to trust him? Had I even begun to care for him a little? The very thought brought blood rushing to my cheeks. Unexpectedly, he put his hands on my shoulders and shook me gently.

"Listen to me, Suzanna." His voice was low and earnest. "You're blaming the wrong man! I'm not after your blasted money or Leo's business. Even if you can't see how I feel about you, you must know that I'd have given my life for Leo. Do you really believe I'd try to swindle him now?"

I couldn't look at him. I felt suddenly giddy and the room was stifling. I wished fervently that I could believe him. Some alien animal attraction urged me to give in and lay my head on his chest and let his arms surround me, but the temptation of it terrified me. I ripped myself away and fled down the hall to the rear parlor, throwing open the patio doors to burst out onto the decking surrounding the swimming pool. I was mortified to find Darla LaTrobe lounging gracefully on one of the deck chairs with David seated next to her, his long legs stretched comfortably in front of him, an amused smile still playing on his lips. They were sharing a bottle of wine.

My hands flew automatically to my face where hot tears still coursed. Without pause, I pushed open the pool gate and, thankful for the blessed darkness that instantly engulfed me, stumbled off down the gravel path that wound through the garden. I didn't stop running until I reached the bluff overlooking the beach, and there I stood, exhausted, alone, and drowning in a flood of shocked enlightenment.

It was true, I couldn't deny it. Part of me was drawn irrepressibly to Grant Fenton, and worse still, I had begun to trust him—even like him—and I knew it was a terrible mistake. I should have faced it long ago, but like all the things that worried me lately, I'd chosen to ignore it. It hadn't happened overnight. It had been there years ago, perhaps even before David. I had been too young, and mistook the attraction for weakness. Even that evening in the gazebo, when Grant had found me with David and had flattened David with one blow, mistaking our innocent wrestling for something more intimate—even then, I had found his overdramatized chivalry flattering. But to squelch my admiration, I'd turned to David even more fervently and had spent the subsequent years avoiding all those impulses that had flooded me whenever Grant was near.

I squeezed my eyes shut, trying to force reality into

oblivion, but it was no use. I began to descend the wooden steps. It was very dark. The moon hadn't yet made its appearance, and there were no lights to show the way. But the whiteness of the sand below and the roar of the rising tide guided me, and I reached the beach without mishap. Here I paused uncertainly, letting the steady, unseasonably warm wind dry my tears and cool my flaming cheeks.

Something about the lake always calmed me. The power that lay dormant, the patient drift and pull that spoke of many decades gone by and of those yet to come, made my small existence, my trivial woes and worries, pale into inconsequence. Within a few moments, I felt my tense muscles begin to loosen and the inner turmoil ebb. I began to think more clearly and allowed my rational side to speak. I had said nothing to Grant. Thankfully, he didn't know how I felt. No one knew. Grant would merely think I was upset about the stockholders' meeting. Darla and David? Well, it hardly mattered what Darla thought, and David would probably just say I was "overstressed." None of them need ever find out what I now knew—that I felt more than a sisterly affection for Grant. This was probably what Grant had been aiming for all along. I scoffed inwardly at his feigned sincerity. Oh, but he was a good actor! No wonder he was so successful in the courtroom. He'd probably been taking lessons from Alicia!

Alicia. I recalled Grant's ruthless interrogation, and his accusations that she'd been taking drugs for some time. Well, it didn't surprise me. Everyone knew that she drank too much, and alcohol was its own form of drug. I pitied her. Would she ever recover from her ordeal? How long had Colin known about her problem?

I began to stroll along the beach. The moon was just beginning to cap the dunes. It was waxing one-quarter, and just the tip of it could be seen above the spectral sands. The rhythmic rumble of the surf soothed me, and I removed my shoes automatically to feel the chilly wetness beneath my feet. The sand squeaked like buffed glass at each step.

"Suzanna!"

I jumped uncontrollably. Giles materialized suddenly in front of me. He had been running, for he was still dressed in a loose tracksuit, his hair was tousled and his face was red from the exertion. He was frowning and seemed agitated.

"Thank God! I was just coming over to Beacon to speak to you."

"What is it?" I asked, concerned, "Is something wrong?"

"I must speak to you," he said, breathing heavily. "I think you may be in danger."

"What?" A shiver ran up my spine. He seemed genuinely upset. "What sort of danger? What do you mean?"

He all but wrung his hands in consternation. "I probably shouldn't be telling you this. I may be wrong and I don't want to alarm you unnecessarily but, well, I overheard something that frightened me."

I waited expectantly and he opened his mouth to continue, but his eyes strayed over my shoulder and he shook his head impatiently.

"What's this? A secret liaison? How are you, Giles?"

I swung around. Grant was striding toward us, his suit pants rolled up to his knees, his shoes and socks held in one hand, and his tie loose and flapping in the breeze. I would have laughed if I had been less annoyed.

"What do you want?" I demanded rudely.

"I was worried about you, Suzie. You shouldn't go running off in the dark. It's dangerous."

"Spare me your concern!" I retorted.

Giles shifted uncomfortably and greeted Grant with a stiff nod.

"It's a bit late for jogging, don't you think?" Grant asked.

Giles smiled nervously. "Perhaps. I try to fit it in when I can."

"And I suppose you'll be up at the crack of dawn for your swim, eh? You fitness buffs are so dedicated." Grant, too, seemed a bit nervous, and I eyed him curiously. He was gazing up and down the beach, almost as though expecting someone.

"The water is so refreshing first thing in the morning," Giles said, "though I'll have to give it up soon; it's getting a bit too chilly."

Grant nodded absently. "Well, old man, I really must get Suzanna home. I don't think she's even had her dinner yet—have you, darling?"

I tossed his hand off my elbow irritably and turned back to Giles. His eyes communicated a plea. I bit my lip.

"I'd better go," I said. What Giles had to tell me was for my ears only, and I cursed Grant for his inopportune arrival. "How would you feel about some company tomorrow morning?" I suggested. "I run better on an empty stomach and, if you're willing, we could jog a ways together."

He smiled tightly. "Yes. That would be perfect. What time?"

"Around seven?"

He nodded. "See you then."

He saluted Grant, and I turned back the way I'd come. Grant watched him disappear but I didn't pause, striding off in the direction of Beacon, so Grant had to run to catch up. He caught my arm and spun me around.

"What's the idea of coming down here in the dark? Don't you know there's a murderer loose?"

I jerked myself free of his grip. "Leave me alone!" I cried, my rage by now well beyond civility. "Why did you come back, anyway? Things were great around here until you showed up! How will the firm survive without you?"

He fell into step beside me. "Did you ever think that maybe I was concerned for your safety?"

I laughed harshly. "Don't try to con me, Grant! Do you really think I'm so gullible? My guess is that you're more concerned with Alicia, although you could have fooled me, the way you were tormenting her up there. Don't tell me you're tired of her already? Oh, but that's right! I almost forgot, it's the grand Miz Darla LaTrobe now, isn't it? I have a hard time keeping up. Just don't pretend you're worried about me. The only person you're really interested in is yourself!"

"What the hell are you talking about?"

I stopped then and faced him, my jaw set stubbornly, my eyes flashing. "I won't play your game, Grant." I spoke with as much control as I could muster. "I know what you're trying to do, and it won't work. All I'm asking is that you stay away from me. If you can manage that for twelve months, we'll get along just fine."

I didn't give him time to respond, but turned abruptly and ran lightly over the beach and up the steps.

When I reached the top, I stopped in surprise. David was waiting there, and for once, his emotions were openly displayed. Pure jealousy radiated from him as he stood there, legs splayed, hands clenched at either side. He could have been some primitive god, ready at any moment to call down thunder and lightning from the inky sky. His thick blond hair lifted in the changing wind, and his eyes shifted from the beach below to me. The expression in them was one I'd never seen before. Without a word, he strode over, pulled me into his arms and kissed me with a ferocity that set my head spinning. His arms crushed me to him. His mouth bruised mine.

I was stunned, and hardly had time to react before he jerked his head up abruptly and stepped back. He was trembling, aghast at what he'd done. If I'd had time to think, I might have been angry, but his horrified look instantly aroused my sympathy and, after recovering myself, I took a step toward him to offer what comfort I could.

"No!" he said hoarsely, "Leave me be! I don't know

what came over me. I guess it was the state you were in when you came running out onto the patio. And then, seeing you down there with him…" He lifted his eyes and his expression was pleading, hurt. "Suzanna, you aren't…you aren't becoming involved with him, are you?"

I studied him sadly. It was never my intention to hurt him, though selfishly, I'd hardly thought of it at all. Now, seeing him like this, afraid and unsure, I wanted to comfort him, to convince him that he was all I'd ever wanted. At the same time, I knew that it would be a lie. So, ignoring his protests, I went to him, wrapping my arms around his lean waist and laying my cheek against his chest until I felt his tension subside. His arms, after a moment, encircled me, tenderly this time, and I answered his question calmly, knowing he couldn't see the lie in my eyes.

"No, David, I'm not involved with him. In fact, at this moment, I could almost say I despise him."

There was movement behind us. Grant mounted the last step and regarded us coolly from behind veiled lids. I lifted my head and stepped aside, feeling ridiculously guilty.

"Oh, please!" Grant spoke sarcastically. "Don't stop on my account. You do make such a lovely couple! Just try to be a little discreet, will you? I don't want the two of you splashed on the front of Time magazine; it wouldn't be good for business."

David stiffened and his eyes glittered dangerously. "Listen, Fenton," he said, his voice barely controlled, "a piece of paper doesn't give you the right to torment Suzanna. If it's the business you're worried about, then why don't you go back to Chicago and tend to it? Suzanna has had enough worries, without you adding to them."

Grant gazed at David humorlessly, then glanced at me. I was frightened. I thoroughly expected a replay of that long ago day in the gazebo, but this time, I knew that it wouldn't be one-sided. They stood there poised, the tension between them tangible, as though a challenge had been made and accepted, and it was merely the time and place that was in question.

Finally, Grant spoke and his voice was determinedly cool. "If I've upset you, Suzie, I'm sorry." He lifted unreadable eyes to David and added, "But I'd suggest that you pick and choose your company very carefully. I don't think I need to remind you that there are plenty of vultures around just waiting for the chance to pick at Dirkston bones."

He nodded stiffly and, with unruffled composure, strode off. We heard the squeak of the gate and then silence. Instantly, I flung myself back into David's arms and he held me comfortably, his cheek resting warmly on my head. I felt the stiffness gradually drain from my limbs and, when we finally pulled apart, we didn't need to speak, for our eyes met in quiet understanding: His, elated, victorious, protective; mine, gentle, accepting and determined. Grant meant nothing to me. David was all I needed. That was the way it should be. The way I wanted it.

I fell into bed that night exhausted, and slept immediately. When I awoke, gray dawn was just filtering through the gauzy curtains. So deeply had I slept that for a moment, I was disoriented, thinking I was still back in that quiet, uncomplicated cabin deep in the woods. I stretched lazily, and the events of the previous night came back in snatches. But with the bolster of solid rest, they seemed much less dramatic. I smiled as I thought of David, aware that he had finally declared his love for me as surely as if he'd spoken it. I couldn't expect more from him and I was satisfied, for it wasn't in his nature to be demonstrative. This feeling of belonging seemed to mute the intensity of my other troubles. It was as though I were finally able to lower a few of my mounting defenses and let him shoulder some of the burden. I was no longer one against the world, and it was an enormous relief.

Suddenly, I sat up and looked at the clock. Giles! He'd be waiting for me!

I leapt out of bed and donned a light tracksuit and joggers. Running a brush through my hair, I tied it back in a ponytail, then hurried downstairs and into the crisp morning air.

Despite the previous day's warmth, frost had fallen in the early hours, the first one of the season, and it powdered the manicured lawn and wove patterns on the foliage, sucking out what little life remained. I traversed the short space between pool and garden, my shoes crunching over the delicate white lace, leaving green tracks. I rubbed my hands together to warm them and blew white clouds with each breath. The air tingled with clarity. It was exquisite!

No one else was about. Even the industrious black squirrels seemed loath to leave their snug hideaways. A huge raven perched atop a distant pine rasping out his views adamantly. Somewhere deeper in the woods, an answering cry resounded, which sent the first caller into a raucous barrage of abuse marked by impressive wing flapping and neck stretching. A fat gray rabbit squatted near the modest vegetable garden some distance beyond the hedges. He was eyeing a clump of mottled pumpkin runners and bean bushes that were sagging under the weight of the frost. His nose twitched rapidly. His soft coat was plumped against the cold, and his ears twisted and turned like antennae. I paused to watch him, enthralled. He crouched and cocked his head and suddenly, as though he'd sensed disaster, a crack reverberated through the stillness and he leapt into the air, ran a few short paces and fell, twitching, to the ground.

I was horrified. Instinctively, I dropped to a crouch and peered about, wide-eyed. There was a movement near the woods to the left and I watched, my heart pounding, as a figure unhurriedly stepped around the grave markers and sauntered toward the fallen animal. I could tell by his halting gait and faded dungarees that it was Rudy. He held a rifle loosely over one arm, and didn't look right or left but plodded on with bovine resolve, skirting the sweep of lawn that cupped the vegetable patch and bordered the shrub-lined paths where I crouched. I rose slowly, still aghast at what I'd witnessed, and followed a branching track that would take me out onto the open grass.

Rudy didn't look up from where he squatted over the carcass until I was standing over him. He seemed unsurprised to see me, and merely tilted his head to look up. I realized with revulsion that he was gutting the rabbit where it lay. The red and purple-blue entrails steamed in the frosty air.

"What in God's name are you doing, Rudy?" I gasped.

"Gotta gut 'em right away if you're gonna eat 'em," he responded briefly.

His nonchalance galled me, and disgust turned to indignation.

"Do you think it's a good idea to be shooting off guns so close to the house? Someone could get hurt!"

He squinted from under the limp brim of his weathered hat, considering, then he resumed his work undeterred.

"I s'pose you'd be a might gun-shy after what happened down by the river," he said, matter-of-factly. "Didn't know you was around or I'd-a held off." He flipped the carcass over, lay his knife to one side and reached into the bloody cavity to scoop out the remaining entrails. "This fella's been helpin' himself to the crop. I've been tryin' t' nail him for weeks."

I frowned. Rudy was so used to having free rein that he was oblivious to any suggestion of change. I watched with distaste as he shoveled up the leavings with a small trowel slung from a loop in his overalls. He carried them to the edge of the garden, where he dug a hole and buried them. He half smiled at my grimace.

"'S mighty good fer th' garden, Miss Suzanna. The good Lord don't look kindly on wastin' any part of His critters."

I wondered at the sick logic that made it all right to slaughter an innocent creature, as long as it was put to good use. It gave me a slightly uncomfortable feeling that perhaps Rudy Coleman was much more complex than I'd suspected.

"How long have you had that gun?" I asked.

He straightened, slipping the trowel back into its place and the knife into its sheath. His gaze was openly insolent.

"Can't say," he said. "But I've had it since long before you was born."

"Well, I don't want it to be used on my property anymore," I said in my most officious tone. "Not only is it dangerous, but I'd guess that it's highly illegal as well."

He knotted a bit of rope around the rabbit's hind feet and slung it over his shoulder, then picked up the offending weapon and cradled it protectively. When he looked at me again, he was sullen and his watery blue eyes were stubborn.

"Hate t' have t' set traps, miss," he said. "Once seen a fox chew his own leg off t' get out o' one. But," he added, pleased by my look of horror, "you're th' boss!"

He turned and limped briskly away, leaving me fuming. He may have won this time, but it was imperative that he learn that I was the boss now that Leo was gone. Still, I had to tread carefully. Rudy had been with us for many years and despite his simple, unassuming demeanor, his pride was a fragile thing and must be handled with care. My father had allowed him total freedom, and it would take a large amount of diplomacy on my part to change that.

I was suddenly aware that the sun's warm rays were already shooting over the treetops, and most of the frost had disappeared. I glanced at my wristwatch and cursed. Giles would think I wasn't coming! Half walking, half running, I made my way over the remaining grounds to the rear fence and followed it along to the gate. It was partially open, and I wondered if we'd latched it properly the previous night or if Rudy had been down this way and left it ajar. I didn't give it another thought as I flew nimbly down the steps.

The wind was even cooler on the beach, whistling across the water in long, mournful sighs, kicking up sand, which stung my eyes and pricked my skin. There was no sign of Giles, and I struck off toward Spindrift, certain that he'd have gone there to wait for me. I passed the boat-house and noted that the speedboat was tied casually to the outer pier. I must scold Colin for not securing it inside. He was hopeless when it came to putting things back where they belonged.

Some twenty minutes later, I was clambering up the well-worn path that led to Spindrift. The sun, after its initial attempt to break through, bowed to defeat as a thick threatening blanket of cloud rolled slowly in.

David met me at the door, obviously pleased to see me but unhelpful as to his father's whereabouts.

"He usually goes for a swim early on, but it was pretty cold for that this morning. Have you checked the beach? Of course, you have. Well, sorry, but I don't think I can help you. Perhaps he went for a walk on the dunes. You wouldn't have seen him there. Was it something important? Why don't you sit down and have a cup of coffee? He's bound to be back soon."

I shook my head. "You may be right, but all the same, I'd like to go back and wait for him on the beach. He seemed pretty anxious to talk to me."

David looked disappointed. He appeared to have recently showered, and wore only a navy velour robe emblazoned with red initials on the lapel. Despite myself, I hesitated. Even with his creamy blond hair wet and uncombed and his face unshaven, he was undoubtedly good looking. It was one of the few times I'd seen him less than perfectly groomed, and I liked it. I offered to meet him for lunch at the marina and left quickly, before he could coax me to stay.

I'd been gone for less than ten minutes by the time I retraced my steps to the water's edge, but already the sky had blackened further and streaks of rain were rapidly approaching from the northwest. I decided to jog, enjoying the brisk exercise and the cooling wind on my face. I hadn't gone far before I slowed to a walk. Up ahead, a large chunk of driftwood rocked back and forth with the lapping tide and I eyed it curiously. There was something about it that seemed odd and I approached with caution, remembering the occasional dead salmon that washed ashore and their gruesome appearance after being feasted upon by scavenging crabs and birds. Already, a swarm of seagulls were circling, screeching ghoulishly against the mournful sough of the wind.

I stopped abruptly and my throat constricted. What lay on the beach wasn't driftwood or a large fish. I could see from where I stood that it was a human body, and there was no doubt in my mind that whomever it was most certainly was dead.

TEN

Render an honest and a perfect man
Commands all light, all influence, all fate.
Nothing to him falls early, or too late.
Our acts our angels are, or good or ill,
Our fatal shadows that walk by us still.

    John Fletcher
    Upon an "Honest Man's Fortune."

It was probably some instinctive sense of self-preservation that kept me from inspecting the body too closely, though now I regret not having done so. Despite assurances that Giles would most certainly have been beyond help, I can't help think that he might still be alive today if I'd only thought to check for a pulse or attempt to resuscitate him. Like a coward, though, I turned and ran blindly back to Spindrift for help. David paused only long enough to ring the emergency rescue number before returning with me to the scene. He did all the things I should have done earlier—listen for a heartbeat, and commence cardio-pulmonary resuscitation until the Coast Guard arrived to take over.

I stood well back, my hands clasped so tightly that the knuckles stood out. I watched the men squat around the prone figure, working methodically, lifting the eyelids and feeling the bloodless wrists. Eventually, one of them stood up and turned to David, his face grave. I knew before he spoke that there was no hope.

The other men lifted Giles onto a stretcher and zipped him into thick plastic. It had begun to drizzle, lightly at first, and then with intensity, turning the sand to riveted pea soup, the plop of the drops like bursting bubbles in a boiling pot. I remained frozen to the spot until I saw Grant approaching; then, I automatically crept closer to David for support, even though he was much too caught up in his own grief to notice. Grant spoke in low tones to the rescue team and inspected the body before they closed the bag completely, nodding grimly in verification. He helped put the gruesome bundle into the boat, spoke again briefly to the man in charge, and finally pushed them off. Only then, after the Coast Guard was gone, did he turn and peer through the blinding rain toward us, still rooted like statues in the gloom.

He spoke to David sympathetically, shouting to be heard over the thunder of the surf and spatter of rain. "Come on, Dave, you'd better get in out of this weather." I noticed for the first time that David was still dressed only in his robe. His feet were bare.

Dazedly, we followed Grant back to Spindrift. No one spoke, but as we went, I glanced up at David and realized that he was sobbing. I took his hand. It was cold and unresponsive, but it seemed to comfort him slightly. My own tears followed the path of the raindrops down my face.

Grant organized everything with the help of Darla, whom he rang the minute we reached Spindrift. After being coaxed into dry clothes, David retired to his room, preferring privacy to deal with his grief. When Darla arrived, she took charge immediately, ringing Lottie and organizing for a pot of chicken soup to be sent over, and agreeing to stay at Spindrift to look after David. I was still too bewildered to care. I was wrapped in something dry and driven back to Beacon, where Grant ushered me up to my room, ran a hot bath and commanded me to soak for at least a half-hour because my lips were blue.

The horror of what had happened took some time to sink in. I bombarded myself with recriminations. If only I hadn't paused to speak to Rudy! If only I had been on time! If only…! Even my normally reliable logic couldn't lessen the guilt, and I cried until there were no tears left and my face was blotched and swollen.

When at last I'd regained enough control to join the others downstairs, I was acutely conscious of all eyes on me. I was certain that everyone must blame me as I blamed myself.

Martha appeared briefly, her face drawn and white, and I remembered how close she had been to Giles. She made an apology for not feeling up to staying, and disappeared to her room. Colin and Grant sat at the long dining table along with Alicia, who still looked wan and fragile, while Lottie served up steaming bowls of soup. Grant rose dutifully and pulled out a chair for me.

"You'd better have some of this," he said. "It'll make you feel better."

I looked up at him, but he avoided my eyes and wandered to the far end of the room, a cigarette clamped between his lips, his fists thrust deep into his pockets. I picked up my spoon, gazed at the broth, then put it down again. Alicia had begun to sob softly and Colin turned to her solicitously, placing an arm about her shoulders.

Grant cleared his throat and spoke quietly. "Suzie, I'm afraid the police will want to speak to you. I understand that you were supposed to be meeting Giles?"

I looked at him dumbly. "The police?"

He nodded. "I'm sure it's all routine, but you're the one who found him, and there's always the possibility of foul play."

"Foul play?" I knew I sounded like a parrot, but my brain seemed to be working in slow motion.

Grant crushed out his cigarette. "There will have to be an autopsy, of course, but most likely drowning will be found to be the cause of death. Still, there was the gash on his head…"

This time I stiffened with surprise. "What gash?"

He frowned. "Surely you saw it? It was pretty severe. But we don't know if it happened before or after death."

Alicia began to sob more loudly. My eyes clouded as thoughts tumbled randomly. Of course, Giles's death was no accident! He'd planned to tell me something; something that frightened him; something he'd overheard—perhaps something that might identify Leo's murderer. Whoever it was must have known Giles was meeting with me and… But who could have known? There was only one person who might possibly have overheard our conversation. My throat constricted, and I pushed back my chair so abruptly that I nearly upset it. My head was spinning. I had to get away before anyone read the primitive fear in my eyes.

Grant was saying something, but I didn't listen. I bolted from the room, ran down the hall and back up the stairs to my room. I slammed the door shut and turned the lock. My heart was thumping wildly, stark reality enveloping me. Whoever had murdered my father had murdered Giles as well and I knew, now, that it couldn't possibly be some faceless stranger—it had to be someone close, someone who knew the workings of Beacon, someone who had access to our intimate lives. I remembered Grant's furtive look when he'd approached us on the beach the night before, as if looking for someone else. Had he overheard us? I thought of Rudy Coleman casually gutting the dead rabbit, and his macabre sense of righteousness. I thought of David, moved to passionate outbursts of jealousy and barely controlled rage over Grant's callous accusations. Anyone could have followed me to the beach and hidden among the dunes. Voices carried too well in the open air.

I hugged my arms around me and sat on the edge of the bed, racking my brain for some clue as to what Giles might have wanted to tell me. Failing with this, I tried to concentrate on what might have happened that fateful morning.

I'd agreed to meet him at seven. By the time I arrived on the beach, it was close to seven twenty-five. When I found him, he was wearing a wetsuit, so he'd obviously decided to get his swim in before I came. Since there was no evidence that he'd brought a change of clothing with him, it was safe to assume he'd intended to have time to return home to change before our scheduled meeting. That meant that he'd died sometime before seven. Someone who knew his habits must have been waiting for him, brutally struck him over the head—just as they'd struck my father with the iron poker—and left him dead, on the beach.

But, no. The beach was empty when I'd arrived. His body must have washed up on shore sometime during my first visit to Spindrift. Perhaps he'd struck his head on something while swimming? It seemed impossible. There were no rocks near that section of the beach, and the idea of another swimmer overpowering him mid-water and battering him didn't seem plausible. Then, I remembered the speedboat. It was tied negligently to the pier, as if abandoned hurriedly. I rubbed a hand over my face. It all fit. Someone had used the speedboat to run him down. It must have been an act of desperation, for anyone could have witnessed such an attack. Whoever it was must have counted on the early hour and the cold to deter unwelcome spectators.

There was no point now in pretending that there was no danger. Whoever was guilty of these murders was obviously close enough to Giles to know his schedule, to have access to the keys for the boathouse, the powerboat and to Beacon itself. Leo had been struck with the poker taken from beside the fireplace in the parlor. This meant that the attacker had come from inside the house. This same person had killed Giles to silence him. Could I be sure that they knew he'd been silenced before sharing his secret with me? If not, I'd most certainly be next in line!

I shuddered. Those shots at the river must have been meant for me. But what possible reason would someone have for murdering me? Either they hoped to gain something from my death, or I was dealing with a maniac who killed for pleasure and needed no real motives. This was the most frightening scenario of all—that someone close to me, someone who I'd known most of my life, someone I trusted, could kill simply for the sake of killing. I longed to go to David. He was the only one who could make me feel safe—the only person I felt I could share my fears with. But now wasn't the time, not when his own tragedy was so new.

I thought of Darla LaTrobe. I didn't like the idea of her hovering over David when he was so hurt and vulnerable. I had to trust that he cared for me enough not to be so easily swayed. I seriously doubted that Darla's shabby overtures would have any effect on him, but I still wished she'd go back to wherever she'd come from.

I needed a friend, and my thoughts automatically turned to Jenny. It had been a couple of days since I'd visited the hospital. There, at least, I could feel safe. Impulsively, I donned my raincoat and crept down the back stairs. I didn't want to meet anyone and have to explain where I was going. There was no one in the house I dared to trust.

It was still raining, though not as fiercely. The sky was leaden. The rain had abated to a soft drizzle, seemingly content to linger for some time. I gained the sanctuary of my car and turned on the engine, waiting only momentarily for the wipers to clear the windshield and the blower to disperse the fog. Backing the car around, I glanced nervously toward the windows across the front of the house. Was that Grant peering out at me? I didn't wait to find out but drove off, relieved once I had reached the open road.

I took my time driving into town. The rolling acres of mottled trees were muted by the mist. Leaves stripped from their branches littered the road, the combination of the frost and rain too much for their frail life-holds. Nature's quiet, unhurried dealing of death seemed to amplify the violence which had taken my father, and now Giles. It frightened me most of all to think how easily a life could be ripped from existence at the whim of a maniac.

Jenny was propped up in bed and seemed somewhat recovered, though she was still hooked up to an intravenous drip and a heart monitor. She looked gaunt and tired, but was pleased to see me, and smiled weakly.

"Are you up to a visitor?" I asked tentatively.

She nodded. "They've just given me another needle full of something, but I refuse to give in. It seems all they want me to do around here is sleep!"

I smiled and sat down on a chair near the bed. She turned her head on the pillow and her brow knitted as she studied my face.

"Something's happened," she said.

I looked down at my hands. It was useless trying to hide anything. I nodded dully, knowing that I shouldn't burden her with bad news. She waited patiently, her eyelids heavy but her gaze fixed, curious.

"It's Giles Lancaster, Jenny. He's...dead."

She drew a sharp breath and her hand tightened on the edge of the blanket.

"My God!" she breathed. "How? When?"

"This morning. I went down to the beach to meet him. We were supposed to go jogging together. I found him there. He must have...have drowned."

Stupidly, I began to sob, resting my head on my arms on the edge of the bed. Jenny lifted a hand and placed it on my hair comfortingly.

"Mad!" she murmured. "Must be mad!"

"What?" I sniffed. But her eyes were closed, the drug undoubtedly stronger than her will to fight it. I groped in my purse for a tissue and wiped my nose and face, then placed her limp hand across her chest and stood up to go. But, as if waging one final struggle to avoid sleep, she rolled her head slightly and her lips moved. Her eyelids fluttered open and she looked up blearily, her hand groped the air, beckoning me.

"What is it, Jenny?" I asked, concerned.

"Grant…" she said, "Must find Grant…" Her voice was thick and her lids wouldn't stay open. "Suzanna, he knows…"

There was no more. Her eyes shut and her lips, though still parted, were mute, her breathing deep and regular. I adjusted the blankets and left, puzzling over her words and chilled by their possible meaning.

There was no point in waiting for the police to come to me. I drove to the station and asked to speak to Sergeant Davison. He was naturally anxious to see me and led me into his private office, diplomatically not mentioning the telltale signs of tears puffing my eyes. This evidently wasn't a part of the job he enjoyed.

He pulled out a chair for me and retreated to the safety of his own on the opposite side of the desk. He produced a form of some kind from a drawer and scribbled something at the top, then, with finger poised over the button on a cassette recorder, asked if I'd mind if he taped the interview. I shook my head resignedly.

Most of his questions were predictable. How long had I known Dr. Lancaster? Were we on friendly terms? When had I last seen him alive? How often did he visit Beacon? Was I aware of his habit of having an early morning swim? Wasn't it unusual to continue these swims when it was so cold? I answered absently, battling with myself over my own suspicions. After some minutes he paused, switched off the machine and leaned back in his chair.

He gazed at me speculatively. "Would you like a cup of coffee, Miss Dirkston?"

I shook my head, but relaxed a bit as he set aside formality. "If I'm not mistaken," he said, "you have your own theories about this accident. If you don't mind, I'd like to hear them."

"Why?" I asked suspiciously, "The last time I gave you my opinions, you weren't exactly encouraging."

He made a wry grimace and fiddled with the papers in front of him. "Suzanna—may I call you Suzanna?— Suzanna, a lot has happened since we spoke last. I believe that you have a right to know some of what's going on, especially after the unfortunate episode at the river. By the way, how is Miss Hampton?"

"As well as can be expected, I suppose."

He nodded. "It was unfortunate that I couldn't be more candid with you at the hospital. I'm sorry if I've seemed, uh, less than helpful, but my hands have been tied."

I eyed him mutely, wondering what devious trickery he was up to this time. Something in his world-weary brown eyes, however, told me that he was making an effort at sincerity.

"Before I tell you anything," he said, "I must have your word that you won't share this with anyone."

I nodded my promise.

"Well, then…there's an official federal investigation being conducted into your father's death. I wasn't at liberty to share this information with you before and, if they find out I'm telling you now, they could very well have my badge. Your father was a powerful man and, as you probably know, even the slightest hint that his death may have been anything but accidental could start a landslide of unwanted press coverage that would slow things down considerably. However, I personally believe you have the right to know, and I'm counting on you to understand the need for discretion."

Slowly, my mind processed this information and I

thought back to my conversation with Grant in the car by the lake. I looked up hopefully. "Is Grant, uh, Mr. Fenton, helping with this investigation?"

Davison frowned. "I really can't give you all the details, only what you've probably already guessed. We're obviously dealing with a very intelligent person, or persons, who could very well have access to Beacon. And since we've been able to rule you out as suspect, it's been suggested that I speak to you and try to convince you to remove yourself from the area until the investigation is completed."

I gazed at him dumbly. "You want me to go away?"

He nodded.

"Why?"

He cleared his throat. "I think it must be apparent even to you that there is an element of risk involved if you choose to remain here."

I narrowed my eyes. "How do you know? And why just me? Sergeant Davison, do you have any idea who killed my father? Because, if you do…!"

He held up a hand. "No, no—and please, call me Bill. I really don't. I'm not even supposed to be working on the case, though I can tell you I'm not at all happy about it. The FBI contacts me through official channels and tells me very little, only what they want me to know. But since they bothered to suggest to me that you should leave the area for your own safety, I can only assume that they have good reason."

I sighed. "Well, it seems we're both in the dark, then. I don't suppose there's any reason for me to ask for the name of someone I can contact at the FBI?"

He smiled. "Sure, I could give you a name or two, but I think you know that you'd only get the run-around."

I nodded wryly, knowing very well about bureaucratic double-talk.

"I won't go," I said.

He didn't seem surprised. His face was a picture of

weary resignation. "I won't waste my time trying to coax you. It's obvious your mind is made up. At least, I can say I warned you and urged you to be extra-careful. I'm sure that what happened to Miss Hampton has made it clear to you that we aren't dealing with a rational human being."

"Those shots were meant for me, weren't they?"

He shrugged. "I don't know. We've recovered two of the bullets, but Forensics hasn't been able to come up with any leads. If you want my personal opinion, though, I'd have to say yes. You must keep in mind, however, that there's no proof that anyone was actually firing at you. It's still possible that someone was out hunting and wasn't even aware that you and Miss Hampton were in the area." He smiled at my look of disbelief. "Yes, I know it sounds farfetched, but accidental shootings take place more often than you realize. People go out with rifles and shotguns and don't know how or where to use them properly. We have to look at all the angles."

"What about Giles?" I asked. "That was no accident!"

His face suddenly closed and he studied me seriously. "What makes you say that?"

"Oh, come now!" I said impatiently. "My father was murdered. Giles tells me he's got something urgent to tell me—something that makes him believe I'm in danger—I go to meet him and find him dead! Do you really think I'm stupid enough to believe that was an accident?"

Bill leaned forward and put his hands flat on the desk. "I'm afraid you've lost me, Suzanna. Perhaps you can start at the beginning and tell me exactly what happened."

I shrugged and waited for him to switch the tape recorder back on, then I launched into a summary of my experiences of the past few days. I felt more comfortable with him now. At least, he was no longer treating me like a mindless bimbo, and this small spark of human kindness gave me the incentive to confide in him.

By the time I left the police station, I was feeling considerably less dejected. Giles's death still hung heavy in my heart, but at least now I knew that I wasn't overdramatizing things. My suspicions about Leo had proved correct and, though Bill reminded me emphatically that an autopsy hadn't yet been completed, my deductions about Giles's "accident" were shared by more than a few. At least, this was something the local police could get involved in. They'd send experts to inspect the speedboat and keep me notified as to the coroner's findings.

He shook my hand warmly when I stood to go.

"Tell me," I asked, "how did you rule me out as a suspect? And why is it that no one from the FBI has approached me? I would think they'd be extremely anxious to pick my brain for information."

"Yes," he said. "I've wondered that myself. All I can guess is that for some reason they don't need to, that they're on to something that neither you nor I know anything about. Still, I'd appreciate it if you'd come to me if there's anything else you can remember, or any other suspicions you might have. They may not want me on this case, but I'll be damned if I'm just going to sit on my hands and do nothing." He smiled. "And as for ruling you out…well, we have our ways. I can't give all our tricks away."

"All of them?" I said wryly. "I'd settle for one or two!" But I didn't pursue it, satisfied that at least there was something being done, and someone who cared what I thought.

After assuring him that I'd keep in touch and call him at the least sign of danger, I left, more determined than ever to get to the bottom of this gruesome puzzle. Time was of the essence now, for whether I wanted to admit it or not, my life might depend on finding the answers.

Grant's involvement in the affair was becoming more and more confusing. It seemed that he had at least been telling the truth about the FBI's involvement. This, however, didn't necessarily rule him out as a suspect. The best place for a murderer to be in this situation was at the heart of the investigation, where he could always stay one step ahead by removing clues or silencing anyone who might appear to be a threat, as with poor Giles.

Mentally, I skimmed over my private list of suspects and realized that it was by no means growing smaller. The only substantial clue I had uncovered was the poker, and that was gone now. I was certain that Grant would have handed it over to the authorities. He would have no alternative. But he was smart enough to know that his fingerprints on it would prove nothing, since he and I had handled it carelessly the day he'd wrested it from my grasp. I was surprised, however, that the police hadn't dusted for fingerprints in and around the fireplace where the poker had been kept unless, like me, they knew that the murderer had to be someone who lived in or frequented the house.

I drove toward the marina and noted that it was open for business. With David away and Colin preoccupied with Alicia, Mike would undoubtedly be taking care of things. On impulse, I turned into the drive.

It was still drizzling and the place looked deserted. The door to the office was unlocked, but no one appeared when I entered and I peered over the counter, trying to see into the small room behind. The appointment book was open on the counter and I perused it, noting only one fishing reservation scheduled for ten a.m. The clock on the wall said one. Unless Mike had captained the cruiser himself, he should be somewhere around.

I followed the path around the side of the building and onto the boardwalk, against which a number of vessels bobbed rhythmically in the dreary rain. At the far corner, tied well away from the boats, was the Dirkston sea-plane and it was there that I found him, squatting at the rear of one pontoon, apparently engrossed in manipulating some attachment there. I hailed him from the pier and he looked up, his face shadowed within the hood of a bright yellow slicker. Without hesitation, he rose and made his way agilely over the rocking pontoon, ducking beneath the wing and stepping neatly up beside me. I pulled my own hood closer about my face.

"I was in town, so I thought I'd stop and see if I could help out here, but it looks as though it'll be a slow day."

He regarded me curiously, then nodded. "It's been pretty quiet lately. Gettin' close to the end of the season."

"You left the office open. Aren't you worried that someone might rob the till?"

He flashed a broad smile. "There's nothin' to steal in there. We did the banking yesterday."

I glanced over his shoulder. "Is something wrong with the plane?"

"No. Just checking things out. It pays to go over it regularly." He brushed some water from his face. "No point in standing out here. Come inside and have a cup of coffee."

I followed him back to the office, and he disappeared into the back while I removed my dripping raincoat and hung it on a coat rack near the door. The waiting room was far from luxurious. I sat down on one of the four deck chairs arranged around the cheap blond laminate coffee table. When Mike returned, he was carrying two steaming mugs and had discarded his own sodden rain gear. He didn't sit down, but propped an elbow on the counter and regarded me over his coffee, making me feel suddenly uncomfortable.

"I suppose you've heard the news," I said.

"About Dr. Lancaster? Sure."

"It was quite a shock to us all."

He nodded. "Guess all that health and fitness stuff makes no difference, eh? When it's your time to go, well…" He smiled, not needing to complete the thought.

I shifted, biting back a tart remark. I didn't like his nonchalant attitude. His insensitivity made me unsettled. He seemed to be waiting for me to say something. I changed the subject. "Where are you staying these days, Mike? Still in town?"

He nodded.

"And I suppose you've got enough work around here to keep you busy?"

"For now. But they'll be shutting the place down for the winter soon."

"You'll still be flying for Dirkston, though."

His brows drew together and he took a noisy slurp of coffee before responding.

"You'd know more about that than me. Mr. Fenton seems to want to do most of his business over the phone lines. He's made it pretty clear that I should start looking for work elsewhere."

"What?" I asked, surprised. "Did Grant say that?"

He shrugged. "Not in so many words, but he and I never hit it off too well, and I'm not one to hang around where I'm not wanted."

I mulled this over. It was true that the sea-plane was rarely used once the snows set in, but there was the helicopter which was kept on its private pad at the Dirkston offices or, when Leo needed it here, at the small airport in Ludington. A pilot was essential no matter what time of year, not just for Grant, but for the other executives as well. It didn't make sense to me that Grant might suggest otherwise.

Mike was frowning into his cup sullenly and I almost felt sorry for him.

"I can't understand why Grant would want you to leave. Perhaps you misunderstood? Maybe I could talk to him. Do you have any idea why he would take this sudden attitude?"

His voice fairly dripped with bitterness. "You'll excuse me for saying so, but Mr. Fenton seems to be getting rid of anything or anyone that reminds him of your father. Now that he's got his fingers in the honey-pot, he's not interested in what happens to the people who were loyal to Mr. Dirkston."

I frowned, wondering with renewed apprehension just

what Grant was up to. Setting my coffee cup down, I stood up and reached for my raincoat, my mouth set determinedly.

"Thanks for the coffee, Mike. Don't worry, I'll speak to Grant immediately. As long as I've got a say in things, you'll have a job with Dirkston."

He raised his brows in surprise and flashed me a charming smile. "That's mighty kind of you," he said, adding as I opened the door to leave, "Tell David, if you see him, that I'm real sorry about his dad, and that I've got things under control here."

I nodded and left, grateful that the rain had let up sufficiently to allow me a dry run to the car. I wondered angrily just how many other changes Grant was instigating behind my back!

I stopped at Spindrift to check on David on my way home, surprised and more than a little annoyed to find Darla still fawning over him. She had obviously made herself right at home, greeting me at the door and ushering me through as though she'd lived there all her life.

David was immensely improved since I'd last seen him. He was dressed and shaven, sitting on the sofa sipping a cup of frothy coffee that reeked of whisky. He greeted me over his shoulder and patted the seat next to him.

"Why don't you fix one of these for Suzanna, Darla? She could probably use one, too."

Darla smiled stiffly but acquiesced. I waited until she'd disappeared into the kitchen, then turned to him.

"How are you?" I asked in concern.

He made a feeble attempt at a smile. "I'll be okay. How about you?"

"I've been to the police." I saw no reason to beat around the bush. David needed to know what was going on, and I preferred to tell him without Darla present.

He raised his eyebrows. "So soon? I suppose they'll be

knocking on my door any minute. What did they want?"

I hesitated, torn between an instinct to protect him from further hurt and the conviction that he should hear about Giles from my lips and no one else's.

"David, the police have their suspicions that Giles's death might not have been an accident."

Slowly, he raised his pale blue eyes over the rim of his cup. The shock in them made me regret my bluntness. I looked down at my hands folded tightly in my lap and proceeded to tell him what I knew. He set the cup down and I noticed that his hand shook slightly. After a few moments of thought, he rubbed the back of his neck wearily.

"Murder!" he breathed. "I can't believe it! Who would want to...? Do they have any idea?"

I laid my fingers gently on his arm. "I really don't know. They aren't saying much. But I think we can assume that it all ties in with Leo's death. Your father had something important he wanted to tell me. I think he knew something about Dad's murder. He may well have known who did it. I think that's why he was killed."

David stared at me blankly. Before he could reply, Darla returned and, oblivious to our somber expressions, began chattering about the unpredictable weather and the inconvenience of having to change clothes almost hourly to suit it. She nodded in the direction of the huge windows.

"See what I mean? The rain's stopped and the sun's out! Now, things will heat up and I'll be simply sweltering before the end of the afternoon. It's September, for heaven's sake!"

I grimaced and sipped the warm drink she'd placed before me. Darla sat opposite and her bright eyes darted between us with open curiosity.

It was David who broke the silence. He stood up abruptly, downed the last of his drink and flexed his long legs. "I think I'll go over to the marina. I'll go mad if I sit here much longer." He smiled apologetically at Darla. "Not that I don't appreciate all you've done. I just need to get out."

She nodded benignly. "I'm glad to be of any help. Grant hasn't had much work for me lately, and I feel like a bit of a freeloader at Beacon."

I didn't trust myself to respond politely to this, so I set aside my barely touched drink and stood up as well. "I must be going, too. I've got a few bones to pick with Grant."

David lifted a curious brow but said nothing. Darla, seeing that she had no alternative, gathered up her belongings and followed us out.

David walked with me to my car and kissed me lingeringly before shutting me securely in the driver's seat. I couldn't help shooting a victorious glance in Darla's direction before driving off, feeling as though I'd scored a winning point. It's surprising what baser instincts surface when faced with a bit of competition!

Grant's car wasn't in the drive when I arrived home, but I noticed Alicia in the living room chatting candidly on the telephone. By the time I'd removed my raincoat and placed it on the rack in the hall, she'd hung up and was scribbling hastily on a pad of paper.

"You seem better today," I commented, coming into the room.

She looked up and her face was lit. The change in her was indeed remarkable. She had washed her hair and applied makeup. Even her long nails were newly painted, and she seemed to have revived much of her old energy.

"I feel better," she responded brightly. "I needed something to take my mind off all the horrid affairs of late, and I've found just the thing!"

"What is it?" I smiled. "I could use some of it myself."

"Colin suggested I get together with some of my old friends, and I thought the best way was to have a little party."

"Party?" I echoed, sitting down and taking the list that

she offered. There were at least a hundred names. A few I recognized, but most were unfamiliar. "If all these people come, this will not be a little party."

She waved a hand and her bangles clinked. "I couldn't decide, so I just invited everyone. It's a Halloween party," she went on. "Don't you think it'll be fun? Everyone can dress up and we can have jack-o-lanterns and cider, just like when we were kids!"

I eyed her dubiously. It seemed to me that a party was the last thing we needed, especially with reporters still lurking behind corners waiting for any juicy gossip. But, at the risk of dampening her healthy enthusiasm, I didn't say so. Instead, I gestured to the list. "Who are all these people?"

"Oh, most of them are friends of mine from the stage; I haven't seen them in ages. That one there," she pointed with one coral nail, "is one of the most famous mediums around. I knew her when I was working in LA., and she'll be lecturing in the area. She's agreed to come along and conduct a séance!"

I frowned and glanced at the name: Madam De Luna. I hadn't heard of her, but that didn't mean anything. "Alicia, I really don't like the idea of a séance. It seems pretty morbid, considering…" I stopped. What was I saying? It was only a bit of harmless fun. I certainly didn't believe in communicating with the dead. Or did I? No. I was worried about Alicia. She was so easily influenced and, despite her newfound enthusiasm, she still wasn't fully recuperated.

I'd witnessed a couple of amateur attempts at contacting the spirit world. Every teenager dabbles with ouija boards and slumber party séances. We used to get a kick out of turning out the lights and frightening the daylights out of one another. Nothing ever came of it, but each experience had left me with an uneasy sensation in my gut and I soon avoided them altogether. I was certain that a more 'professional' approach wouldn't change my opinion, despite the fact that I knew most of the production was staged—arranged with cheap props and theatrical special affects. Besides, Alicia was too recently recovered to risk being traumatized. Who knew what tactics this woman might use just to enthrall her audience?

Alicia laughed. "Oh, I know what you're thinking! But I'm not such a ninny as you think, Suzanna. I know this stuff is mostly for show, but I like to keep an open mind. If Leo or Giles could talk to us, I know a lot of people would be interested!" She lowered her voice and leaned closer. "We may even discover what really happened!"

I stared at her. The suggestion made the hairs on the back of my neck prickle, and I didn't like the odd glint in Alicia's eyes.

I handed the list back and stood up. "Well, frankly I don't approve, Alicia. But, if it's what you want, I can't stop you. I just hope you remember that it could make things a lot worse than they already are."

She smiled, undaunted. "I knew you wouldn't be a wet blanket! You'll come, won't you? I mean, I'd really like you to be here—for moral support."

I sighed. I was beginning to realize that Alicia had a talent for manipulation. She was right. If she was going to go ahead with this thing, I felt duty-bound to be on hand in case anything went wrong. "Yes. I'll come."

She clapped her hands and put a large check mark next to my name. "Thanks!" she said. "Oh, I know you'll enjoy it!"

I pursed my lips doubtfully and left her to her phone calls. I supposed it wouldn't hurt to let her have her fun. Heaven knew, we could use something to ease the oppressive pall that hung over Beacon.

ELEVEN

The Past—the dark unfathom'd retrospect!
The teeming gulf—the sleepers and the shadows!
The past! the infinite greatness of the past!
For what is the present after all but a growth out
of the past?

Walt Whitman
Passage to India

Kong sat expectantly at the door of the attic, his slanting yellow eyes assessing me casually as though he knew what I planned to do, and felt it his duty to supervise.

I went immediately to the trunk and opened it, finding the spiral notebooks on top where I had left them. I removed the most recent one, determined to find out whom it was my mother had likened to a "coiled cobra." It was very possible that this same person might be the one we were all looking for. Perhaps Anna, with her quiet perceptive instinct, had sensed some manic streak in someone that the rest of us couldn't see.

I sat down on the chair near the window and thumbed slowly through. Eventually, I located the passage I'd glimpsed before and flipped past it, only to find torn stubble where a number of pages had been ripped out. The rest of the book was empty. I stared at the ravaged edges blankly, then went back to the trunk and removed each of the other diaries and shook them, hoping against hope that the missing pages would fall out. I knew it was useless. If Anna had indeed put a name to her suspicions, someone had made very sure that it wouldn't be discovered.

I leaned back in the chair and stared out the window dejectedly. Who could have known about the diaries? David came quickly to mind. Had he seen through my little white lie about them? Perhaps he had seen more when he casually thumbed through the notebook than I'd realized, and had come back later to destroy any damning evidence. But no, anyone could have ripped out those passages. Chances are they had been severed even before I'd laid eyes on the book. Those diaries had been in that trunk since my mother's death, and in all those years, any member of the household could have come upon them.

Sadly, I opened the book again and read the pages just prior to the end. Leo had brought Grant to live at Beacon. Anna was skeptical about the arrangement, finding Grant a "...sullen and uncommunicative young man." Colin was becoming harder and harder to discipline. There were reports from school about his fighting. She suspected that the other children taunted him about his father's precipitous marriage.

"I can't seem to talk to Colin about it," Anna wrote. "He probably blames me for everything. Leo has no patience with him, and seems to be more interested in Grant than his own son. No wonder the boy is so resentful." And later: "Giles tells me not to worry. He says I should be taking it easy, but I find it impossible. My nerves are always on edge. Leo is forever running off to Chicago, or wherever the company needs him, and I'm expected to sit in this museum and amuse myself! At least, I have Suzanna. She's such a good girl. I only wish I didn't have to stay in the house alone."

I read the next passage through. "Grant Fenton is entirely too ambitious for my liking. It seems unnatural for a boy of that age to spend all his free time studying, or tagging after Leo. And I've seen the way he looks at Suzanna. She's still just a child! As if I don't have enough to worry about."

I considered this paragraph, puzzled, unable to remember Grant looking at me in any particular way unless it was with aloof disinterest. I knew that Grant had considered me a "spoiled rich kid" from the start and, in my own rebellious way, I had done nothing to alter his perception. In those days, I set great store by my father's fame and would never have admitted to myself that I could be attracted to someone like Grant. I realized now that he had been on my mind often, and by avoiding him I was also avoiding my own feelings.

It seemed obvious to me that my mother must have been speaking of Grant in that final entry. The Grant of those days had indeed been wound tightly like a spring, as though with obsessive diligence he could make up for all the early years of poverty and ignorance. He seemed to have no time for anything or anyone who couldn't help him in his struggle up the ladder of success.

I'd never considered that driving force behind Grant. As children do, I merely accepted his presence, secretly admiring his rough manners which were so different from the studied charm of the nouveau riche with whom I was used to associating. Grant said what he meant and did what he wanted without pretense—or so I'd believed. Now I wondered. Anyone born into such a desperate situation as his would certainly carry the scars for a long, long time. It would be only natural to develop a deep resentment toward others born with the proverbial "silver spoon" in their mouths. It also seemed likely that such resentment could very well fester and turn violent.

I shivered and put the diaries away. I was having second thoughts about confronting Grant with his handling of the business, becoming more and more suspicious that he could be the one responsible for the deaths of my father and Giles. The fact that I was now married to him wouldn't protect me, should he decide I was interfering with his plans. I was still unsure what these plans were, but if Mike's beliefs were accurate, Grant was set on remodeling Dirkston Enterprises to suit his own personal ambitions, and would dispose of anyone who stood in his way.

But he knew that I still held the purse strings. If he felt I wasn't going to relinquish them to his care, he would simply have me removed. Even if the money didn't pass directly to him after my death, Colin could easily be managed, since he'd never had any interest in the company. He'd gladly turn it all over to Grant, as long as his own comforts were assured.

It was this point that convinced me that Colin had to be innocent. He didn't possess the ambition necessary to commit murder, and I could see no other motive that might evoke such ruthlessness. Still, I wouldn't rule him out altogether. There was the marina, which he admitted was floundering. He'd solve most of his problems by collecting the inheritance. But even this theory had a gaping hole. It was Colin who had uncovered the contents of Leo's will long before it was officially read. If he had known that he wouldn't inherit directly, what was his motive for murdering Leo? Resentment? Perhaps. He had good cause to despise my father, but I doubted it. The crime was too well executed—as though it had been planned—or, at the very least, considered for some time beforehand.

It all came back to Grant.

I closed my mother's trunk and latched the shutters at the window. Kong watched me intently.

"If only you could talk!" I said absently and bent to stroke his thick coat. He endured my caress stoically, even going so far as to arch his back against my fingers and purr loudly. I was ridiculously pleased that he chose to accept my friendship. At least, he was one member of the household I could trust.

~ ~ ~

After Giles's funeral, David spent more and more time at Beacon. I, for one, was pleased. I enjoyed seeing more of him, and I knew it was healthier for him to be with people than to sit and brood in the empty house where his father no longer dwelled. We developed a deeper empathy for each other. We had both experienced the death of a parent by violent means and, though I'd have preferred to have found a closeness some other way, those tragedies formed a common ground where we could share feelings more intimately than we had ever done. I think, for the first time, David needed me as a friend. Colin, of course, was there, but he would never fully understand the depths of sadness that David felt. Colin had felt nothing similar at the death of his own father and he was too young to remember much about his mother's death. There was no one else for David to turn to, and I liked it that way.

The guestroom near my own was prepared and David preferred to stay there most nights, away from the haunted emptiness of Spindrift. I could see that, despite his brave front, he suffered deeply, and though he never admitted it, I knew he wanted me close. He insisted on accompanying me most places, purporting to worry about my safety, and I didn't object. I told him of Sergeant Davison's suggestion that I leave the area, and he knew as well as I that, by staying, I was taking a big risk.

Grant came and went unannounced. I could tell by his rigid face and gruff manners that he wasn't pleased with David's residency, and I was careful not to allow him the opportunity to confront me face to face.

At David's suggestion, I locked my door carefully each night. However, this didn't prevent the recurring dream that woke me frequently and left me shaking and drained. The dream was unlike any other I had ever experienced, and the intensity of its realism was horrifying. Each time I felt the "presence" that had beckoned me at the cabin, had surrounded me the first night in the swimming pool, and on the beach. The presence itself didn't frighten me, but the desperation it transmitted did. After the dream, I awoke in a cold sweat, racking my brain to remember details, but was only able to piece together a hodge-podge of sensations and disjointed images.

I must have called out in my sleep, for often it would be David, hammering on my door, that brought me awake. On these occasions, I fell tearfully into his arms, allowing him to comfort me with soothing words and hot tea, which he fetched from the kitchen.

I tried to ignore the effect these late night disturbances had on me, though I found myself sleeping later and later and having to drag myself about during the day with little or no energy, longing only to return to the soft security of my bed and the oblivion of sleep.

Alicia, on the other hand, seemed to have recovered completely from her close call, though no one but Grant would have the temerity to question her about her use of drugs, and he seemed too preoccupied with the business to worry about it. With the party only a week away, she was ambitiously organizing costumes for everyone in the house, and suggested I find something from the attic. She was ridiculously excited when I mentioned Anna's wedding gown, and insisted that it would be the perfect thing. I could be the bride of Dracula, or Frankenstein's bride. Personally, I didn't care. Together, we brought the dress down and I tried it on halfheartedly. It was too small in the bust and hips, and there were a few brown stains on the full white satin skirt, but with the help of Martha and Lottie, the garment was cleaned and altered until it looked practically new and fitted me well enough.

I felt ridiculous wearing it. I suspected that it had been chosen by Leo rather than Anna, for it was much too elaborate for Anna's quiet tastes. It was intricately embroidered with pearls and sequins, with a high lace collar and long, fitted sleeves. The skirt was meant to be held out, bell-like, with hoops and petticoats, but I drew the line there and instead had the hemline raised so that it could drape naturally.

I endured the fittings apathetically, grateful to pull on a pair of comfortable jeans afterward. I thought wryly of my own so-called wedding, and wondered if I would ever have another. The logical side of me viewed large weddings as a waste of time and money, though the romantic in me longed for all the frills and frippery of a traditional ceremony.

Darla had made herself quite at home at Beacon, despite her professed insecurities, and I couldn't see that she was accomplishing anything much in the way of secretarial duties. Occasionally, she shut herself into my father's—now Grant's—office, and I heard the click of computer keys or the whir of the fax machine. Still, it seemed that the woman was more than dispensable as an employee, and I deeply resented her presence. I tried my hardest to avoid her, but she seemed set on confronting me at every turn and was forever popping up "coincidentally" at the oddest times and places.

My mother's diaries drew me like a magnet. I brought them down to my room and read each one carefully, particularly attentive to the last one. The more I studied it, the deeper was my conviction that Anna was genuinely afraid of Grant. She never said so directly, but her references to him were emotion-packed, and it was obvious that she wished he hadn't come to Beacon.

The idea that Anna's fall might not have been the accident we'd all assumed came suddenly upon me one evening as I sat working on my neglected manuscript. At first, I tried to put it from my mind, telling myself I was getting paranoid. But surrounding events and occurrences began to slide into place, giving the suspicion ample fuel to grow. I switched off my computer and went downstairs to the library, hoping to find something to distract me.

Martha was sitting quietly in a wingback chair, reading. Her hair was curled with clips, and a pair of bifocals were balanced on the end of her nose. She was covered from neck to ankles in a warm lavender dressing gown, and her feet were encased in soft, fluffy white slippers. She glanced up, surprised.

"Don't get up," I said smiling. "I didn't mean to disturb you."

She removed her glasses and held up the book.

"It's very good," she said.

I recognized it immediately. My novel. The one I had so proudly discussed with Leo as proof of my talents. Now it seemed like a stale memory, written by a novice who had still been filled with boundless ambition and enthusiasm. I realized, unhappily, that I would be hard pressed to recapture that spirit and zeal again.

"It's a bit sappy, don't you think?"

She shook her head. "Not at all. It's very romantic."

Romantic! What did I know about romance?

"Is something wrong, dear?"

"No. I've just hit a snag with the new novel, and thought I'd take a break. Thought I'd see if I could find something to read."

She nodded. I hesitated, then sat down opposite her. "Actually, there's something on my mind," I said. "I've been thinking of Mother. I found her journals. Do you remember the ones she used to write?"

Martha nodded sadly. "I put them in the attic after the accident."

"Some of the pages are missing. It looks as though they've been ripped out. Do you know if anyone else has read them?"

She raised her eyebrows. "I don't think so. Who would want to, other than you? Your father wanted me to destroy them, but then, he wanted everything of your mother's removed. Her death was so hard on him. I just couldn't burn them, though. I thought that one day you might want them."

"I'm grateful for that. Just reading them makes me feel I know her so much better." I paused uncertainly, then plunged on. "Mother talks of Grant in her journals. I get the impression that she really disliked him. Do you know why?"

Martha shifted uncomfortably, and I fully expected her to try to sidestep the question. Instead, she sighed and met my inquisitive gaze with resignation.

"She didn't talk about it much," she said, "but I think she resented your father's attachment to Grant. Your mother was a bit insecure. You know she came from pretty humble beginnings, and to find herself suddenly thrust into a world of wealth and fame—well, it was overwhelming, to say the least.

"It was difficult for her to function in that role without Leo's constant support and, you know your father, he was always jetting off, leaving her alone here at home. I'm sure he would have taken her with him more often, but she didn't feel comfortable in his world. The times he did spend with her she treasured, and I think when Grant came onto the scene, she felt Grant was taking a bit of that time from her." She shrugged. "Your mother spoke to Leo once about sending Grant away, and it was the only heated argument I recall them having. Leo stubbornly refused to discuss it, and Anna went to her room in tears. Later, he tried to make it up to her by spending more time at home and, as far as I know, the subject was never discussed again."

"And what about Grant?" I asked, intensely interested. "Did he know how Mother felt?"

Martha shook her head. "I really don't know, dear. He was such a broody boy in those days. If he did, he was tactful enough not to mention it. After the argument, Anna was careful to avoid Grant. I think she might have even been a bit frightened of him. It would only be natural, since she knew he had once been a petty thief and had grown up under unsavory conditions. But what difference does all of this make now?"

"I really don't know," I hedged. "I'm just trying to understand some of what she wrote. What about the accident? Do you know any of the details?"

"Probably no more than you," she said. "Your mother and father went out riding, and she fell. That's all I know."

Her answer was brisk, and I knew I must drop the subject. It wouldn't do to frighten Martha with my suspicions. Any further questioning would surely arouse her suspicions, and I wasn't ready to share what could very well be plain paranoia.

Unfortunately, Martha knew me too well, and she eyed me skeptically. "You're worried about something, Suzanna," she said, putting the book aside. I frowned, but didn't meet her eyes. "I know that these past weeks have been a great strain on you," she said, "on all of us, but I don't think that digging up the past will help anyone. I also know that you married Grant only out of a sense of duty to your father. It's only natural that you would resent it, but if my opinion means anything to you, I think it was the right thing to do. Grant is a fine man, take it from me. He's held this family together, in one way or another, for years. Perhaps in his younger days, he was a bit callous and distrustful, but those days are gone and I really feel he has only good intentions when it comes to the business and the family…and you." She looked at me intently and her eyes glistened. "He loves you, you know. Has for a very long time."

I stiffened. "Why, that's ridiculous!" I sputtered. "I mean, excuse me, but how could you ever get such an idea?" I was certain that Martha must have lost her marbles.

She smiled patiently. "You can't see it because you don't want to." She held up her hand as I opened my mouth to retort. "I only want to put your mind at ease, dear. Grant isn't the person you should fear. He worries about you. Why do you think he's trying to run the firm from this house? He's trying to protect you. No, don't scoff. Whether you want to believe it or not, it's true. Still," she fingered her robe nervously, "there is someone on the loose who is very, very dangerous. I only wish Grant could be here more often than he is." She shuddered visibly and I softened. The memory of Giles and his recent tragedy was obviously still too vivid. In my preoccupation, I had all but forgotten the personal loss Martha had suffered.

"I'm sorry. I've been selfish," I said. "You've been under just as much strain as anyone, and I shouldn't be bothering you with my problems."

"Our problems," she corrected. "I'm afraid that we're all in this together. It seems to me that there's no rhyme or reason for Giles's death. And now, if what they say about your father is true, well, it makes me shudder to think of it!"

I nodded. I didn't know how much she knew or guessed about Leo's "accident," but it wasn't a secret that the police were investigating Giles's death as a homicide. They had been to the house numerous times to question everyone, including Martha, but so far there was nothing substantial to go on.

They had taken the speedboat away after going over it carefully for clues. As expected, nearly everyone's fingerprints were on it somewhere, and the rain that had soaked the beach that morning had successfully washed away whatever other evidence might have been left. Still, they wanted to inspect the hull and propeller, so they had impounded the craft for an unspecified period of time. I wasn't sorry. I doubted that any of us would ever want to set foot on it again, anyway.

I left Martha some time later. I was still uneasy, and more confused than ever. It was obvious that Grant had a firm ally in our housekeeper, and it would be pointless to try to sway that loyalty. Grant had learned his trade well, and knew how to win people over. Martha's belief that he was somehow in love with me was probably just another part of his scheme—a way to present himself in the best

possible light—as a caring, concerned, if not misunderstood, husband who had only my best interests at heart.
My affection for David would only serve to martyr him in
the eyes of those who supported him. His own question-
able association with Darla LaTrobe had, as yet, offered
nothing overtly illicit. He would be too cunning to let a sordid dalliance interfere in his game plan.

David met me on the stairs with obvious relief. "Here
you are! I was worried. I knocked at your door, and there
was no answer."

I sighed. Sometimes his concern was stifling. I wished
he would at least give me space to breathe.

"I was just in the library," I said. "Where have you
been?"

His hair was windblown and his face flushed. His canvas shoes were wet, and I detected the fresh scent of lake
spray on his clothes.

"Just walking. I went down to the beach. It's nice this
time of night."

I nodded thoughtfully, still preoccupied.

"Come on," he said taking my hand. "I could use a cup
of something hot. Let's raid the kitchen."

"Sure," I agreed, welcoming the distraction.

Together, we foraged in the pantry, deciding on hot
cocoa. "With marshmallows!" I insisted, catching his
enthusiasm.

David prepared the cocoa as I spread honey on butter-
milk biscuits that were left over from breakfast.

We were comfortably settled at the kitchen table, chatting through mouthfuls of fluffy dough, steaming mugs
cupped in our hands, when Grant came in. He entered
through the side door from the garage, his briefcase in
hand and raincoat slung over one shoulder. A gust of cold
air followed him in and his look, as he took in the com-
panionable scene, did nothing to lessen the chill.

"Well, well, isn't this cozy?"

I lowered my eyes, feeling a deep blush creep up my

neck. David smiled, undaunted. "Want to join us? Or are cocoa and biscuits too mundane for your tastes?"

"As a matter of fact, it sounds like just the thing!" He dropped his coat over a chair in the corner and tossed the briefcase onto the floor nearby. His suit coat came off, along with his tie, and he casually rolled up his shirt-sleeves as he searched the cupboards for the necessary ingredients.

"Sit down," I said. "I'll get it. I know where everything is."

He didn't argue, but settled himself in the chair next to mine while I poured more milk into the pan and put a few more biscuits on the platter. The silence that ensued was distinctly uncomfortable. David and Grant eyed each other coolly while I nervously rattled the spoons and cups. When I finally sat down, Grant turned his gaze on me and smiled. "You look cute with a moustache."

"What? Oh!" I reached for a paper napkin and wiped the cocoa from my top lip.

"There's marshmallow on your nose," he added and made to wipe it with his own napkin, but I shrank away instinctively and rubbed the spot with my palm. His brows lowered and his eyes hardened, and I cursed myself for being so transparent.

"How are the family fortunes?" David asked pointedly, successfully diverting attention.

"Still intact, despite an increasing number of freeloaders." Grant's sarcasm wasn't lost, and David's eyes narrowed.

"Suzanna was just telling me that you're letting a lot of the staff go, including Mike. Are you planning to replace him, or are you going to join the ranks of lowly commuters?"

I could have kicked him. I hadn't planned to confront Grant with that information just yet, and the fact that I'd confided in David certainly wouldn't enhance the situation.

Thankfully, Grant appeared unperturbed, stirring his

drink nonchalantly as he replied. "It's impractical to keep Mike on the payroll permanently when he's only needed occasionally. There are plenty of pilots around who'll work on a standby basis; it's more economical. Besides, I thought Mike was working for you now."

"We give him what work we can."

"Surely, we can afford to keep him on?" I piped up, "He's been with Dirkston for so long. I don't think it's fair to just fire him."

Grant eyed me tolerantly. "How much do you know about Mike Kensington, Suzie?"

I met his gaze boldly. "I know that he's been a loyal employee for at least three years, and that Dad trusted him implicitly."

"And do you also know that he's been arrested on three separate occasions for drug offenses?"

My gaze faltered. "I...No. But surely, a man's past record shouldn't affect his present employment."

"Past record?" He snorted. "The last arrest was six months ago. He spent three days in jail for possession of cocaine."

"As I understand it, the case was thrown out of court," David said quietly.

"Only because the evidence was tampered with," Grant returned.

"There's no proof of that."

"Yeah! There's no proof, because someone stole the goddamn evidence right out of the police station!"

My eyes darted between the two. I felt ridiculously uninformed, and I resented both of them for their patronizing air.

"It was obviously a case of the police acting on a hunch," David said, his own temper fraying slightly. "It's their word against Mike's that they ever found anything on him. Who could steal a half kilo of cocaine right out from under the DA's nose?"

David's eyes glittered with conviction, but Grant's face

was rigid. He leaned his forearms on the table, his hands flat, his fingers splayed, hunching forward as if he fully intended to grab David by the throat and throttle him. When he spoke, however, his voice was controlled, patient—slightly supercilious. It was the voice he used so often in court when he was about to deliver a verbal blow below the belt.

"Who? Yes, indeed, who! Someone with enough clout to be able to stroll into a respected, well-manned precinct house, pick up the cocaine and stroll out again without a shred of resistance. Got any ideas, Einstein?"

David's face reddened considerably and the muscles in his jaw twitched, but he managed a stiff laugh. "I don't think the officers in charge would appreciate your slur on their honesty, and if you think Mike's mixed up in organized crime, you're out of your mind!"

"Funny, I don't remember mentioning organized crime, but now that you've brought it up…?"

Having endured this verbal sparring with mounting frustration, my temper finally snapped. "Stop it!" I shouted, springing to my feet and surprising even myself at my vehemence. There was instant silence, and both men stared at me in surprise. My cup had overturned, but I didn't even notice the cocoa splashed across the white table-top and dripping in muddy rivulets onto Lottie's gleaming floor. "Just who do you think you are? You're acting like a couple of bull elephants trumpeting your territorial rights! This isn't about Mike Kensington, or Dirkston Enterprises or—or, or…!"

I put a hand to my head. What was I saying? Why was I so angry? I was suddenly aware that the room was shimmering with pastel lights, and moving—like ripples over a mirror. I looked down at my hands where they gripped the edge of the table, and they seemed to belong to someone else, as though my arms were detached and had become beings unto themselves. I felt as though there was nothing to anchor me to the ground and that at any moment, I'd whirl off into infinity. A wave of panic unlike any I'd ever known gripped me and, in painful slow motion, I turned stricken eyes to Grant just before I collapsed and blackness washed over me.

I stood on the beach, gazing up at the lighthouse. It towered over me like a fortress. Huge, ink-black clouds whirled with uncanny speed across a multicolored sky. I was rooted to the spot. My feet were sunk to the ankles in cloying sand, yet my body was weightless, swaying with the gusting air. The changing cloud patterns distorted the lighthouse with their shadow and seemed to give it life. It seemed to be coming closer—growing larger—its beacon fixed on me like a menacing cycloptic eye. I struggled to pull my feet free of the sand, but the action only intensified my predicament. I heard voices drifting with the roar of the wind—Grant's, David's, Leo's, Giles's. I tried to reply, tried to call for help, but my voice caught in my throat, choking me. My eyes were drawn to a window high in the tower. A glimmer of undulating light hung suspended there and I watched, frozen, as it gained depth and substance. I recognized the wedding dress and the face, blurred by tendrils of fawn-colored hair. My mother's mouth opened and, though no sound came forth, I knew she was trying to warn me, willing me to go back. A darker figure loomed up behind her and, in exaggerated slow motion, I watched as she turned, struggled briefly, and fell.

"Suzanna!"

It was Grant's voice. I forced my eyes open a fraction. His face was close to mine. I felt the warmth of his breath. Gradually, sensations returned. My fingers ached, and I realized that I had hold of both his arms in a grip that hurt. My mouth was dry and my throat was sore.

"Suzanna!" he repeated. "It's all right! You're all right now!"

I loosened my hold, and the muscles in my body began to relax. The room swam slightly, but I knew where I was: in my own room, in my own bed.

"God," I croaked, "what happened?" I squeezed my eyes shut for a moment to try to still the spinning room. My head throbbed painfully, but when I opened my eyes again, the dizziness subsided.

"You passed out. How do you feel?" His face was lined with tension and his eyes were filled with concern.

"Not too good," I admitted. "I think I'm going to be sick."

He carried me to the bathroom and held me up while I retched miserably. When I'd finished, he mopped my face gently with a cloth and put me back in bed, laying another cool, damp cloth across my forehead. I felt better, though my head still ached and my limbs were weak.

"I had a dream," I rasped, swallowing hard. Grant put a glass of water to my lips and I sipped gratefully.

"You were screaming."

"Was I? No wonder my throat hurts. It was horrible! Mother was in the lighthouse and—and someone pushed her…"

Grant set the glass aside and took my cold hands, chafing them gently. I watched him, and the intensity of my gaze made him look up. Curiously, his eyes were glistening with tears.

"Jesus, Suzanna, you sure know how to frighten the hell out of me!"

I smiled weakly. "Really? I didn't know you cared!"

He looked away. "I thought it was pretty obvious."

I curled my fingers through his and, for a moment, gave in to my emotions, accepting the comfort of his presence, setting aside my suspicions and allowing myself to drift with the flood of emotions that tumbled in. I was too weak to fight it and, for that instant, felt no desire to. His touch sent a thrill through me that I'd never felt before.

But the moment was short-lived. David suddenly

appeared over his shoulder, his face also lined with worry. I released Grant's hand immediately.

"Thank God, you're awake!" David said. "How are you?"

"Better, I think," I said wryly.

He came around to the side of the bed and hunkered down, tracing a finger gently down my cheek. Grant retreated tactfully to the other side of the room and absently began to finger the knickknacks that cluttered the bookcase.

"I rang the doctor. He's a friend of Dad's," David said. "He can't come to the house, but he said to keep an eye on you and if this sort of thing happens again, you're to go straight to the hospital. He said there's some flu going around that's pretty potent."

I nodded. "I have been feeling a bit run-down lately."

Grant came to stand behind David, and the scowl on his face made it apparent that he didn't approve. "I think we should take you over right now and see what's wrong."

"No." I grimaced at the pain that shot through my head as I shook it adamantly. "I'll be all right. I'm sure the doctor's right. It's just a bug. Thanks for all the concern, but I think all I need is some sleep."

Martha appeared at the door, and it took nearly twenty minutes to convince them all that I didn't need anything and didn't want anyone sitting by my bedside. I agreed to leave the door ajar, so that someone could look in on me occasionally, and eventually they drifted out, leaving me to sink into a deep, thankfully dreamless sleep.

In the morning, I opened my eyes tentatively. The dizziness was gone and my stomach was no longer queasy. I was just about to attempt to sit up when Grant popped his head around the door.

"Awake? How do you feel?"

"I don't know yet. So far, so good, though."

"Can I come in?"

I nodded.

He entered, balancing a tray dexterously on the finger-tips of one hand, a white cloth draped over his arm.

"Your breakfast, madame," he announced with exaggerated aplomb. He set the tray down on my bedside table, shook out the napkin and placed it over my lap. With a dramatic flourish, he lifted the lids on the dishes one by one. "Dry toast. Unadulterated oatmeal. And an excellent vintage Jello water."

I grimaced. "You're joking, I hope."

He looked pained. "I made it all myself. It's what my mother used to give me when I was sick. Try it."

I inspected the offerings ruefully and bit dutifully into the toast, surprised at how hungry I suddenly felt. Grant sat down on a chair nearby and kept vigil until I'd finished, encouraging me with nods of approval and a fierce scowl if I balked. Afterward, apparently appeased, he removed the tray and grinned.

"My, we are better this morning!"

"M-m-m," I agreed around a mouthful of porridge. "I didn't know you could cook."

"This is nothing. You should taste my Fettuccine Marinara. Magnifique!" He kissed his fingertips expressively.

"Good Lord, don't let Lottie hear you!" Anyone dabbling in Lottie's kitchen courted serious bodily injury.

Grant cocked a brow confidently. "Lottie's a lamb. You just have to know how to get on her good side."

"And I'm sure you're an expert at that!"

He winked conspiratorially and I had to smile. Despite all my doubts about Grant, he could be irresistible when he put his mind to it. Try as I might, I couldn't stop the rush of affection that filled me when he smiled just so, or the tingle of excitement when his fingers brushed mine. I'd rarely had trouble with self-control, but the charm or charisma, or whatever it was that Grant exuded, seemed to scramble my brain. I lowered my eyes, afraid he might see the turmoil there, and reminded myself that Grant might very well be a cold-blooded killer.

"How come you're not in Chicago?" I asked, noting his faded jeans and bulky sweatshirt.

"It's Sunday. Even I'm not that dedicated." He paused, considering. "I was wondering, though, if you'd feel up to a drive? That is, if you're recovered enough? It looks like it's going to be a nice day, and I have a feeling it may be our last chance to enjoy the fall colors before the snows set in."

I didn't answer immediately, and he sighed. "You still don't trust me?"

I shrugged. "I'm finding it hard to trust anyone."

"Except David," he glowered.

"That's not fair."

"Isn't it?"

At my look of stubborn defiance, he softened. "Never mind. I suppose logically, I'd make a prime candidate for manic perversion. If I didn't know better, even I'd suspect me!"

I smiled grudgingly. I knew I should turn him down, but something in me wanted desperately to trust him. If he'd wanted to do me harm, he'd already had plenty of opportunities.

"All right," I said finally. "I'll go. It'll be nice to get some fresh air."

"You're welcome to take along a bodyguard."

"Don't be ridiculous."

He threw up his hands. "Hey, I'm only trying to make you feel at ease!"

"Then, get out of here so I can get dressed!"

He flashed me that winning smile, lifted my hand and kissed it. The brush of his lips sent a shiver through me that had nothing to do with fear. He looked up, searching my face. Our eyes locked, and time froze as battles raged within. Finally, and, I thought, with reluctance, he released my hand and left without another word. I stared after him, still frozen with strange, unbidden emotions. Martha's words echoed in my mind: "He loves you, Suzanna. Has for a very long time." This time, they didn't seem so unbelievable and, inexplicably, a surge of exhilaration swept over me.

So much had changed, and yet so little. There was still David, and my feelings for him were more muddled than ever. I was certain that the bulk of them had to do with habit and a need to cling to old securities. They were nothing like the awakening emotions I felt for Grant. Still, I was finding it more and more difficult to trust my instincts. Logic reminded me that I was leaving myself wide open for, at best, disillusionment; at worst, mortal danger. But, for once, I refused to listen. It was time I faced up to and accepted my own long repressed desires.

In the past, the pressures of living up to the Dirkston name, the inbred fear of disappointing Leo, had effectively inhibited my personal relationships. It must have been the same with Anna. I was beginning to wonder if it was Grant that Anna feared, or the raw attraction that he exuded. She would know that her only daughter, so much like herself, would be all too susceptible, and a such a romantic alliance would certainly be discouraged. Or would it?

It was Leo who had forced our marriage in the first place. Why? David would surely have been a better match—well-bred, well-known, stable, reliable, a friend of the family since birth. Perhaps we had all misjudged my father. Perhaps he had known me even better than I knew myself and, in his own inimitable way, had tried to force me to accept what lay in my heart all along. If only I could talk to him now, I thought sadly. His death had left so many unanswered questions.

I was surprised at how well I felt, considering the previous night's episode. If I was indeed suffering from a virus, it had come and gone with uncanny speed. Aside from a moderate weakness of muscles and overall sluggishness, I felt no other ill effects.

I dressed warmly. The mild temperatures of our recent Indian summer had disappeared overnight, replaced by a crisp chill of impending snow. It wasn't unusual at this time of year to enjoy a comfortable swim in the pool one day, only to find a layer of ice on it the next. As Darla pointed out, it was next to impossible to dress correctly.

As if I had mentioned her name aloud, there was a cursory rap on the door and Darla appeared. Initially annoyed at the intrusion, I bit back an inhospitable remark and kept silent, refusing to let anyone destroy my good mood.

"Oh, you're up. Well, that's a good sign. How are you feeling?"

"Much better, thank you."

"David's taking me out fishing today. If I'd known you were better, I'd have asked him if you could come, too."

I finished pulling the coverlet up on my bed and gritted my teeth. So, she had come to gloat. Well, two could play that game! "As a matter of fact, Grant and I have made other plans."

Surprisingly, this didn't seem to bother her. She merely nodded and smiled. "Well, just don't overdo it. You never know about these bugs. One minute you feel great, and the next…!"

"Don't worry, Darla; if I feel another attack coming on, I'll be sure to let someone know."

She disappeared with a wave of her hand and a smug grin on her face. I felt a childish urge to stick my thumbs in my ears, poke out my tongue and waggle my fingers at her retreating figure. Instead, I pummeled the pillow violently before placing it on the bed. I was sick of everyone treating me as though I were an invalid. They probably all assumed I was on the verge of a nervous breakdown. This thought in itself was disturbing, for they only knew a small portion of the strange illusions my mind had been playing on me over the past weeks, and this latest episode had been truly frightening. I'd had various types of influenza before, but they'd never affected me like this!

Grant was in his office when I finally went downstairs. He had several papers spread out before him, and was dictating into a small, handheld tape recorder.

"...despite fluctuations in market averages, it's been a favorable year with positive gains on all fronts. We look forward to..." He looked up and took his thumb off the button. "Ah, you're ready."

"Don't let me interrupt," I said, and flopped down in the deep leather chair opposite him.

"No problem. Just working on the annual report."

"A good year?"

"Not bad, so far. Could have been better." He sighed. "Your father was a helluva lot better at this sort of thing."

"Too much for you, eh?" I smiled slyly.

He shrugged and turned to gaze thoughtfully out the window. "It's funny how you dream of doing something all your life, and then when you actually have the opportunity, you find it's not really what you wanted after all."

"Isn't being chairman of Dirkston Enterprises rewarding enough?"

"Oh, sure. It definitely boosts the ego. But it takes a certain hardness of character that I'm afraid I haven't developed yet."

"Haven't you?"

He smiled, but chose to ignore the barb. "Your father had it. He could let a man go who'd worked with him for years without blinking an eye. And yet, at the same time, he could hire someone just because they were down on their luck—even invent a position for them, if there was nothing available." He shook his head. "I never understood him. I don't know if I would have wanted to."

I was silent, thinking bitterly of Grant's hypocritical treatment of Mike Kensington. But I didn't want to start another argument. Instead, I chose to encourage his sudden confidence.

"Don't try to be like Dad," I said. "For one thing, it

would be impossible, and for another, I wouldn't like you as well if you were."

He turned and looked at me with a deep seriousness that made me acutely uncomfortable. "And do you?" he asked in a low voice. "Like me, I mean?"

I laughed. "What a question! No. I hate you! You're irritating, unpredictable, overbearing, chauvinistic..."

He came around the desk and pulled me to my feet, silencing me with a kiss that left me stunned. Electric sensations shot through me, and I pushed him gently away.

"What was that for?" I asked shakily.

His gaze was warm and all too knowing. "Because you're right about me. And because you're also stubborn, inflexible, argumentative and exasperating. And because I like you, too."

I smiled, though I knew my cheeks were flaming. He smiled back and I noticed that, for the first time in a long time, the line between his brows, etched from months of strain and worry, had smoothed and his eyes were clear and unveiled.

I turned away and gathered my coat from the chair, trying not to wonder if he was sincere or merely concentrating his efforts on swaying my allegiance. My hands trembled. "Let's go," I said. "It's stuffy in here."

TWELVE

Man is a torch borne in the wind; a dream
But of a shadow, summed with all his substance.

> George Chapman
> Bussy d'Amois, act 1, sc. 1

We drove north along the lakeside, following less
frequented roads which cut through the burnished forest
and provided an uninterrupted pageantry of autumn's brilliant fashions. Maples were mottled orange and yellow, silver birch topped with russet and gold. Poison sumac
thrusting up soft crimson spears as though begging to be
stroked. And rising over them all, the stolid, thickly
plumed pines, unaffected by temperature change, were
still heavily robed with blue-green needles and brown
cones.

There were a number of signs to warn motorists to be
on the lookout for deer. They made themselves scarce during the day, but at dusk could be seen grazing close to the
roadside, occasionally darting across in front of oncoming
cars in response to mysterious, instinctive urges.

Grant was silent, and I was happy to watch the passing scenery. Despite my familiarity with the beauty of the

local terrain, I never grew tired of it. Too soon, the colors
would slip to the ground and leave only slick, bare limbs
to wait pathetically for the winter clouds to dump their
load of snow and wrap them in crystalline whiteness for
the interim. Today, the sun shone brilliantly but with a
waning warmth, as though in a last feeble tribute to summer.

Grant lit a cigarette and offered it to me. I took it automatically and opened the window a crack while he lit
another for himself.

"You're a rotten influence," I muttered, inhaling the
noxious smoke and trying not to feel guilty.

"No more than you are. Do you realize what hell I go
through every time I try to light a cigarette in the house?"

I smiled. "Martha?"

"Martha, Lottie, Colin...even Alicia, the little hyp-
ocrite!"

"Alicia doesn't smoke."

"Yes, and that's about all she doesn't do!"

I glanced at him. "You seem to know a lot about Alicia's
habits."

"It would take a blind, deaf mute not to know she's got
a problem with drugs," he said defensively. "It's been getting worse the last couple of years. That accidental overdose came as no surprise to anyone."

I didn't comment, preferring to think my own naiveté
was a result of my prolonged absences. My information
regarding Beacon's private melodramas was apparently
sadly out of date.

"Things have changed since you moved out," Grant
said, reading my mind.

"Not as much as I'd have liked," I muttered, thinking
bitterly of the undercurrent of antipathy and mistrust that
surrounded us all.

We fell silent again. The car slowed perceptibly as we
passed through Elberta and Frankfort. To our left, I could
just make out glimpses of Lake Michigan beyond the rise

of dunes, while to the right, Crystal Lake glittered invitingly through the trees.

This smaller lake and its environs had grown into a popular resort area. In summer, visitors clamored to share in the fishing, hiking and trailbiking or, for the less sports-minded, sunbathing, beachcombing or shopping at the quaint boutiques huddled along its shores. One could spend quite a few pleasant days perusing the plethora of antique shops, sampling the cuisine of neat little restaurants, or just strolling along cobbled walkways lined with old-fashioned gingerbread cottages. In winter, Crystal Lake Ski Resort opened its arms to those who enjoyed that dubious activity called skiing. I was an armchair skier myself, preferring the safety and warmth of the lodge and a cup of hot mulled wine

The road continued along the coast, and the dunes to our left rose to towering heights. This was Sleeping Bear Dunes National Park, the largest moving sand dune in the world. Each year some twenty-five miles of heaped sand rose, fell, flattened or dipped with the whims of the weather so that each day presented a changing landscape.

Grant pulled the car to a stop at one of the "Scenic Platform" signs. There was an arrow indicating a steep path that wove its narrow way up through the underbrush. I frowned. I didn't relish accompanying Grant to a cliff edge with only a small retaining wall separating me from a sheer drop.

He must have sensed my lack of enthusiasm. "All right. Forget it," he grumbled. "I just thought you might like to stretch your legs."

"Hey, I didn't say anything!" I cried defensively.

"You didn't have to. You know, Suzie, sometimes you're as clear as glass. Do you think I plan to throw you from the precipice to the jagged rocks below? You've been reading too many of your own novels!"

I glared at him. "My novels don't have precipices. Nor do they have women being lured to their demise by evil husbands. If it's all the same to you, however, I'd prefer to have the courtesy of a few witnesses."

He grunted and started the engine again.

"Where are we going, anyway?" I asked. "Or have I already ruined your plans?"

"As a matter of fact, I hadn't really made any plans. You may find this hard to believe, but I actually thought the drive and change of scenery might help you to relax a little."

"I am relaxed."

"Is that why your face has been puckered with frown lines ever since we left?"

I forced my brow to smooth, and realized he was right. The muscles ached from the intensity of my scowl. "Sorry," I muttered.

"I know you still don't trust me," he said. "But I suppose that's good. It means you have a healthy respect for the danger you're most probably in."

I shot him a concerned glance. "What do you mean?"

"Didn't Davison spell it out for you? I assumed he would have asked you to make yourself scarce until they catch whoever's been murdering your friends and relatives."

"As a matter of fact, he did, but I said I wouldn't go." I stared at him suspiciously. "But how do you know that?"

He sighed. "I told you I was working with them, didn't I? What do I have to do to convince you that I'm on your side?"

"Well, you could catch the real culprit or show me a badge—or 'take me to your leader.'"

The slump of his shoulders indicated his unwillingness or inability to comply with any of these conditions.

"I don't suppose, then, that you'd tell me if you uncovered anything in the way of clues?" he asked.

"No," I returned. "Would you?"

"If I could, I would, but…"

"You're sworn to secrecy!" I finished for him in an exaggerated, furtive whisper. "Oh, come on, Grant! This isn't a James Bond flick, this is real life. I suppose you're going to tell me next that you're keeping this all a secret for my own protection?"

"Well...."

I snorted. "Just as I thought."

"You could always torture me into talking—thumb-screws, boiling oil?"

I smiled. "Too obvious; they leave marks."

"How about sleep deprivation?" He cocked a suggestive brow. "I might even be willing to go along with that, if you used the right methods."

"Sorry. You'd enjoy it too much."

At least, the brief swing to levity had lightened the mood. Grant's hands relaxed on the wheel, and I felt the rigidity of my spine ease.

I decided on a different approach. "I really don't understand why, if you're working with the FBI or whatever, you can't let me in on it. Excuse me for being a naive female, but wouldn't the old adage, 'forewarned is forearmed,' apply here? I mean, it's not like I plan to call the New York Times or something!"

He didn't reply immediately, and I could see he was struggling with an answer. "All right. I suppose there's nothing they can do to me anyway, if I tell you some of it."

I waited eagerly. Finally, he spoke.

"Drugs," he said.

"Drugs?" I repeated.

"Heroin. Cocaine. Smack. Ecstasy...you may have heard of them?"

"Don't be sarcastic."

"It's got something to do with organized crime. They bring the stuff into the country through various channels. Some via the west coast, some via the east coast..."

"I have listened to the news on occasion!"

He scowled. "You're not making this easy."

"All right," I relented. "I won't interrupt. Go on."

"Anyway, they've infiltrated one of the rings and are currently following up on its distribution network. Which brought them to this area. They don't want to move in until they've collected enough evidence to pin down the head honcho."

"But, what's this got to do with Dad? Don't tell me he–"

"You said you wouldn't interrupt." His look softened at my obvious distress. "I don't want to be the one to disillusion you, Suzie, but Leo was no saint. But, to be honest, we don't know whether he knew what was going on or not. There's a possibility that he might have accidentally stumbled on the truth, and had to be silenced. Either way, we're pretty sure his death was directly related to this racket."

I digested this information slowly, and its ramifications sprouted distastefully. On the one hand, the Leo I knew wouldn't sit quietly for long if he became aware of a drug smuggling ring. I could imagine him bellowing threats and shaking his fist with all the relish of a man who considers himself invincible. That he might be at risk wouldn't have even entered his mind. In that way, I suppose he displayed his greatest weakness: Blindness to his own mortality could have led to his demise.

On the other hand, I remembered stories I'd heard over the years about Leo's shady dealings and, although I'd chosen to put them down as unfounded rumors, I knew that in the early days he could have done anything to further his ambitions—had even married a woman he didn't love to get a foot in the door. It wouldn't be such a long leap to become involved in the massively lucrative drug trade. When everything was said and done, what did I really know about my father's character or ethics?

I shivered. I wasn't willing to accept this sinister portrait of the man I'd loved. "I thought the mob had more succinct ways of disposing of people," I argued grimly. "Jimmy Hoffa's body still hasn't been found. People disappear everyday without a trace. And Dad wasn't exactly unknown. A blow over the head in his own house isn't my idea of a contract murder."

"No." Grant made a wry grimace. "That's what doesn't fit. It appears that Leo was killed by an underling. That's assuming it was a mob-related murder. Someone got scared, and decided to take matters into their own hands."

"And this underling was someone close to Dad? Someone at Beacon?"

"Very likely."

I shuddered. Up until now, my ignorance had acted as a cocoon, protecting me from the immensity of the situation. Avoid the unpredictable whims of a lone lunatic was one thing, but a lunatic coupled with the vast resources of a huge crime syndicate was quite another.

My mind flitted from one Beacon resident to the next, slotting each too easily into the role of drug dealer. Logically, anyone might fit: Alicia, with her addiction; Colin, sympathetic to his wife's weakness and desperate for independence; David, in need of more and more money to keep his business alive; Rudy Coleman...well, who knew what motivated him? And Grant—despite his calm narration of the situation, it didn't make me feel any easier about his position. His had a trained mind—trained to shadow or enhance guilt or innocence. If he could perform admirably in court, how much better might he do in real life where imagination, misconception and innuendo need not be overruled? Then there was Lottie who, I suppose if stereotyped, could very possibly have a close relative hopelessly involved in the drug trade—someone using her position to advance their own sinister purposes. Martha? I smiled. Somehow I couldn't see her smuggling packets of white powder or syringes about in her dressing gown. But who knew? Sometimes the least obvious ones were the most deadly.

"I think my mother may have been murdered." I don't know why I blurted it out—perhaps to see what sort of effect it would have. I felt temporarily better for having voiced it aloud, but I was surprised that, aside from a side-

ways glance and the play of muscles in his jaw, Grant barely flinched.

"What makes you think so?"

I didn't want to go on. Suddenly, I wished I had never
opened my mouth; but now that it was said, I couldn't
brush it aside.

"I think she was frightened of someone…someone in
the house."

"How do you know?"

"I was reading her journals and…"

"Journals?"

"Yes, diaries, sort of. She used to write in them regularly. Anyway, it seemed to me that she was frightened,
especially just prior to the accident."

Grant was very interested. Too interested. I felt his tension, and the air fairly sizzled with anticipation. My palms
were sweating and I cursed my stupidity.

"Do you still have them?" he asked. "I'd like to see
them…and I'm sure the, uh, police would be interested."

"No! I mean, you can't. I—I got rid of them."

"You what?" He was incredulous and angry. It only reinforced my suspicion that it had been a mistake to tell him.

"They were too…painful," I lied, theatrically rubbing a
hand across my eyes to hide the truth that I was sure was
flashing like neon in them.

"I suppose you—"

"—burned them." I nodded sadly.

He cursed and riveted his eyes on the winding road
ahead. I let out my breath slowly, satisfied that he didn't
suspect.

"I don't suppose your mother said who it was she was
afraid of?"

"No."

Did he look relieved or exasperated? I didn't offer to
explain about the missing pages. Instead, I veered the conversation back to where he'd left off.

"Tell me more about the operation. Do your colleagues

have any other leads? What's their next step?"

"I can't. I don't know. I don't know," he replied crisply.

"You're despicable!"

He raised his eyebrows. "Why? Because I don't have all the answers?"

"Because you tantalize me with tidbits and then leave me hanging."

"And I suppose you don't do the same?"

He was right. We were both playing games—holding back, keeping that safe distance. I wished fervently that I could take the plunge and tell him everything, but self-preservation is an instinct too strong to ignore.

"You're not being fair," I complained. "You're still under suspicion. I'm not."

He smiled. "Is that what they told you?"

I blinked. "As a matter of fact…"

"You've been around, Suzie. You could very easily have fallen in with some unsavory characters. You've always wanted to make a name for yourself without Daddy's help. What better way to build up your own assets than—"

"Good Lord, Grant! You know I can hardly handle two glasses of wine let alone…"

"I'm not saying you're using the stuff." He shot me a meaningful look.

I clamped my mouth shut, fuming. We were silent for some time before he finally relented.

"How's it feel?" he asked quietly.

"What?"

"Being on the receiving end of suspicion? Especially from someone you've known most of your life?"

I considered this objectively and finally nodded. "Point taken. Let's drop it."

"Fine," he said grimly and slowed the car as we approached civilization.

We had lunch at the harbor restaurant in Leland. It was very quiet, with only a few other couples and a handful of salesmen sharing the split-level establishment.

We discussed the business. Grant shared some of the problems of his new position with me, and seemed interested in my thoughts on the matters. By unspoken agreement, we didn't bring up the investigation again. I had some very serious thinking to do, and I got the impression that Grant was regretting that he'd told me as much as he had. At least, the interlude helped to lessen the tension that seemed to hover constantly over me, for I was able to put it aside temporarily and concentrate on other issues.

After lunch, Grant humored me by tagging along as I poked about the little shops nearby, examining silver and turquoise jewelry, purported to have been handmade by Navajo Indians, and admiring a display of carved candles created on the spot by an aging hippie. We strolled along the dock and Grant pointed out the various differences in the yachts anchored there, his voice full of fondness for the subject. I listened intently, aware of how little I really knew about his personal likes and dislikes. At one point, a woman pointed at us covertly and whispered something to her male companion, and I realized that they'd probably recognized us from one of the newspaper reports. It occurred to me that, in the eyes of the world, we were newlyweds and the brunt of all kinds of media speculation, and I felt suddenly exposed and vulnerable, angry that even in this quiet, isolated spot there was no escaping public scrutiny. When we finally made our way back to the car, it was with a sense of regret. Our freedom was short-lived, and we both knew that Beacon awaited us like a tomb.

That night, I tossed all the latest revelations around in my head until I was thoroughly agitated. It seemed there were never any answers, only new questions; and by morning, I was fiercely determined to investigate a few theories of my own.

The first investigation had to do with my mother's fall. I wanted to believe that her death had been an accident, but I was increasingly suspicious, and I knew there was only one person who might shed some light on what had happened that day.

I found Rudy outside the old stables, half-hidden beneath the ancient tractor which was used to tend the vacant field between the main house and the disused horse sheds. He took his time emerging, tossing out a wrench and an oilcan and wiping his grimy hands on his already stained overalls.

I didn't know how to broach the subject, so decided on directness. "Rudy, what do you know about the day my mother died?"

If I'd expected him to be shocked or surprised, I was disappointed. He assessed me from under his shaggy brows and allowed the glimmer of a smile to touch the corners of his mouth. "That's a mighty long time ago, Miss Suzanna. Seems t' me there's enough goin' on around here right now without disturbin' th' dead."

I steeled myself, determined not to let his casual attitude daunt me. "Who saddled Mother's horse that day?" I persisted.

He studied me intently and, after apparently concluding that I wouldn't be swayed, shrugged. "I did. I always saddled up fer yer ma and pa."

I nodded. "Did anyone else come down to the stables before they left on their ride?"

Rudy turned his head and squinted across the open pasture. "Don't really recall. Seems like there was someone…yep, I remember. Mr. Grant came down. He sometimes liked t' help me groom th' horses. Never was one t' think he was too good t' get his hands dirty."

"Was there anyone else?"

"Well, I don't think so. But th' other two boys was always scamperin' in and out. Never knew where they'd be hidin'. Always up t' some mischief, those two." He chuckled fondly.

"You mean, Colin and David," I said half to myself.

Rudy turned back to the tractor and lifted a cover to expose the engine.

"Rudy, do you think it's possible that someone might have caused my mother's accident?"

This time he was surprised and he turned and stared at me, his face puckered in a frown. "What makes you ask that, Miss Suzanna?"

"I don't know. It's just that we've had three deaths here at Beacon and the police are investigating Giles's. I'm beginning to wonder, now, if any of them were accidents." I hurried on, knowing that Rudy wouldn't confide in me unless I made him see my reasoning. I told him about Anna's diaries and her uneasiness. I knew that Rudy had been extremely dedicated to my mother, and had taken her death quite hard. Certainly, he'd want to expose any foul play—unless he was somehow involved.

When I'd finished, he pulled the cap from his head and ran a hand over his shaggy hair, considering. "P'raps you'd better come inside, missy," he said. "We'll have a cuppa."

The small apartment set over the stables had been home to Rudy since he'd come to Beacon many years before. The last time I could remember visiting, it was as a child in the company of my mother. Oddly, Anna had felt comfortable with Rudy, and often came for a cup of tea and a chat. I became bored easily, as young children do, and quickly escaped to play among the haystacks or wander about outside in search of wildflowers.

The apartment hadn't changed much since those days, except that it seemed smaller than I remembered. The main room was bare of unnecessary furnishings, with only a few threadbare mats scattered about to relieve the worn wooden floor. An old, square television stood against one wall with a huge sagging armchair pulled up in front. Over in one corner was a kitchenette with a small refrigerator, an electric oven and a sink. A small drop-leaf laminate table was placed in front of the only window, which looked out across the pasture and framed Beacon. There were curtains of a sort, also threadbare and of an indistinct color bordering on brown. Two straight-back chairs were drawn up to the table, their yellow vinyl seats cracked in places and randomly patched with aged tape. I sat down on one of these while Rudy switched on an electric kettle and placed two chipped, mismatched mugs on the table. Everything was surprisingly clean. Even the floors looked as though they'd recently been mopped. It made me wonder about the eccentric old character before me. What sort of background had he come from? As far as I knew, Rudy had no family or close friends. He lived reclusively in this small set of rooms, and if he had any hobbies or special interests, they weren't shared with any of us at Beacon.

After the coffee was made, he sat down and assessed me speculatively, his eyes sharp, waiting for me to speak. Now that I'd come this far, however, I was hesitant to continue.

"I remember," Rudy finally said, obviously taking pity on my loss for words, "when you was a scrap of a thing. Your mother thought th' world o' you. She'd sit in that very place where you are now and watch ye' out th' winder, an' she'd smile. She had a beautiful smile." He took a slurp of his coffee and gazed out the window, as though seeing the past spread out before him.

"What was she like?" I asked, trying to capture the image.

"Oh, she was purty—natural, though, not all painted up—and gentle. I don't think I've ever met anyone so gentle. She even spoke gentle, you know. Never raised her voice. Listenin' to her was like puttin' lotion on a sunburn." Rudy took another slurp of his coffee and frowned. "She come to see me after my Connie died. She was good t' me then."

"Who was Connie?" I asked, interested.

He paused momentarily, then gave a quirky smile. "She was my missus."

"But Rudy, I never realized you were married! Did she

live here with you? How come I don't remember her?"

"No, you never met her, missy. Y' see, Connie had a problem with her brain. They called it schizophrenia. She was okay for the first few years we was together, but she got worse and, well, I had to take her to Kalamazoo—t' the hospital. And that's where she died."

I stared at him, suddenly aware of how blind I had been all these years to this man who had always been a peripheral part of our family.

"How...?" I couldn't finish the question. I suddenly felt nosy, as if I'd come across a packet of love letters that were hidden away in someone else's room.

Rudy didn't seem to notice, however, and answered calmly. "Killed 'erself, she did."

I didn't ask any more. Couldn't. We were both quiet, and I could see that Rudy's eyes were moist.

"My—my mother helped you ?" I asked quietly.

He nodded. "She was a good woman, yer ma. If I was t' think that anyone harmed her a-purpose...!" He didn't need to finish the sentence—the steely edge of his voice and his clenched fist said it all. Suddenly, the vision of him scooping the steaming entrails from the freshly killed rabbit, gun held comfortably, flashed before my eyes.

"I'm probably just imagining things," I said reassuringly. "You know what a vivid imagination I have."

He stared at me, unsmiling. "Y'd best let things be, Miss Suzanna," he said. "No tellin' what can o' worms ya might open if ya don't watch yer step. Y' can't bring none of 'em back now, anyway. If yer ma or pa or Mister Lancaster come to foul play, they'll take care of it. The dead don't forget. An' they got ways o' gettin' even."

I shivered involuntarily. "What about your dream?" I asked. "When Dad said, 'Don't let them get away with it!' Doesn't that mean we should do something?"

He looked at me and smiled, but his eyes were like bright, hard stones. "Now, missy, that was jest a dream! You don't believe in dreams, now, do ya?"

I suddenly felt an overwhelming need to get away; away from that room, away from the memories—away from Rudy.

"Well, thanks for the coffee," I said as I stood up and backed toward the door. "And thanks for the chat."

Rudy didn't move but simply nodded, turning to gaze back out the window as I fumbled with the doorknob and escaped into the fresh freedom of outdoors. I ran back across the field as fast as I could, certain that I could feel his eyes burning into my back all the way. At least, something Rudy had said made sense; there was no telling what can of worms I might open. I'd opened too many already!

THIRTEEN

The seal is set. Now welcome, thou dread power!
Nameless, yet thus omnipotent, which here
Walk'st in the shadow of the midnight hour
With a deep awe, yet all distinct from fear;
Thy haunts are ever where the dead walls rear
Their ivy mantles, and the solemn scene
Derives from thee a sense so deep and clear
That we become a part of what has been,
And grow unto the spot, all-seeing but unseen.

    George Gordon Byron, 6th Baron Byron of Rochdale
    Childe Harold's Pilgrimage, canto 4, stanza 145

When I went to visit Jenny, I was surprised to find her room empty. I was told she had been transferred to another hospital, but no one could—or would—tell me which one. Her mother was similarly reticent, unwilling to speak to me at all. When I went to her home to visit her, she left the chain lock fastened and peered out suspiciously through the crack of the door. She told me that Jenny was much improved and was recuperating slowly, but couldn't say when she'd be coming home.

"I'd like to see her," I said.

Mrs. Hampton shook her head adamantly. "She can't

have visitors," she said. "At least, not for a few weeks. Doctor's orders." She wouldn't discuss it further, and closed the door with barely a civil goodbye.

I puzzled about the mystery in the car on the way home. Perhaps Jenny had been transferred for her own protection. After all, whoever had shot her was still very much on the loose. I preferred to believe that this was the case, and not that Mrs. Hampton considered me a threat. Her attitude, however, worried me. It was one of mistrust and something else—something very much like fear.

Halloween arrived sooner than I'd hoped. It dawned bright and sunny, despite a pronounced chill in the air. The weather was probably the only aspect of the day that Alicia couldn't organize. She had been buzzing around the house over the past weeks with a new vitality that I'd never thought her capable of. She even looked healthier, and I wondered if it was because she'd controlled her addiction. I knew that she now attended therapy sessions at a drug rehabilitation clinic once a week. The hospital had been very strict about this, and surprisingly, she didn't seem to mind. She was now thoroughly absorbed in her role as hostess to what she called, "the party of the year," and I had to admire her industry.

The house had taken on a very real Halloween atmosphere. Sheaves of cornstalks tied with huge orange ribbons fronted by grinning jack-o'-lanterns graced the corners of the rooms. Crêpe bats dangled from chandeliers and ceilings, while yards of white gauzy material was draped over makeshift frames to resemble ghostly specters. Black cats with fiery red eyes, witches on broomsticks and ghoulish monsters were painted on the windows, and a full-sized skeleton sat on the piano stool, wearing an incongruous tophat and tailcoat as though ready to entertain.

All of the guests had responded, and I was surprised to

learn that most of them were coming. I supposed that the recent media hype regarding Dirkston Enterprises and the family had a lot to do with it. I was glad that Alicia had found a sense of purpose but, personally, I'd be happy when the whole affair was over. I still felt it was too soon after two tragic deaths for this sort of thing.

Grant had been gone for the past week, this time to Washington D.C. on business—or so he said. Darla had gone with him, which was a relief in one way, but irksome in another. I didn't like to think of her having all that time alone with Grant.

David and Colin were preoccupied with the marina. David had flown to Chicago to consult their accountant, while Colin was busy preparing for the onset of winter, poring over new advertising campaigns for the next year and making endless lists of repairs, equipment and improvements that were needed.

All three men had assured Alicia that they would be back in time for the party, but I had my doubts. I didn't mind having a few days to myself for a change. I hadn't realized how stifled I'd felt with both David or Grant hovering at my elbow. I tried to ignore the fact that Rudy was always lurking somewhere about the estate. Since our conversation, I felt I knew him even less than before, and it made me uneasy.

The lethargy and tiredness that had plagued me ever since the evening of my "spell," as everyone now called it, had eased somewhat. For the first time in weeks, I felt my strength returning. I cancelled an appointment I'd made to see a doctor, for it seemed probable that I had indeed been simply the victim of some potent viral attack.

When I came downstairs, Alicia was already on the phone to the caterer. I waved briefly as I passed, and she smiled distractedly. I followed the aroma of fresh-brewed coffee wafting from the kitchen.

Lottie was standing in the middle of the room, hands on hips, scowling as she gazed about at her domain. Every

available surface was covered with food. Platters of
morsels with colorful toothpicks sticking up, crustless
sandwich wedges, fruits, vegetables—all perfectly
wrapped in cellophane.

"Now you tell me, Miss Suzanna, how am I s'posed t'
get anything done in here?"

I smiled. "Maybe you shouldn't bother," I said. "Why
don't you take the day off? I think Alicia is having fun running the circus."

"Well…" Lottie shook her head doubtfully.

"She's having a catering firm supply most of the food
and drink. This is only the start. I understand it will take
three trips. By the time they're set up, no one will be able
to fit in here."

"Well…" she repeated, her lips pursed. "If you're sure
you won't need me?"

I smiled and hugged her. "We'll always need you,
Lottie. But I don't think you'd be able to stand what
they're going to do to your kitchen. Go home and have a
rest."

She nodded and smiled. "All right, Miss Suzanna, I
might jes do that." She looked around the kitchen once
more and sighed, "Never thought I'd see th' day that I
couldn't call this room my own!"

After Lottie left, I poured my coffee and took it
upstairs. It seemed to be the only part of the house that
didn't look like a scene from a horror movie. When I
reached the upper hall, I was surprised to see Martha just
shutting the door to my room. Martha firmly respected our
privacy, and never entered our bedrooms unless invited.

"Martha?" I queried.

She whirled, startled, and put a hand to her chest.

"Suzanna! You scared the daylights out of me!"

"Is there something you're looking for?" I asked, puzzled.

She blinked. "No, dear. No. I was…well, I did knock
and you didn't answer, so I thought…I know it's silly, but

since Alicia's—um—accident, I've been worried." She dropped her eyes and I could see that she was embarrassed.

I smiled and placed a comforting hand on her shoulder. "Don't worry, I'm not the overdosing type."

"Oh, no! I didn't mean…" She put a hand on my arm. "It's just that there have been so many accidents."

I nodded. "Yes, I see what you mean. Thanks for your concern." I bent down to stroke Kong, who had appeared from nowhere and was rubbing himself against my shins. "Is there something you wanted me for?" I asked.

"No. Nothing, really," she said. "I just thought that, since you haven't been feeling too well these past few weeks, that maybe you'd like to sleep in, and have breakfast in your room."

I smiled. "You really are trying to spoil me! Actually, I feel pretty good today. I must have finally shaken whatever it was."

"Well, that's good news, dear. Anyway, I'd best be getting downstairs. Alicia has a list of things a mile long for me to do."

"Don't you let her overwork you," I called after her.

Kong led the way into my room. I put my coffee cup down, went to the wardrobe and took out the altered wedding dress that I was compelled to wear that evening. Kong stood outside the closet and meowed.

"What's the matter, Kong, don't you like it?" I asked, amused.

He yowled again. Then, he got up and went into the closet. I watched, puzzled, as he stood up on his hind legs and stretched his front paws up the front of the set of drawers on one side of the hanging clothes. I followed the direction of his stretch, and suddenly felt a chill of apprehension. Pulling over a chair, I climbed up and felt along the shelf at the top of the closet, sighing with relief as my hand touched the box which I'd hidden there some days before. I pulled it out and carried it over to my bed. My mother's journals were inside. I gazed at them, puzzled. Something wasn't right. I was sure I'd put them in order before placing them in the box. Now, the most recent journal was on top instead of on the bottom. I took it out and thumbed through it. The blank page facing the section where the pages had been ripped out stared up at me. There, scrawled with thick, black marker in large, childish lettering, were the words: GET OUT WHILE YOU STILL CAN!

I sat down on the bed. I felt as though a heavy weight lay on my chest, making it hard for me to breathe. Blood pounded in my ears. Reality hit me with the full force of a falling boulder. This was danger—no longer ambiguous, no longer undirected—this was a direct threat, and it was meant for me!

I put the book down with shaking hands and tried to think. Could Martha have done this? My mind wanted to reject such a ridiculous premise, but the facts were there. She had been in my room. Anyone could have been in my room, logic reasoned. There was nothing to show when this message had been put in the book. I hadn't looked at the journals for at least two weeks.

Questions flooded in. Why had the message been scrawled in the journal? Why not left in a note in full view, where the perpetrator could be sure I'd see it? Perhaps for the very purpose of veiling the time. Whoever had put it here was willing to take the chance that I might never see it—or else, they knew me well enough to know that I'd bring the journals out again soon.

Who had access to my room? I had to admit that anyone could have done it. As far as I could remember, I had only spoken to three people about the journals: David, Martha and Grant. I'd told Grant about them in the car on the way to Leland. I'd also told him I'd burned them, but I wasn't certain he'd believed me.

Martha had always known the journals existed. It was she who put them in the attic in the first place. I had spoken to her about them. She could easily deduce that I'd brought them down to my room.

I had also discussed my suspicions regarding my mother's entries in the journals with David. He had listened, but hadn't seemed overly interested.

I stood up. I had to face it, anyone or everyone might have known of the journals, so I was back to where I'd started. I'd have to take the journal to the police. They'd know what to do. They might even be able to employ a handwriting analyst, though I didn't hold out much hope there. Whoever had written the words wouldn't be doing so in his or her regular hand.

There was a knock at the door. I thrust the journal swiftly back into its box and put the box back onto the top shelf, replacing the chair and shutting the wardrobe. Then, I opened the door.

"Suzanna, you've just got to help me!" It was Alicia. "I've just had a call from Madam Valenia. She's here, Suzanna, right here in Ludington! I've told her to come right out. She needs time to absorb the atmosphere of the house, she says. I just don't know what to do. I've got the caterers coming at one o'clock, and I'll have to give them their instructions and help set up the bar. I haven't even finished my costume yet!" She paused and looked at me curiously. "Are you all right? You look as pale as a ghost!" She laughed. "But I suppose that will help you fit right in, eh?"

I ignored the quip. "I'll take care of Madam what's-her-name, Alicia. You go finish what you were doing. Try to take it easy. You'll end up back in hospital if you don't slow down."

She flashed me a broad grin. "Oh, no, darling, no more white walls for me! This is just what I need!" And she turned and disappeared back down the stairs.

The police, I thought distractedly, would have to wait.

Madam Valenia wasn't what I would term your typical clairvoyant. I'd expected flowing crimson robes, bangles, beads, and dark gypsy features, but the woman I met at the door surprised me. She was younger than I'd expected, or perhaps she merely gave the impression of youth; either way, her face was smooth and unlined, with a porcelain complexion and a fresh, natural beauty. She was very petite, no taller than five feet, with flowing blonde hair that was tied back by a simple gold ribbon. She wore an expensive white woolen pantsuit with a high-collared black silk blouse. Her jewelry was impressive but tasteful: earrings of black onyx and gold, a gold chain at her throat, and a gold watch with a thin band that accentuated her delicate wrist. The only thing that could be construed as remotely ostentatious was the huge square ruby that flashed from a solitary ring on her finger. She smiled at me and stretched out her hand, which I took in stunned silence.

"You are surprised," she said. Her voice, too, was delicate, with a musical lilt.

"Yes," I said, regaining some composure. "I was expecting…I mean, I thought…"

"Don't be embarrassed," she said, and her hazel eyes twinkled. "It's a very common misconception. Television and cinema have a lot to answer for."

I smiled. I liked her immediately.

"Come in," I said, standing aside. "I'm Suzanna Dirkston. Alicia asked me to show you around. Would you like to freshen up? We've set aside a room for you."

"Actually, I've just come from the hotel. I make it a rule not to stay at my place of focus. It is often…mm-m…disruptive. But I'd like to put my things somewhere, if that's all right?"

I looked down at the large leather case and nodded. Together, we took it upstairs to a guest room not far from my own.

Afterward, we went on a tour of the house and

grounds. Valenia, as she preferred to be called, was interested in everything. Her eyes devoured every detail of every room; her small, graceful fingers gently touched furniture, walls, decorations and woodwork. I could almost observe her absorb the essence of the house, and I couldn't help but admire her capacity for information. Deep down, however, I was still skeptical.

When we reached the den, she stopped dead and I looked at her, puzzled. "Is something wrong?" I asked.

She held up a hand and her eyes roamed around the room. Then, purposefully, she strode across to the sliding doors and looked out at the pool.

"There has been violence here?" she asked.

"Well, yes and no," I replied. "My father died a few months ago; as you've probably heard, it was an accident. He struck his head on the side of the pool. But violence? Not really."

It was a lie, but the media hadn't been told about the murder investigation, and I wasn't going to be the first to mention it. For all I knew, Valenia might be fishing for information.

She turned and looked at me, and I could see that she didn't believe me. But she didn't pursue the subject, gesturing instead toward the pool, which was now hidden beneath its winter cover. "May I have a look?"

"By all means," I said and followed her out onto the patio. The wind was cold and I shivered, watching her as she made her way around the pool. At one point, she bent and placed a hand palm-down on the surface of the paving, closing her eyes as though in meditation. It struck me how angelic she looked, with her soft blonde hair wisping out from its ribbon like a halo, and her creamy skin almost translucent in the sunshine. Finally, she stood up, frowning, and stared off into the distance.

King Kong wandered out of the shrubbery and padded across the patio to her side. He sat down next to her and curled his tail around his legs. After a few moments,

Valenia turned her head and looked down at him. She smiled. "Ah, there you are," she said softly and bent to stroke the cat. He purred loudly and arched his back to her fingers. She looked at me. "He is for you," she said.

I didn't understand what she meant, but before I could ask, I heard the door open behind me and was surprised to see David.

"Suzanna!" He greeted me warmly. He caught me around the waist and gave me a quick kiss. "Did you miss me?" he murmured.

I pulled away, embarrassed. Wouldn't the tabloids like a photo of this! "David, this is Valenia De Luna, the clairvoyant."

David squinted against the sun, then smiled broadly. "Ah, our entertainment, eh?" He held out his hand. "Pleased to meet you, Madam!"

"Valenia, please," she corrected, taking his hand. Then, she turned suddenly to me, frowning. "Suzanna, if you don't mind, I think I might go to my room for a few moments. I am feeling a bit tired."

"Of course," I said. "Are you all right? Can I get you anything?"

She shook her head. I could see weariness and tension in her face. "No, nothing. I'll be all right after a quick rest. Please don't worry. I often feel overwhelmed at the start. I just need time to assimilate. You needn't come. I can find the way." She nodded to David and disappeared into the house.

"Well," David said. "Was it something I said?"

I gazed after her. "Perhaps it was something you did."

"What do you mean?"

I sighed. "Oh, David. You know what Grant said about creating further scandal."

"What scandal?" he asked. "What's wrong with giving an close friend a kiss?"

I looked at him and could see the irritation on his face, and I knew without a doubt that it was plain and simple jealousy. This time, however, instead of feeling pleased, I felt only pity.

"All right," I said, "I'm sorry." I went to him and reached up and kissed him. "I did miss you," I lied. "How was the trip? Did you sort out all your problems?"

He wrapped his arms around me, assuaged. "The trip was boring. I was stuck for three hours at O'Hare because of flight delays. The accountant was late for the meeting. But, I think we're finally seeing some light at the end of the tunnel. If we can just see a good season this year, we might even see our way out of the red. Now, how about you? Any problems while I was gone?"

I pulled away from him gently. "No, not really." I wouldn't tell him about the message in the journal. I wanted to take that particular information to the police before I told anyone. "I'll just be glad when this party is over," I said.

"Yes," he agreed. "Alicia will certainly be in her element! But I personally don't go in for big shindigs. Especially so soon after..." He put his hands in his pockets and turned to look out over the lake.

I placed a hand on his arm. "I know," I said feelingly.

He looked down at me, and I saw the pain of grief in his eyes. He nodded. "You're probably the only one who really does know," he said. I went back into his arms and we held each other, finding comfort in the sharing of loss.

Guests began arriving throughout the afternoon. The majority of them were from out of town and, once they'd checked into hotels, motels or bed-and-breakfasts, came directly to Beacon. It was like a great reunion where I was the odd man out. I knew very few faces and fewer names. Some of the guests were quite famous in their own right, and arrived in limousines or Cadillacs, having flown in by private plane or jet. It was probably one of the biggest events in the history of this small, unassuming area, but because we had been meticulously careful to avoid publicity, there were, as yet, no reporters or camera crews. Still, we had hired additional security—four more men, two to check visitors at the house and two to roam the grounds at random and keep an eye on the beach access. It wouldn't be the first time the media tried to sneak pictures of Beacon parties by approaching via the beach. We didn't want any surprises today.

The ballroom had been opened up for the first time in years and, though it was normally a cold room even in summer, tonight it glowed invitingly. There was a raised dais at one end where a string quartet, at the moment, provided background music for the guests milling about. There was indirect lighting along the walls while two enormous crystal chandeliers lit the dance floor like something out of Cinderella. Later, there would be a dance band.

The costumes that I'd seen so far were stunning. Already there were four vampires, three witches, a banshee, a hunchback, three Frankensteins and at least two aliens. I felt somewhat unremarkable in my mother's white wedding dress. Alicia had helped me with makeup, powdering my face and hands so that my skin was deathly white, brushing dark shadow around my eyes to give them a sunken look, and painting my lips blood-red. I refused to wear the fake fangs. It was impossible to speak clearly with them, and I felt they were just too childish.

Alicia looked magnificent in a black gauzy creation that clung to her thin frame from neck to ankle. A filmy shroud covered her head and face, and draped over long sleeves that were also hung with black, cobweb-like veiling. She carried a long cigarette holder and her nails were painted black. She looked like a macabre wraith, drifting from group to group as though on roller skates. I could tell she was enjoying herself, even though she only lifted the veil occasionally to sip a drink or eat a tidbit.

Velenia appeared as the antithesis to Alicia, dressed in a flowing white caftan with golden serpents at her wrists and around her forehead, and golden sandals on her feet. She truly looked like a goddess.

David was quite handsome, dressed as Don Quixote, with a black, red-satin lined cape and form fitting black tights and doublet. His blond hair, however, looked somewhat incongruous beneath the jaunty plumed hat. I couldn't help but smile.

"Is it that bad?" he asked, concerned.

"No, no!" I said, chuckling. "You look wonderful! I was just noticing your fair hair. I'd never thought of Don Quixote as a blond."

He smiled. "I had a wig, but it was one of those curled white pompous affairs, and I absolutely refused. Alicia thought this up."

"Yes. She has a talent for it, doesn't she?" I said sarcastically. I let my gaze wander around the room. "Have you seen Colin? Or Grant? I thought they promised to be here."

He shook his head. "I haven't seen Grant, but Colin is getting dressed at this very moment. Wait until you see what Alicia has come up with for him!"

I didn't have long to wait. Five minutes later, I looked up to see Colin descending the stairs, a huge scowl on his face, wearing a voluminous pink frilled, floor-length dress, a long blonde wig and carrying a shepherd's crook. It was too much for me. I burst out laughing. Colin turned at the sound and glared at me darkly, before Alicia drifted up to claim him and integrate him into a chattering group near the base of the stairs. David had turned aside to hide his own smile.

"Little Bo Peep?" I chortled.

"It's Alicia's way of getting even, I think," David nodded. He glanced at his watch. "They're planning a séance in a few minutes. I think I'll make myself scarce and check on the new security guards. I don't think I could stand sitting through all that hocus-pocus nonsense. Do you mind?"

"No, not at all. Maybe I should go with you?"

He shook his head. "No, you stay. You might enjoy it. Besides, one of us should keep an eye on Alicia—just to make sure she doesn't overdo, if you know what I mean. I don't think Colin really notices."

I nodded seeing the sense in this. I'd been watching Alicia. It seemed that she was only drinking apple cider, but I was certain she'd be strongly tempted to take something alcoholic. Besides, despite my reservations, I was curious to see how Madam Valenia operated. I'd never attended a professionally conducted séance.

The séance itself was limited to ten people, all of whom were nominated by Alicia. The rest of the party moved to the ballroom, where a variety of semi-famous musicians with names like Nudist Monks, Nuked Kittens and Hell's Toilet had already begun to perform. I was glad in this respect that I'd been selected to join in the séance. It assumed it was my midwest conservatism that kept me from appreciating their style of music.

The chosen ten assembled in the living room. Cushions were placed in a circle in the middle of the floor, and candles were lit to create an aura of mystery and suspense. I sat quietly next to the skeleton on the piano bench and assessed the people assembling. Alicia chatted with Robert and Louisa Masterson, both out-of-work actors, who were dressed as Henry VIII and Anne Boleyn. Colin, who had discarded his wig and crook, stood near the fireplace sipping a large glass of bourbon. He looked understandably uncomfortable. He had never learned to enjoy Alicia's crowd of people and, dressed as he was, must have felt ridiculous. I silently applauded him, though, for bowing to Alicia's whim. It took a certain strength of character to allow oneself to be put on display in such a manner.

There was Jonathan Hutchins, the famous hairdresser, who came as the Scarlet Pimpernel complete with lace-cuffed shirt, tailcoat, buff-colored leggings, red-velvet knee-boots and an elaborate powdered wig. He was happily chatting with Edna Murcheson, a costume designer. She was an exceedingly large lady who, despite her profession, had made little effort to create her own costume, wearing simply a voluminous multi-colored batik caftan with matching turban, which was wound masterfully around her head and fastened with a huge shimmering blue brooch. From what I'd heard, she had helped with a good many of the costumes worn by others, and most probably gleaned satisfaction from those.

Alicia excused herself from her friends and hurried over to me. "Suzanna, where's Grant? He and Darla are supposed to make up the rest of the party."

"I haven't seen either of them, Alicia. Have they come back from Chicago?"

"Yes. I saw them ten minutes ago. Oh, thank God! Here they are." She hurried off with a swish of veils.

Grant and Darla stood in the doorway, gazing about the room. Grant had chosen the old west as his motif, dressed in boots, buckskins and sporting a Stetson hat. He'd even managed to find some very real looking six-shooters, which were slung low on his hips. Darla was the perfect saloon girl in a red-flounced, form-fitting dress that revealed more of her bosom than it covered. She had one side of her hair pulled back with an artificial rose fastened in it. They both caught my eye at the same time. Grant winked and smiled; Darla lifted the corners of her mouth and slipped her hand through the crook of Grant's arm.

"I think that we're all here." Valenia's quiet voice somehow penetrated the din of multiple conversations. "Why don't you all choose a cushion? Please try to keep the circle as closed as possible. I shall sit here, at the end. Alicia, perhaps you could get the lights?"

With much chuckling and groaning, we did as directed. Alicia pulled the doors shut and lit candles around the room with a long taper. There was one large candle in the center of our circle. It was already dark outside, so there was no need to draw the draperies. Valenia sat very erect and poised, her face relaxed, her eyes shut.

"You should have worn that dress at our wedding, Suzie," Grant said, taking the cushion next to mine.

"A bit too elegant for signing a short-term partnership agreement, don't you think?"

He smiled, and his teeth were very white in the flickering candlelight. "You'd better watch what you say; these guns are real, you know."

"Be careful not to shoot your foot off, then—although that would probably be difficult, considering it's usually in your mouth."

"Are we all ready?" Valenia asked.

Alicia squirmed into her place between Colin and me and nodded.

"We must join hands to form an unbroken chain. It's easier for the other world to speak through us if we present a strong channel. Please take the hand of the persons on either side of you, and don't let go for any reason or the channel will be broken."

I took Alicia's hand. It was clammy and cold, and my misgivings returned. Despite her seemingly happy-go-lucky attitude, she was nervous. Grant's hand was warm and strong, and I felt slightly comforted.

"We must be silent. We must concentrate. Watch the candle. Open your minds. Allow the other world to speak." Valenia sat very straight and still. I could see the flame dance in her eyes. The other faces around the circle were cast in goulish shadow. I shivered. Grant's hand squeezed mine.

The room was hushed, except for quiet breathing. There was the dull thrum of the music from the other side of the house, but it only seemed to accentuate the silence in the room. I stared at the candle flame, letting my thoughts drift, fascinated by the dance and flicker of the yellow glow and the thin line of smoke rising from its point.

Valenia began to speak even more softly than before, a

dull monotone, soothing to the ear. "We are open to you. We are here. Come to us. Speak to us. We are open."

Her voice lulled me. The candlelight drew me. I felt my breathing slow. Alicia's hand was relaxed in mine.

"I feel a great warmth." Valenia's voice hadn't changed its pitch. "Is there someone there? Speak to us. We are open."

My eyes were feeling heavy. The candle flame blurred. Valenia's voice droned on. I couldn't keep my eyes open any longer. I shut them, and felt myself float free and drift away into blessed darkness.

"Suzanna, wake up!"

I groaned and opened my eyes to a blinding glare. I raised a hand to shield my eyes. Faces were grouped over me. The chandelier above bored light into my brain, making my head throb.

"Give her some water, someone. Suzanna, are you all right?"

"Yes—yes, I think so. What happened?"

I struggled to sit up, placing a hand to my throbbing temples. Someone shoved a glass of water under my nose and I took it shakily.

Alicia squatted in front of me, her eyes as big as saucers.

"You said: Don't let them get away with it, Suzanna. What did you mean?"

"She's been under a lot of stress." This was Grant's voice.

"But her voice! It was so deep—like a man's!" Jonathan Hutchins was obviously awestruck.

"Suzanna." I looked at Grant; his eyes were wary. "Do you remember anything?"

I frowned. "No, not really. I remember the candle and Valenia's voice. Then, I remember feeling very, very tired and I closed my eyes and...and then I woke up."

"It isn't uncommon for the other world to choose its own channel." Valenia seemed unconcerned. "You will be all right in a moment. Drink the water."

I did as she said, realizing that my throat was slightly parched.

"I felt a presence in this house the moment I came," she said. "Perhaps more than one. I also felt a strong frustration. There is a great need here. Does the message mean anything to any of you?"

There was a great deal of low muttering, but no one seemed to want to suggest anything. Finally, it was Alicia who said what was in everyone's minds.

"Perhaps it was Giles—or Leo," she said, her voice shaking. "Perhaps he's telling us that he was murdered!"

The last word came out a bit too high-pitched—strained.

Grant turned to Colin and murmured something. Colin nodded dazedly and went to Alicia, coaxing her to her feet and escorting her from the room She was sobbing, and leaned heavily on his arm.

Valenia extended a hand to me and I stood up. I felt better and my head was clear. She smiled. "You've missed your calling," she said, then turned to the others. "Obviously, we're finished. Thank you all for your cooperation. I, too, am feeling a bit tired. I will go to my room."

With Valenia's departure, the rest of the company began to disperse with curious backward glances in my direction. I took my empty glass over to the table, still confused and more than a little concerned. Why couldn't I remember? And what was it about the message that rang a bell?

"That was an excellent performance, Suzie." Grant stood at my elbow, his mouth twisted in wry amusement.

"What do you mean?"

"Oh, come now! Are you going to say that you and Madam Valenia didn't put this whole concoction together this afternoon?"

"I don't know what you're talking about!"

He shrugged. "Right. Well, suit yourself. But I think it was a pretty vicious thing to do to Alicia."

I was too astounded to do anything but gape at him.

"Grant, I could really use a drink, how about you?" Darla beckoned from the doorway.

"Yea, a double—on the rocks." he said, and left before I could gather my wits.

His accusation hurt. And worst of all, there was no way I could prove him wrong. I wondered shamefully if Grant was alone in his belief, or if everyone suspected I had manufactured the episode. This was too much! The news would spread quickly throughout the rest of the party, and I'd be a laughing stock. I needed to get away from them all. I needed to talk to David.

The night was cool, and I immediately regretted not grabbing a jacket. I stood on the sandy bluff at the top of the beach steps, staring out across the inky expanse. The wind blew strongly, moaning morosely, setting the reeds and grasses shivering. The house behind me was lit like a birthday cake. The sound of music and laughter, the clink of glasses and the gabble of voices drifted out, muted by distance. I wrapped my arms around me and searched the beach. David must be out here somewhere, unless he'd gone back in during the séance and was hiding out upstairs.

I was just about to turn and go, when a light caught my eye. I stared through the dark and was rewarded to see it again—just a flash, then gone. I frowned. It was coming from the room at the top of the lighthouse. No one should be up there. The entrance had been boarded up long ago, the structure itself deemed unsafe. Leo would have had it pulled down years ago, if not for the local historical association who were continually trying to raise enough revenue to restore it. If one of the guests had decided to do some exploring, they could very well end up hurt.

I wondered vaguely where the security guards were as I hurried down the steps and across the beach, making my way to the rocky spit. The tide was rising, but it would be a while before it reached its full height. I stood on the rocks and peered up the sheer walls to the small balustraded walkway that ringed the top. There was a window just below it, and I could barely make out a dull glow coming from within.

Slowly, I felt my way across the rocks. I was stupid to have come without a flashlight but, I reasoned, if I went back for one, whoever was in there might be gone before I could confront them. My dress hindered my progress. I pulled the white skirt as high as possible and tied it up on one side to keep it from encumbering my movements. I was glad that I'd worn flat shoes.

The entrance appeared untouched. All the boards were in place. I pulled at them tentatively and found that one whole side had been loosened and came away easily, leaving a good-sized gap to squeeze through.

Don't let them get away with it! The message replayed in my mind. Where had it come from? Why had I said it? And why now, of all times, did it suddenly fill my head? And then I remembered: It had been Rudy Coleman who had said those same words—words spoken by my father in a ghastly dream. Coincidence? I shivered and reached a hand out in the dark interior to touch a heavy spider web. I must concentrate on what I was doing. There would be time later to ponder that incident.

The moonlight fell across the stone floor through the gap where I entered, barely illuminating the winding staircase. The steps were of stone, set against the wall, circling up into the blackness above. I started up, one hand on the wall, the other on a banister that felt none too secure. I heard a faint scuffling coming from above. I should call out—there was really no need for me to go up at all. But something kept me mute. Some inner voice bade me to go slowly, carefully, and most of all, quietly.

I crept on, feeling with each step, keeping as close to the wall as possible. I soon stopped holding the railing, for I found that it was very loose and there were huge sections missing altogether. The darkness was all-consuming, stifling, like the air which was stale and musty, heavy with mildew and mold. The wall under my hand was damp and furred, fissured with cracks that attested to the deterioration of the foundation.

By the time I was halfway up, my heart was beating uncontrollably and I had to pause, a cold sweat beginning dampen my palms and underarms. I knew now why I hadn't called up. The movements above weren't reckless. There was no laughter or raucous noise, as one would expect from people who may have left the party for a bit of exploration. Whoever was here, was here for a reason, and instinct told me that he or she wouldn't welcome discovery.

For a moment, I hesitated. I should go back and get help. If I could find David or Grant or Colin—or one of the security guards…! But, having come this far, I was unwilling to retreat. Pure, illogical curiosity kept me moving upward.

FOURTEEN

By these storm-sculptured stones while centuries fled?
The stones remain; their stillness can outlast
The skies of history hurrying overhead.
  Jean-Paul Satre
  The Heart's Journey, pt 9

It didn't take long at all to reach the top, although at the time it seemed a very slow, painstaking ordeal. The last arc of the stairs was illuminated by the wash of light coming from the room above. At this point, I was able to see instead of just feeling my way on. The light flickered and danced on the wall opposite the steps, interrupted intermittently by a huge, distorted shadow that could barely be identified as human.

When I reached the top, I leaned flat against the wall to one side of the doorway and tried to calm my breathing. My palms were perspiring, and I wiped them on my hoisted skirt. Finally, with thudding heart, I peeped around the door jamb. There, in the small upper gallery, a man squatted. His back was to me, and a lantern stood on the wooden floor nearby. I couldn't make out what he was doing, but I recognized who it was instantly and felt a flood of relief that nearly made my knees buckle.

With a chuckle at my inanity, I stepped through the door. "David! What are you doing up here?" I asked. "I've been looking everywhere for you."

I'd obviously taken him by surprise, for his back stiffened and his head jerked around, and in that split second I glimpsed a large briefcase lying open on the floor in front of him. He slammed it shut immediately and stood up to face me, but I had already seen what was inside, and there was no way I could disguise this fact.

"Suzanna!" he said gruffly, "You shouldn't sneak up on a person like that." He searched my face, reading the surprise and confusion there. He took a step toward me. In the dancing lantern flame, his face was unreadable and threatening and I automatically took a step back.

"What are you doing up here?" I asked again. Something inside me had grown very alert.

David tilted his head to one side and smiled. "You shouldn't have come, Suzanna."

"I saw the light," I said. "I thought someone might be in danger. This place isn't safe, you know."

He didn't reply immediately, still searching my face. Finally, he sighed, squatted down to the briefcase again and threw the lid open, stepping back so I could see clearly.

"It'll bring in a lot of money," he said proudly.

I stared at the neat bags of white powder, racking my brain for a logical explanation. Perhaps he'd found it up here. Perhaps it wasn't what I thought it was. But deceiving myself was useless. Like an animal that smells danger, I smelled corruption, and David was at the center.

"Where did you get it, David?" My voice was cold.

"Get it?" he smiled. "Oh, don't worry, darling, I don't use it. I merely pass it on to some friends of mine. They pay me well for my help."

I frowned. "Who are these friends, David? How could you get mixed up in this sort of thing?"

He shrugged. "It's a long story. Come here. I'll show

you something."

He moved to the little window in the stone wall. I hesitated, but went to look where he was indicating.

"See that light out there?"

I followed his pointing finger, peering into the night gloom, stiffening when his arm dropped casually around my shoulders. Far out on the water, I could make out a signal beam.

"Who is it?" I asked.

"I'm meeting them," he said, his breath tickling my ear. "We've got business to do."

"David," I tried to make my voice calm, "what sort of games are you playing? Does this have anything to do with the marina? Are you in some sort of financial dilemma?"

"No," he said. "Not the marina. This is just for me—at least now, anyway. It was going to be for both of us—you and me—but you turned your back on me. You see, I knew you wouldn't want to be married to a pauper. Especially after all the luxuries you've been used to."

"What do you mean?"

He snorted and his arm tightened around my shoulders. "Oh, come now, Suzanna! Little rich Suzanna? Don't tell me you'd accept anything less than what Daddy has given you all these years?"

I tried to pull away, but he tightened his grip. "David, I don't know what you're talking about. Let me go!"

But he didn't relinquish his hold and, as I looked up into his face, I saw an expression of pure malice which made me suddenly very afraid.

"No, Suzanna, for once you're going to listen. You're going to hear all of it," he said. "You couldn't leave well enough alone, could you? Well, it doesn't matter now. All this could have been for us. Now, it's only for me. It's my turn for a piece of the cake."

I struggled to get loose, but it was useless. He pushed me up against the wall and pinned my shoulders. I felt the rough stone biting into my back.

"You know, it's all your fault," he said through clenched teeth. "Yours and Leo's!" He was breathing heavily, and I could see his eyes were dilated and dark. "I was the only one besides Leo who loved Beacon! I was the one who should have had it. You—Colin—you've never learned to appreciate it. If you'd married me, Beacon would have been mine, and none of this would have happened. But then, how was I to know that Daddy had other plans for you?"

He was squeezing my shoulders so tightly I had to bite my lip. "Please, David. You're hurting me!"

Abruptly, he seemed to come out of his thoughts and focus on my face. "Am I?" He loosened his grip slightly, but didn't let me go. "You know, you've hurt me, too, Suzanna. More than you'll ever know." Suddenly, his eyes misted. "How could you marry that bastard? How could you throw away what we had?"

"You know why, David." I was trying to sound calm, but I'd never seen him so erratic. I didn't want to provoke him. "If I hadn't, we all would have lost Beacon."

"Yes. Yes," he murmured, as if to himself. "We wouldn't want that…"

I watched as a muscle worked in his jaw. I must take advantage of his confusion. "Let me go, David. We can work all this out. I'm sure there's a logical way to explain the drugs and…and, well, Grant is a good attorney. Surely, he would…"

But I knew the minute I said the name that I'd made a tragic mistake. He shoved me hard against the wall; my neck snapped back and my head hit with a stunning force.

"Grant! Grant! Grant!" he shouted. "It's always been Grant with you! It only proves that you're not worthy. Anyone who could love a whore's bastard doesn't deserve Beacon!"

He was fumbling with his belt, and for one wild moment, I thought he was going to rape me. Instead, he whirled me around roughly and brought my wrists together behind my back, wrapping them tightly with the belt and fastening it so that my hands were useless.

"David, please! I don't understand what you're doing!" I was sobbing, now, confusion mingling with fear. This was a David I'd never known. This was a David out of control—maybe even mad. I didn't know what to do—didn't know what he would do.

"Shut up!" he snapped, slapping me hard so that lights danced in my head and I fell backward to the floor. Before I was able to recover, he grabbed my skirt and ripped a long strip from it, tying it firmly around my ankles so that I was totally powerless. My head still spun from the slap, and it took some minutes to catch my breath. He stood over me, fists clenched, as I writhed helplessly.

"Beacon should have been mine!" he said in a low growl. "Leo took it away from me! He found out about the drugs. I tried to tell him it was for us—all that money. Do you know how much money you can make trafficking drugs? No, you wouldn't. You're too lily white! Always had plenty, haven't you?" His mouth lifted in a sneer and I cringed, afraid he would kick me.

Instead, he began to pace. "Leo was going to tell everyone, forbid you to marry me. He'd even threatened to turn me in to the police. I had to kill him. He wouldn't listen to reason."

I was too stunned to speak. That David was running drugs was unbelievable. That he had killed my father was totally incomprehensible

"This was to be the last time, you know," he said. "After Dad found out and…" He rubbed his eyes hard.

"It was you who ran your father down with the speedboat?" I whispered incredulously.

"Dad overheard my arrangements for this haul. He was going to tell you—he always sided with you, with Leo—it was his own fault! If it hadn't been for him, I never would have started selling. It was easy, you see. He always left his big black 'I'm-a-respectable-doctor' bag lying around.

And then mother—she always had plenty of pills. She never even missed them. I found out at school how rewarding pill-pushing could be! And Jenny? Well, a nice target she was! Did you know that she and I were an item? No, I didn't think so. We kept it very quiet. I spent a lot of time in New York. She's the one who introduced me to Benny. 'Want to make some big bucks?' Benny said, and within months I was rich. All they wanted was a middle-man. Someone to move the stuff. Is that so bad?"

I listened, aghast, to his rambling tale, wondering if this was some sort of cruel joke. But my throbbing head and wrists told me otherwise.

He moved to the window, stooped to pick up a pair of binoculars and gazed for some minutes into the blackness outside. He seemed calmer now, and continued to talk, half to me, half to himself.

"Jenny shouldn't have come back. I warned her to stay away. She never knew all of it, mind you, but I wasn't going to take any chances. She was having pangs of guilt—could have ruined everything."

"So, you were the sniper at the river?" I said, trying to keep my voice calm, testing my restraints.

"I wasn't trying to kill her, you understand, just warn her. It did the trick."

"But why the drugs, David? If we'd married, Beacon would have been yours and you would have had access to my inheritance."

He laughed harshly. "That's what I thought, too, at first. But Leo was a wily old devil. He wasn't going to let me have a penny that I didn't earn. He wanted me to sign a prenuptial agreement ensuring that Beacon would stay in your name, along with the money and holdings. I wouldn't have been any better off than I am now. I'd have had to grovel for every penny, and that's one thing I'll never do. No, I want Beacon, but I want it in my own right. Besides, I get a great deal of satisfaction from using Dirkston Enterprises to make me rich."

"What do you mean?"

He glanced over, smiling. "The plane, Suzanna! We bring the stuff in in the seaplane! Smack, Fantasy, Ecstasy, Crack, Cocaine—whatever the latest craze—in the pontoons! It's as simple as ABC—though I can't take all the credit for working it out. Mike's the one who came up with the idea."

I remembered the day I had seen Mike Kensington squatting over the pontoon on the seaplane. He had seemed intent on something, now I knew what. David saw recollection in my expression.

"Yes," he said, "Mike insisted that you hadn't seen anything that day, that even if you had, you wouldn't have put two and two together. I wasn't so sure. You were a problem from the beginning, Suzanna. If you'd only minded your own business…but no, you had to start snooping. It's a trait in you that I've always abhorred—meddling curiosity. I would have cured you of that, given time.

"Once you found the poker, I knew there was no going back. I knew you wouldn't rest until you'd put the puzzle together. And when you married Fenton, I tried to convince myself that you only did it to save Beacon. I thought that after the year was out, you'd leave him and come back to me, until I began to watch the two of you together. Then, I saw the truth. It became obvious that I wasn't going to get Beacon by marrying you, so my only alternative was to invalidate your inheritance."

At my puzzled look, he waved an expansive hand.

"It all seems complicated to you, I know, but really it's quite simple. Who would inherit Beacon if something were to happen to you?"

"I—I don't know."

He snorted. "Little Miss Naive! No, I suppose you wouldn't. Well, it would go to Colin, and Colin is nearly as easy to manipulate as you. He's so far in debt that he'd sell his own mother, if someone offered him a cent! Not to mention that his lady fair, Alicia-dahling, has been under my power ever since she arrived."

"You gave her the drugs?"

"Sure. She had an itch, and I had the means to scratch it."

"But she's off them now," I said with false conviction.

He looked at me and cocked an eyebrow. "You really are an innocent, Suzanna. All I'd have to do is…" and he snapped his fingers with a click, "…and she'd be right back onto them—worse than ever."

"Does Colin know? About the drugs?"

"Hell, no. He's blind to anything he doesn't want to see. Besides, he's never had a head for business, and is quite happy to let me do the bookkeeping and organization at the marina. Without me, Colin would be nothing."

I bit my lip and tried to get more comfortable. The floorboards were digging into my hip, and I was losing sensation in my fingers. I wanted to keep him talking. I didn't know what he planned to do with me, but I knew my only chance was to stall him long enough for someone to come looking for us.

"So, you decided to get rid of me, then?" I prompted.

He made a wry face. "No, more's the pity. Actually, I'd grown quite fond of you. I guess I even hoped I was wrong, and that you'd see sense and come back to me. But I did figure I could alter your credibility a bit—make people wonder about your mental state."

I felt chilled. "How?"

He reached into his pocket and held up a smaller bag of powder. "It's all here. Mind control in a bag. A bit in your cocoa…a bit in your tea." He made an exaggerated shudder. "Nasty dreams! Strange hallucinations!"

I gaped at him. His teeth were very even when he smiled.

"Actually, you gave me the idea yourself," he said. "The night you nearly drowned in the pool—said you saw Daddy. They all thought you were having some sort of breakdown. Well, I figured I might just help it along."

"And my mother?" I whispered. It was too much to

believe. The man before me now was a stranger.

"Yes." He thrust his hands deep into his pockets and turned back to the window. "Anna. She never liked me, you know. Shouldn't have written all that about me in her diaries. How could she possibly know what I was like? I hated her, rich bitch! But did I kill her, you ask?" He looked at me again and shrugged. "Unfortunately, no. That was Colin's doing."

I gasped. "Colin?"

He waved a hand. "Oh, not like you think. It was just a prank. You know, like the ones we used to do back then? A practical joke. He was actually trying to get Grant into trouble. After Rudy saddled up the horses, Colin loosened the cinch; no one saw him. After Anna took a tumble, he was going to blame Grant. Colin really resented Grant in those days. He'd do anything to get Grant in hot water with Leo. He hadn't meant for her to die. I suppose he felt pretty bad about it afterward. But it worked miracles for me."

"What do you mean?"

"Mind control, Suzanna! There's only one thing better than drugs to control the mind, and that's guilt. All this time, I was the only one who knew Colin's secret. How do you think I managed to keep him in line all these years?"

I let out my breath in a long sigh, squeezing my eyes shut, trying to block out the disgusting revelations that were spilling from his mouth. "So, you're the one who tore the pages from Mother's journal?"

He nodded. "I'd nearly forgotten about them. Then, when I heard you'd been poking around in the attic, I remembered." He chuckled. "I must say, I had to stay on my toes to keep one step ahead of you!"

"And the message? 'Get out while you still can'?"

"Yes. You see? I never really wanted to hurt you. If only you'd done as you were told, you wouldn't be in the predicament you're in now."

I felt sick. He turned away from me and raised the

binoculars to his eyes. His silence accentuated the sound of the wind moaning around the upper parapet and gusting through the window. I craned my neck, searching for something sharp, something that might cut my bonds.

Suddenly, he turned to me, his face set. "They're coming to get me now," he said. "I've got to go. I'm sorry it had to end like this, Suzanna. I'll miss you."

He picked up the briefcase and the lantern and disappeared through the door, leaving me in darkness, alone and helpless, but immensely relieved that he hadn't seen fit to kill me first.

I allowed my eyes to become accustomed to the dark, and was eventually able to make out moonlight coming in through the window. I rolled onto my stomach and squirmed over to the wall. Feeling carefully, I found a bit of raised ridge in the stone, testament to the rough masonry of past decades. I struggled to a sitting position, my back against the wall, and began to drag the leather belt binding my wrists up and down over the jagged ridge. I felt the stone slicing into my skin, but forced myself to persevere. After some minutes, I paused, my arms aching. I sniffed the air, curiously aware of an acrid smell that I hadn't noticed before. I began to rub harder, feeling blood trickle down and drip from my fingertips. The odor was growing. In a flash, it dawned on me what is was: smoke!

I peered through the dark toward the door and saw a vague, incandescent flicker. My heart began to thud in my chest. David hadn't shown mercy after all. He had set the lighthouse on fire and left me here to burn!

Frantic, I scraped harder at the belt. Despite its stone exterior, there was plenty of wood inside this old building, and all of it brittle enough to easily catch alight. By the time the belt snapped, I was oblivious to any pain. The smoke was heavier now, and my nose and eyes watered fitfully. Coughing uncontrollably, I fumbled with the bindings on my ankles, cursing my slippery, numb fingers. After what seemed an eternity, the knot came free and I stood up shakily and stumbled to the door, covering my mouth and nose with one hand. Flames danced far below, and I could see they had already started up the stairs.

I whirled and ran to the window, thrusting my head out, away from the smoke, gasping desperately for air.

"Suzanna!"

I looked down. Grant was making his way across the rocks below, while further along I saw Colin sprinting down the beach from the steps.

"Grant!" I cried. "The lighthouse is on fire! I can't get out!"

"I'm coming up!" he shouted.

"You can't," I began, but he'd already disappeared.

It was only a matter of moments before he burst into the room, slapping frantically at his clothing. He'd doused his shirt in water and wrapped it around his head. It, too, was steaming and he threw it off quickly.

I stared at him numbly, unable to move, feeling my legs become weak.

"Oh, Grant!" I whispered. "Thank God!" My knees buckled.

He was across the room in an instant, scooping me into his arms, holding me close so that I could feel his heart beating and smell the singed hair on his chest. There was no need to speak. All the feelings that I had tried so desperately to deny broke free, and it was as if our spirits met and merged. The sensation lasted only a few seconds, but it was enough to topple all barriers, and we both knew there was no turning back.

It was a guttural yowl that broke us apart. Spinning around, we stared in mutual surprise at Kong, standing, tail erect, in the center of the room.

"How did he get up here?" I exclaimed, through fits of coughing.

"I don't know," Grant replied. "But I think he's trying to

tell us something. Look."

The cat began to pace in a circle, tail twitching, crying plaintively, his eyes fixed upward. I followed his gaze, my eyes streaming with tears from the smoke. But I was just able to make out an outline in the ceiling.

"Grant! Look there! I think it's a way out."

He looked to where I pointed, and hurried over to the spot. Sure enough, it was a trap door. By standing on tip-toe, he was just able to reach the handle. It took some moments of tugging, but finally, in a whoosh of dust and cobwebs, it came free and a narrow set of steps concerti-naed down.

"Get up!" Grant said, giving me a quick shove.

I didn't need encouragement but climbed the rickety steps quickly, squeezing through the small hole above to find myself at the very top of the lighthouse. I crawled away from the hole on my hands and knees, heedless of the shards of broken glass cutting my flesh, grateful for the clean night air. Grant was up behind me, and pulled the trapdoor shut to keep the smoke contained below.

I looked around me. In the center of the platform was the working part of the lighthouse: the beacon, its mirrors shattered, its lamp long since destroyed. The glass beneath my hands and knees was all that remained. Our perch was protected by a stone parapet that rose to about three feet. It had crumbled in parts, and I saw huge cracks where stone and mortar were ready to fall to the sea below. Seagulls had left inordinate amounts of droppings, which had hardened over time and made the surfaces even rougher.

Grant was inspecting the walls, peering down over the edge.

"What will we do now?" I asked, exhausted from coughing, wiping my eyes with a piece of cloth I'd ripped from the skirt of my dress.

But Grant didn't answer immediately. He waved an arm in a wide arc. I stood up and went to stand beside him. Far down below was Colin. He was holding a high-powered spear gun, one that we kept in the boathouse for scuba fishing.

"Go ahead, Colin!" Grant yelled. Then, he turned to me. "Get down low, Suzie. He's going to shoot."

I dropped automatically. Within moments, I heard a pop and a chink.

Grant cursed. "Not high enough," he muttered, then yelled, "Hurry, Colin!"

There was another pop and a zing, and I saw the spear clatter across the floor a few feet beyond me. Grant grabbed the line attached to it and began to haul it in, hand over hand. I jumped to my feet and watched as he pulled up a rope which had been affixed to the end of the line. I waved an arm at Colin. At the same time, I saw flames licking out the window of the room where we'd just been.

"Grant, look!" I gasped.

Grant's face paled slightly. "We'll have to hurry."

The frame around the spotlight was of steel, and it was the only thing safe enough to tie the rope to.

"You're going down first," Grant said. "Get out of that dress. It's too cumbersome."

I didn't argue but pulled the now torn and filthy gown off, watching, shivering, in my underwear, as he made a harness in the end of the rope. He held it open. and I slipped it over my head and down around the back of my thighs.

"I'll lower you down," he said, "but you'll have to keep yourself steady. Just hold your feet out to keep from swinging into the wall. Are you okay?"

I nodded, trying not to tremble, my teeth chattering with fright and cold.

He didn't give me time to think but lifted me over the edge of the wall, facing the open lake. This was the only unbroken expanse of wall. We couldn't take the risk of the fire catching the rope aflame by going too near the window.

I was petrified. Suddenly, I was dangling in mid-air, the rope biting unbearably into the flesh at the back of my legs, the wind icy on my skin. Far, far below I could see the dark shapes of the huge boulders surrounding the lighthouse base. The rising waves were already foaming around them, breaking over the tops. I clung tighter to the rope, feeling suddenly dizzy.

"Don't look down, Suzanna!" Grant's voice snapped me out of it. I looked up. He was there, above me, the rope wrapped around one arm and around his waist, his face tense and flushed with the effort of holding me in place.

"Use your feet!" he yelled.

I nodded and put my feet out tentatively, feeling the cold, slimy surface of the wall.

"I'm going to lower you now! Try to walk down the wall using your feet!"

I did as he said, moving my feet numbly, my heart stopping each time he let a loop of rope loose with a lurch. Slowly, very slowly, I made my descent. My hands throbbed with the ferocity of my grip. The bite of the rope was almost unbearable. Halfway down, I put out a foot and it slid on the wet surface. The movement overbalanced me and sent me spinning out of control. I heard Grant curse, but all I could do was hang on as the wall came up to meet me with such force that I thought I would black out.

"Use your feet, Suzanna!" Grant bellowed. I heard the strain in his voice, and it was this that helped me thrust my legs forward to prevent a second collision with the wall. If I was struggling, I knew that he was struggling more.

"I'm okay now!" I yelled as best I could, and was able to continue the slow descent.

It seemed like hours before I reached the bottom. Here I encountered more difficulty. The rising tide had made the rocks inaccessible by land from this side of the lighthouse. I managed to cling to one huge boulder while I disengaged the rope. The spray and waves doused me instantly, the shock of the cold water helping to clear my head.

"Stay where you are, Suzie!" Grant called. "I'm coming down!"

He pulled the rope up and I watched, dazed, as he wrapped remnants of my mother's wedding dress around his hands, then carefully climbed over the edge of the parapet. With one arm holding the rope under him, the other gripping it above, he took one look, then pushed off, abseiling down in three giant leaps. What had taken me an eternity, he'd managed in a matter of seconds! My relief was tangible. He clambered over to where I clung to the rock, his face mirroring his concern.

"We're nearly home, Suzie. Can you bear a short swim?"

"I—I don't know," I said truthfully. My teeth chattered uncontrollably, and the numbness in my fingers and toes was spreading. He crawled over nearer to me and pulled me into his arms. I was shaking fitfully, and it was some moments before the warmth from his body made any impression. The crashing spume still doused us mercilessly, and I knew that we'd have to get out before the tide rose any higher. Still, I felt safe in his arms and wished I could stay there forever. His lips touched my forehead, soft, reassuring.

Then we heard the motor.

"It's Colin," Grant said, his voice relieved. "We won't have quite so far to swim."

I looked out over the water and saw Beacon's fishing boat chugging in. Colin was standing up at the wheel, and had a spotlight trained on us. He cut the engine to an idle some fifty yards off the rocks and hailed us. "It's as close as I can get!" he yelled. "You'll have to swim out."

Grant looked down at me, questioning. I nodded. "I'll make it."

He squeezed me briefly, then raised an arm. "We're coming!" he called. Then, to me, "When we get in the water, put your arms around my neck and just hang on."

"I can swim," I insisted.

"Don't fight me on this, Suzie," Grant said. "Please, just do as I say."

I frowned, but realized I was in no shape to argue. We crept down to the very edge of the rocks. Grant held my hand tightly and we waited as a swell broke over us, nearly sending me toppling backward. As the water whooshed back out, Grant slipped into the black depths, pulling me after him. Together, we flailed out past the boulders and into deeper water before another swell could push us back. Once there, Grant treaded water while I obediently wrapped my arms around his neck. Then, he began to swim strongly toward the boat, towing me like a useless bit of flotsam.

The water was freezing and after a few seconds, I could hardly feel my extremities. I was glad, now, that I hadn't tried to swim myself. As it was, my muscles weren't responding to anything I told them to do. My fingers wouldn't cling and my legs wouldn't kick. I felt myself losing my grip, and I gave a strangled cry just as I lost my hold and sank into the inky depths.

~ ~ ~

The next thing I knew, I was lying on the deck of the speedboat, coughing water from my lungs, a coarse blanket rough against my skin. Grant, too, was wrapped in a blanket and crouched over me, his wet hair dripping onto my face. He touched my cheek tenderly when I opened my eyes, then turned to Colin.

"She'll be okay," he said. "Let's go."

Colin revved the twin engines and we were off, bouncing across the waves in the direction of the boathouse. I struggled to sit up and Grant put an arm around me, pulling me close so that I could lean against him, feeling suddenly too weak to even speak.

As we pulled up to the pier, I looked over at the lighthouse and gasped. Flames leapt out of the roof now, and the walls were ablaze. Great tongues of fire licked into the night air, illuminating the rocks and the sand all around. I could see the shadowy figures of people milling on the beach; people from the party, no doubt. As Colin cut the engine, I heard the roar of the fire over the crash of the waves.

Then, I heard another sound and I turned my head in time to see a Coastguard cutter and a police launch roar past. But they weren't heading for the lighthouse, they were heading further out onto the lake. I watched, fascinated, as their spotlights picked out a large yacht bobbing at anchor.

"They're only here to assist," Grant said.

I looked at him, puzzled. He smiled.

"Darla—or I should say, Pauline—and company bagged them just as David boarded. They had to catch them in the act to make it stick."

"Darla?" I queried through numb lips

"She's FBI, Suzie. They've known about David for some time—about the drugs, that is—but they wanted to identify his contacts. That boat out there holds the key to busting a syndicate that has operations in Colombia, Cuba, Canada and at least six major cities in the U.S."

"Darla is a federal agent?" I said weakly.

He laughed. "Yes, darling. Her real name is Pauline Petrowski. Did you really think I was so infatuated with my secretary that I had to bring her to Beacon? Don't feel too bad, it's what you were supposed to think. It was the only thing we could come up with to get her into the house. She was there to keep an eye on things, and to make sure nothing happened to you. Also, she had to keep close tabs on David—check his movements—do a bit of, and please excuse the expression, undercover work."

I smiled at him ruefully. "I was jealous, you know."

He cocked an eyebrow. "I'm glad to hear it. I thought all this time that you really didn't care."

I looked up at him then, feeling the warmth of his arm around me, and regretted all those months and years of confusion and denial. Tears of pure relief filled my eyes. "I love you," I said simply. "And I think I always have."

He looked down at me, his own eyes shining conspicuously. "That makes two of us," he murmured and lowered his head to kiss me, long and lingeringly.

Alicia met us at the boathouse and was surprisingly in control, holding out warm clothing for both Grant and me, then ushering us over to where paramedics waited to tend our bruises, burns and abrasions. They suggested we come with them to the hospital for a more thorough examination, but we both refused, our eyes glued in morbid fascination to the flaming lighthouse.

The rest of the partygoers stood about in groups, also transfixed. Their Halloween costumes made the beach look like the set of a horror movie. Someone handed me a hot drink, and I sipped it gratefully.

A CoasGuard cutter appeared out of the gloom and trained a hose on the burning building but, after a few moments, they gave up and shut off their pump, bobbing at anchor to watch, like the rest of us, the final death throes.

Suddenly, I remembered. "Grant!" I cried, "Kong! Where is he?"

Grant grimaced. "I don't know, Suzie. After you went up the ladder, I looked around for him and called, but he'd disappeared. Perhaps he knew another way out."

I stared at the roaring flames and tears filled my eyes. "How could he get out of that?" I murmured.

Grant looked down at me and, seeing my distress, wrapped me in his arms. "Cats have a sixth sense when it comes to these things," he said. "He'll probably show up without a mark."

I knew he was just trying to comfort me and though I wanted to believe him, I had grave doubts. But I didn't have time to worry about Kong. One of the police launches was making its way towards the pier at top speed. It pulled up too quickly, sending a huge bow-wave arching over the boards. Before it had even made fast, three dark clad figures leapt out and ran toward us. I sat up straight, sensing that something wasn't right.

Grant had seen them, too. "Stay here, Suzie; I'll see what's up."

I watched wearily as Grant strode to meet them. I could make out one of the figures as Darla—or Pauline—looking decidedly out of character in a plain black sweater and black trousers. Her hair was whipped into tangles, her face pale in the dark. She was flanked by two burly men. As they met Grant, they all began gesturing extravagantly, their faces grim. Grant listened, nodded, ran a hand through his hair, turned to gaze up the beach, and then spoke again. Seconds later, they separated. Pauline and the two men ran up the beach toward Spindrift while Grant turned back to me.

"I want you to go up to the house, Suzie," he said. His face was tense.

I shivered and pulled the blanket tight around my throat. "What is it, Grant? What's gone wrong?"

He crouched down in front of me and took one of my cold hands in both of his. "I don't want you to worry," he said. "It's just a minor hiccup. He can't get far. They've got police patrols all up and down the coast roads, and…"

My body went rigid. "Who can't get far?! David? Are you telling me that David got away?" My voice shook.

He pulled me to my feet and hugged me tightly, but I still felt a chill that went beyond comforting. "Go up to the house, Suzie. Go to your room and lock the door. You'll be fine there. I'm going to help them find him. He slipped overboard just as they were making the arrests. He'd have had quite a swim in this icy water. He won't be in very good shape. We think he'll head for Spindrift." He kissed me quickly, passionately, then put me away from him. "Will you do as I say?"

I looked at him—his fierce eyes, the set of his jaw—

and I nodded. He turned to go, but I put a hand on his arm. "Please…" I said, my whisper reflecting my fear, "he's killed two people already, Grant. Please, be careful."

He smiled, that clear beautiful smile that I loved, nodded and was gone. I watched as he disappeared down the beach, then I turned to go, having lost any desire to involve myself further.

The wind had picked up, blowing in cloud-cover to blot out the stars and moon. With the flames from the lighthouse dwindling to flickering embers, there was very little light left. Most of the guests had dispersed. The few who remained were being rounded up and escorted to their waiting limousines and cars by Alicia, Colin and two security guards. No one protested. None of these people would want their names linked to headlines of a large drug bust. There were plenty of reputations still in their infancy, and any hint of impropriety could destroy them altogether. I didn't worry about Dirkston Enterprises. It had already survived enough scandal to test its mettle.

I didn't feel like speaking to anyone, so I hurried up through the dunes, avoiding the steps, following a path through the reeds and grasses that zigzagged up gradually. It would, I knew, bring me out closer to Beacon's west boundary. From there, I could skirt the grounds quickly, enter the house through the servants' entrance and go straight up to my room without being disturbed. All I wanted was to soak in a hot bath and crawl into bed. The cuts on my knees and arms were throbbing, and my head was dizzy—probably from delayed shock.

I took off my shoes to make better progress in the shifting sand, and it felt cool and soothing on my bare feet. I worried about Grant. If he found David first, there would be a showdown. I didn't doubt Grant's ability to take care of himself, but I didn't trust David. He could be armed. Even if he wasn't, I knew how desperate he would be—

and desperate men resort to desperate measures.

I reached the top of the dunes without incident. There was a gap in the iron fence there, behind a clump of heavy evergreen shrubs, so well hidden that no one who didn't already know it was there would find it. It was one of those little chinks in security that Leo never found out about. If he had, he'd have had the fence fixed immediately.

I pushed my way through the tangle of boughs, bruising the needles so that the heavy scent of pine filled my nostrils. I felt carefully for the gap in the rails, and, finally finding it, squeezed gingerly through. It wasn't as easy as I'd remembered, and my shirt-front caught and ripped. At this point, however, I didn't care. The thought of familiar surroundings and a tub full of warm, soothing bubbles left no room for concern.

After struggling through more bushes on the other side, I came out in the clearing, only steps from my parents' graves. It was too dark to see much of anything, but I was able to find the two markers without a lot of searching, and I paused there—drawn—wanting comfort, but finding only cold marble. I felt relieved that the mystery was solved, but I was still struggling to accept the fact that the man I had once intended to marry had murdered my father and Giles, had seriously injured my friend, and had contributed to the death of my mother. I took a gasping gulp to stem the tears. If I let myself cry, I was afraid I'd never stop.

I turned to go, but a small sound caught my attention and I hesitated, listening. There was nothing, only the incessant rustle of wind in long grass and the dull rush of distant surf. It might have been an owl I'd heard, or some small night creature scouring the underbrush. I scanned the forest beyond. The trees rose black against black, and I suddenly remembered the dark figure I'd seen silhouetted against the edge of the tree line the day Rudy had told me of his dream. I shivered. The sooner I got back to the house, the better!

I'd taken only one step before I heard footsteps running up behind me. I whirled just as a huge, shapeless hulk burst out of the bushes. I opened my mouth to scream, but it launched itself at me and drove me backward. I fell, and as I hit the ground, my neck snapped back and lights exploded in my head. Then, everything went blissfully black.

I'd made my way down to the lighthouse. I stood at its base and looked up. The moon shone brightly and the clouds skidded recklessly across the sky. At the top, a woman leaned over the parapet. She was wearing a long white gown and her hair streamed out in the night wind. I felt a desperate urgency to reach her, but I looked down and discovered my feet were sinking rapidly into the sand. I tried to pull them out, but they sank even faster until I was mired up to my knees. I looked at the woman, and she lifted an arm to hail me. At the same time, I saw a dark figure come up behind her, arms outstretched. I opened my mouth to scream, but it was too late. The woman tumbled out and over the low wall, falling in slow motion toward the black, glinting rocks.

But it wasn't my mother tumbling to her death. This time, the woman was me.

I must not have been unconscious for long. When I woke, it was still pitch dark and I could feel damp grass under my back. My head throbbed and I groaned involuntarily.

"Get up!" The command was hissed, but I knew who it was. My heart began to beat wildly.

"David?"

"Get up!" he insisted again, and this time he pulled me roughly to my feet. I swayed and would have fallen, but he caught me and held me against him, propping me up like a lifeless puppet.

He was wet. I could feel the cold moisture of his clothing, and water dripped from the end of his nose as he peered into my face. I tried to focus, but his features were blurred and distorted.

Without further hesitation, he dragged me over to the deeper darkness of the forest and dropped me with a thud onto the hard, prickly ground. He squatted down beside me and waited as my head slowly stopped spinning, and the throbbing behind my eyes abated to a dull ache. When I was able to focus properly, I could just make out his face. It was pale, too pale. His hair was matted and his lips were blue. His eyes flicked about wildly, and I knew immediately it would be useless to try to reason with him. This wasn't a man. This was a cornered animal.

He must have seen my expression, for he grabbed me by the hair and thrust the cold barrel of a gun hard against my throat. "Not a word!" he said. "You scream and you die. Understand?"

I nodded dumbly, unable to summon enough saliva to swallow.

He released me, but kept the gun pointed steadily at my head.

"You were very lucky to have escaped my little fire," he said. "You must be more resourceful than I've given you credit for. But I'm glad that you did, Suzanna, because now you're going to help me get out of here. If you do everything I say, you may even live to tell the tale. Do you understand?"

I nodded again.

"Good," he said. "First of all, we're going to get your car. I'm going to hide in the back while you drive me to the marina. Once I get to the plane, I'll be as good as free. If anyone stops you or asks any questions, you'll tell them that you're going to the hospital to have those nasty cuts better tended to. Any questions?"

I shook my head. I couldn't speak. I was shivering

uncontrollably, and my throat had constricted.

He smiled, a cruel grimace. "I like you like this, Suzanna—nice and obedient. If you're a real good girl, I might even take you with me. Now, get up!"

He jerked me roughly to my feet. I reeled dizzily but stumbled forward where he shoved me, concentrating only on putting one foot in front of the other, feeling the icy eye of the gun staring at the point blank target of my back.

It wasn't too difficult making our way to the garage without being seen. We followed the topiary maze, keeping well away from any sounds of voices or footsteps. Once or twice, he pushed me roughly to my knees when something sounded particularly close, but it took relatively little time to gain the shelter of the hedgerow behind the house, and then the shadows at the rear of the garage. If I'd been able to think logically, I would have realized that no one would be looking for him here. Grant, Pauline and the rest of the FBI would be scouring the beach and dunes around Spindrift, assuming he would head there first. The security guards we'd hired were helping Colin and Alicia round up guests. As it was, my mind was a blank. I did as he directed, and that was all.

We entered the garage from the rear. It was dark, but I could see all four vehicles lined up docilely. I got into the driver's seat of my own car and waited, shaking, as David climbed into the back. He curled up on the floor and pulled a tartan travel rug over himself. I didn't bother to wonder what would happen if my keys weren't in the ignition. I merely waited until he told me to start the engine, and then did so. I pushed the remote button to open the garage door and backed the car out.

I wasn't prepared for the glare of floodlights. They made my head begin to spin again, and I fumbled with the gear shift, trying to find first, hearing the cogs grind painfully. Suddenly, there was a tap at the window.

"Remember what I said!" David hissed.

I rolled down the window and tried to smile at the

guard's face peering in at me.

"You goin' somewhere, Miss—er—Mrs. Fenton?"

"Yes," I croaked. I coughed. "Yes," I said, more clearly. "I'm, uh, going to the hospital. Just want to get a Tetanus shot. The paramedic suggested it."

He peered at me, his brows furrowed, then he nodded. "Probably a good idea. You don't look too good. Would you like someone else to drive you?"

"No!" The word came out too high-pitched. "Sorry, uh…John, is it?"

"Roger, Ma'am."

"Oh. Roger. Sorry. I'm a bit on edge, that's all." I laughed, a sick, grotesque parody. "I'll be fine. Thanks, anyway."

I didn't give him time to say any more, but put the car into gear and drove off. The blood was thumping so loudly in my ears that I barely heard the hammer of David's gun click back into its resting place.

The guard at the gate waved me through and, without further delay, we were on the road, flying toward Ludington. David threw the blanket off and sat up. I glanced at him in the rearview mirror and saw that his shirt was torn and his right arm was bloodied at the shoulder.

"You've been shot," I said dispassionately.

"Yeah. That woman, Darla—bitch! I should have known." He flexed the shoulder and I saw him grimace. "Nothing serious. Just keep driving."

I turned my eyes back to the road. There were no other cars. I put the headlights on high beam, and suddenly he was there, right in front of the car, standing stock-still in the middle of the road. Without thinking, I slammed my foot on the brake and the car screeched out of control. With tires squealing, we careened sideways. The steering wheel jerked in the opposite direction, snapping my wrist and throwing my hands off. As if in slow motion, the trees loomed up. The car rose on one side and flipped onto its roof. The headlights went out and darkness engulfed us.

I wasn't unconscious. My seatbelt had saved me from serious harm, but I couldn't move. I hung suspended in the vehicle, aware of the whir of the tires and the unusual angle of the sky. Inexplicably, through the cracked windshield, I saw King Kong. He was upside-down and his yellow eyes bored into mine, as though trying to tell me something.

"Get out, Suzie!" It was Grant. He had the door open and was grappling with my seatbelt. Still, I couldn't move. I was frozen. My limbs weren't my own. I felt the belt come loose, and Grant pulled me out. Then, I was in his arms and we were moving away from the car, out onto the road.

I was aware of red and blue lights and fuzzy figures dancing at the corners of my eyes. I was being caccooned in soft blankets, and I closed my eyes to savor their warmth. The last thing I remember was Grant's voice saying, "It's all right, Suzie. I'm here now. You'll be all right."

EPILOGUE

The knowledge that you cannot have is inexhaustible,
and what is inexhaustible is benevolent.
The knowledge that you cannot have is of the riddles
of birth and death, of our future destiny and the
purposes of God. Here there is no knowledge,
but illusions that restrict freedom and limit hope.
Accept the mystery behind knowledge:
It is not darkness but shadow.

Northrop Frye,
1988 Address,
Metropolitan United Church, Toronto

"I still love it up here," I said.

I was sitting on High Dune. Grant sat beside me, his arms wrapped around his knees, his blue eyes crinkled against the afternoon glare. It was cold, despite the brightness of the sun. There would be snow soon. Even now, flat gray clouds lined the horizon ominously. I huddled in my warm parka, a soft woolen cap pulled over my ears.

"I feel privileged," Grant said.

I looked at him in surprise. "Why?"

He smiled. "I've never been up here. This is the first time you've invited me."

I leaned my head against his shoulder, and he automatically put his arm around me and pulled me closer. "I'm glad you're here now," I said.

We were quiet, enjoying the peace. I gazed down at the burned-out ruins that were once the lighthouse. Surprisingly, most of the main structure still stood, but it was charred and blackened and parts of the upper walls had caved in. I shuddered, thinking back to that night.

David was killed in the crash. Without a seatbelt, he'd had little chance; his neck was broken when the car flipped.

"How did you arrive so quickly?" I murmured.

Grant was obviously remembering as well. "The accident happened just past Spindrift," he said. "I'd seen your car go by, and knew you wouldn't be out joyriding, so I grabbed one of the officers and we got there just as you went off the road. By the way," he asked, pulling his head back to get a better look at my face, "why did you lose control?"

I smiled up at him sheepishly. "You'll think I'm crazy."

"No, I won't."

I hesitated. "I saw Leo. He was standing there—right in front of the car."

Grant considered this for some moments. "When we got there," he finally said, "the cat was sitting in the middle of the road—Kong. He ran off toward your car."

"Yes," I said. "I saw him afterward! I saw him through the windscreen. I remember thinking he looked silly upside-down." I turned to look up at him. "Grant," I asked earnestly, "do you believe in the supernatural?"

He thought for a moment. "If you'd asked me that six months ago," he said, "I'd have said no. But, given everything that's happened…

I smiled, and snuggled more closely into his embrace. "Will you mind being married to someone who, as Madam Valenia puts it, is 'receptive to messages from the other side'?"

Grant chuckled. "Certainly not. As long as that some-one is receptive to this."

He kissed me then, with a tenderness that made me melt inside, his lips searching, his arms warm—comfort-ing. I kissed him back, with all the love and passion that I'd kept hidden for so long; my joy so intense that I felt giddy.

And from somewhere nearby, at the periphery of my senses, I heard the sound of a cat purring.

Watch for Maureen McMahon's new novel *Return of the Gulls*, coming from Avid Press in September 2001!

Maureen McMahon was born in Niles, Michigan. She pursued her education in English and creative writing, earning an English Major/Creative Writing Emphasis from WMU and obtained elementary teaching certification as well as certification for teaching English/Creative Writing at all levels.

Fascinated with her mother's country of birth, Maureen traveled to Australia in 1981 to visit relatives. She met her husband, Peter, and they were married in 1983. She now resides in Wallington, on the Bellarine Peninsula, Victoria, with Peter, her two teenaged children, James and KatyAnne, two Labradors, two cats, a cockatoo (who she claims to be the reincarnation of a long-lost, beloved cat) and a number of very happy "chooks"

Shadows in the Mist is her first published novel.

Watch for this exciting Avid Press release
in early 2001....

The Divided Child
by
Ekaterine Nikas

A vacation in the Greek Isles turns into
danger and romance as a young woman
saves the life of a young boy.

Here's a sneak preview...

"Who paid you to follow Michael?" he demanded.

I stared at him in disbelief. "You're crazy! Nobody paid
me to do anything. Why would anyone have a little boy followed?"

"Dammit, you know why!" he said, seizing me by the
shoulders. "How did they know I was meeting him?"

"You're hurting me!" I cried. He let go abruptly. "I think
it's time I was going," I said, trying to sound calmer than
I felt.

"We're not finished yet."

I didn't answer. Instead, I struggled to sit up, stiffly swinging my legs out of the bed and dangling them toward the floor. Unfortunately, the bed was an expensive antique and ridiculously high off the ground.

Hoping to get a more solid footing, I launched myself forward, but my knees buckled and I started to fall. There was a muffled crash. Then I found myself on the floor cradled in Geoffrey Redfield's warm, strong arms.

"Do you make a habit of collapsing onto every man you meet?" he inquired acidly.

"No one asked you to catch me," I snapped back, tears of pin welling up in my eyes. His arms dropped away.

"Are you all right?" he asked through clenched teeth.

My cheek was burning, my neck ached, and I found myself shaking so hard it hurt. "I'm fine," I whispered, turning my head away so he wouldn't see the tears starting to spill.

He turned my face back toward him and swore. Taking out a handkerchief from his pocket, he wiped the tears away with surprising gentleness. Then he picked me up and placed me carefully back on the bed. For a moment, his arms lingered around me, then the nearby murmur of voices seemed to snap him from his reverie. He straightened abruptly.

"Look, I've no more time for games," he declared in an urgent undertone. "I need answers, and I need them now. Can't you understand how important this is?"

"Can't you understand," I retorted, "that I haven't the vaguest idea what you're talking about?"

For the first time, uncertainty flickered in his green eyes. "You truly don't know?"

"No!"

He raised a finger to his lips.

"No," I repeated more softly.

"But you speak such fluent Greek --"

"So? Since when is that a crime?"

"You didn't ring my hotel? You didn't leave a message

saying Michael was in hospital?"

I stared at him, flabbergasted. "Of course not! Why would I do such a thing?"

Suddenly outside the room I could hear the approaching click-clack of high heels.

"Perhaps I've leapt to some hasty conclusions."

"I'll say!"

He held up his hand. "If I have, I apologize. If not, at least we both know where we stand." He backed away toward the French windows, his eyes on me, his attention fixed on the approaching footsteps. "But if it's true you simply stumbled into this . . . well, then someone ought to warn you."

"Warn me? Warn me about what?"

The footsteps had stopped, and I heard the door open. I turned to see who it was. Michael's mother glided in, followed by her brother.

"Ah, Miss Stewart, you are awake," she said, casting a significant look back at her companion. "I told my brother it was so, but he would not believe me. ou see, Spiro. Did I not tell you I heard voices coming from this room?"

Her brother flashed me a quick appraising look, then gazed past me.

"And to whom, dear sister, would Miss Stewart have been talking? The room is empty. There is no one else here."

Startled, I looked back toward the French windows. Spiro Skouras was right. Geoffrey Redfield was nowhere to be seen.

Coming from Avid Press
in early 2001!